PRAISE FOR SHOLES & MOORE'S
AWARD WINNING BESTSELLING THRILLERS

THE BLADE

"Sholes & Moore are at the top of their game in this dark, chilling cat-and-mouse race to stop an unimaginable act of terrorism. THE BLADE is full-throttle thriller writing." -- David Morrell, *New York Times* bestselling author of MURDER AS A FINE ART.

"Completely kept me guessing. THE BLADE delivers a razor edge of suspense. As fast as you think you know what's going on, you're wrong. An absolute thrill ride." -- Lisa Gardner, #1 *New York Times* bestselling author of CATCH ME

"History and suspense entangle from page one, forming a plot rife with deceit and deception. Sholes & Moore write with a confident, assured hand --- always keeping the reader primed and ready for the gut punch. This is another terrific outing. I highly recommend that you sink your claws into this entertaining nugget." -- Steve Berry, *New York Times* bestselling author of THE COLUMBUS AFFAIR

"THE BLADE by Sholes & Moore is an epic thriller, combining contemporary suspense and historical mystery. From the opening scene in Iraq to the final explosion at Big Bear Lake in Colorado, this is one hell of a thrill ride. Well-crafted, with vivid settings and a premise that will blow your mind, this thriller is not to be missed! Highly recommended." -- Douglas Preston, #1 *New York Times* bestselling author of THE MONSTER OF FLORENCE

"Fast. Fresh. Fascinating. THE BLADE is another razor-sharp thriller from one of my favorite writing teams!" -- Brad Thor, #1 *New York Times* bestselling author of BLACK LIST

"You will need THE BLADE to cut the tension as you turn the pages to the shocking climax. Sholes & Moore have painted a stunning portrait of suspense that leaves you wanting their next collaboration." -- *Suspense Magazine*

THE PHOENIX APOSTLES

"Fast-paced, exciting story that grips the audience." -- *The Mystery Gazette*

"Once again, Lynn Sholes & Joe Moore have produced a novel that is as revelatory as it is packed with action and suspense. THE PHOENIX APOSTLES takes their talent to new heights in a story that will leave readers breathless and wanting more. Bold, taut, and masterfully told, here is a book that demands to be read in one sitting." -- James Rollins, *New York Times* bestselling author of THE DOOMSDAY KEY

"A fascinating, compelling page-turner. Lynn Sholes & Joe Moore hit all the right notes with THE PHOENIX APOSTLES!" -- Carla Neggers, *New York Times* bestselling author of COLD DAWN

"Lynn Sholes & Joe Moore have created a knockout apocalyptic thriller with THE PHOENIX APOSTLES. An epic tale of gold, archaeology, mass murder, ancient prophecy and terrorism, it propels the reader at light speed from its opening chapters to its stunning climax. An outstanding read!" -- Douglas Preston, #1 *New York Times* bestselling author of IMPACT and THE MONSTER OF FLORENCE

"An ingenious thriller with an audacious plot. Awesome; a reminder why fiction is fun." -- *Library Journal*

"What do you get when you cross Indiana Jones with THE DA VINCI CODE? THE PHOENIX APOSTLES, a rollicking thrill ride with so many twists and turns that you won't have time to catch your breath!" -- Tess Gerritsen, *New York Times* bestselling author of ICE COLD

"Sholes and Moore have been writing stellar thrillers that use religious themes for some time, and their fifth effort, the first to feature archaeologist Seneca Hunt, is their best yet. Hunt and her fiancé are on a dig near Mexico City when explosions rock the site. Hunt is the only survivor. Still grieving, she teams up with a journalist who has evidence that the explosion was meant to cover up a robbery. All over the world, tombs are being invaded and bodies stolen, while valuable jewels and gold are left behind. Who are the thieves, and do all the missing bodies belong to infamous mass murderers throughout history? The breakneck pace and sharp characterizations immerse the reader into a surprising and frightening story that posits what the future might look like if science is allowed to run amok. Fans of historical thrillers and mysteries with a religious tint will devour this one while eagerly awaiting the next Seneca Hunt adventure." – *Booklist*

THE GRAIL CONSPIRACY
#1 Bestselling Kindle Book on Amazon

ForeWord Magazine Book-Of-The-Year

Independent Publisher IPPY Award Nominee

"Cotten Stone is a heroine for the ages." ~ Douglas Preston, #1 *New York Times* bestselling co-author of RELIC

"Action-packed, twenty-first century Indiana Jones." ~ Harriet Klausner, ReviewCentre

"If you love books by Steve Berry and Dan Brown, you will love this one, too. The search for the Holy Grail is an exciting adventure and definitely worth reading." ~ Bookreporter.com

"In this time of Dan Brown, here are fresh voices. THE GRAIL CONSPIRACY is everything a mystery should be." ~ Stuart Hecht, The Book Vault

"Gripping!" ~ *Mystery Scene Magazine*

"Spellbinding!" ~ *BookSense*

THE LAST SECRET
"Sholes & Moore have the magical ability to keep you on the edge of your seat. From the first page to the last, you won't be able to put it down." ~ ReaderViews

"Skillfully crafted page-turner." ~ Debra Hamel, Book-Blog.com

"A blend of international thriller and religious fiction, it's an attention-grabber that kept me up at night feverishly turning pages because I just had to know what would happen next. (THE LAST SECRET is) one for those who want a really good "DA VINCI CODE"-esque read." ~ Lelia Taylor, Creatures 'n Crooks Bookshoppe

"Superb thriller. Sholes & Moore write some of the best apocalyptical thrillers on the market today." ~ Harriet Klausner, ReviewCentre

"Demonic possession, strange suicides, and Biblical prophecy collide in THE LAST SECRET, an intelligent religious thriller with bite. Once again, Cotten Stone proves herself to be a heroine for the new millennium. A female Indiana Jones with a press pass! Insightful, engrossing…but more importantly, a suspenseful thriller from first page to last!" ~ James Rollins, *New York Times* bestselling author of BLACK ORDER

"Fascinating and breathless, THE LAST SECRET will leave you glued to your chair. The story sweeps across centuries in a quest for the secret key to surviving Armageddon. Sholes & Moore are true story-tellers with unerring eyes and the souls of artists. You'll love this one!" ~ Gayle Lynds, *New York Times* bestselling author of THE LAST SPYMASTER

"THE LAST SECRET grabs you and won't let go. This is a page-turner with an awesomely creative premise and a surprise around every corner." ~ Lewis Perdue, *New York Times* bestselling author of DAUGHTER OF GOD

"Engaging. Sholes & Moore are experienced authors whose expertise is evident. THE LAST SECRET is entertaining and recommended." ~ BookPleasures

THE HADES PROJECT

"THE HADES PROJECT is an exceptional novel, a dark labyrinth of suspense, international intrigue and apocalyptic horror. The characters, the pacing and the amazing premise of this series are all first-rate. Sholes & Moore are very talented writers indeed." ~ Douglas Preston, #1 *New York Times* bestselling co-author of RELIC

"Short chapters and a pulsating storyline make this a quick read, and those looking for well-drawn characters will be pleased as well. Fans of religious-themed thrillers like THE DA VINCI CODE will enjoy. Recommended for all public libraries." ~ *Library Journal*

"A compelling thriller!" ~ Harriet Klausner *The Mystery Gazette*

"Smoothly-written, nicely paced page-turner." ~ Book-Blog

". . . the tension builds as Stone and her mortal and otherworldly allies race to avert catastrophe." ~ *Publishers Weekly*

"THE HADES PROJECT is a briskly-paced read combining Christian fantasy with mystery. Fans of THE DA VINCI CODE should find THE HADES PROJECT a satisfying read. ~ *Mystery Scene Magazine*

THE 731 LEGACY

"Sholes & Moore are the new Preston & Child. From the very first chapter, THE 731 LEGACY wraps a rope around your neck, pulls it tight, and never lets go! This is what masterful storytelling is all about!" ~ Brad Thor, #1 *New York Times* bestselling author of THE LAST PATRIOT

"What an outrageous and terrifying read. I can't get enough of Cotten Stone!" ~ Lincoln Child, #1 *New York Times* bestselling author of DEEP STORM

"A superb blend of science, myth, history, and imagination. Strap yourself to the chair and get ready for a heart-thumping ride. Sholes & Moore are clearly ahead of the pack, able to satisfy even the most finicky of reader. THE 731 LEGACY is a labyrinth of mystery, crisply plotted and paced, with throat-grabbing twists." ~ Steve Berry, *New York Times* bestselling author of THE TEMPLAR LEGACY

THE 731 LEGACY "has a bit of everything found in popular thrillers: destruction of civilization, ancient religious lore, modern science, and non-stop action. It could be entitled Angels and Demons, and is far superior to the book that bears that title." ~ *Mystery Scene Magazine*

THE BLADE

LYNN SHOLES & JOE MOORE

THE BLADE

Published by Stone Creek Books
Edited by Jodie Renner (www.jodierennerediting.com)
Interior design by Joe Moore
Cover design by Joe Moore
Cover image © 2013

Excerpt from THE SHIELD
© 2014 by Lynn Sholes & Joe Moore
Published by Stone Creek Books

ISBN: 0692226176
ISBN-13: 978-0692226179

Dedication:
Lynn Sholes dedicates this book to Ashleigh Oliver
Mac McKee, Alexis Arce, their spouses and children.
And for Tommy. Thank you. Love you.

Joe Moore dedicates this book to Friendly Finley,
mentor extraordinaire

The authors wish to thank the following for their
assistance in adding a sense of realism
to this work of fiction.

Cary E. Moore
Former Special Agent
United States Air Force
Department of Defense
Office of Special Investigations

Frank N. von Hippel PhD
Former Assistant Director for National Security
White House Office of Science and Technology
Professor of Public and International Affairs
Princeton University

Dale Beauchamp
Branch Chief Digital Forensics
Office of Information Security
Department of Homeland Security
Transportation Safety Administration

John C. Darrin
Radiological Emergency Preparedness Consultant for
Federal, State and Local Government Agencies and
commercial enterprises.

"And Abraham stretched forth his hand,
and took the blade to slay his son."
~ Genesis, 22:10

CHAPTER 1 - BETRAYAL
Three years earlier, North of Kirkuk City, Iraq

I lay flat on the ground beside the five-thousand-year-old Assyrian settlement wall and watched the smuggler through my night vision goggles. My partner, OSI Special Agent Aaron Knox, was concealed among the ruins fifteen meters to my right.

"Maxine, what's he doing?" Aaron's voice whispered in my earbud.

"I'm not sure," I said. "Looks like he's fumbling with some boxes in that van."

Just moments earlier, the smuggler had emerged from the farmhouse, glanced in my direction as if he sensed my presence, then headed toward an old panel van twenty meters away. With it parked facing away from me, I had a back view of him as he opened the cargo doors. He kept looking toward the road a hundred meters to the east, probably anticipating the arrival of the transfer truck any moment.

A faint odor of cattle manure drifted from a nearby dusty pasture as I turned my head to the left. A ridgeline ran at an angle across the back of the property, making a perfect hiding place for the Iraqi National Police commandos waiting there.

I shifted my focus back to the van. The smuggler, a twenty-year-old Sunni Kurd, remained at the rear by the open doors. At such a young age, he had already made a name for himself on the black market as part of a smuggling ring that pilfered Iraqi artifacts out of the country through the neighboring Sulaymaniyah Province. Recently, he'd gotten his hands on a few of the valuables looted from the Baghdad National Museum during the chaotic start of the war back in 2003. Our intel said the treasures included several small Sumerian relics and a number of gold and silver pieces dating back to 2000 BC. The smuggler's take would be hundreds of U.S. dollars, but as the goods moved up the food chain to the ultimate private collectors, they could be worth millions. Because the artifacts were believed to have been originally stolen by U.S. Air Force personnel, the Office of Special Investigations had sent in Aaron and me.

"Truck." The voice in my earbud was now the Iraqi police captain.

I heard it before I saw it. Through the night vision goggles, its headlights glowed green—a ghostly image of a lumbering farm truck appeared over the crest of a hill and headed toward us along the old Kirkuk highway. The Iraqi police would perform the actual apprehension. The two of us were there to observe and assist in the recovery and identification of the artifacts. Nothing more.

I glanced back at the van. "Shit!"

"Max, what's wrong?" Aaron asked.

"He's gone." The van doors stood open like a gaping mouth, but the smuggler had vanished.

I swept the space between the van and the house. Empty.

Back to the van. Dark interior. No movement.

"Maxine?" Aaron's voice was louder.

I looked in the opposite direction and spotted our target hauling ass on foot toward the road. "The little prick is bailing!"

I saw the blurry image of the smuggler running across the flat, barren space toward the highway at a full sprint. He gripped the straps to a bulging backpack, and I realized he had duped us with the cargo van full of cartons. Instead he had all the goods on him. Chances were, nothing of value would be in the van.

"Agent Decker?" The captain was waiting for my signal.

"Hang on." I spotted my partner running behind the

smuggler. He was within a meter of being able to tackle the target.

But something wasn't right.

I stood and signaled to the Iraqi commandos to begin their assault.

"Aaron," I called, "Take him down! Stop the bastard!"

My earbud filled with orders from the captain shouting to his men. They were already swarming over the ridge.

Shots came from the van. Someone had been hiding inside. The shooter seemed to be ignoring the commandos and instead was firing at me. *What the hell?* I dropped behind the ancient wall and pulled my SIG Sauer.

Pieces of clay burst from the wall as slugs slammed into my hiding place. *How do they know my exact location?* I heard the Iraqis yelling. More shots. Within seconds, the sound of automatic weapons was everywhere. The guy in the van was relentless.

Crouching low, I maneuvered around the wall toward where my partner had been positioned. New shots fired. I popped up my head for a second and determined they were coming from the farm truck. It had stopped beside the highway, and at least four men were firing at the commandos from the truck's canvas-covered bed.

Whoever was still in the van was spraying bullets across the top of the ruins to keep me occupied. Then I saw him jump out and start to make a run for the truck before the commandos got to him. I moved to the end of the wall, rose, and fired three shots at the gunman. He dropped and didn't get up.

Several Iraqis swarmed the house while the rest headed for the farm truck, their tracers lighting up the night. I took off running to back up my partner but immediately caught the attention of someone in the truck—bullets were now coming at me. The commandos had to seek shelter behind the van as the men in the truck laid down cover fire for the smuggler's escape.

"Aaron, get down!" I yelled into the mic. He was running in

the open area. I felt my belt to make sure I had a fresh clip ready before racing along the perimeter of the pasture. I had to help him before he got himself shot.

The smuggler veered off the direct course toward the highway to avoid the line of fire, with Aaron right behind him. They left the open space of the pasture and weaved through the ruins. I took advantage of their detour and sprinted straight toward them for an intercept.

Just before they emerged from the last ancient clay structure, they charged right into me.

I aimed my gun and the smuggler froze. Aaron bent over, hands on his knees catching his breath.

"Aaron!" A voice shouted above the gunfire coming from the truck.

It was American. Not Iraqi.

I ripped off my goggles and glared at my partner. "Who's that? How does he know your name?" The smuggler sidestepped. "Freeze!" I ordered. "Aaron, who's that in the truck?" I had to shout for him to hear above all the racket. "What's going on here?" The pieces were coming together and I thought I already knew the answer, but I desperately wanted to be wrong.

"This has nothing to do with you, Max. Just turn around and walk away." Aaron straightened. "This is my ticket out."

"Have you forgotten that you're a federal agent?"

"Just back off. You're not supposed to get hurt. That was part of the deal."

"Deal? What deal? I'm not backing off. This isn't going to go down. Not like this." Bullets pelted the opposite side of the structure protecting us.

The voice from the truck roared out my partner's name again.

Aaron still hadn't caught his breath, and his words came in a staccato rhythm. "Don't make me do it. I don't want to shoot you."

The truck engine revved.

"Maxine, I'm sorry—"

As he brought his gun up I fired twice.

He collapsed.

"You bitch!" The scream came from the direction of the truck, but closer.

The American. Without my goggles, he was nothing but a dark form rushing at me.

The smuggler took off.

Then a flash.

The bullet struck my side just below my vest. Another slammed into my right thigh. The pain was white hot.

I dropped to my knees and fell forward.

The odor of the cattle manure seemed stronger this close to the earth.

Or was it the smell of death?

CHAPTER 2 - THE VISITOR
Present day, Big Bear Lake, Colorado

As I crested a hill, half a kilometer from my cabin, I spotted a Jeep in the distance. For an instant, the last orange from the setting sun glinted off its shiny paint even as it sat partially hidden in the shadows of the Douglas firs below.

Quickening my pace, I slipped along the path, protected from view by the Gambel oaks and mountain mahogany. I wanted to get a better look at the vehicle.

The Jeep might belong to hikers or wilderness lovers fancying a view of the Rockies in springtime. But this area was not a popular spot, which is one reason I had chosen the location—for solitude. And the signs declaring private property were hard to miss where the dirt road to my place turned off the county blacktop. The Jeep either belonged to a lost soul or to someone looking for me. The latter made me nervous.

The trail leveled off as I came down to the southern end of Big Bear Lake. The path hugged the lake's perimeter in a sweeping arc. Tall blades of grass and sedge kept me partially concealed. Combined with the onrush of night and my dark clothing, I was just a shadow.

I came to the edge of the clearing that cascaded from my cabin down to the lake. Crouching behind a thick fir tree, I poked my head around and scanned the rear of the cabin. That's when I saw him.

The guy was dressed in jeans and a heavy jacket with a baseball cap pulled low over his forehead. Dark hair. Maybe six foot one. Trim. Between 160 and 170 pounds. He walked slowly along the back porch. Judging by the way he moved he was agile and I bet fit beneath the bulk of the jacket.

At each window, he paused to peer in. As he reached the back door, I instinctively went for my sidearm, but the SIG Sauer had long been replaced with a five-inch hunting knife and a Maglite. I hadn't touched a gun since I shot Aaron Knox.

Time to improvise.

I waited until he cracked open the door and entered. Keeping low, I moved through the grass and took advantage of an occasional tree to evade the clearing until I made my way to the side of the cabin. With extra care, I eased open the storm door and slipped into the basement.

It was pitch-black and dank smelling—I'd had every intention of cleaning and reorganizing it, but it was still down near the bottom of my to-do list.

I kept my flashlight off. Moving blind, I felt my way around boxes, tools, and general junk. A rattling thud came when I bumped my shin on an old bedframe. "Damn!" *Had he heard both the collision and my curse?* When I found the thick supports of the wooden stairs, I slid underneath and waited.

The soft creaking of the floorboards told me he was in the kitchen. His steps were slow and light, obviously exercising caution as he searched each room. With my old F150 parked out front and the back door unlocked, it was no mystery that I was home or not far away. Since he wasn't ransacking and rummaging, I concluded that he was not there to burgle. That left one alternative, and I didn't like it.

Narrow slits between the floorboards lit up as the intruder swept his light around each room. He approached the door to the basement.

At the sound of the door hinge squeaking above me, I pushed back against the wall.

He took the first step on the stairs, and his light beam came to rest on an old refrigerator sitting next to a workbench. The Frigidaire didn't function, and the tools on the bench were worn and rusted, left behind by the former owner.

The second step creaked and then the third, slow and easy. A dark leather hiking boot settled on the step level with my face. The next step down, I grabbed his boot laces and he flew forward, head first. With a grunt, he hit the dirt floor hard. I ran out from under the stairs and before he could move, I had my knee planted firmly in his back at the base of his neck and the butt end of my Maglite pressed into his skull.

"Move and you're dead." I stabbed the Maglite against his head for emphasis, hoping it felt like the real thing.

"Maxine, sweetheart, is that any way to greet your long-lost love?"

CHAPTER 3 - KENNY GATES
Big Bear Lake, Colorado

"What did you expect me to do, Kenny? You broke into my home and sneaked around like a burglar. We've got electricity up here in the backwoods. Next time, ring the doorbell. Or call first."

I leaned against the porch railing with my arms folded and watched him baby a cut on his forehead with a Ziploc bag of ice. He sat in a high-back rocking chair and glanced up at me with his apologetic hazel eyes.

"Knocked at your door. No answer. Car was here. You live way out in the middle of bum-fuck Colorado. Anything could have happened to you. I was just checking the place out to make sure you were okay. Of course I loved the extra element of surprise. "

"I'm sure you adored your little perk of scaring the hell out of me."

"So you were going to blow me away with a Maglite?"

"If I had to. It was locked and loaded with double-As."

Kenny smiled as he shifted the plastic ice pack to a new position on his head and looked at the lake in the distance. The stars and fireflies were coming out. "Nice place, Max. You've done good."

He was right. This was what I needed after the long recovery and rehab from my gunshot wounds in Iraq, not to mention the additional hell of going through endless grilling by the Inspector General's Office on the shooting of Aaron Knox. The actual gunplay took a few seconds—the inquiry seemed to go on forever. It didn't take much to push me over the edge. I decided to retire after being shot at three times during my eighteen years as a Special Agent with the OSI.

The first time was an airman who stood in the parking lot of the Eglin Base Exchange and decided to shoot his girlfriend and any other females within line of sight. I was three cars over. He got the girlfriend and my driver's side window.

Second time, I was conducting an interrogation at MacDill on an officer caught smuggling stolen Peruvian artifacts out of Florida. He came to my hotel room and knocked. When I asked who it was, he fired three bullets through the door. One grazed my arm. I went to the hospital and he went to prison.

The first two weren't anything like Kirkuk. There was also the mental and emotional wrecking of having shot my partner and friend. To make things worse, I was then under suspicion of involvement in the smuggling operation. That nailed my decision to leave the OSI. I didn't just retire, I fled. I *needed* to get out. And I needed to go someplace and be alone for a long time. Big Bear Lake was perfect.

Kenny and I had a long history. We'd met when I joined the OSI. I was only 23 and green. Kenny, on the other hand, was an experienced agent and a good one. While others let me flag and flounder, Kenny found time to coach me through the maze of my new job. He was my personal mentor, even though our fields were different. He was an OSI Computer Crimes Investigator specializing in computer forensics, while mine was the antiquities black market. If a crime was committed by military personnel, we were usually called in to investigate. Kenny had to deal with everything from kiddy porn to falsifying documents, while I dealt with stolen art objects and smuggling.

"Must be boring up here." He put down the ice pack and took a long pull from the Coors.

"Not when I've got people sneaking up on my place and breaking in." I took a drink from my beer. "And why did you park your Jeep up the road? You're lucky I don't like guns anymore."

"My intent was to happily surprise you. But when you weren't around, I got worried. I screwed up, okay? So sue me."

I shook my head. "And people wonder why I got out of the military."

"What do you do up here all day?"

"Well, I do some painting. Lots of reading. And I've started writing—"

"Really? What kind of writing?"

"Fiction. I've got a few ideas for a novel. I write longhand, then type my work into my laptop. It's fun. They say everyone has at least one book in them."

"Am I in your book?"

I resisted a smart reply and zapped him a *give me a break* look.

"Just asking," he said.

"And I fish. There's some decent trout fishing in the lake. A boat came with the house, so I go out on the lake once in a while. I like being around nature. As a matter of fact, I was coming back from checking on a litter of foxes about a kilometer from here when I saw your Jeep. The mother's been missing for a few days, and I was worried about the kits. But mom showed back up today, although she looked the worse for it."

"Probably a slut fox.

"Or a battered wife."

"Touché," Kenny said, hoisting his bottle.

"So, now that we've had the obligatory idle chitchat and the complimentary beverage, why are you here?"

He set down the beer, rubbed the dark stubble on his chin, and let his face go serious. "We want you back."

I stared at him, wondering if this was someone's idea of a joke. "Back? Back to what? Kenny, there is no back. There's only forward. I'm moving forward with my life. This is my life. Look around you. What could be better than this? There's nothing the government could possibly offer that would entice me to return to active duty."

"Max, you're living in downtown boredomville. OSI is in

your blood. You've had your R&R. Now it's time to get back to work. Catch some bad guys. Find an ancient relic or two. Do your magic. I know you."

"Well, for once, you're wrong. This *is* me. And I like me." I walked a few paces away and turned toward the lake, now only a dark mass under a brilliant, star-filled sky. I rubbed my upper arms, enjoying the brisk Colorado mountain air before turning to Kenny. "There's nothing that could bring me back."

"Don't be so sure."

I didn't like the way he said that. He understood me well enough to know what blew my skirt up. Maybe he was just playing with me. He had an annoying habit of doing that. "What do you mean?"

"We think we've got a line on the Blade."

I felt a tingle in my belly and my pulse quickened. Suddenly, that old rush of the chase shot through me. Just to clarify, and with a great deal of anticipation I asked, "What blade?"

"The Blade of Abraham."

CHAPTER 4 - THE ROAD
Austria, 18 months earlier

"Debbie, check this out," she heard her boyfriend call out.

"Where are you?"

"Over here." She looked toward the sound. He was waving at her from among the deep shadows of the forest. He stood in knee-high brush about twenty paces from the remote mountain hiking trail.

"What've you got, Scott?" It took her a few moments to make her way through the brush. "And why did you have to come this far just to take a leak?"

"Took advantage of the moment to see what the woods are like off the trail." He stooped and lifted the edge of a large piece of metal off the ground.

"So what's your big discovery?"

"I found this underneath some brush and ground cover." He pulled the plate up so she could see the bottom. The faded lettering was barely visible among the rust and corrosion. "What's it say?"

Debbie stared at the words. She'd learned German from her mother and maternal grandmother. It was her interest in her heritage and Scott's graduate studies in history that had inspired their summer backpacking trip through central Europe.

"It's German," she said. "Basically says to turn back, that if you go on you'll be shot."

"Turn back from what?" He glanced about at the dark forest as it followed the curve of the mountain. "There's nothing here."

"Well, nothing *now*," she said. "But by the looks of its condition, the sign must've been around for years. Chances are the only reason it's still here is because it's made of metal rather than wood." She leaned forward. "Hang on a sec." Bending, she gave the sign a closer inspection. "Hold the edge up higher. There's something else near the bottom." She brushed away the dirt and caked-on debris. "Wow!"

"What?"

"I'll hold it while you take a look." Tilting the heavy metal plate upright, she waited until he came around. "See it?"

"A swastika. I'm not surprised. The Nazis took over Austria in 1938. Near the end of the war, Hitler had a plan to make a last stand in the Alpine areas of Austria, Bavaria, and northern Italy. They built a number of heavily fortified bunkers to house the army. When that didn't work out, some say they used them to hide all their looted treasure."

Debbie dropped the sign. "I wonder if we're close to one of those treasure bunkers?"

"Plenty of the stuff stolen by the Nazis is still missing. But it's not likely we've found anything after nearly seven decades. Let's get back on the trail or we won't make it to the next hut by sundown."

"Now it's my turn to have to pee." She waved with both hands, motioning for him to turn away. "I'll just be a minute."

Debbie headed for an area a few meters further into the woods. Coming to the top of a slight rise, she looked down onto what she thought was an irregularity below. The brush there was less dense, less lush, and it seemed to form a pattern, like a trail through the thick forest. "Scott," she called out. Her voice sounded small among the thick oaks and sycamore maples.

She ambled down the slope. Kicking at the brush and vines, she noticed the ground felt especially hard and rugged beneath the scrub here. Ripping out some of the plant growth revealed a swatch of cracked and pitted pavement.

"A road," Debbie said. "An old road." So that was why the

brush was less dense. It struggled to survive atop pavement.

Looking around, she saw more evidence of crumbling pavement riddling the area. The remnants of the road continued through the forest up a gradual incline to the left until it curved out of sight.

She wondered if Nazi transport trucks loaded with gold bullion or rare art objects had once traveled along it. A scrabbling sound and a grunt caused her to turn.

Scott had lost his balance as he came down the embankment and landed on his butt.

"That was graceful."

"What are you doing?" He brushed off the dirt before re-securing his backpack. "All of a sudden I turned around and you were gone."

"Look what I found." She gestured like Julie Andrews on the mountaintop in *The Sound Of Music*.

"What?" Scott said, eyeing the surroundings.

"This." She pried loose a piece of the pavement and held it up. "A road. It must date back decades. Certainly hasn't been used in a long, long time."

"That's impressive. Now can we get back on the trail? The hut is hours away. We're losing valuable time."

"But don't you think this is so cool? You found the old Nazi sign, and now I've discovered a hidden road. Think where it might lead. A German treasure bunker could be right around the next bend." She turned, adjusted her backpack and started walking. "Come on, let's explore a little."

"Not a good idea."

"Why? It's headed in the same general direction as the trail. If we get bored, we can work our way west and jump back on."

Reluctantly, he fell in beside her. "We're going to wind up sleeping on the ground, mark my words."

"Where's your sense of adventure? Everyone takes the trail. We're the only ones following this."

"It's just an old road."

"Yes," she said, picking up the pace, "but one with a Nazi warning that beyond this point we'll be shot. You won't find that kind of adventure on the trail."

They followed the road through the forest as it wound around the side of the mountain. After a couple of miles the trees thinned enough for them to see the rugged incline of the mountain.

"I still don't think we should have taken this side excursion," Scott was saying when they rounded a bend and came to an abrupt halt.

What was left of the pavement seemed to run right into the side of the mountain—at least right into a large pile of rocks and debris.

"Landslide?" Debbie asked.

He shrugged. "If it was, it happened a long time ago. No wonder the road isn't used anymore—it doesn't go anywhere."

"So it went somewhere but there was this landslide and now it ends here."

"Now that we've solved the mystery of your phantom highway, can we try to work our way back to the trail? If we move fast, we might be able to make the hut before nightfall."

"Do you think it continued on past the rockslide?" she asked.

"It doesn't look like there's anything beyond the rocks." He walked to the far edge of the debris pile. "I don't see any road beyond. My guess is that it ended right here."

"That makes no sense," Debbie said, heading over to the opposite side of the slide. "Why build a road that dead-ends on the side of a mountain?"

"Deb, we really need to get a move on."

Ignoring him, she passed the base of the rockslide and wandered into the trees and underbrush. She didn't have to look back to know Scott was following her. His grumbling was loud and clear.

"Why are you obsessing over this place?"

"I'm curious, that's all." She climbed over an outcrop by pulling herself up using low hanging branches. "Don't you think it odd?"

"What? That someone a long time ago built a road that

dead-ended into the side of a mountain?"

"That's just it." Standing on a rock, she turned to face him. "I think the road runs *into* the mountain."

"You mean like a tunnel?"

"Maybe. Why would the Germans threaten death to anyone who came up here if they didn't have something to hide? We could be right on top of your treasure bunker."

"So what are you looking for?"

"What's the one thing you need if you're in a bunker inside a mountain?"

"I don't know. Flashlights? Schnapps?"

"Air."

Scott stared at her for a moment before nodding. "So you think if there's a bunker, there might be some kind of ventilation?"

"Maybe. It shouldn't take too long to find out." She started climbing over the next grouping of rocks.

He looked at his watch. "You might as well take your time, now. There's no way we're going to make it to the next hut. We'll sleep back down on the road and head over to the trail tomorrow."

"Be looking for some unusual feature."

They spent the next twenty minutes investigating, climbing, parting vines and weeds, searching the landscape for some anomaly. At last, just as she was ready to give it up, Debbie spotted something. "Over there," she said pointing and heading toward her sighting.

Scott climbed to join her.

"Look at this," she said, pushing the undergrowth aside to expose a man-made stone and mortar slab. "I should be a detective rather than an engineering major." Protruding up from its center was a metal tube about thirty inches in diameter with a cone-shaped lid mounted on top. The lid sat at an odd angle, having been the victim of wind, rain, rust, and more than one falling rock.

Looking inside the small space between the cone lid and the tube, Scott saw a layer of straw and twigs from generations of bird nests. "Well, I've got to admit, you were right. Somewhere inside is a tunnel or bunker, and this probably leads to it." He looked at his girlfriend. "But finding it isn't enough, is it? You're still not satisfied, are you?"

She slipped her backpack off and tested the strength of the cone-shaped lid supports. "Of course not. Now we go inside the mountain."

CHAPTER 5 - EBAY
Big Bear Lake, Colorado

"You're kidding!" I stared at Kenny as I recalled the first time I'd seen the Blade of Abraham. When I was a teen my family took a vacation to Egypt. During our visit to the Cairo Museum, one exhibit especially intrigued me. I remember standing transfixed and staring at the age-worn twelve-inch-long knife with its simple wood and leather-bound handle that rested in a wooden box. I was drawn to it because of the dramatic story it told, one I'd read as a child in Sunday school. Unlike the cold stone statues and endless rows of pottery in the museum, this simple knife suddenly became a direct connection for me to an event over four thousand years ago.

It was the tale of ultimate faith—how Abraham obeyed God's command to sacrifice his son, Isaac. Only at the last moment did God send an angel to intervene. It had a profound effect on me as I stood there staring at the relic in the exhibition case. Throughout my life the Blade of Abraham was my personal symbol of faith and sacrifice.

Not long after our family vacation, I read that the relic was stolen. I suppose that's what helped lead me to pursue my profession. I started following news accounts of other ancient artifacts being stolen and sold on the black market. After I graduated from college, one of my professors told me of his time in the military as an agent in the Air Force Office of Special Investigations. When I found out they needed an archaeologist and welcomed civilian agents, I joined up. But no matter how fulfilling it was to solve hundreds of cases over the years, I never lost my hope of someday finding and recovering that simple blade: the Blade of Abraham.

"We've been down this road before," I said. "Always a dead end, or the piece turns out to be a fake. What's different this time?"

He set the empty Coors bottle on my porch deck. "When was the last time it showed up on your radar?"

"There were rumors of it surfacing in Damascus five years ago and then a year later in Istanbul." I handed Kenny another cold one from an ice chest at my feet.

"Thanks." He twisted off the top. "And nothing since?"

"Right."

"Until last week. You'll never guess where it popped up. eBay."

I almost spit out my beer. "Are you shittin' me?" Wiping my mouth on my sleeve, I decided to drop into the companion rocker beside Kenny. "What kind of moron would auction a priceless religious relic online?" I looked at him. "And a stolen one at that."

"It appeared under the Holy Land Antiquities category. The auction lasted one hour before it disappeared."

"Any bidders?"

He shook his head. "By the time we got wind of it, the listing was gone. Turns out someone hacked the seller's account to post it."

"I can't believe someone would use a public internet site to try to sell a relic like the Blade. Had to be a hoax."

"That was my reaction at first."

"And they actually called it the Blade of Abraham?"

"Takes balls."

"I'll say. What makes you think it was the real thing?"

"We had eBay send us the cached images, which we forwarded to the Cairo Museum. The pictures were high res, so it was easy to compare to what they had on file. Interestingly enough, it was actually the container the Blade was displayed in that gave the most proof. One of the guys at the museum confirmed a small identifying mark on a corner of the wooden box that matched their records and photos perfectly."

"I remember that box from when I first saw it years ago. So the big question—why is OSI involved?"

"The hacked account belonged to an Air Force officer."

I stared at the starlight reflecting off the dark lake, wishing it had gone that easy for me after… My cat suddenly appeared, winding around my ankles and purring. I put him in my lap, stroking his head and back. "Another of my simple pleasures."

"I never knew you were a cat lover."

"After all these years? Surprise, surprise." I hesitated a moment. I was being bitchy and decided to let it go. "Even as a kid I wanted a kitty, but Mom and Fran were allergic. Now that I'm retired and live alone, I tend to indulge myself. So I got a cat. Named him Nanki-Poo. Nank for short. From *The Mikado*."

"Speaking of Fran, how is your sister?"

"Still a free spirit with a big heart. She took off a few months ago on a humanitarian mission to Haiti after the earthquake. They say twins act and think alike, but I never got her wanderlust. She's with a UN-sponsored relief organization. After her work in Haiti, she headed to Cuba to help out with the victims of the hurricane."

I rocked for a few minutes, petting Nank, enjoying his attention as much as he seemed to enjoy mine, and deeply missing my sister. "I have to admit I'm interested."

Kenny gave me that "I know you so well" grin, the one that had rankled me so often over the years—mostly because he did know me so well, and he knew it. But just for an instant, I felt an old cold trail turn warm, maybe even hot. Then the distant sound of a fish jumping out on the black water and the memory of what I'd done that day three years ago in Iraq near the Assyrian ruins brought me back to reality.

"Despite your tempting news, I'm going to have to pass, Kenny. I wish you luck, but I gotta tell you, I'm perfectly happy right here." I leaned back in the rocker and inhaled the fresh mountain air, clearing my head.

"Come on, Max. What's put out that spark in you? Get

back on the horse, as they say. You aren't afraid. Of that I'm sure. The only thing I've ever known you to fear is heights. So why not?"

He wasn't going to quit, and I could feel the fire of my temper flaring. My posture stiffened, and I glared at Kenny. "It's not about fear. How could you even ask me such a thing knowing what I went through after Iraq?"

"Look, Max, I've put my neck on the line for you."

"Maybe that's what you should have done three years ago."

"You're right. I should have. But that's Monday morning quarterbacking. I was wrong. I've told you that before. But I can't change that."

"No, you can't."

"Time and distance make us see things more clearly. I'm not trying to make up for anything. I'm just trying to do what's right."

There wasn't much I could say to that. Yes, he should have done more in my defense and not let me get beat up so badly with the investigation. But looking back, I realize that at the time he was angry. Interesting that I wasn't as bitter anymore. Maybe a tinge of sourness still rose up now and again—that accounted for some of my snippiness with him. Tangled, tangled webs we weave.

Kenny paused a moment, then continued. "You know, at OSI there's still a black cloud that hangs over the name Maxine Decker. People get all weird when your name comes up. Just so you know, when I suggested bringing you in to help with this case, not everyone got excited. I had to remind them that there was never a shred of evidence that you were involved in that smuggling plot, and that killing Aaron had nearly killed you—emotionally. No way would you have shot your partner without just cause. Oh, they agreed that you were the best one suited for this job, but there was resistance in getting you involved. I pushed hard to turn them around. They relented, and I volunteered to come out here and recruit you. They don't have anyone with your level of expertise. You're it, Max, and if you don't say yes, I guarantee they won't get to the bottom of the Blade issue."

I looked away, lowered my head and rocked a few times before I spoke. "Sorry, Kenny." I faced him again, looking into his disappointed eyes. "I just can't. After the Aaron incident, I was severely depressed and I about lost my sanity. It's been a long road back. I finally get out of bed in the mornings instead of finding no reason to get up, take a shower, or get dressed. And I don't think about hurting myself anymore."

He stared into the night for a long time. "I'm so sorry you had to go through all that, Max. I can understand why even a chance at finding the Blade isn't enough to bring you back. No sense in discussing it any further." He stood. "I hope you have a nice life in your mountain hideaway. I'll just be running along. There's no reason to tell you the best part."

I stared up at him and saw a hint of a smile playing at his lips. God, he could be exasperating. "What best part?"

CHAPTER 6 - INTO THE MOUNTAIN
Austria, 18 months earlier

"Give me a hand." Debbie pushed up on the cone-shaped cover of the ventilation shaft. "It shouldn't take too much to pop this thing off."

Scott removed his backpack and joined her. He planted his feet firmly apart and, with a grunt, pushed.

The cover didn't budge.

"No wonder it's managed to last almost seventy years." She stepped back, inspected the area, and spotted a thin rock shaped roughly like the head of an axe. She studied the rock for a moment before taking a firm grip. Choosing the rustiest of the four support posts holding up the cover, she struck it with a solid blow. The result was a slight bend in the metal.

"Nazi steel was good steel," Scott said. "Let me take a whack at it."

He gripped the stone and repeated her blow. The support gave a little. Three more strikes and the metal broke.

"One down," Debbie said as they shifted their position to attack the next post. Five minutes later, she shoved the now-separated cover out of the way. The old metal cone clanked its way down the side of the mountain and disappeared in the underbrush near the road.

Scott cleaned off the thick layer of twigs, branches and debris. Then he took a firm hold of the metal grate on which all the rubble had rested. Unlike the cone lid, the grate had weakened over the years, and it gave way with his strong yank.

Tossing it aside, Debbie leaned over and peered into the

dark shaft. "I don't see anything."

"Hang on." He dug into his backpack and pulled out a flashlight. "Here you go."

She clicked it on and aimed the beam. "I see ladder rungs. Looks like a maintenance access." She turned to him with a smile. "That means it was designed for a human to pass through. Wanna see what's down there?"

Scott glanced at the sky barely visible through the trees. "It's going to be dark soon."

"So? Can't be any darker down there than it's going to get up here."

"What if the rungs are rusted and corroded like the grate? We don't know if this goes down two feet or two hundred. If one of them breaks, it could be a long fall."

"We've both got rope in our backpacks. You can tie one end around my waist and I'll go first. That way if I get into trouble, your brawny he-man strength can pull me up. Make sense?"

"None of this makes sense. We should be almost to the hut by now rather than climbing down an old German ventilation shaft."

"Getting to the hut isn't going to matter much if we find a pile of gold bullion or a priceless van Gogh. What if this really is that treasure bunker you said might be around here?"

"I guess you have a point."

She patted his cheek. "Get the rope."

Soon, Debbie had climbed over the rim of the ventilation shaft and lowered her weight onto the first rung. Gingerly she tested it with a slight bounce. Scott held the rope firmly. "Seems okay," she said.

"Try the next one. But go slow."

She eased herself down to the second iron rung. Grinning up at him, she said, "See, this—whoa!"

With a grinding noise, the rung gave slightly but held.

"That was scary." Debbie hung to the lip of the shaft, supporting most of her weight with her arms.

"You sure you want to do this?"

She blew out her breath. "We just have to keep thinking: gold, gold, rich."

"Or fall, fall, splat."

"Okay, I'm ready." She stepped to the next rung and with a tepid bounce confirmed that it was solid. "Piece a quiche," she said with a wink. Slowly, she continued.

Pausing every three or four rungs, Debbie took hold of the flashlight strapped to her wrist and aimed it downwards. After about fifty feet, she saw what looked like a pile of more debris. It had collected at a point where the shaft formed a ninety-degree bend.

"What do you see?" Scott called.

"Tie off the end of the rope and come on down. If we have a problem we'll use it to climb back out."

Debbie untied the rope from around her waist and started pushing the litter out of the way while she waited for her boyfriend to join her.

Then she got on her hands and knees and began to crawl along the pipe. The flashlight beam showed large amounts of dust, dirt, and cobwebs. She heard Scott making his way behind her.

Aiming the beam forward revealed more blackness. Although the shaft was big enough to move through on hands and knees, Debbie started feeling claustrophobic. The first tingling of panic flickered in her head. She paused in an effort to shake off the uneasiness growing inside.

The air felt heavy and stale. It seemed oppressive and lacking oxygen. Suddenly, her quest looked less like an Indiana Jones adventure for gold and more like a search for fool's gold.

"You okay?" Scott's voice sounded hollow.

"Yeah, just getting my second wind. The air down here is hard to breathe." She didn't want him to think she was ready to reconsider and turn back. "Give me a second."

Debbie tried filling her head with images of shiny ingots or ornately framed masterpieces. She imagined the newspaper headlines declaring that two Canadian backpackers had stumbled across a massive trove of Nazi loot. Even if Austria claimed possession of the treasure, there would have to be a reward—one big enough to keep her and Scott in the black for years.

"Deb?"

"Sorry." She started forward again. This time, the flashlight beam revealed something up ahead: the shaft was obstructed by a fan and motor assembly mounted on a brace. In front of the fan was a screen to keep animals out.

Approaching the screen, Debbie shined the light past the fan assembly. "The ventilation shaft widens, Scott. It's much bigger on the other side. Looks like it splits off into at least three directions." She moved over against the side of the shaft so Scott could get a look.

"How are we going to get past that?" he asked.

She shined the light on the ends of the supports. Three were corroded enough to have already separated from the mounts. And the protective metal screen didn't appear to be in much better shape. "If I can squish myself into a ball and maneuver around, I might be able to kick the screen and the fan out of the way. It all looks like it's hanging by a thread."

Scott backed up out of her way. "Give it a try, but don't get stuck."

"Gee, I really want to do that."

"Want me to try?"

"Nope. I think I can handle it."

She began by lying on her side and bringing her knees up into a fetal position. Pressing her chin to her chest, she wiggled and squirmed until she had reversed her direction.

"Never knew you were a contortionist."

"Years of acrobatics and interpretative dance classes just paid off." She gave him a quick kiss, then maneuvered onto her back. Sliding forward and bending her knees, she braced herself and kicked at the screen. Unlike the cone cover on the top of the shaft, this obstacle gave way almost immediately. Using the screen as a large surface area on which to kick, Debbie struck with the hardened soles of her hiking boots and soon knocked the fan assembly aside. Then she scooted forward on her butt until she was ready to cross the threshold into the area beyond the fan.

"Careful with the sharp edges," Scott said. "It would be impossible to get you out if you were cut and injured."

"Yes, doctor." Heeding his warning, she moved slowly over the edge of the screen frame and what was left of the fan mounts. Beyond, she entered a junction of three tunnels that were somewhat bigger than the entrance tunnel. Scott joined her as she sat upright contemplating which direction to follow. She aimed the beam in all three shafts but saw only darkness down each. "What do you think?"

"Seems like the left duct would lead toward the front side of the mountain nearest the road and landslide, while the others look like they head more toward the interior. I say we start with that one."

"Left it is." With flashlight in hand, Debbie crawled into the left-hand shaft. A short distance later, it made a turn and continued on. She was constantly brushing cobwebs and dust out of her path as she tried to concentrate on the task at hand and not the panic that was just a heartbeat away.

"You good?" Scott was close behind her.

"So far."

Out of the blackness, her flashlight beam lit up another obstacle. This time she saw the parallel slats of a large, round vent cover. What lay beyond could be the Nazi loot. This might be the biggest moment of her life.

Kneeling in front of the vent, she pushed on one of the horizontal slats. It held firm. She pushed harder and felt a slight, reluctant give. She tried again and the slat creaked like an old door hinge and moved. Along with its fellow slats all connected together, the vent swung open.

She aimed the flashlight into the void.

"What do you see?"

"Nothing." She moved the beam back and forth. "Just a big black space."

"Maybe the vent is mounted on a wall. Try aiming down."

She did, and the light fell on a large box-shaped object.

"You're right. Looks like we're about six or seven feet above something." She repositioned the light until she clearly saw the edges of the shape below.

"Well?"

"It's a truck. I can see the top of a cargo or transport truck. It's open in the back with what looks like a swing-down tailgate."

"That's it? We found a truck?"

"Will you just be patient? Let me see if I can move over . . . wait. There's something on the floor beside the truck."

"So what is—?"

"Oh, my God!"

CHAPTER 7 - NATURAL
Big Bear Lake, Colorado

I motioned an invitation and Kenny dropped back into the rocking chair. He said, "Actually, I had my doubts that the Blade would be a big enough reason for you to leave your piece of paradise and come home to the OSI. Even if that relic has been a long passion of yours." He rocked back. "But there is something else. I don't think you can pass it up."

"Jesus, Kenny, just get to it and knock off all the drama."

He took his time, teasing me, licking his lips and taking a few more rocks in the chair. "I figure you're going to flip when I tell you the name the fake seller used."

I swung around to face him head-on. "I give up."

"Aaron's brother, Travis."

"Son-of-a-bitch!" Travis Knox was who shot me. Standing, I swallowed the rest of my beer then held up the bottle. "This isn't going to do it."

The screen door whined closed behind me as I went inside. Leaning on the kitchen counter I took in several deep breaths through my nose and blew them out my mouth. My mind conjured up the images and sounds of that night in Iraq, causing my stomach to coil and kink with a wave of nausea.

I could still see the dark figure racing toward me from the direction of the smugglers' truck—screaming, shooting. Again, I felt the white-hot pain of his bullets slamming into me. In a fraction of a second, I had seen the fury in his eyes, the baring of his teeth in rage. Something told me I knew him, but it wasn't until a week later while I was still in the German hospital that word filtered back to me of his identity. Our guys, working with Turkish undercover agents, had tried to buy the goods from the Iraqi raid. They positively identified the black market trader as Travis Knox. Before their sting operation went south and he slipped away, Travis admitted to shooting me because I'd killed his brother. He told the Turks he'd carried Aaron's body away and buried him in the mountains. Now Travis had surfaced after so long. And in such a strange manner. Why?

I got my act together and fetched two glasses and a bottle of Johnnie Walker Black.

When I walked back out on the deck Kenny said, "You okay, Max?" He stood and took the bottle. "Want to eat dinner first?"

I shook my head and held out a glass. "Two fingers."

After he poured my drink I offered him the other glass.

"Not done with my beer yet. Maybe later." He crossed the porch. "How's about sitting over here?" He parked himself on the cedar porch swing that hung by chains from the exposed beams. "For old times' sake." He patted the space beside him.

My better judgment whispered *no way*, but my less astute reasoning kicked in. "What the hell." I plopped down beside him. "You always were a persuasive S.O.B."

"Yeah, well, what can I say? By the way, I like your haircut. Didn't think I'd like you with shorter hair, but I do."

He'd also changed some over the last several years. Temples were grayer and threads of silver laced his dark hair, which flattered him, especially set against his slight tan and those hazel eyes. Age hadn't fazed those good looks for which I'd been such a sucker. Damn, it wasn't fair. Getting older didn't treat women that way.

Kenny put his hand on my knee as if regrouping. And that's exactly what it was. He changed the subject.

"I thought I should let you in on this Blade thing. And of course we could always use your expertise. You're damn good. But listen, Max, if you really don't want to, don't do it. Just thought you'd want to know. You deserve the right to say yes or no. Nobody else should make that decision for you. You earned it. I was wrong to badger you."

I sipped the scotch. Drinking it neat, the whiskey blazed a hot trail into my belly. I took another mouthful and closed my eyes when I swallowed. "Knox is a known antiquities smuggler. He's wanted by half a dozen countries. Why would he do something so stupid?"

"Here's my theory." He pushed back so the swing moved a little. "I think he's calling you out."

"You mean like in the old west? High noon showdown?"

"Maybe. What if he found out how attached you are to the Blade, got his hands on it, and figures flashing it around might get you to take the bait and come after it. Killing Aaron certainly had to enrage him. He wants to finish the job he started back in the desert. I doubt he enjoyed burying his brother's body."

"Seems a little farfetched to me."

"Revenge is a strong motivation. He can't come to you because he can't enter the country. But if you went looking for the relic outside the U.S., well… If I were him, that's what I'd do."

I took another sip. "He can run it up the flagpole if he wants. I'm not going anywhere."

Kenny massaged the back of my neck. "What do you have in the fridge? Never mind, I'll just go have a look. I'll whip up something for the two of us. How's that?"

"Thanks," I said, but didn't look at him.

Over the next ten minutes I listened to Kenny banging around in the kitchen as I rolled through my options and the emotions that flurried around his news. I would *absofuckinglutely* love to get that bastard, Travis Knox. For a couple of reasons. Not only had he nearly killed me, he'd corrupted what was once a good and decent man—the Aaron I had so often trusted with my life, the Aaron who had propped me up during my divorce, the Aaron I'd cried with when his wife and daughter died in a car crash. Travis Knox was a despicable human being. It had only been Aaron's hesitation that let me shoot first. At the very end I don't think he had it in him to pull the trigger. But at that instant, I couldn't take the chance. I suppose that'll haunt me forever. The last thing I wanted to do now was get sucked into a trap fueled by vengeance. And yet, it would be a real high to recover the Blade and capture a piece-of-shit like Travis Knox. I looked up as the screen door squeaked open.

"Dinner is served." Kenny emerged with two plates. "Western omelets suit the lady?"

How could he be so frustrating one moment and then so endearing the next? He handed me a plate, fork, and paper napkin, then sat beside me.

"Maybe I'll do it," I said, immediately thinking I would regret the commitment.

"I'm not going to hold you to it yet." He nodded toward the half-empty Johnnie Walker bottle sitting on the railing. "I can't let you make a decision while under the influence."

"It never stopped you before." I realized that was uncalled for. "Sorry." I took a bite of the eggs. "You always were a good omelet maker."

We sat in silence eating. After the last bite, I was full and totally mellowed out. Of all the people in the world, Kenny was the only one who knew all my secrets, all my vulnerabilities and fears.

He extended his hand. "Give me your plate. I've got a pan of hot soapy water waiting. I'll drop them in and we can worry about it in the morning."

I didn't have much resistance left so I handed over the bare plate. Kenny disappeared for a couple of seconds before rejoining me on the swing. His arm slid around me and it seemed so natural.

"Tired?" he asked.

"Pleasantly." I leaned my head on his shoulder.

"I've missed you, Max." He lifted my chin and kissed me. Not hard. Just soft and affectionate. Cautiously, as if he might hurt or offend me. And that felt natural, too.

"It should have worked out," I said. "We messed up."

"What's done is done."

I lifted my head and looked at him. "There were times you made a damn good husband."

CHAPTER 8 - SKELETONS
Austria, 18 months earlier

Debbie drew away from the ventilator shaft as she turned to Scott. Her heart raced. "There's a skeleton down there."

"Really? Let me have a look."

She moved so he could get to the vent. "Shine the light on the floor beside the truck."

He squeezed past and took the flashlight. "I see it. Looks like he was a soldier. He's wearing a military uniform."

"Maybe we've found a Nazi storehouse, or barracks."

"Well, we definitely found something. Let's check it out." He slipped through the opening feet first.

"You should be able to drop to the floor with no problem. It's not that far."

Scott took a final look before letting go. He dropped about four feet. Sweeping the flashlight, he scanned the area.

"Don't start searching for the loot until I get there. I want to find the gold bullion with you." She followed Scott's technique and let her legs go first. Squirming out of the opening, she dropped to the floor.

"It's some sort of a vehicle parking area." Scott shined the light on a half-dozen trucks and military autos lined up along the wall.

The air had an oily smell mixed with rot and the bitter odor of what Debbie figured was rodent feces. She could even taste the rot. "Watch out for rats," she said as they took their first steps. A fine layer of powdery dust covered everything. Each footfall threw up a tiny cloud, like astronauts walking on the moon.

"This is big-time creepy," Scott whispered as they stepped past the skeleton. He swept his light beam ahead. "There's another one."

Debbie saw the second set of bones lying in the middle of the floor. The layer of dust turned the bones and soldier's uniform to a ghostly gray. The bony fingers still gripped a rifle. Scott moved past the soldier's remains but stopped short. "Wow, take a look at that!"

Debbie followed the beam as it fell on two colossal steel doors, so large and heavy they were mounted on train tracks. "Wanna bet the rockslide is just on the other side of those?"

"That's probably what killed these guys. They couldn't get the bunker doors open."

"I don't think so."

"What do you mean? They were trapped by the rock slide and probably starved to death."

"If they were trapped, why didn't they try to escape through the ventilation shaft? Why does it look like they dropped in their tracks? Know what I think?"

"I give up, Detective Debbie."

"I think they were murdered."

Scott turned to shine his light on two more skeletons a short distance away. "You figure someone sealed the place and then poisoned them?"

"The Nazis were pros at gassing people."

"What if some of that gas is still in here?"

She shrugged. "After all these years? Doubtful. The ventilation system is still bringing in air. I'm sure the gas dissipated decades ago or we'd be dropping just like those guys." She turned away from the doors. "Come on, let's go find the treasure."

They moved beyond the trucks, bunker doors, and what looked like a guard station before entering a tunnel wide enough to drive one of the trucks through. The walls were made of brick, with a high, arched ceiling. They almost tripped over a few more dead soldiers. Stepping carefully over them, they passed a number of doors marked with names that Debbie translated as Electric Works, Water Works, Ventilation, Fire, and others.

Scanning from side to side with the flashlight they emerged from the tunnel through a set of double doors. Scott shone the light into an expansive area with a number of partitioned rooms lining the walls. In this new area, more skeletons were found, but these wore civilian clothing, work overalls or laboratory coats.

Checking each of the partitioned rooms, they found a few offices, a machine shop, what appeared to be a large and very serious-looking chemistry lab, a kitchen, toilets, showers, and sleeping quarters. Two skeletons were still in their beds.

"Poor souls died in their sleep," Scott said.

"Never had a chance." Debbie felt her enthusiasm start to dissolve as they followed the perimeter. "This is looking more like a military installation than a Nazi treasure trove."

"There was definitely some kind of scientific work going on here," Scott said. "But why murder all these people?"

"Maybe the murderer didn't want news of what was going on here to ever get out. I'll bet what they were working on was top secret. Best way to keep it a secret is to eliminate everyone who knows about it."

"You think we should go find the authorities and report what we've found?"

"Absolutely. We tell no one until we can talk to the police."

"Let's climb back out, cover the opening with rocks, and get to the next village."

"The sooner we get out of here, the better. I don't like wandering around a tomb." She pointed. "Let's cut across to the tunnel."

Moving cautiously so as not to trip over a skeleton, Scott aimed the beam on the floor ahead. Suddenly, he grabbed her arm and pointed the light on an imposing object blocking their path.

She looked up and gasped. "What the hell is that?"

CHAPTER 9 - MAE WEST
Big Bear Lake, Colorado

The sun pierced the window blinds like knives aimed at my eyeballs. I rubbed my lids from the sting of the light and slowly opened them. Cobwebs as thick as Spanish moss clogged my head.

I heard a snort that made me look to the side. *Shit.* Kenny was sprawled next to me in bed, mouth agape, snoring like a bulldog. I flinched and became acutely aware of the throbbing in my temples. What had I done?

Through my bleary vision, I glimpsed the clock: 7:30 a.m. Maybe we had simply fallen asleep last night after a few drinks. Old friends—you know. I'd cried on his shoulder and he'd held me until I drifted off. But that over-used cliché just didn't work, much as I wanted it to.

Was it possible to slip out of bed without Kenny noticing? Not waking up at the same time in the sack together might make it easier for both of us to ignore whatever had transpired last night. So I carefully maneuvered my legs over the side of the bed, but before I stood I realized I was buck-naked. *Goddammit, Max.*

If I pulled the sheet to cover my body, that tactic would likely wake him up. My only choice was to climb out of bed, grab my clothes, and head to the bathroom. There I was, bare-assed, trying my best not to disturb my ex-husband as my feet hit the hardwood floor, when no sooner had I stood than I felt a hearty slap on my butt.

"Come back here, Maxine Gates."

"Decker," I corrected. I'd taken back my maiden name after the divorce.

He pulled on my arm hard enough for me to plummet onto the mattress. Keeping my back to him, I said, "Kenny, I made a big mistake. *We* made a big mistake."

He chuckled, low and melodic with a sleepy, sexy tone. "That's not what you said last night." He reached around to my breast with one hand as he propped up on his other elbow.

"Well, thing is, I don't remember last night. Johnnie Walker was in bed with you, not me."

He tugged at my shoulders, lowering and twisting me around, his lips suddenly encircling my right nipple. He climbed atop me, and a famous Mae West quip snagged in my thoughts. *Is that a pistol in your pocket...?* How did I possibly find humor in that moment? Then another piece of Mae West trivia flittered to mind. A movie. *I'm No Angel. You can say that again, Maxine.*

I bristled, mostly because of the hangover, but also because I felt a little tingle inside at his touch and was oddly pleased that I still mustered his arousal. I elbowed Kenny and pushed him away. Sitting up, I said, "Listen, we need to forget last night ever happened. Or maybe I should say *you* should forget, because I already have."

I dragged myself out of bed, tugged the sheet free and wrapped it around me.

"Why do you always have to be such a tough wench? Go with the flow. Enjoy the moment."

I snatched my clothes from the floor, and as I closed the bathroom door behind me, I heard Kenny say, "Last night was nice."

He said it softly, but loud enough that I could faintly hear. I wasn't sure if he had said it to me or to himself.

As the shower beat down it cleared the fog from my head, like wiping away murkiness on mirror glass. But that didn't prove to be such a good thing because as the haze moved out, memories from the night came into view—Kenny holding me as we slow-danced barefoot on the porch, my head nestled in the crook of his neck, eyes closed. A romantic stroll to the bedroom with a detour in the hall as he unbuttoned my shirt while I balanced by leaning my back against the wall.

Vigorously I worked shampoo into my hair as if I could scrub away what should not have happened. But worst of all, I kept thinking, *He's even better than I remember.*

———

Between the shower and the coffee Kenny had brewed I was beginning to feel like I might live after all. The java was strong and doctored with milk and three packets of artificial sweetener. Just the way I like it.

I held my cup up toward Kenny like an informal toast. "Thanks," I said after my second swallow. "And listen, let's just leave the elephant in the room alone for now, okay. Let's not talk about it. Never happened."

Kenny sat in the chair across from me at the kitchen table. "We don't have to talk about it, but it *did* happen."

I didn't want to talk about it and I wished it hadn't happened. He had such a way about him that I'd never been able to resist. Now that all those feelings had been stirred up, he'd soon disappear from my life and I'll have to get over him again.

I stood, walked to the sink, and poured out the rest of my coffee. My stomach wasn't ready for anything yet, just like my head wasn't ready to deal with renewing our relationship.

"If you don't want the coffee, you should at least drink something. It might make you feel better if you give it a chance."

I ignored him and went about putting away the coffee can. I decided to go ahead and bring up the OSI business, get it over with, then he could leave.

I propped against the counter. "I've given your offer some thought. I'm not going back to work for the OSI."

Kenny shuffled in his chair. His disappointment was obvious.

"If that's your decision, guess there isn't anything else I can do about it."

That got my dander up a little, wondering if he'd played Casanova last night as part of his plan to lure me back to the organization.

I guess my face betrayed my inner thoughts because Kenny got up from the table, came over and gave me a tender hug. "It's okay, Max. I hear you."

Well, that made me feel like a jerk for thinking he hadn't been sincere the previous evening. As he pulled away, I said, "However, I will go back as a consultant. But on this job only."

CHAPTER 10 - THE HUT
Austria, 18 months earlier

It was late the next morning when Debbie spotted the hut as she and Scott rounded a bend in the trail. They were above the tree line, and although fresh green growth covered large portions of the ground, a fast summer snow had left behind spotty white patches. In the distance, she saw the ridgelines of the Alps.

Most of the over five hundred "huts" along the thousands of miles of Austrian hiking trails were not huts at all but stone and wooden houses maintained by locals, some large enough to sleep and feed forty or more hikers. Debbie had researched it and they had both been pleased to discover the Alpine hut system, which allowed hikers to travel with scaled-down backpacks since they didn't need to bring along cooking supplies, tents, or bedding.

As they approached, Scott said, "Okay, remember, no mention of the bunker or what we found. We tell no one until we get to the next village and contact the authorities."

The front room was paneled with dark pine. A reception desk sat to the left in front of a small room filled with hiking supplies, trail snacks and essentials. Straight ahead was a dining room with three tables and a few booths. Checkered cloths covered the tables, with a small vase of freshly cut mountain flowers sitting on each. To the right was an open-bunk sleeping area with rows of cots. Debbie noticed a sign listing the prices for meals and overnight stays—private bedrooms were available upstairs at an additional cost.

The two were checking in with a polite, well-worn looking middle-aged woman at the desk, when a man approached them.

"Please, meet my husband," the woman said.

"Josef Haupt," the man introduced himself. "I see you've met my wife, Uta."

"A pleasure," Scott said.

Josef's eyes wandered over their soiled clothes. "Looks like you've had a rough time of it."

"We strayed from the trail. Deb likes adventure. But as it turned out, it wasn't a good idea. Lesson learned."

Josef gave them another once-over glance then said, "You'll be staying with us tonight?"

Debbie nodded.

"Open bunking or a private room?"

"Private." Scott pulled out his wallet.

"Your room fee includes dinner and breakfast, and a hot shower," Uta said. She handed Debbie a key. "Room three at the top of the stairs."

Josef added with a smile, "My wife makes the tastiest *kipferl* you'll ever have."

"We'll look forward to it," Debbie said. "I love fresh pastry."

"And tonight for dinner, there's hearty beef stew and some of Styria's famous Schilcher wine." He broke into a big smile. "And of course, we always have plenty of *Weizenbier* on hand."

"You had me at hot shower." Debbie knew they were both filthy from crawling through the bunker's ventilation shafts, and probably smelled worse than they looked.

As Scott paid the forty euros for their stay, Debbie headed past the bunk room to the stairs beyond. She found the room right away. Although it was private, it was also tiny and sparse; two cots, pillows and woolen blankets, a small table with a hurricane-style lantern, and a crucifix on the wall. She planned for a quick shower and then down for a nap, thinking only of the taste of wheat beer and beef stew.

———

Debbie and Scott sat at a table on the front veranda and sipped another *Weizenbier*. Fed and rested, they were the last of the hikers to remain outside enjoying the cool weather and the spray of stars. The handful of others that had arrived that evening had already turned in.

While Debbie hummed a quiet tune, Scott clicked through the hundreds of photos they had taken so far on their week-long hiking vacation. Every so often, he would turn the camera toward her and comment on the current photo.

"So where are you kids from?" It was Josef Haupt. He had wandered onto the veranda.

Debbie looked up as he approached. "Winnipeg, Canada."

Haupt motioned to an extra chair at their table. "May I join you?"

"Of course," Scott said, pausing his review of the photos.

"I visited Winnipeg once many years ago. Saw the Jets play just before they moved to Phoenix to become the Coyotes. Lovely city, great food. Too cold in the winter, though."

Scott nodded.

"So where do you two go to school?"

"University of Manitoba," Debbie said. "We're both in grad school—Scott in history and I'm studying engineering."

"Interesting," Josef said. "I would have thought it the other way around." He motioned to Scott's camera. "Got a lot of good shots?"

"I don't think you can take a bad picture up here."

"Could I have a look?" Josef gestured toward the camera.

Scott held onto the Coolpix a moment, then said, "Sure." Reluctantly he surrendered it.

"Beautiful," Josef said as he advanced through each photo. "Amazing quality of these small cameras."

Scott's chest tightened as Josef kept clicking the arrow to view the next picture. "Yes, they are." He reached out for the return of the camera.

But Josef kept tapping the arrow key.

For a few moments, only the soft beep of the camera's

advance button was heard.

"What is this?" Josef's voice had a hard edge as he turned the LCD toward them.

CHAPTER 11 – DC3
Department of Defense Cyber Crime Center (DC3)
Linthicum, Maryland

Two days after Kenny's surprise visit to my Colorado cabin, I stood next to him in one of the transparent walled cubicles at the DC3 image forensics lab. Surrounded by the constant and somewhat comforting hum of servers and computers, we studied the information received from eBay regarding the listing of the Blade of Abraham.

"Can you zoom in and sharpen both pictures?" I asked the technician at the workstation. Side-by-side, the eBay picture and an authentic Cairo Museum photo split the screen. I waited for him to complete the task. Then he rotated one of the photos and made an overlay. "Looks like it's the real thing," he said. "If it's a fake, it's a damn good one. They match nick for nick."

I turned to Kenny. "What'd you find in the latest computer analysis?"

"Same as we're seeing here. Details are identical. Measurements. Everything. Though we haven't found any indication of manipulation, admittedly, an expert Photoshop geek can produce just about anything he wants."

"Or *she* wants." I said, bringing a smile to the technician's face. "What else have you got?" I asked Kenny.

"The description on the auction doesn't give us much. *You are bidding on a knife from the Middle Bronze Age (about 2000 BCE), which is believed to be the knife the Old Testament prophet, Abraham, was going to use in the sacrifice of his son, Isaac.* It lists the measurements and specifics of the handle and metal blade."

"Go back to the top for a sec." When the tech did, I said, "That's so odd."

"What?" Kenny asked.

"The price: $1,435,121. Don't you think that's a bizarre asking price? Why not an even number like one-mil-five? Weird." I tapped my forehead in thought. "Not only that, but it's just too low. Travis Knox isn't new to the game. He's a world-class black market antiquities dealer. He's savvier than that and knows his prices"

"Maybe the odd asking price was also intended to get your attention."

"Well, it worked. I think if he went to all that trouble, there's got to be additional intel embedded in the listing. We're just not seeing it. Travis wants more than my attention. I'm starting to agree with you that he intends to draw me out in the open so he can get to me."

"He'll never forgive you for killing his brother."

I felt a flush of sickness and had to look away. I'd never forgive myself for it, either. Oh, I can rationalize with the best of them. Of course I had no choice. Aaron was going to shoot me. It was self-defense. But then that one little thought always creeps in. He had told me to just back off, that I wasn't supposed to get hurt. It wasn't part of the *deal*. Maybe Aaron never would have pulled the trigger. As partners we were as close as brother and sister. We had trusted one another for years with our lives.

"Max?" Kenny said.

"Sorry."

"You realize Travis hacked the account so Joe Blow eBay shopper wouldn't know who he was, yet the whole reason for doing it was that he wants to be found. He did it so sloppily it had to be purposeful. He knew we'd contact you, and he also knew you'd jump at the chance to find the Blade."

"Well, so far he's been right on the money, hasn't he?"

"He didn't do much to cover his trail except for hiding his real location. The city given on the auction is the Air Force officer's hometown. We've already eliminated that."

"If he wants me to come looking, why no location? I'm getting more and more confused."

"Maybe he figured if we had known where he was, we'd go straight for him and not get you involved."

"But exactly $1,435,121? Just doesn't make sense. It's not a phone number. Maybe an address?" I shook my head even as I said it. This was really pissing me off. My head ached. "I'm going to catch a cab and go back to the hotel. Maybe something will come to me."

I thanked the forensics technician and told him we would try again tomorrow. Kenny walked me out of the sprawling space filled with investigators' cubicles and down the ramp from the floor that was elevated to hide the thousands of miles of cables and data transmission lines. Stopping at the elevator, he said, "Interested in dinner?"

I gave him a smirk.

"No, really, Max. Just dinner."

"Trick me once, shame on you. Twice. You know the saying."

The elevator doors opened and we both got in.

"I'm not out to trick you. Just wanted to have a bite to eat and some company. But, hey, you want to keep up that attitude, have at it."

It actually made me feel good that he could be on the sharp-tongued side sometimes, too. I watched him in the reflection of the metal doors. He did look good in his fatigues. Always had. And when in his dress blues, killer. Damn him.

"Not tonight, Ken. I'm beat. But thanks."

"That's better," he said. "Big improvement on the attitude."

Yes, it was an improvement. I was working on it. We'd been divorced for over five years, two already when the Iraq incident occurred—the event that nearly destroyed me and so profoundly changed me. At that time he was still confused and hurt about the divorce. It was hard to admit, but I'd neglected Kenny, his dreams, his aspirations, his desires. I was selfishly career-driven, wanting to spend more time working on my career and less time working on our marriage. I know it hurt him. It was only in recent hindsight that I had come to terms with that. And it didn't make me proud. But too much time had passed to start going down those same roads again.

Because of the bitterness after the divorce, Kenny didn't go out of his way to defend me during the investigation. It felt like a knife in my back. In a matter of two years we had essentially deserted one another. Still, even with all the pain we caused each other, buried under all that baggage I knew that none of it had been because we didn't love each other. If I could turn back the clock, things might have been different. I almost chuckled out loud. After all, look how my career worked out for me.

The elevator doors slid open, and I headed to the front entrance. Outside I hailed a cab. It wasn't three minutes into the ride when I told the cabby to turn around. I grabbed my cell phone from my purse and punched in Kenny's number.

"You still there?" I asked.

"Yeah, why?"

"Don't leave."

CHAPTER 12 - JOSEF
Austria, 18 months earlier

Debbie stared at the photo on the LCD. Her mind raced through a dozen plausible scenarios for what she could say the object was. She felt a queasy twisting in her belly, the same one she had experienced when they first saw the large rocket-shaped object mounted on thick steel support gutters in the middle of the bunker. She had sensed in an instant that it was some kind of a horrific weapon the Nazis had developed—the stark black swastika painted on the tail fin had sent chills through her body. Was it an atomic bomb like America had dropped on Hiroshima and Nagasaki? Or worse? Unlike the skeletons scattered throughout the bunker, she believed this thing was still somehow alive. It appeared to sit in the dark, patiently waiting for its time to be awakened...to kill.

"Where did you see this?" Josef asked, his voice filled with apprehension.

Scott cleared his throat. "We found it in the mountains."

The man studied the photo again. "In a bunker?"

"Yes." Debbie answered.

Josef nodded slowly before handing the camera back to Scott. "The rumors have been part of our history since the end of the war. I heard my mother whisper of it—*Der Thor-Bunker.* Growing up, we suspected the Germans built many mountain strongholds throughout this portion of Austria. Some people theorized that it was to stage a last stand against the Allies. But one fortification in particular was surrounded in deep secrecy. The Thor Bunker was the most obscure. Its location was never revealed. But my mother always believed it to be in this region."

"What did they do there?" Debbie asked.

Josef shrugged. "What did they do at any of those Nazi hellholes? No one knows. There were always mysterious comings and goings. Strangers would pass through, heading into the mountains on hidden roads. But there was a belief that at Thor, they experimented with secret weapons—bombs, perhaps even an atom bomb. I once heard someone refer to it as the Uranium *Projekt*. But it was always considered nothing more than rumors. And when the war ended, no one spoke of it again." He motioned to the camera. "Until now." He rubbed his fingers through his thinning gray hair. "What else did you find there?"

Scott gave Debbie a concerned glance. She returned a hesitant nod of approval. He said, "Bodies. Actually, skeletons. Soldiers and civilians. They appeared to have died at the same instant, all dropping in their tracks."

"Probably poison or gas," Josef said.

"The bunker was heavily fortified." Debbie felt the upheaval in her gut start to subside. "A set of huge doors protected the entrance, and outside we discovered a rockslide covering the entrance. We think it might have been deliberately staged to hide the existence of the bunker."

"Inside was a great deal of old scientific equipment." Scott pointed to the camera. "The way it was laid out, the whole place seemed focused on that object."

There was a long pause as the three sat staring into the night and the faint outline of the distant Alps beyond.

Josef said, "Where is the bunker?"

Debbie looked at Scott. "Actually," she said, "we want to speak to the authorities before we disclose the location."

"Very wise of you. You can never be too cautious who you confide in."

"We hope you'll respect our confidentiality, too, Mr. Haupt."

"Call me Josef."

"Of course, Josef," she said. "It's just that we hadn't planned on telling anyone what we discovered until we spoke to the police."

"Your secret is safe with me." Josef started to get up but settled back into the chair. "You know, you might want to have some sort of legal representation as you relate your story to the police. And it just so happens that I'm a retired attorney."

"Thanks, but I'm not sure why we would need legal advice," Scott said. "We just want to tell the authorities what we found and then be on our way."

"It was just an offer in case you need it."

"I doubt that we will," Debbie said. "But thank you just the same." She slipped the camera into her pocket. "What type of law did you practice?"

"Criminal prosecution. I worked in the Public Prosecutor's Office in Graz."

"That must have been an interesting career."

"I helped put many very bad people in prison—murderers, thieves, smugglers. One of my most famous cases involved the successful prosecution of the man who stole Benvenuto Cellini's Silver Cup, which was made for the cardinal of Ferrara. It was taken from Vienna's Art History Museum. I'm sure you've heard of it?"

Debbie shrugged. "I'm afraid I haven't, but I'll bet it was an impressive case."

Josef stood. "Well, that's enough for tonight. We'll have breakfast cooked for you in the morning to start your day." He turned and walked across the porch, calling over his shoulder, "*Gute nacht.*"

As Debbie watched him leave, she felt the resurgence of queasiness. Just above a whisper she said, "I hope we don't regret telling him."

———

It was a strange dream, one that made her feel uncomfortable. She was crawling through the ventilation shaft again. But this time, it was narrower than before and she fought to breathe. She was suffocating. Dust and dirt clogged her nose and mouth. She labored to brush away the obstructions and take in air, but the force…

"Don't move." The voice was just a whisper, close enough to her ear that she felt the moisture from the man's breath. His strong grip over her mouth kept her from calling out.

Even with the pale light of the moon seeping through the small window above the cots, Debbie saw her assailant was Josef. Then she felt the cold edge of a large knife pressing into the flesh under her chin. She heard Scott's heavy breathing as he slept on the cot next to her. She tried to turn her head.

"I said don't move."

Scott stirred. "What?" His words were thick with sleep. "Who's there?"

"Quiet!"

Scott sat up and swung his feet to the floor. "What's going on? What do you want?"

"Both of you get dressed. Don't make a sound or I'll cut her open." He pushed the blade into Debbie's flesh and she whimpered. "I'm going to take my hand away. Scream and I'll slice your throat."

He removed his hand from her mouth and she sucked in air.

"What is it you want?" Scott asked,

"You'll find out soon enough." Josef stood and pulled her up beside him. The point of the knife was now poking into her side. "Get your things. Hurry up."

"Where are we going?" Scott asked as he pulled his backpack from under the cot and slipped into his jeans and shirt.

"For a walk in the mountains. You're going to show me Thor Bunker. And the weapon."

CHAPTER 13 - HUNCH
DC3

I walked up the ramp into the DC3 forensics lab and headed for Kenny's office, glancing at the giant video screen on the far wall where the organization presented their dog 'n' pony show to visiting VIPs. He was there waiting for me. I know Kenny wanted me to say I'd changed my mind about his dinner invitation.

"What's got you so wound up?" he asked.

"A hunch. Can you pull up a world map with latitude and longitude?"

"Planning a trip?" He sat at his desk as I came around and watched over his shoulder. "Here you go."

I repeated the asking price of the Blade on the eBay listing. "Okay, let's start with the first two numbers: one and, four or fourteen." I touched the screen on latitude fifteen degrees south, then nudged up an estimated single degree. As I ran my finger along the fourteenth parallel I called out some of the countries it crossed. "Bolivia, Brazil, Zambia, Madagascar." Then I did the same for fourteen degrees north. "El Salvador, Nicaragua, Guinea, Nigeria, Sudan. Or I could try the first parallel, latitude one south, then try one north."

"There are hundreds of different ways to plug in those numbers to latitudes and longitudes."

"Let's just try some. Bear with me."

"Too many combinations," Kenny said. "Look, let's run these numbers through an algorithm and see how many hits we get. It'll take us days to do this on our own. Maybe it's one degree, forty-three minutes and five seconds north or fourteen degrees, three minutes—"

"I hoped that maybe something would strike me right away."

"Let me send the asking price number to one of my guys and tell him what we want. We'll take a look at all the hits in the morning. What do you say?"

"Okay. I'm convinced his location is buried in those numbers. I'd bet my life on it. He knows the sophistication of this department and doesn't doubt that we'll unravel his code. I'll be back at seven in the morning. Let's get to work on this early."

Kenny spun around in his chair and faced me. He hesitated before saying anything, as if he deliberated whether or not to mention dinner again. He didn't, and this time I think I was the one who was disappointed.

"In the morning, then," he said.

———

I was up by five. Bad dreams had tormented me the little bit I'd slept. The recent events brought a lot of old baggage back to the surface. It served as a fresh reminder of why I had chosen the peace of my mountain cabin, where the biggest concern lately was the return of a mother fox to her den or whether my cat had enough to eat while I was away.

To my surprise, Kenny was already in his office when I arrived.

"I thought I was early," I said, sitting across from him.

"You are. Couldn't sleep so I came in to work. How about you? Sleep okay?"

"Not really. Do you have the results?"

"They should be coming through shortly. Apparently there are more important demands on our analysis department than turning a price on eBay into hundreds of global locations."

"So what kept *you* awake?"

"The puzzle. How do the pieces fit?" Kenny looked at me. "This guy's a badass, Max. Antiquities smuggling, art theft, extortion, fraud, identity theft, not to mention attempted murder of a federal agent—you. And as far as I'm concerned, treason. An Air Force lieutenant colonel who suddenly walks away from his command and disappears without a trace, for his own personal gains, is a traitor. And now he's hell bent on vengeance. You're his target, Max. I don't like the smell of this. You know what? I say, fuck the Blade. It's time for you to walk away. My bad call to drop this on your doorstep."

"It's too late. You know me. I've already stuck my toe in the water. And not just because of the Blade."

"Go home and put it behind you. Let the department do its job."

"You didn't go all the way to Colorado just to bring me here and then tell me to hang it up."

Kenny reached across the desk and touched the back of my hand. "I'm one selfish son-of-a-bitch. Maybe I just needed to see you again."

I pushed the rising emotions down and pulled away, unable to allow myself to fall into that dark hole. "And it's been good. Up at my cabin— that was nice. But it was a one-time shot."

We stared at each other for a moment or two. I was picturing a better time in our relationship when we first fell in love—passionate, heady whirlwind that it was. We met and married within a year. And I bet Kenny was thinking of those days, too. I said, "I'm glad you brought this to me. It was good to see you again. But now it's business. You, of all people, know how I feel about Travis Knox and what he made me do to Aaron. Our job is to focus."

I didn't need to say more.

Kenny leaned back. He let out a sigh that seemed to deflate him. A chime alert from the computer made him glance at the monitor. "Okay, here it is." He clicked on print and scanned the data on the screen while it printed. "I don't think this is going to be of any help."

I heard the whir of the laser and three pages rolled out. Kenny handed them over. I ran down the long list of locations that were the combination of all the lats and longs. Nothing jumped out at me until I spotted an item near the bottom of the second page.

CHAPTER 14 - DECEPTION
Austria, 18 months earlier

Winded and his clothes covered in dust and dirt from crawling through the ventilation shaft, Josef eased down from the vent opening onto the floor of the secret German lab. It had taken them over four hours in the predawn darkness to hike to the old road and the bunker, then another half hour to pass through the shaft. During the trek, the two students said nothing. After a slow and cautious journey into the depths of Thor Bunker, they came to a halt. In the light of their combined beams, they stood before a large metal hulk. Josef swept his flashlight beam over its surface while keeping a pistol pointed at the young Canadians.

"So it is true," Josef said, looking up at the weapon, his gaze falling on the swastika. "I never would have believed it had I not seen it for myself." Awestruck by the bomb's intimidating bulk, Josef noticed the hammering of his heart. He stepped forward and touched the cold metal skin. "It is as if the madness of those years is suddenly reborn right before my eyes."

"Now that we've shown you the way here, please, let us go," the annoying girl said.

"All in good time, my friends."

As Josef continued to inspect the weapon, the young man asked, "Do you think it could be a Nazi A-bomb?"

He shrugged. "I'm no expert by any definition, but when you add up all the stories and combine them with this, it certainly looks like the real thing." He turned back to them.

"There is a great deal of money to be made here. Perhaps millions of euros. The demand for an undocumented, unclassified weapon of mass destruction could bring a fortune on the black market."

"Are you crazy?" the young man turned his lantern's beam toward Josef. "The only purpose this has is to kill. Do you want that on your hands?"

Josef smiled. "I want money in my hands."

"Just who would you sell it to?" she asked.

"There are numerous organizations around the world that would pay virtually any price to possess a weapon of this sort. Especially a device that the world never knew existed."

"Herr Haupt," the girl said, "you must reconsider. If you do this, thousands or even millions could die. It's not worth it to place a weapon like this into the hands of terrorists. I can't believe you're that heartless." Her expression changed to revelation. "Everything you told us was a lie wasn't it? All that crap about being a prosecutor."

"Actually, no. I *was* a prosecutor. I spent years sending criminals to prison while living off a meager public servant's salary. I also watched the guilty go free through bribery and corruption. The rich play by a set of rules different from the rest of us. But now I have the chance to be like them—wealthy beyond my dreams."

"It's wrong," she said. "You don't want the blood of others on your hands."

"Can you imagine how little I make managing that hiking hut and trying to live off a trickle of a government pension? No, this is my one and only chance to—"

The young man lunged forward, swinging his lantern at Josef's pistol. But before he could make contact, Josef pulled the trigger. A deafening blast filled the mountain bunker. In the next instant, the student slumped over and collapsed to the floor, groaning and clutching his midsection. A dark pool formed beside him as blood oozed from between his fingers.

"My God! What have you done?" the girl screamed, dropping her lantern. She knelt beside her boyfriend, trying to press the wound and staunch the blood flow. "Why?" She glared up at Josef, fury and fear in her eyes, tears streaming down her cheeks.

"I told you!" He clenched his jaw. "There may be millions to come from this. Don't be a stupid girl. It's too late for him." She moved his head into her lap. "Oh, God, don't die. Hang on, baby. I'll go get help." But there was no way she could miss seeing the blood spilling onto the floor or the rattling in his chest growing louder.

The young man's eyes were open but blank. He had uttered a few moans, but now was silent.

"You murderer!" Jumping to her feet, she leaped toward Josef, screaming as she grabbed for his gun.

The second blast echoed through the hard-walled bunker, followed by the soft drop of her lifeless body onto the floor.

"Pity," Haupt said, sparing only a moment to glance at her. He shined his beam once more on the imposing Nazi weapon. A few moments later, he headed back along the tunnel to the ventilation shaft entrance, already forming in his head an extensive list of equipment he would need to open the bunker doors and remove the bomb.

CHAPTER 15 - BROTHERS
DC3

"That's it," I said, tapping my finger on the printout. "Manila."

"What makes you think that, Max?" Kenny said. "Look at all the possibilities. There are three pages of locations, single-spaced, for god's sake."

Memories gushed out, convincing me that Manila was the right choice. "When Aaron's wife and child died in the car accident, he was destroyed. I had to scrape him up off the floor. You remember how dark a time it was for him? You and I both thought he was going to lose it. He told me the only family he had left was his brother, Travis. When Aaron skidded along the bottom of his sanity, he reached out to Travis. He really thought it would help him heal. His brother was all he had—good, bad, or indifferent. Their parents had died when they were youngsters. Aaron went to foster care and an aunt took in Travis. They grew up geographically separated but never emotionally estranged. Anyway, after deserting the Air Force, Travis had hidden out in Manila. When Aaron suddenly took leave and disappeared, I had a feeling he was going to find Travis. His brother was AWOL, but Aaron knew where he was.

"It was a bad time for Aaron, and all I could do was try to support him through it. He never got over losing his family, and frankly he was always a bit unstable after that. When he returned, he admitted to me that he had gone to meet Travis in the Philippines. We agreed never to talk about Manila again. I felt sorry for him, so I turned away from the legalities. I knew it was wrong, even at the time, but Aaron was a true friend. Being blind to his misconduct took precedence." I shoved my fingers through my hair. "Travis knows Manila would mean something to me and nobody else."

"It's a long shot. You might be reading way too much into this one location."

"No. You called it. He's drawing me out." I threw a hard glare at Kenny who responded with a maybe-you're-right expression and shrug. "So, let's play. Check on flights to Manila."

"Slow down. We should get some confirmation that he's actually in the Philippines. And even if he is, there's no reason for you to go. We'll arrange through Interpol to have him found and arrested. Then we'll set up the extradition. It's got to go through channels—you know that."

"Come on, Kenny. The paperwork would take forever, and if he got wind of it, he'd be gone in a heartbeat. He's way too slippery to hang around. And you know the extradition treaty with the Philippines is shaky. There's twice as much breaching as there is observing the agreement. Only one route we can take."

"Extraordinary rendition?"

"It's the only way. Snatch him."

Kenny sat back. "I love the way the government uses a sly legalese euphemism for kidnapping."

"Do you see that as a problem?"

"Possibly. The U.S. has lost a lot of respect from across the world because of avoiding due process—at least that's the perception. So I can't justify it, Max. Can't do it."

I gave in to Kenny, though my gut didn't want to. "Then use me. I'm the bait. Dangle me."

"No. If we set this up, let the agency do its job. There's no need for you to get involved any further."

"But I want Knox to believe he's one up and then nail his ass. That would be such sweet victory. I want to see it go down, and I want him to know that I'm part of it, watching and enjoying it happen."

Kenny drummed his fingers on his desk, thinking.

"I really want this guy." I took Kenny's hand. "Let me do this."

Standing, he said, "I can't. We can handle it without putting you in jeopardy. You've already done your part of the job, as far as I'm concerned. Like I said, I never should have dumped this on you. It was just an excuse. Wave at me from the plane on your way back to Colorado."

"Kenny . . ."

"No smooth talking, Maxine. I already said twice that I was wrong about getting you involved."

When Kenny was like this there was some puppy-dog innocence about him that tugged at my heart. But I had to change his mind about my participation. Going after and finding Travis Knox might set me free from my nightmares and my guilt. Kenny had opened the gate the day he showed up at my cabin—now he had to let me run.

My smartphone vibrated and I pulled it from my pocket. What I saw caused my body to go stiff.

"Everything okay?" Kenny asked.

"It's a message—from Travis Knox."

CHAPTER 16 - HIGHEST BID
Austria, 16 months earlier

Josef sat at a table in the backroom of the farmhouse a few kilometers from the small city of Leoben. From his window, he saw the Mur River sparkling in the distance. Nearby was the barn that concealed the cargo truck holding the weapon. The farm had been in his family for over a hundred years and was where he and his wife spent the harshest of winter months, when there were no hikers. She had remained to tend the hiker's hut after he gave her a bogus reason for him to make the trip. She was unaware of the discovery of the Nazi weapon and his plans to sell it. Nor was she aware her husband had murdered the two Canadian hikers. And if he sold the weapon for the amount he intended, he would quickly vanish and she would never know what happened to her beloved Josef.

The recovery project had taken over a month, and had to be conducted without arousing suspicion. First, he located the access point to the remote road leading to Thor Bunker. He then rented a backhoe and spent a week clearing the debris blocking the bunker doors, telling Uta he was helping to clear some blocked road a few miles away and hauling away debris. Next came transporting a generator and lights up to the location and running the power cables through the ventilation shaft. Bringing the motors back to life that powered the doors took days of replacing rotted hoses, belts, and broken pulleys. Once the doors were opened enough, he brought in a forklift and carefully moved the weapon into the back of the truck. The final stage of the recovery involved closing the doors, sealing the ventilation shaft, and using a number of dynamite blasts to re-block and conceal the bunker entrance. With the operation complete, the last step was to send out feelers to the long list of black market and fencing contacts he'd gleaned from years as a prosecutor. He knew all the potential buyers, many of whom had gone free after paying off the police and government officials. In his wildest dreams, he had never thought he would be looking to those criminals as the answer to all his prayers. He'd set the bait and he now waited in the farmhouse for the first bite.

Josef was glad he had set up the computer and satellite at the farmhouse, even though they only spent the winter months there. Sometimes they received reservations for the following summer which helped business, and surfing the internet was a fruitful pastime, especially now, as he searched for potential buyers. Excitement swept over him when an email arrived from a known weapons smuggler and terrorist sympathizer in Algeria requesting a photo of his find. Luckily he had taken a few pictures before removing the weapon and securing the bunker. Josef sent them along, and an hour later received a bid for a quarter of a million euros. Notifying all the parties concerned of the first bid and reminding them of the four-hour time limit, he waited. Within an hour, a second bid arrived—this one for €350,000.

As the remaining hours ticked by, more bids and counter bids came in until there were only five minutes left. The highest bidder so far was from an arms dealer in South Africa for €745,000.

A flurry of bids came in simultaneously from associates in Colombia, Sudan, Uzbekistan, South Yemen, and Azerbaijan, the highest hovering just under one million euros.

Josef watched the second hand on the clock mounted over the computer. As he was about to send his conclusion-of-bidding email, a final offer pinged, this one for exactly one million euros. He recognized the name, but had never dealt with the bidder before. Still, the man's reputation was extensive, especially in the area of rare antiquities and heavy arms.

He clicked on the send button and launched the email to all bidders thanking them for their offers. Then he composed a new email to the winner along with payment instructions to his Swiss numbered account. The email also included details on how the winner could acquire the prize.

Once all the messages were in his sent folder, Josef rose and went to a cabinet nearby. He removed a bottle of peppermint schnapps and poured a generous amount in a crystal glass. Staring out the window, he toasted toward the barn.

"Congratulations, Mr. Travis Knox. You are now the proud owner of a nuclear weapon of mass destruction."

CHAPTER 17 - SALVAGE
DC3

I read aloud Knox's instant message. *Luv Manila this time of year. Same 4 Bear Lake. Here is a pic a friend took. Enjoy. What a pretty little pussy you had. Cat, that is. Maybe the smoke got him before the flames.*

No! I looked at the photo and gasped, suppressing a sob. It's gone. All ash. The bastard. The fucking bastard!

"What is the picture?" Kenny said as he came around the desk.

A knot coiled in my gut and I thought I was going to throw up before I could talk. "It's my cabin. Oh, dear God, Nank. Poor Nank. He killed Nank and burned my home to the ground."

"Jesus, Max." Kenny put his arm around me. "Don't look at it."

I hung my head, bracing my forehead with my palm when my phone chimed again. I glanced back at it as a second MMS message came through. I stared into the face of Travis Knox. The dark eyes distorted through thick lenses, the wavy red hair, the sarcastic mocking smile. He sickened me.

"He's obviously got contacts in the U.S. Somebody set my cabin on fire and took the pictures. I live up there alone. He could have had me killed thousands of times over the past year. And Nank, for god's sake. What's the purpose of killing a cat?"

"Appears he doesn't just want to kill you, he wants you to suffer. Strip you of the things you love. Retaliation for taking away the only person in his life who cared about him."

"But it's been over three years since Iraq," I said.

"You know the saying—revenge is a dish best served cold."

"Yeah, but I'm not buying that. I think this goes deeper."

"He's a diabolical barbarian, not just a simple-minded hoodlum. A sociopath with no conscience. He's determined to first torment you and then kill you. Maybe he hasn't let anyone else do it because he wants to be the one. He's sick, Max. Hand me the phone."

I gave it up. "What are you doing?"

"Checking the number the message was sent from." He scribbled on a desk pad, then went around to the computer. I was still too shocked to even follow him. I sank into the chair, thinking of Nank and my cabin, and how my dream had just turned to ashes.

Another message came through. It was from a neighbor several miles down the road from my cabin who checked on Nank every few days to make sure he had enough food and water. His text was one of sympathy telling me he'd gone to look after my cat and found the cabin burned to the ground. I started crying.

"Got it," Kenny said. "Sixty-three is the country code and two is the city code for Manila. Looks like we've got confirmation he's there."

I wiped my tears away. "So start the arrest and extradition process. And you can tell the Philippine authorities I'm going along for the ride."

"Max—"

"Didn't you see those pictures? He torched my life. Travis Knox has taken the last thing from me that he ever will. No more." I hesitated before I spoke again, because I knew if I went on I risked feeling an avalanche of vulnerability. It would be like standing naked in front of the world. Before I knew it I heard the words bumbling out of my mouth. "There is something else I've never told you. That night in Iraq, Travis did a lot more than shoot me. I'd worked hard to get where I was in my career—you know that better than anyone. And I believed that I was a good agent. A smart agent. Worthy of being an agent. But in the matter of a few seconds I became acutely aware none of that was true.

"I was blindsided. I never saw it coming, Kenny. Never saw any signs in Aaron that he'd gone sour. I wasn't on point. If I had been, I could have stopped Aaron, and he'd still be alive. In just those few seconds, a simple flicker in time, in the dark of the desert, I lost all faith in myself along with my dignity. I wasn't who I thought I was at all. Travis Knox has executed so much emotional and physical destruction that I don't think I'll ever be the same. I've lost a part of me. If I can bring him to justice it may salvage some of my self-respect. I don't just want to do this—I *need* to."

"I get it, Max. But you're wrong. No one could have seen it coming, not you, not me, not anyone. These pictures are nothing but a ploy, a tease. He's pushing your buttons with a bunch of—"

"What?" I asked.

Kenny swung his chair around to face his computer. He pulled an adapter cable from a drawer and connected one end into the Blackberry with the other into his desktop.

"What are you thinking?" I leaned forward, fascinated.

With a sly smile, Kenny turned to me. "He just made his first big mistake."

CHAPTER 18 – APPLEWHITE
Las Vegas, 10 months earlier

Reverend Hershel Applewhite groomed the crown of gray hair and peered into the hand mirror. He rubbed his front teeth with his forefinger, making them shine to his satisfaction before handing the mirror off to the makeup assistant.

"You look fine, Reverend Applewhite," the woman said as another assistant adjusted the robe over his shoulders.

Lank and tall, some of his bones created sharp angular plains and juts. His shoulders were one of those places. His disproportionate cheekbones another, creating sunken flesh beneath them and shadows under the eyes. Sometimes he looked more like an undertaker than a man of the cloth.

"Stand by, everyone. Recording in three, two, one." The technical director's voice was calm and soothing in Applewhite's ear prompter as the stage manager pointed to the televangelist, and camera one's red light lit up.

Applewhite heard the fifty-member choir begin the angelic theme of the non-denominational Applewhite Ministry of Deliverance as their voices filled the ethereal-like Golden Throne Cathedral mega-church in the desert northeast of Las Vegas. Someone once told him the gleaming spires and lofty recesses of the church reminded them of a scene in *Star Wars*. And in many respects, it did look like a towering, futuristic movie set. But wasn't that the idea? To remind his flock of the uplifting glory of God and the promise of the sparkling towers of Heaven?

And what a flock it was: eight million U.S. households

tuned into his ministry each Sunday, along with millions more around the globe. God is great, he thought. And so is his work on earth.

The special-effects fog machine had already been churning out billowing clouds, and as the camera and the live five-thousand-member congregation first saw Applewhite's image, it appeared as if he were emerging through heavenly cumulus. And in Applewhite's mind, he was. He'd known since he was a boy that he was more than simply human, he was a spiritual being, belonging to a special rank of heaven. The memory of his childhood epiphany was painful, but he believed it was through pain that man redeems himself.

Applewhite found his mark on the stage and outstretched his arms to his viewing audience. "Brothers and sisters, let us begin by giving thanks." He recited a prayer from memory while his mind wandered back to childhood. When he was seven years old, it was a trying time for the family. His father decided that they should fast to prove their love for the Almighty, and in return, God would lead them out of their financial despair. It was the second day of the fast and he'd been so hungry as he attended to his daily chores. When he went to feed the chickens he caught sight of the blueberry bushes, rich with the deep royal blueberries. His mouth watered and his stomach grumbled. He grabbed a handful of the berries and crammed them into his mouth. Never in his young life had anything tasted so deliciously sweet and succulent. Manna from Jehovah.

Unfortunately the blueberries left a stain in the corner of his mouth. When his father noticed the discoloration, he went into a rage, dragging Hershel out to the barn by a hank of his hair. Hershel expected a switching but instead was told to go to a dark corner in the rear of the barn where they stored old furniture and appliances. "Here," his father said, slapping the top of an old rusted washing machine. "Give me your hand. Your right hand."

Hershel had no idea what to expect as he obeyed.

His father gripped the boy's wrist and shoved the fingertips between the rollers of the wringer atop the washer.

"Papa!" Hershel cried, realizing what was about to happen.

But it was too late.

Keeping a firm grip on his son's wrist so he couldn't pull away, his father turned the crank, crushing the fingers of the right hand, all the while praying, his voice rising above Hershel's screams.

When the deed was done, Hershel collapsed, his breath so sucked from him that he wasn't able to cry.

"Now you know what eternal damnation would be like, boy. If you sin, you will spend eternity in such suffering. That is the pain of hell. Let this be a lesson. Seek forgiveness." His father headed out of the barn, shouting over his shoulder, "Repent."

Hershel lay on the dirt and straw for over an hour writhing in pain before having the strength to go into the house. His mother caught a glimpse of his mangled hand as he climbed the stairs to his room.

"Hershel?

"Quiet, woman," his father said. "Let the boy be. He needs to get right with God."

Hershel crawled onto his bed, his hand throbbing, excruciating pain radiating all the way to his shoulder. But he had to pray through the pain if it was to end. With tears streaming down his face, he prayed for forgiveness, begging God for mercy. The pain was so great that sleep would not come. Sometime in the night, he was certain he heard the voice of God, as clear as if the Almighty stood beside the bed. His repentance had been accepted, and God told Hershel that he was special and should devote his life to tending to His work. At last the boy drifted into an exhausted slumber. When he woke the next morning the throbbing in his hand had been replaced by a dull ache—confirmation from God that he'd been forgiven. But the crippled fingers would remind him for a lifetime of his calling to serve.

The reverend's memories faded and turned to the awareness of his audience.

As Applewhite stared out onto their faces and played to the camera, he was thinking that sinners had to be punished if they were to be brought to God. Sincere repentance was born out of punishment *and* pain.

"Let us raise our voices to the heavens. Wherever you are right now, lift up your hearts and words to God." The music cued into his ear prompter, and he led his congregation in a rousing gospel version of "We Are Going to See the King.".

The crowd stayed on their feet even after the song ended, still clapping and swaying as Applewhite spoke out.

"The day of judgment is coming. We're going to see our God. Hallelujah."

A burst of Hallelujahs and applause rang out from the group.

"Glory, glory," Applewhite repeated, crisscrossing the stage with a theatrical strut, bending deep into the hand-held microphone, then stretching high. "Glory to God in the highest. As it was in the beginning, is now, and ever shall be, world without end. Praise to the Lord. Praise to the Father, the Son, and the Holy Ghost." Voice ringing, exaggerating, and drawing out words. Rising and falling dramatic tones. "Yes, friends, brothers, and sisters. The day is coming when we must account for our sins. We are going to see our Maker. Soon. Very soon. There will be no troubles then. Glory be to God." He was giddy with bliss. "Oh, God I want to see you."

The crowd roared, some sobbing, some shining with joy.

Oh yes, Applewhite thought, he was at home here in these moments on the stage before his flock. Peace and elation filled him. The money, though more than bountiful, was secondary. "We will all see the face of the Almighty. We will spread the word of the Holy Book to the ends of the Earth. We will pick up those who have fallen, those sinners who must come to God, and carry them on our backs through the door of repentance. Hallelujah."

He wondered if his followers understood how deeply he meant that. Yes, he was special. God had told him so as a boy. And he was convinced that one day very soon God would reveal His extraordinary plan.

Fifty minutes later, when the service ended and the production credits rolled, Applewhite bid his flock farewell, disappeared in the fog and left behind a cathedral-filling, thunderous rendition of "Amazing Grace".

"Father." Carl Applewhite waved at the televangelist from off stage. "You've got a personal phone call."

"Take a message, son."

"He insists he speak to you. He says he has something that should be in your hands only. Something about Abraham."

CHAPTER 19 – LAPTOP
Manila, the Philippines

From behind the darkened windows of the black SUV, I watched the Parañaque City cross streets fly by. Kenny sat beside me—the driver and front passenger were members of the Philippine National Police. Three more sat behind us, and an additional three SUVs followed, each filled with heavily armed assault specialists.

"We're two minutes out," said SPO2 Dela-Cruz as he glanced back at me from the passenger's seat. With a physique like an oversized fireplug, he filled the seat with every inch of his body.

"Thank you, Sergeant." I watched the congested traffic of jeepneys and cars move out of our way as the police sirens warbled into the hot, sticky night. Kenny and I had arrived at Ninoy Aquino International Airport just over forty-eight hours after routing the investigation through Interpol and requesting the PNP surveillance of the house believed to be where Travis Knox was staying. The PNP picked us up at the terminal and whisked us directly to the suspect's location.

It was nice work on Kenny's part back at DC3. After examining the pictures Travis had attached to the text message, Kenny downloaded them into his computer while explaining to me that most current smartphones have a built-in locator system. Using what he called EXIF data (Exchangeable Image File), the latitude and longitude of each picture taken with the phone's camera is embedded into the digital photo's metadata, along with date and time stamps, the phone serial number, and exposure settings. We quickly determined that the three pictures of my Colorado cabin were taken with a different camera than the photo of Knox. And what Kenny concluded was Travis's big mistake turned out to be the exact location of the Manila suburb house. As smart as the black market smuggler was, we were both convinced he had unknowingly sent us a confirmation that he was not only hiding in the Philippines, but his exact address.

I'd convinced myself that after Iraq I never wanted to come back to this line of work. But I had to admit that the excitement of the chase was addictive. And I liked the feel of my newly-minted OSI ID and badge in the pocket of my jacket.

"Sixty seconds," Sergeant Dela-Cruz said over his shoulder as the sirens were silenced and emergency lights extinguished. "Okay, here's the deal. We'll be approaching the house from the front and down the side to the rear. Two fifteen-man teams—Tiger and Alpha. The back of the building is high-walled in so there is no escape from that direction. A man generally fitting your suspect's description was seen entering the house six hours ago and has not come out. Understand that you two must remain in this vehicle until we gain access to the building. Once we confirm that the suspect is apprehended and the structure is secured, I'll alert you." He handed Kenny a two-way radio. "We'll let you know when it's safe to approach. You'll be able to hear everything that goes down, so you won't miss a thing. Any questions?"

I glanced at Kenny, then shook my head. "None, Sergeant. We'll wait for your all-clear."

Our rapid trip from the airport through the streets of Manila suddenly slowed as we glided to a quiet stop at the curb in front of a dark townhouse. When the assault team opened the doors to the SUV, I got a whiff of smoky meat cooking. There were faint sounds of rap music coming from a nearby house and a dog barking in the distance. This was a quiet suburban neighborhood about to be rocked by a thirty-man federal police assault operation. Knox was such a prick to drop this mess into the middle of innocent lives.

I noticed the interior dome lights didn't come on when the vehicle's doors were opened. That way the doors didn't need to be completely closed, thus creating no sound and no lights.

Sergeant Dela-Cruz and the rest of the team wore black combat gear, body armor, helmets, and black "Jason" masks that concealed their faces. They carried Colt M4 automatic assault rifles. I watched them form two lines along a wall by the sidewalk before slipping silently into the darkness—each man's hand on the shoulder of the one in front.

Our two-way radio crackled.

"Tiger team?" It sounded like Dela-Cruz.

"Position one."

"Alpha team, position one." It was Dela-Cruz again. "Tiger team, advance to position two."

All the voices were just above a whisper. A moment later, the second team leader said, "Tiger team, position two."

"Stand by." Dela-Cruz was as calm as if ordering a pizza. "On my mark. Three, two, one, mark."

Like black ghosts, alpha team rushed the front steps. I couldn't see tiger team, but I guessed they were storming the back of the house. The assault was followed by the shattering of glass, and a series of white flashes from concussion grenades lit up the interior of the house. The front door disappeared. A second later, the ghosts rushed inside, weapons at shoulder-ready.

Now the voices turned from whispers to shouts and commands: "Police! Police! Police!" Soon, the shouts turned to: "Clear. Front room clear. Kitchen clear. Bath clear."

Each room in turn was called out as the assault officers determined that it was searched and safe. Within twenty seconds, the radio fell silent. I could hear breathing but no voices. Dela-Cruz said, "Agent Decker, you and Agent Gates need to see this. Back bedroom, second floor."

Kenny and I exited the SUV and moved with caution along the sidewalk to the front entrance. The calm and quiet of the neighborhood turned into shouts and concerned voices as residents came out of their homes to see what had caused the loud booms and commotion.

As we approached the blown-out doorway, lingering gray smoke hung in the air. We passed through the living room, empty of any objects, furniture or rugs. An assault officer motioned to a set of stairs. I took a quick glance around as we climbed the steps. It appeared that all the rooms were equally empty. Tattered soiled sheets covered the windows.

Once at the top of the stairs, another officer pointed to a doorway at the end of a hall. Stepping into the bedroom, I saw Dela-Cruz and a number of other members of his assault teams standing in a small group with their backs to us. I approached and a couple of the men moved out of the way. Sitting on the top of a plain, three-step wood ladder was an open laptop computer. The soft light of its LCD screen gave off an eerie glow in the semi-dark, barren room.

Kenny and I approached and leaned forward, trying to make out the image on the screen. It was slightly out of focus and grainy, as if originating from a location with poor lighting.

"Is it a photo?" I asked.

"Maybe a webcam," Kenny said.

I realized that the grain in the photo was unstable as if the autofocus of a digital video camera was trying to grab onto a light source or object. Then I noticed the small blue light from the laptop's built-in webcam had just turned on. At the same time, a face moved into frame on the LCD.

Travis Knox.

"Hey, bitch," he said. "Welcome to Manila, the armpit of the universe." He turned his gaze slightly to the side. "No offense, Sergeant Dela-Cruz."

"He can see us," I said just above a whisper.

"Of course I can see you." Knox grinned. "It's like we're havin' a party. Where's the drinks and chips, Kenny Boy?"

"What is this shit?" Kenny said.

"I just told you—it's a party. You guys know what makes for a great party? Party poppers." He held up his hand. In it was a device with a button on top—his thumb resting firmly on it.

"Clear the building!" Dela-Cruz yelled. "Everyone, out, out, out!"

Kenny and I turned simultaneously, but I hesitated. Spinning back around, I grabbed the laptop, slammed it shut, and cradled it under my arm like a football. A second later, we were taking the stairs three steps at a time. We burst onto the street and ran to the safety of the SUV, crouching behind it and bracing for the explosion and shock wave.

Kenny still held the police radio and I could hear heavy panting from the members of the assault teams as they found a safe place to hunker down. No one spoke.

We waited.

Thirty seconds ticked by. Then a full minute. No explosion. The night turned strangely silent. And then I heard it. Laughing. Thin metallic laughter. It was coming from the laptop.

CHAPTER 20 – FIRST CONTACT
Las Vegas, 10 months earlier

"Hello," Applewhite said into the phone.

"Reverend Applewhite, I hope this is a good time. If not, I'll call back at a preferred hour."

"Who is this, and what is it that you're calling about? My son said something about Abraham. I don't mean to be rude, but I have a busy schedule, so please make it quick."

"Reverend, I am a faithful follower of your ministry. I believe in everything you preach, and know that you have indeed been hand-selected by God. One of the things that convinced me to contact you is that even though chosen by the Almighty, you have not elected to declare yourself as His chosen one, His anointed prophet on Earth."

"I appreciate your vote of confidence and your dedication, but I am nothing more than God's humble servant here to do his work."

"Reverend Applewhite, I have read between the lines, and I hear your message coming through loud and clear. God has spoken to you and promised that you will become his warrior on Earth. You will prosecute His justice and proclaim His glory."

"Again, I appreciate your interpretation of my sermons, sir, but right now I must be about my business."

"I have an artifact that only you merit possessing. For you are the single person alive who is truly here to do the bidding of the Almighty."

Applewhite's eyebrows rose as did his curiosity, but only

slightly. "Is that so?" He thought of the many crank calls he had received over the years. And in between the calls from the wackos were the pleas for some off-the-wall cause or charity. Most only wanted to fatten their own pockets. It seemed that inside the deeply religious community there were numerous skewed and unscrupulous people. Everyone wanted his attention, and they would do or say anything to get a piece of the one hundred thousand dollars in contributions his ministry averaged each day worldwide. This sounded like just another con, another scam. He let these urchins have their say, then blessed them and sent them on their way. But this caller did mention one thing that piqued his attention. An artifact. Something to do with Abraham. That was a new ploy for sure. "Go on."

"It's a relic destined for you. Only you."

Applewhite slipped off his robe and pitched it to a stage hand as he prepared to bid the caller farewell and hang up. "Get to the point and tell me what you're talking about. I have a lot to do and can't spend time on the phone going around in circles."

"I assure you that this is not a waste of your time. I am convinced that you are the new leader of God's army and an extension of His will. It is imperative that you listen to me. I have the one object that can, without any doubt, lay claim that you are the one who will direct the sinners of the world and set them on a path of repentance and redemption."

Maybe his first instinct had been correct, Applewhite thought. This was just another nut job.

"I hold in my hand the blade that Abraham was prepared to use to sacrifice his son. I have the Blade of Abraham."

Applewhite gasped. *My God, if this were only true! Abraham, the patriarch of the Jews, the Muslims, and the Christians.* "Excuse me a moment, please. Don't hang up." He dismissed a trailing assistant, and with the cordless phone in hand, headed to his dressing room, where he closed the door. "Sorry. I thought I should speak to you in a more private location."

"Of course."

"How did you get this artifact, and what proof do you have that it's real?"

"As I'm sure you're aware, Reverend Applewhite, Abraham, along with his sons Isaac and Jacob and their wives, was buried in Canaan in the land east of Mamre at a place called the ancient Double Cave of Machpelah. His resting place has been revered since at least one thousand BC. Herod the Great constructed the Tombs of the Patriarchs in Hebron over the burial site in the first century BC."

"Let me stop you. I have doctorates in theology and Biblical history. What you're telling me I learned in Holy Land history studies in my sophomore year."

"I'm sorry. I don't mean to be condescending, but I want to establish a timeline that you'll find convincing. May I proceed?"

Applewhite glanced at his Rolex Submariner. "Thirty seconds is all you've got left."

"Thank you. After the 1967 war, Israeli archaeologists exploring the Cave of Machpelah discovered numerous Iron Age artifacts and Crusader relics. As they went deeper into the underground, they came upon the crypts of the prophet and his family. The only object buried with Abraham was a simple blade with a wooden and leather-bound handle, exactly fitting the ancient description and dimensions described in the Scrolls of Canaan discovered by the Crusaders in the twelfth century. Those writings told that the Blade was buried alongside the great prophet and gave an exact description.

"After the Egypt-Israel peace treaty, many cultural exchanges were made between the two countries. One of the artifacts on loan to the Cairo Museum was the Blade of Abraham found in the Tombs of the Patriarchs. In 1982 it was stolen, along with a number of other Israeli treasures, some say to embarrass the Egyptians and anger the Jews."

"Your time is up."

"Six months ago, while I was in Iraq acquiring a number of rare pieces from the former Baghdad Museum, the relic came into my possession."

Applewhite felt his pulse quicken. Not only because of the chance that this might be true, but because it just might be *the* sign. The sign he prayed for each day. The sign God had promised him on that terrible night as he lay suffering the pain from his crushed fingers. Perhaps, at last God would reveal his mission. And what a splendid one that would be if he was destined to be the new Abraham. "So what you're telling me is that you're a dealer of stolen property? You trade on the black market."

"Reverend, you can call it whatever you wish. The point here is that one of the rarest religious objects in history has made its long journey down through four thousand years to this time and this place. God has used me to deliver it to the one man who will do His work. You yourself preach that God works in mysterious ways. By whatever means this has taken place, I have what you want—what you need. Move past how it came to you and concentrate on why. It came because God willed it."

Applewhite wiped the sweat from his forehead. He looked at his right hand and the mangled, deformed fingers. At last he was to understand God's plan for him. He was to become the blade of God and wield His power in the name of the Almighty.

"Reverend Applewhite, are you still there?"

"Yes." He sank into a nearby chair. "If I wanted to view this object, how would I go about it?"

"It can be arranged, but it would have to be a most private undertaking. You could never disclose any details of the meeting. And if you decide to possess the Blade, you must never make public that you possess it. I'm sure you understand."

This would be an illegal exchange with serious consequences if found out. But he saw no problem with either the confidentiality or the secrecy. "What is the price of this relic?"

"That's the best part, Reverend. There is no price. It's my gift to you."

CHAPTER 21 – THE BIG BANG
Manila, the Philippines

I sat on the street behind the SUV and carefully opened the laptop. The face of Travis Knox still filled the LCD, his laughing poured out of the tiny speaker. The light from the laptop's webcam still glowed. He had configured the computer to remain on even if it was closed.

"You should see your face," Knox said between chuckles. "What's the matter, can't take a joke?"

Sergeant Dela-Cruz had moved to the back of the SUV to watch. "This was a joke?" he said through clenched teeth.

"A dry run, Sergeant," Knox said. "Consider it a dress rehearsal for what's in store for Agent Decker."

Knox checked his watch. "Sorry, Kenny Boy. Look at the time. Gotta run." He reached toward his computer but hesitated. "Just to let you guys know, there are no explosives in the house. At least I don't think there are. Can never be too sure, can we? I'm saving them up for the big bang. Until next time."

The screen went dark, and the laptop's webcam indicator light died.

"Get the bomb squad down here right now!" Dela-Cruz said. "And evacuate everyone within a two-block radius."

"Let me see that," Kenny said, reaching for the laptop.

I watched as he used the built-in mouse pad to click on the *show hidden icons* arrow on the task bar. Next, he clicked on the internet access network icon. "It's connected to a wireless network called *Paco*." He looked up at Dela-Cruz. "The router is probably no more than a few hundred feet away. Once the bomb squad is done, have your men search the surrounding houses. Chances are, Knox, or whoever his accomplice was, hacked into the router, and the owner has no idea our friend was stealing his Wi-Fi signal. But he might be able to identify Knox or the guy who set this up."

"Sergeant," I said, "didn't you mention that a man entered the house earlier but never came out?"

Dela-Cruz nodded. "We assumed no one would go over the high wall in the back. Mistake." He turned to his men, who had gathered around. "You heard the agent. As soon as the house is clear, start knocking on doors. Find that wireless router. I want the owner standing right here." He pointed to the ground.

Kenny went to the front of the SUV and rested the laptop on its hood. The sergeant and I joined him. "Can we see the route of his webcam's connection and where it originated?" I asked.

"You're reading my mind." Kenny opened the network configuration window and started examining the internet provider's login data. A moment later, he said, "No big surprise here. Knox used Tor—The Onion Router network."

"Onion?" Dela-Cruz said.

"Tor is a free network of virtual tunnels that create layers just like peeling an onion. Running a trace route shows that his connection bounced all over the world through dozens of router points. Impossible to find the source. It's virtually anonymous."

"So he could be next door or thousands of miles away." I said.

"Afraid so." He closed the laptop. "I'd like to take this back to DC3 for analysis, if that's okay, Sergeant?"

"You can have it when our lab is through examining it. Wait around for it or we'll ship it to you, it's your call."

"We specialize in this sort of thing."

Dela-Cruz held out his hand. His expression was firm. "We have an excellent forensics lab, Agent Gates."

"Of course you do." Kenny reluctantly handed over the computer. As the officer walked away, Kenny added under his breath, "Let's hope they've moved beyond DOS."

I heard the rumble of a large truck. The bomb squad rounded the corner at the end of the street and pulled up in front of the townhouse. While four men got out and finished putting on their protective gear, I turned to Kenny. "So what the hell was this all about?"

He watched the beehive of activity around us. "Knox is playing a game. Trying to prove how much smarter he is. It's all about control. But to what end? That's the big question."

"I've got an even bigger question."

"Which is?"

"What's the big bang?"

CHAPTER 22 – COCKFIGHT
Puerto Rico, 9 months earlier

Herschel Applewhite drove east from San Juan in his rented Nissan. Along the potholed Highway 3, he passed shanties and ramshackle buildings, this route delivering the impression that the entire island was poor, the exception being the exclusive beachfront resorts and hotels. Such a waste of a beautiful island eaten alive with human pollution, he thought. Even from a distance he could see the giant verdant hunk of El Yunque Mountain rising into blue sky, the pinnacle of the rainforest shrouded in mist. Perhaps after he completed his mission, he would have the opportunity to visit what his imagination conjured as a splendid tropical paradise, complete with exotic creatures and flora. Even the croaking of the tiny coqui frog last night at twilight outside the hotel had helped create the appealing foreign atmosphere. Oh, to be able to sit back and luxuriate in this environment would be a blessing. But he had been given a different blessing, and he was, at the moment, undertaking part of that task.

Upon Applewhite's arrival at the Ritz Carlton yesterday afternoon, the desk clerk handed him a sealed envelope that had been delivered earlier. Inside were directions to the town of Fajardo and a small cockfight arena off the beaten path. When originally contacted, Applewhite asked why he should travel to Puerto Rico. The response was simple. Traveling to and from the island wouldn't require a passport, nor would Applewhite need to go through customs, an important element considering what he would be taking back with him. And why the cockfight arena? he'd also asked. Because no one would ask questions. This was not a big commercial arena, but rather a family business passed on through several generations where traditions were embedded in the culture. Here, discretion was an understood and respected code. No one needed to reveal their identity, nor anything else they cared not to share.

Applewhite parked in the dirt lot in front of the orange arena that looked much like an aging barn. The fights had not yet begun, but men were already gathering at the bar and also checking in their fighting cocks for examination and weighing. Some sat with partners, both men and women, young and old, inside the arming room where they bound artificial spurs to the cocks' feet.

Floor-to-ceiling cubbies began to fill with roosters waiting for their numbers to come up to do battle, sometimes to the death.

Applewhite bought his ticket for the front row and took a seat in the circular wooden stands. A pulled-down cap and dark sunglasses helped to hide his face from any possible members of his worldwide congregation. To his surprise, there was no reeking odor of chickens or blood. After another thirty minutes the stands filled, not just with men as he had expected, but families with small children, too. The first cocks were carried into the ring in cloth sacks, strung on a scale, and weighed again to assure a fair match. Then they were released and teased with a toy chicken before being shoved into a divided Plexiglas box where they could see each other and work up a temper. One side of the box was streaked with blue, the other side red. The betting had already begun.

To Applewhite's left, a shaved-headed young man held up five fingers on one hand and with his other outstretched arm pointed to an older gray-haired man across the stands, a sign that appeared to mean, *You're on!* "*Azul,*" he yelled. The deal was done—fifty bucks on the rooster in the blue side of the box. The arena was alive with men betting, waving hands and fingers, calling out red or blue, pointing to one another. Gentlemen's bets. The timer started, and the cocks were released, immediately on the attack. The betting continued.

So where was his contact? Applewhite wondered, scanning the crowd. How long was he expected to wait?

About ten minutes into the first fight, the owner of the rooster from the red box stepped into the ring and picked up his exhausted bird, calling the end of the fight. Applewhite watched the gray-haired man wind around the stands and peel off bills to pay the young bald fellow.

Applewhite sat through two more fights and was about to give up and leave when a bulky, muscular man scooted next to him. He wore a flowered shirt, cargo shorts, and sandals.

"Enjoying the local color, Reverend?" the man asked.

Applewhite tried to place the man's distinct accent—perhaps Russian or Ukrainian. "I'd prefer you didn't use that reference here. Hershel will be fine."

The man nodded, and Applewhite glimpsed the wooden box on the man's lap. His gaze jumped to the man's eyes, shocked at the lack of security, if indeed the Blade was inside the box.

"Is that *it*?" Applewhite questioned.

"Would you like to see it?"

Applewhite's eyes darted about the arena.

"No need for you to be so anxious," the man said.

"You are not who I spoke to on the phone."

"No. I am a liaison. Does it matter from whose hands you take possession?"

"I suppose not."

The man lifted the lid about an inch. "Can you see?"

Applewhite tilted his head, the rectangle of tubes of overhead fluorescent lighting bright enough for him to catch an image of the object inside. It was a knife with a simple leather-bound handle. Nothing ornate that he could tell, yet the fleeting sight made his heart thud heavily.

The Blade of Abraham sat just inches beside him. But was it? he wondered. How could he be sure? What proof did this courier have?

Applewhite lifted his cap and scraped his fingernails across his scalp. He had to be rational. This was a gift with no price tag or strings attached. It had to be another of God's tests of his blind faith. He would not, could not, fail. The Blade was a gift from the Lord down through the millennia, and now the Almighty had chosen him. His instant reaction was to fall to his knees, but he couldn't allow that here. A flood of fear gushed through his arteries. It was too much to conceive, to take in, to process. "Can we go outside, sir?"

"The light is better in here."

Applewhite struggled to regain his composure. Deliberately he drew in as much air as his lungs could accommodate, and then expelled through his mouth. Doing this twice, his heart seemed to return to a somewhat normal rhythm.

"He will call you after you have accepted the gift," the man said. "I am to remind you there are no restrictions, no gimmicks. There is nothing asked of you in return. You are to have this because God has willed it. Do you understand?"

Applewhite had a million questions swimming in the haze in his head, wriggling like worms that made him want to clutch his skull and squeeze. But something at gut level persuaded him not to ask anything. His mind squirmed with both ecstasy and disbelief.

Without any farewell, the man rose and placed the box on the white-painted arena bench beside Applewhite, as if it were an empty shoe box or forgotten trash. "Find the mountain of Moriah."

"What?"

The man didn't answer. Instead he smiled, turned, and walked away.

What did he mean?

Suddenly the shouts of the men placing bets grew louder as did the flutter of cock wings. The pungent odor of bloodied feathers floated up to Applewhite. His senses were in overload as he tried to comprehend that the Blade of Abraham sat next to him in a plain wood box, and it had been delivered to him by the hand of God.

He touched his mangled fingers to the lid, without the

strength to open it or stand and leave. He'd been taken over by the Holy Spirit.

God must have some miraculously important plan for him. He'd waited how many years? Now the time had come.

CHAPTER 23 – TWIN
Manila, the Philippines

Since the house was bare wall-to-wall, it only took the bomb squad ten minutes to sweep it for explosives. Once they'd cleared it, a CSI team showed up, and Kenny and I joined them, moving through each room looking for anything that would lead to Knox's whereabouts. We wound up in the room with the step ladder.

"Max," Kenny said, "do you wonder if Knox is sitting at a window across the street watching every move we make, laughing and enjoying his manipulation of two OSI agents and the now dozens of PNP officers and detectives scurrying around the neighborhood?"

Kenny could be so right, and that sent a sick feeling to my belly.

"So was it Knox or an accomplice who set up the laptop, then got out over the wall?" I tapped the ladder with the tip of my shoe.

Kenny went and stared out the window. "The problem is that the way the network was set up, he literally could be anywhere on the planet. I get the feeling he doesn't like being cooped up. Knox likes control. Remote control."

"You want to stick around here or find a place to stay for tonight?"

"Is that an invitation?"

I scowled at him, and he held up his hands. "Sorry, no crime in asking."

There was a commotion from the direction of the stairs.

We both turned to see Sergeant Dela-Cruz coming through the doorway, his big meaty hand grasping a blue plastic box about the size of a hardcover novel. Two rigid antennae protruded out of the top of the device. "Here's your router." He handed it to Kenny.

Kenny examined it and glanced at me. "Linksys, a hundred bucks at any Radio Shack." He turned to Dela-Cruz. "Whose is it?"

The sergeant pointed to a man framed in the doorway. "Paco Alvarez. Lives directly behind."

"Does he know someone was stealing his Wi-Fi?" I asked.

"Oh, he knows." Acting as our interpreter, Dela-Cruz asked the man a question in Filipino, then turned to us. "He was paid a thousand U.S. dollars to come in here and set up the laptop, connect it to his home network, and leave. He's the one our stakeout saw entering the townhouse. He scaled the wall right into his own backyard."

"Why?" I asked.

Dela-Cruz asked Alvarez. "He said it was supposed to be a practical joke on someone, at least that's what he was told."

"When was he contacted?" Kenny handed the router back to the sergeant.

"Two nights ago."

"Can he describe the guy who paid him?" I asked.

The policeman laughed. "I asked him that, too. See, the thing is, it wasn't a guy. It was a woman."

Kenny and I glanced at each other. "No shit?" I said. "What did she look like?"

The sergeant posed the question to Alvarez. The man pointed at me as he answered.

"He says the woman looked exactly like you, Agent Decker."

"Me?" I stared at the man. "You mean she had the same features—hair color, eyes, height, build?"

Once again, the sergeant pressed Alvarez before translating. "No, he says that she looked identical to you."

"That's crazy," Kenny said. "There must be some mistake.

Maybe the woman paid him to say that just like she paid him to set up the laptop."

Dela-Cruz shrugged. "I'm just telling you what he says. If he had to identify Travis Knox's accomplice, it would be you, or someone who looks just like you."

My cell phone vibrated, and I removed it from my pocket. As the screen came to life I scanned the incoming text message, then looked at Kenny. "It's from Knox." Aloud, I read the cryptic texting shorthand, "Hey Btch. By now, good neigh Al prob accused u of being my part n crime. Shocker? Close, but no cigar. Enjoy pix."

The attached picture filled the screen. I could barely whisper, "No, no, no."

"Max, what is it?" Kenny moved to my side. "Son-of-a-bitch!"

Dela-Cruz took a step toward me. "Agent Decker, are you all right?"

I felt my heart pound against my chest as I looked at the photo of Travis Knox standing on a seawall, the imposing form of Morro Castle behind him guarding the entrance to Havana Harbor. Knox was smiling, his arm wrapped around the shoulders of my twin sister, Francine Decker.

CHAPTER 24 – PURPLE IRISES
Las Vegas, 9 months earlier

If anyone had come upon the Blade lying in the gutter on the side of a road or tossed into a back alley dumpster, they'd have paid no attention. But to Applewhite it was more beautiful than the Mona Lisa, Michelangelo's David, or any other work of art by one of the illustrious masters. The Blade was simple and nondescript, as was the leather-wrapped handle. But its beauty rested in its simplicity. This was no legionary weapon of a great king or world-conquering warrior. Instead, it was physical proof of a covenant between a common man and his God. If it had been made of gold and encrusted in jewels, Applewhite thought much of the magnificence would be diminished, instead fashioned for show, not for meaning. Garish. And that would negate its purpose, its specialness.

Applewhite's hands trembled in the privacy of his bedroom as he dared to stroke the Blade cradled within the box. He had not yet gathered the courage to remove it and touch it to his naked body, to press it, so raw and glorious, to his bare flesh. He was not yet worthy.

He stared at the Blade, yearning to grasp it, to embrace it. There was no woman on Earth who could tempt him so. But first he needed confirmation from God that he was deserving. He had to resist holding it in his hands until that *word* came to him.

Again he stroked the Blade with his right hand, the crippled hand, because that was the only part of him that merited the touch. His hand, twisted and deformed, had set him on this path. God would tell him what to do next and when.

With those thoughts, Applewhite closed the lid and tucked the box beside him as he stretched out on his cot, shifting for some small degree of comfort. He could afford the most expensive bed in the world and dress it with satin sheets suitable for royalty. His private mansion inside the ministry compound reflected his stature as a world-class televangelist. But as always, within the sanctuary of his master bedroom suite, Applewhite lived differently because he understood that it was through pain, sacrifice, and tribulation that man is brought to redemption, and that was something he must never forget. The redemption trinity, he called it. Such a minor discomfort as sleeping on an army cot was a daily reminder that kept him focused.

Just as he pulled the sackcloth sheet over his nude body, his cell rang. Applewhite grappled the phone from the floor. "Good evening," he said, glancing at the clock on the vegetable crate beside the bed. 7:30 p.m. He switched on the lamp atop the crate. So early in the evening, he thought, yet all energy had been wrenched from him. His body and mind were completely fatigued from the wonder of the Blade.

"Reverend, are you pleased with my gift?"

Applewhite swung his legs over the side of the cot and sat. His hand touched the top of the box. "I am."

"Do you yet understand the extensive plan for you?"

He hesitated. "What can you tell me? And who are you?" Wonderings tumbled through his brain. Why would this man, whom he knew nothing about, deliver to him such a miraculous gift? Or perhaps he was not a man at all. An angel? God, himself? After all, he had not met him in person, only the liaison in Puerto Rico.

"It doesn't matter who I am."

Applewhite recalled the childhood night when he'd lain in pain nursing his crushed fingers and God had spoken to him. So long ago. So very long... Tears brimmed in his eyes at the thought that God had returned to speak to him directly once again.

"We must halt the fouling of the commandments, the sinful ways of the human race. You have the Blade because it is a symbolic belief that you can be an avenging angel and stop this abhorrent, repulsive, reviled behavior of mankind. You are to lead the way. You are Father Abraham! This is why you have received this gift."

Father Abraham. The thought momentarily locked Applewhite's vocal cords.

"You are the one, the most deserving. As a child, you were singled out and have been tested throughout your life. Abraham, you have found favor. You are trusted and needed to expel the evilness in this world. Rid it of the sinners, the blasphemers, the fornicators."

Yes, Applewhite thought. He was deserving and certainly had been tested throughout his life. A backdraft of memory blazed through his head. He'd always envisioned saving sinners as his life's work, and had spent much time and effort with wayward orphaned and runaway boys. Some he had even taken into his home, had them sit at the dinner table with his wife, Evelyn, and son, Carl. He gave them shelter and provided physical and spiritual nourishment. Some he had brought to God with love. Some were more difficult and had to be shown God's wrath, the way he had been shown as a boy. He remembered the first defiant young man who was so filled with Satan that Applewhite failed miserably. And so God stepped in and took the boy.

The second failure had been another young man, about the time Evelyn was stricken with terminal cancer. He supposed that her sickness was another test for him and for his son. Through the ordeal he had remained focused, even continuing to deal with the evil child he was trying so desperately to save. God stepped in again. Both troubled boys rested beneath the plot of Evelyn's favorite purple irises in the back of his first church, a simple white clapboard house of worship.

When Evelyn passed on, Applewhite decided he would move on as well, leaving behind his failures buried forever. His following grew in abundance around the country. Television became the perfect vehicle to deliver his message. Soon, he became global. He took in many other troubled boys. Some he brought to redemption. Others were simply too filled with Satan. Because of his high visibility now and how much time his ministry took up, he had stopped his work with wayward youth.

God had more work in store for him. More sinners to heal, to bring to their knees, to cleanse. He pressed the phone to his ear. "But how?"

"It will all be revealed in time."

Applewhite attempted to stand, feeling the urge to pace, but his knees folded. Of course he would trust in the Lord. But what was the plan? And my God, how, out of all the millions, had he been the only human on the Earth to be touched by the Almighty in such a way? What if he couldn't execute whatever the mission was? What if he failed as he had with those two boys? Or the other unsalvageables who followed?

"Where do I begin? What do I do next?"

"Declare your name."

CHAPTER 25 – THE PLAN
Manila, the Philippines

I sank to my knees on the floor of the empty bedroom, feeling as though someone had just skewered a knife through my heart. A rush of air escaped my lungs, and for a second I doubted I had the power to draw another breath. The photo of my twin sister standing beside Travis Knox, and the thought of him touching her made me sick to my stomach. I suddenly felt like throwing up.

I realized Kenny was kneeling beside me trying to steady my swaying body. Sergeant Dela-Cruz bent over me studying the photo displayed on my phone in my trembling hand.

"You two do look alike," the sergeant said quietly He crouched beside me. "Is it possible she might be part of this, Agent Decker?"

"She's not involved!" The words shot from my mouth with such force that the big man pulled back a couple of inches. "She couldn't be involved." I tried to calm my reaction. "This is some kind of a sick trick to get to me. Maybe he Photoshopped her into the image."

Kenny looked at Dela-Cruz. "I've known Francine Decker for years. She's about as far away from a black market smuggler as my grandmother. And trust me, my grandmother is so clean, she squeaks when she walks."

Dela-Cruz stood. "If this guy wanted to get to you, looks like he pushed the right buttons." He took the cell phone from my hand and stared at the picture. "Morro Castle. They're in Cuba. Smart. Just out of reach of any law enforcement agency.

Knox knows how to stay at arm's length."

Kenny helped me up. "I'll download the image and check the metadata to see when the picture was taken. And I'll email the image to our photo analysis guys, see if there're any Photoshop artifacts. If it really was Francine who was here to arrange for the Wi-Fi hookup, she's had enough time to get back to Cuba."

"Then he's forcing her to do it. She would never cooperate willingly." I looked into Kenny's eyes, searching for affirmation. He read my thoughts and nodded, squeezing my arm. But then the worst concept rolled through my head. What if he had wormed his way into her life using an alias? Francine had met Aaron a number of times, but not Travis. Plus, he and Aaron bore little resemblance. I didn't know which scenario was worse—if she was being forced or an unwitting participant.

"Do you have your forensic computer with you, Agent Gates?" Dela-Cruz asked.

"Yes." Kenny took the cell phone. "It's in the SUV. I'll do the analysis and be right back."

I watched my ex-husband walk away and turned to the sergeant. "I apologize for yelling at you, but I wasn't ready for this. Normally, I can take just about anything that comes along, but Francine is all the family I've got left. Our parents died a few years ago when my mother got caught at the beach in a rip current and my dad went in after her. Neither one made it out. We had a couple of aunts and uncles, but they passed years ago. Fran is it."

Dela-Cruz shook his head. "This whole thing stinks."

"Knox knows there's no way we can touch him in Cuba. The bastard thinks he's safe. But I'll figure out a way."

"Why is your sister down there, anyway?"

"Relief aid worker. She's assistant director of Pan American Outreach and was helping with the survivors of the recent hurricane and mudslides in the eastern mountains. Hundreds killed and thousands homeless. Fran is always the first on the scene."

Suddenly, an idea came to me. Immediately, I knew what I must do. I was about to go find Kenny and tell him when he walked back into the room.

"It was taken in Havana three days ago." He held my cell phone up like a trophy as he returned. "That would be a quick turnaround trip, but it is possible."

"Good work." The sergeant nodded his approval. He handed the router back to Paco Alvarez. "Let him go." The two policemen guarding Alvarez stepped aside. Dela-Cruz followed them all out of the room.

When we were alone, I took Kenny's hand. "I don't think you're going to like what I'm about to say, but I have an idea how to rescue Francine."

———

I sat at the desk in my Manila hotel room using Kenny's laptop to find the website and contact info for Pan American Outreach. I called and spoke to the director of international volunteer services, asking for the status of my sister.

"Actually, Francine recently made a trip from the countryside into Havana several days ago to pick up more supplies. She hasn't returned to the base camp yet," the director said.

"I'd like to volunteer to join her and help out."

"Normally the paperwork and government license take a few weeks to approve, Ms. Decker. But because Francine is your sister and our assistant director, and we desperately need the help, we might be able to speed up the process."

"I'm in the Philippines, but could be ready to fly out as soon as you give me the okay."

"I have an idea. Hang on." She was away from the phone for a few moments. When she returned, she said, "Our logistics coordinator said there are a number of places from which you can fly directly to Havana. Cancún, Nassau, and Kingston are three of the best choices. If you're interested in making connections through one of those cities, I can overnight your paperwork to your stopover hotel. Just let me know where you'll stay before taking the final leg of the flight into Havana."

"That sounds perfect. I'll call you back with my flight and hotel arrangements. If you don't mind, I'd like this to be a surprise for Fran. And thanks so much for your help."

"No problem. It's our pleasure, Ms. Decker. Francine will be so pleased to see you."

I told the woman good-bye and hung up.

Kenny sat on my bed listening. "This is a very bad idea."

I stared at him. "Then give me an alternative."

"There isn't one. You do realize that Cuba isn't fond of former OSI agents roaming around. The least you'll experience is intense physical and electronic surveillance. Plus, you've lied to that relief organization. You're not going down there to help hurricane survivors, you're going to track down an international fugitive and a possible kidnapping victim. Do you have any idea what the inside of a Cuban prison is like?"

"If you're trying to scare me, you're wasting your time." I turned back to the laptop and started searching for flights from Manila to Cancún and on to Havana.

"Max, you'd be going into the lion's den. Obviously, Knox must have some arrangement with the Cubans. He seems to be able to come and go at will. For all we know, he's beefing up some official's art collection. His payment probably includes free access to and from the island. Think about it. There's a good chance they wouldn't give him up. I'll bet he's doing them a service. First thing you'll do is hit a brick wall. Don't do something stupid that could screw up your whole life and your sister's."

I swung around and took Kenny's hands in mine. "Screw up my life?" I laughed. "What life? My home and everything I own is burned to the ground. The fucker even killed my cat. He tricked me into coming here only to make a fool out of us both. Now he's managed to involve Fran in the selling of a priceless stolen artifact. Kenny, I have no life. There's nothing to go home to, because there is no home. If I don't do this, whatever piece-of-shit life I have left will be worthless. Besides, you don't seem to understand. I'm not going after Knox. I'm going to save my sister. Cuba can have the son-of-a-bitch. Fuck him. Knox can rot forever on that island, but not with my sister!"

For once in our relationship, Kenny was speechless.

CHAPTER 26 – THE DECLARATION
Las Vegas, 8 months earlier

"Father, are you all right?"

Applewhite heard Carl's voice as his son knocked on the televangelist's bedroom door.

Fresh from his habitual routine of morning prayers followed by an icy shower, Applewhite didn't want to answer. So he continued staring at the Blade in solemnity and reverence.

Find the mountain of Moriah.

Was he expected to cross the globe to find Moriah Mountain, where Abraham had been instructed to take his son? None of the biblical scholars had ever been able to positively identify the exact location. How was he to find it? He needed more clarification. Why such a riddle?

"Father?"

"Yes, yes. I'm fine." He pictured his son standing stiffly in the hallway. Applewhite thought for a moment, trying to decide whether or not he should share his secret with his only son before declaring it to the world. It had been a month since receiving the gift—the sign. A month of meditation and prayer. A month of preparation for the biggest event of his life.

He made a decision. "Carl," he said. No answer. He opened the door, then turned and called his name again as the young man trailed away down the hall.

Carl made an about-face. "I'm sorry to have disturbed you, father, but I was getting worried. I didn't want you to be late for your preproduction meeting."

For a fleeting moment, Applewhite caught a glimpse of his wife in his son. Carl had Evelyn's Scandinavian features. His mother was sturdy, a form stereotypical of a Norseman—a Viking—big-boned and tall. His wife's eyes had been a paler blue, more glacial, but Carl's were close enough.

"Come here for a moment." Applewhite returned to the bedroom, his son following.

"Close the door and lock it, please." After Applewhite heard the clicking of the latch, he took the box off the dresser and removed the lid. He held it out for Carl to see inside.

"An old knife?" With a confused expression, he peered up at his father.

Applewhite caught the trace of concern in his son's blue eyes. Was Carl starting to fear that his father walked the edge, that fine line between genius and insanity? Applewhite supposed there were many who thought the same. It was impossible for them to comprehend his journey. When his son was young, Applewhite believed the day would come when he would share all of his deepest secrets, but as time passed he had shifted his thinking. There were just some things that even Carl might not truly comprehend. He had inherited his mother's nature—soft and more fragile than Applewhite's. However, the knife was something his son should know about and appreciate.

"Not just any knife, Carl." He touched his twisted forefinger to the object. "Let me explain."

———

Carl opened the door to the conference room inside the administrative wing of the Golden Throne Cathedral. As Applewhite entered, the attending staff rose and waited for their pastor to seat himself at the head of the table.

When Applewhite settled into his chair, Carl nodded the okay for the others, and he took the seat to the right of his father.

Applewhite lifted his face to the ceiling as if he could see through the roof, up through the sky, and into heaven itself.

When he lowered his gaze he fixed his eyes on each of the other ten around the table, besides his son. "Brothers. Sisters. Today I will make a most significant announcement. It will be a profound declaration, and all of you and the rest of our congregation will be moved by it."

"What is it, Reverend?" asked the lighting director, tapping a pencil on a yellow pad in front of him.

"I will not disclose that until I face the cameras later this morning. When I do, I know you will have questions. You will ask how I have come to this place in my mission. And I will say to you that I am not permitted to answer, yet. But believe me when I tell you that Almighty God has not only spoken to me, but given me proof, tangible validation that this is what I must do. It came to me as much a surprise as it will be to you. But at last, my true mission is being revealed. The Lord will disclose this plan as I need to know it. But He has made clear where I am to begin."

He glanced around the table. Mouths were agape, eyebrows arched, some noses wrinkled in confusion. But Applewhite knew he could tell them no more. They would have to accept his word on faith, a faith for which they had all pledged allegiance.

"Pray with me." Applewhite lowered his head. "A moment of quiet prayer first." He paused. "The Almighty is in his holy temple; let all the earth keep silence before him."

Applewhite gave them a minute of time for their own thoughtful prayers before he began aloud. "God be with you."

Everyone responded. "And with thy spirit."

"Let us pray. Blessed be to thee, Dear God, who hath touched me with thy sacred spirit. And we, thine unworthy servants, do give thee most humble thanks for all thy goodness. Let us clearly hear your voice and follow your direction, for we have erred and strayed from thy ways like lost sheep—followed too much the devices and desires of our own hearts. Your voice has become clear and resounding and we shall follow. We praise thee, we worship thee, we glorify thee, and we give thanks. Holy, holy, holy, is our Almighty God. As it was in the beginning, is now, and ever shall be, world without end. Praise be to God."

"God's name be praised," was said collectively.

Applewhite stood.

"But Pastor, we have to go over today's shoot schedule and production notes before you leave."

"God will guide us today."

Applewhite gave no more explanation and left the room, Carl behind him. They continued to Applewhite's dressing room to get him ready for the taping of the Sunday service.

As Carl opened his mouth in protest, Applewhite said, "Trust me, son."

———

Two hours later, as brilliant light washed the stage, Applewhite appeared through his machine-generated fog and stepped before the cameras, with the Il Divo soundtrack of "Hallelujah" echoing in the background. Though he had received so many emails and letters telling him how his presence at the beginning of each program broke his audience out in goose bumps, this time it was Applewhite who felt his flesh prickle. He glanced at Carl in the wings and smiled, sending his son a sign that he was confident in what he was doing and all was well.

After the traditional opening hymns and prayers, all lights dimmed except for a spotlight on the minister. This had been his only direction to the crew just before the start of the session. It included using specialized diffusion filters, providing a softening effect, reducing blemishes and flaws, all to create the ethereal effect Applewhite wanted.

As the camera slowly zoomed in until his face filled the frame, he spoke. "Today will be an extraordinary day. I will not be delivering a sermon as usual. Instead I will share with you, my devoted flock, a miracle. I, only a humble servant of the Almighty, have been honored and blessed. God has come to me. Spoken to me directly, just as clearly as I stand here speaking to you. He has given me a task, a great responsibility, an awesome privilege. When I was a child, He called to me, and I have faithfully followed even though He waited all these years to reveal what his master plan was for me. But now, He has accepted my fidelity, my loyalty, my blind faith, and has presented me a gift. God, the Almighty, has delivered me concrete proof of my mission and my purpose on this Earth. Listen and I shall tell you my name, for it is a secret no longer. From this day forth, Hershel Applewhite is no more.

"From today on, I am Abraham."

CHAPTER 27 – HAVANA CUBA

I looked down from my window seat in the *Cubana de Aviación* Ilyushin Il-96 as we made our final approach into José Martí International Airport. The flight from Cancún, only taking one hour and twenty minutes, had been smooth and uneventful. Coming in over the water, the air was crystal clear and the sky a dark azure, with the sprawl of Havana extending below, a patchwork of gray and tan buildings that formed a surprising contrast to the deep indigo Caribbean. I could see the broad Malecón esplanade stretching for miles along the ocean front. Hundreds of Cubanos had already started their nightly stroll, and the lights of Havana twinkled on as the city turned shadowy in the setting sun.

I was nervous, having never jumped so recklessly into the unknown. But the mixed forces of hate and denial drove me. Hate for Travis Knox and all he had done to me and his brother, and denial that my sister had anything to do with his foul intentions. He had gone beyond the actions of a criminal to ultimately involving the blood of my family. My twin. There is no way she could have taken a path opposed to the values instilled in us. I knew it in my heart. And yet, there was that transparent shadow of doubt lingering off to the side of my thoughts. The question rattling in my head: What if she really was somehow involved? After all, Travis had convinced Aaron to abandon a career of enforcing the law and turn to a darker profession. But just as quickly as those doubts appeared, I pushed them back. I would not allow them to confuse my mission. It was too late for Aaron, but I had to get to Fran and bring her back.

I reached into my pocket and felt the small piece of paper Kenny had handed me before I boarded the flight from Manila to Mexico. I removed it and reread the name: Yuri Kirkov.

Kirkov was a former Soviet diplomat who had worked in the Russian embassy in Havana during the last years of the Cold War. After the fall of Communism in the USSR, he chose to return and retire in Cuba. Kenny said Kirkov had actually been a secret CIA informant working closely with Kenny's uncle, a field agent stationed in Venezuela during the late 1980s. Kirkov had visited Kenny's uncle in Miami on a couple of occasions a few years back. And that's where my ex had met him. "Uncle" Yuri, as Kenny referred to him, might be of help to me if things got dicey.

———

"Your passport and visa, please." The Cuban Customs officer stared at me with a hard, suspicious expression as he reached out for my papers. His English was surprisingly good.

I handed him my passport, along with the license sent to me by Fran's Pan American Outreach headquarters. He seemed to take much longer examining them than he'd done for the previous passengers in line ahead of me. Several times he inspected my papers and then consulted his computer.

"What is the purpose of your visit to Cuba, Ms. Decker?"

"Charity work. I'm here to meet my sister and join her in helping with relief services in the hurricane disaster zone."

"Very commendable." He turned and said something to another Customs officer standing nearby, then gave him my papers.

"Please follow me." The new man motioned to an office a few paces away.

"Is there a problem?" I stood my ground.

"Not if you follow me."

There were still many passengers in line behind me. Rather than create an incident, having only been on Cuban turf for a matter of minutes, I reluctantly trailed the official into the office.

As my *escort* exited and closed the door, a bearded, pock-faced man behind a metal desk said, "My name is Lieutenant Sanchez. Have a seat." The furniture appeared to be 1950s military issue. Drab gray paint covered the walls; two photos were the only adornment—one of Fidel Castro and the other of his brother Raúl Castro. The air smelled of stale tobacco and mildew.

"Is there a problem with my papers?" I tried to sound confident and in control as I slowly lowered myself into the chair.

"What is the real purpose for your visit to Cuba?"

"As I told your fellow officer, I am here to assist Pan American Outreach with the hurricane relief efforts. My sister is already here. She's been with the Outreach for some time."

Sanchez glanced at his computer. "Customs has sent me some interesting information. You are an agent for the United States Air Force Office of Special Investigations, correct?"

"Former agent. I left the OSI three years ago."

"And why did you leave?"

"I was critically wounded in a shooting incident. After my recovery and rehab, I decided to reenter civilian life."

"During this incident, did you not shoot and kill a fellow agent?"

I nodded.

"Why?"

"I don't see what that has to do with my visit to Cuba. I'm a volunteer coming here to help your country. What happened over three years ago is history."

"Why did you shoot your fellow agent?"

My face felt hot, and I could hear my blood pulsing in my ears as my heart sped up. "Self-defense. I had no choice. He was attempting to smuggle valuable stolen artifacts out of the country. He threatened me, and I defended myself."

"So who shot you?"

"One of the smugglers my partner was meeting."

"And that would be Mr. Travis Knox?"

Now I was sure the heat in my face was causing my cheeks and throat to flush. I hoped the hell he didn't notice. I consciously did a hasty check of the tension in my muscles and took a stab at making them all relax before I responded. "How did...? Yes, Travis Knox."

The son-of-a-bitch smiled at me, knowing he had me. If I'd been in the U.S., I'd have probably mouthed off about his blatant arrogance.

"Ms. Decker, you are here because you believe Travis Knox is in Cuba and has kidnapped your sister."

How does he know that? This was going to be the shortest visit to Cuba in history. I could see that already. I fully expected to be placed in a waiting room until the next flight out. "Okay. You're right. I do have reason to believe that, yes."

"Ms. Decker, we may seem to you and your colleagues like a backward 1960s society, but we do keep up with what's going on in the world, especially when it concerns an international fugitive wanted for attempted murder of a government agent. We saw the PNP reports coming out of Manila. And when your name appeared on a passenger list from Mexico, it didn't take long to figure out that you're not coming here to help mudslide victims. You have lied to the Cuban government. You're here for vengeance."

My gut tightened as I thought of the probable consequence. I wasn't going to be taken to a holding area and hustled off on the next plane leaving Havana. Maybe my ass was going to be locked up in a jail cell. I had to keep my cool. Speak softly and with control. Could I work up even the slightest drip of empathy for me? I pressed my brows with my fingertips, a show of how troubled I was. Then I locked my eyes on his and let the muscles in my face go slack. "Lieutenant Sanchez, I'm not here for vengeance. I only want to find my sister and take her home. I believe she is in immediate danger. My only concern is for her safety."

He said nothing.

Man, this time I had jumped both feet into a pile of shit with no boots on. "So what happens now?" I braced for him to place me under arrest and have me taken to the closest prison. "Does this mean I'm on the next plane leaving Havana?"

"On the contrary, we intend to help you find Mr. Knox and your sister."

CHAPTER 28 – GOD IS GREAT
Las Vegas, 4 months earlier

Applewhite awoke from his dream in the middle of the night, his body sheathed in sweat. The dream had been a surreal flashback of the first time he had attempted to save one insolent little sinner boy that God had to take.

Rising, he traipsed to the bathroom, turned on the water and cupped his hand beneath the faucet to gather up a drink. He shook his head, trying to clear the memory. But then the thought: perhaps God was speaking to him as he slept. Maybe giving him a message. Perhaps he'd been premature in his efforts to dismiss the dream.

Applewhite returned to his cot and tried to drift back to sleep, to seek the dream, search for God's message, but instead he found himself recalling in detail the actual incident.

He could see it clearly, as if it had just occurred, when in actuality it was decades ago. The thirteen-year-old boy knelt barelegged on rice, hands cuffed to an old water pipe in Applewhite's basement, gagged, ankles bound. Why hadn't the lad listened when Applewhite read biblical passages, prayed for him, blessed him, counseled him? No, the kid had been so recalcitrant and insubordinate. Infested with the Devil.

Applewhite had told the heathen child how naive he was. How he'd been deceived by Satan. How he had one last chance at redemption. He was about to show the child the way.

After all, Applewhite thought, that was the job of a pastor, a shepherd. He'd already flogged the boy a half dozen times along with all the verbal persuading. But to no avail.

He unshackled the boy from the water pipe and sat him in a chair, then tethered the chair to the pipe. With the child's arms firmly secured, he tilted the boy's head back into a vise-like contraption he'd built that would hold the head still. Once in place, he strapped the kid's head so it was locked in position. Then he pulled up an old rolling high-backed desk chair and sat. Leaning forward, he lifted the boy's upper lip.

With clenched jaw, the boy bit down on the gag and his eyes opened in terror.

Despite his mangled fingers, the pastor was able to hold the kid's lip up with his right hand. From a TV tray beside him, Applewhite deftly lifted one of the three gleaming darning needles that rested in a pan of rubbing alcohol. No sense in risking infection. All he wanted was for the boy to come to his senses. He found himself finding a speck of humor in the irony of bringing the child to redemption just to have him die of an infection.

Through the years, Applewhite had mastered the use of his left hand to overcome the deformity of his other. It had been a struggle filled with frustration. Practice, practice, practice. Pinching clothespins, cutting thousands—maybe millions—of pieces of paper, finger bends, finger weights, moving tennis balls and marbles across his fingers. Hundreds of dexterity exercises repeated and repeated and repeated. But his determination had paid off.

With his left hand he touched the point of the needle to the underside of the top lip at the fold, just beneath the right nostril. He then worked the needle in, slowly, watching the boy wince and hearing his cry that had been dulled by the gag.

He detected the sound of Carl's small footfalls above and paused. His son was young, too young to understand. "Shhhhh," Applewhite whispered. He didn't want Carl to come looking for him or investigating the noise from the basement. He kept the basement locked, and only he had the key, but he questioned himself. Had he remembered to bolt the door? He sat quietly, listening and unmoving until he recognized the muffled sound of the television cartoons coming on. Then he resumed his task, speaking softly.

"It's for your own good. God wants you to be saved. Give in to Him. He wants you to understand what it would be like to go to Hell."

The boy's body trembled.

"God is great. God is good." His words trailed off to a whisper.

The kid whimpered.

"That's right. That's right," Applewhite murmured. "Come to the Almighty God. You don't want to spend eternity like this or worse." He left the first needle in place and now inserted a second, below the other nostril. "Some of us come to salvation through pain and suffering. God is giving you that opportunity. You want forgiveness, don't you?" The pastor pulled back, retrieving the third needle which he delivered dead center, between the other two.

Tears streamed down the child's face as Applewhite twisted each needle and drove them the slightest bit deeper, jiggling them enough to bring about an escalated round of pain. He knew this because he had experienced the same pain at an even younger age than this boy. At the hands of his father.

Applewhite sat back, set an egg timer for seven minutes, placed it on the tray, and then went upstairs to get a snack. He returned to the basement with a fresh, plump Bartlett pear just before the ding of the timer sounded.

"I think you've had enough." He bit into the pear; its sugar juice dripping down his chin. Placing it aside, he said, "Now, let's see what we can do about these." With a firm grip, he ripped one of the needles free.

The boy wrenched in the chair, trying to break loose. His shoulders heaved in silent sobs and his eyes squeezed shut. Like the juice of the Bartlett on the pastor's chin, blood dripped from the boy's mouth.

"Two more and it's done. A lesson learned." Without attention to any technique that might spare pain, Applewhite withdrew the remaining darning needles. "I'm going to remove the gag now so that you can pray with me. But if you call out, there will be severe consequences." He tapped the sheathed fillet knife fastened to his belt.

Slowly he pulled the gag from the boy's mouth, pausing when partway done, testing the child. But the kid made no sound. "That's good." He finished the task.

Applewhite spewed off his version of the twenty-third Psalm. When ended, he said, "Say amen."

To his astonishment, the sinner said nothing.

The pastor picked up one of the darning needles and held it in front of the boy's face. "How would this feel in your eye?" His voice rose. "Say, amen."

The boy acquiesced. "Amen," he mumbled, but with a defiant tone that rode on his voice like a lance aimed squarely at Applewhite.

"I'm not convinced, but God is merciful and He would want me to give you a second chance." He unlatched the straps harnessing the kid's head.

When at last released, the boy rolled his head and stretched his neck.

"Do you appreciate God's love for you? My love for you, and what I have done for your redemption? Without me you would still be on the path to Hell. Led by Satan."

Applewhite noticed a sudden flash in the boy's dark eyes. A demon lurking?

The child's nostrils flared.

"Speak. Tell God you have given yourself to Him. Tell me how grateful you—"

Spittle sprayed across Applewhite's face.

"Heathen!" The pastor bolted to his feet and slammed a backhand across the boy's cheek and then another, coming at him from the other side. Blood streamed from the kid's nose and mouth.

"Tell me your name, demon!" Applewhite delivered another blow—this one stronger. Then another. "Identify yourself." A fiercer blow and the kid tumbled sideways, the chair yanked on the rope bindings, and the rusted pipe snapped as he went down.

The boy's head smacked the concrete floor and a jagged fragment from the pipe sliced through his neck. Blood spurted out of the wound onto the concrete.

Applewhite stumbled backward. It took a moment for his brain to process what had just happened. He felt his heart thrash brutally out of control, hammering his sternum, his pulse pounding in his skull.

He watched the boy's blood spout, strong at first, but eventually diminishing to a steady flow that pooled beneath the torso. Small twitches and spasms moved through the young body—the demon trying to flee. After many agonizing moments, quiet descended over the boy and his pastor.

This wretch could not be saved. God knew Applewhite had done all he could. But the kid had stirred the Almighty's wrath, leaving no option but to smite him down.

The pastor collapsed into his chair, staring at the lifeless body. In an instant, it came to him that he would bury the child beneath the irises and pray over his grave every day. That was the right thing to do. He'd done all he could—all anyone could. Perhaps on Judgment Day, the poor boy would be forgiven.

Because God is great. God is good.

———

Rousing now from his dream, his heart thumping just as it had that fateful night, the stark memory was slow to dissipate in Applewhite's mind. As his breathing calmed, he slid over the side of the cot and dropped to his knees in prayer.

"Oh merciful Father, I will always do your will. Whatever it is you ask of me, I will comply. I trust you to show me the way. I desire to fulfill your confidence in me as your new patriarch, Abraham. Guide my hand as you did with that hapless child and those tormented souls like him that followed."

He had no sooner finished than the phone rang. Applewhite rose and smiled toward the ceiling. As he lifted the receiver he knew, just knew, God had heard his prayer.

God is great. God is good.

CHAPTER 29 – THE DEAL
Havana, Cuba

"I don't understand." I stared at Lieutenant Sanchez. "Despite the fact that I lied to you, you're willing to help me find Knox and my sister?"

"It's not a matter of being willing, Ms. Decker. And we're not going out of our way to do you any favors. But the fact is that soon after you contacted Pan American Outreach, they informed us that Francine Decker was missing, and they believe she was taken against her will. Mr. Knox has been a special guest of the Cuban government for quite some time. But kidnapping is a crime in Cuba, just like in your country. If Mr. Knox is responsible for the abduction of your sister, an American citizen here to help the distressed storm victims of Cuba, it is our responsibility to investigate, and if necessary, take him into custody."

"So you were going to look into this whether I was here or not?"

"That is correct." Sanchez leaned back in his chair, obviously secure in his position of authority. "Now, let me tell you how this will work. Normally, lying to a Customs officer or a member of the *Policía Nacional Revolucionaria* is a criminal offense punishable by imprisonment or deportation. But since there are extenuating circumstances in this case, I am going to make an exception. You will be allowed to remain in Cuba for a period of no more than three days. You are confined to the city of Havana. If there are any developments in this case, you will be contacted and informed. At the end of the three days, you will be required to leave Cuba, no matter the state of the investigation. Is that understood?"

I didn't like the deal, but it was better than getting booted onto the next jet, and a whole hell of a lot better than ending up in a Cuban prison. But with those restrictions, what good was I going to be in finding Francine? I might as well have been back in the U.S. I'd figure a way to snoop around on my own, so I forced myself to agree. "I understand."

Sanchez must have read my mind because as he stood and handed me my papers, he warned, "Cuba is not like the United States. Don't assume that you can conduct your own investigation or violate our laws. And do not abuse the privilege of my personal hospitality or you will see just how different Cuba can be."

I gave him a nod as I took my passport. "Thank you, Lieutenant."

———

With my carry-on rolling behind me, I left the terminal and caught a taxi, a 1950s-era Chevrolet, which drove me along Avenida Rancho Boyeros.

I watched the city streets pass by, a city of sorrow. Kenny had tried to warn me how depressing it would be. Once elegant and prosperous, Cuba had become a victim of deliberate neglect and isolation. An entire nation drifting in a time warp where virtually nothing had changed in half a century. Many Cubans were born after Castro's revolution in 1959 and had grown up conditioned to accept their dismal, impoverished lifestyle. They simply knew nothing else. But among the crumbling old buildings, dilapidated vehicles, and almost total lack of basic services, there was an island spirit in the Cubans' blood that could not be held down. Laughter and the constant sound of a driving Latin beat drifted through the taxi's open window as we passed parks filled with old men playing Dominoes and children giggling through their games of chase and tag.

Twenty pesos and twenty kilometers later, I was delivered

to the front of Hotel Sevilla, located in Old Havana a few blocks from the ocean, and the place where the picture was taken of Knox and Fran.

I walked to the front desk across the tiled lobby with its colonial columns and archways. A few minutes later, I gazed out of my window at the night lights of Old Havana below. The room was clean and nicely furnished with turn-of-the-century pieces. Speaking in reasonably decent English, the cab driver had told me that the Sevilla was built in 1908 and had been recently renovated to take on its pre-Revolution decor. I felt apprehensive as to what I would find during my short stay. I wondered who would follow if I walked out the front entrance and strolled down the street. Sanchez had made himself pretty clear and obviously suspected that I might do some of my own nosing around. I had to think a little more about how I would test those waters.

I saw the lights of Morro Castle in the distance. My sister had seen it, too. The day the photo was taken. I pulled the piece of paper from my pocket and stared at the name. *Well, Max, you came here to find her. Get to it.* I made a decision about where I would start. I would go find *Uncle* Yuri Kirkov.

CHAPTER 30 – SIN CITY
Las Vegas, 2 months earlier

"Reverend?"

Applewhite immediately recognized the voice on the phone.

"Yes."

"I have been thinking about you and your new role. May I call you Abraham?"

"Please do." For some peculiar reason Applewhite recalled how so many years ago he had tossed a towel over the dead boy's face. The evil had fled from the youngster, leaving behind the remnant of a tortured child—an image he did not care to see then or now. With purpose, he dismissed it.

"I hope you have realized the significance of your calling and the gift I sent you to seal that covenant."

Applewhite sat naked on the bare concrete floor and leaned against the wall. "I do. I do." As if a desert wind blew through his bedroom, his mouth dried, and he sucked in his hollow cheeks in an effort to create saliva. "And I have declared my name, as you suggested."

"Yes, I witnessed that broadcast. You handled it very astutely."

"Thank you. It seems to have been well-received by my followers. I've had emails by the thousands. So many in fact that my son Carl has hired several extra temps to reply with my prepared response."

"Good. That is just what I want to hear. You have taken on an immense task, Abraham. The world is so full of sin—and sinners. I fear there are few innocent souls left, and it grieves me. Together, we need to rid the land of the transgressors."

Applewhite felt a shudder rattle down his spine as he heard the word *together*. He and this person were to minister together? Whose voice was he hearing? Again he wondered. An angel? God Himself? "It grieves me, also," he answered.

"Man festers with Satan's venom. There are whole cities where evil reigns. Filled with abominations."

"I pray for them."

"But is that enough? They continue with their foul ways."

His prayers had not been enough to satisfy. Applewhite's shoulders slumped. Had he failed? His mind wandered to a question he repeatedly wanted to ask, and before he considered the consequences, the question blurted forth. "You have given me a new name. But what do I call you?"

There was silence on the line for a moment. "I have many names, and yet I have none. I am."

Applewhite's head thumped back on the wall. Was he really speaking to God? Had not men through the ages tried to know the Almighty's true name? Elohim. Yahweh. *I AM Who I Am. I Will Be.* Overcome, his eyes stung with tears.

"The outcry against Sodom and Gomorrah is so great and their sin so grievous," the voice said.

The call went dead, leaving the reverend's hands trembling. Those were the exact words in Genesis. He stood, gathered his robe from his closet, and pulled it on over his body. From the top bureau drawer he removed a small plastic bag of rice. The pastor sprinkled several pinches on the floor in front of the private altar in his bedroom, lifted his robe above his knees, and knelt on the grains to pray.

———

Carl shifted in the back seat of the Applewhite Ministry of Deliverance's limousine, his father beside him. "You think this emissary, this mysterious messenger, is referring to Las Vegas when he spoke of Sodom and Gomorrah?"

"Perhaps so. Perhaps not." Applewhite shot a piercing

glance at his son. "God is always testing. Always checking if I understand. Do I believe? Do I give my all? Will I sacrifice? Do I clearly interpret his mystic message? He must always make sure that Satan is not in control." Applewhite's cheek flesh softened. "See our driver? We must trust that he has followed our orders to take us to our intended destination. Now and again we peer out the windows, taking note of the route. It is so with the Father."

Carl made a quick glance through the darkened window. He was devoted to his father's ministry, but as of late his dad seemed preoccupied with something other than their original mission. Since the mysterious calls began and the arrival of the relic, his father had changed. Carl wished he could put his finger on the precise transformation, but he couldn't. The direction of the ministry had always been to save those who were lost, but recently he had detected a warp in that doctrine. Perhaps it was just that his father had become awash with the power of the Almighty, assuming the role of Abraham, and the delivery of the glorious gift of the Blade. So then what was it that nagged at him? Was this trip into Las Vegas really necessary? The world knew Vegas for what it was. Most folks, believers and all, visited, indulged in their devilish cravings, and then went home and returned to their respective institutions of worship on Sundays. Vegas was what it was. But his father had seemed to latch onto the city's nickname and reputation, and even beyond that, had agonized over it.

"We are looking for proof, boy," Applewhite said. "Just as in the Holy Book, if we can find twenty, ten, or even a few who are innocent…that is what we search for."

Carl's stomach lurched from anxiety. He recalled the scripture: *And God said, If I find in Sodom fifty righteous within the city, then I will spare all the place for their sakes.* Finally, *And he said, I will not destroy it for ten's sake.*

What was his father's new calling? And what did it have to do with Las Vegas? Sin City?

CHAPTER 31 – YURI
Havana, Cuba

"Maxine Decker?"

It was dark as I stood on the Malecón esplanade roughly where Fran had stood in the photo. I was engrossed in the sweeping majesty of the Caribbean and the waves breaking over the rocks beyond the seawall when I heard a voice behind me. I turned and looked into the face of a man who appeared to be in his mid-fifties. He was short—about five-five. Balding with a crescent moon of gray hair, his face was narrow and his skin deep brown from too much sun. He wore brown pants, sandals, and the traditional Cuban guayabera shirt. *Police?*

His smile was warm as he stepped forward and extended his hand. "I am Yuri. Welcome to Habana."

I huffed out a sigh of relief. "How did you know I would be here?" I looked around and wondered if I was being watched. But this had to be a stroke of luck. I didn't have to go poking around looking for Yuri. Sanchez couldn't nail me with violating our deal.

"Your husband—"

"Former."

"Sorry. Your former husband called yesterday to tell me about your sister and let me know you were coming. I'm very sorry this is what brings you to Cuba."

I nodded a thank-you. "I'm convinced that she's in trouble. Her outreach organization reported her missing. Did Kenny tell you about the picture?"

"Yes, and where it was taken. That's why I assumed you

would come here first. But to be certain, I followed you from your hotel."

"You're a clever man."

"Years of working for the old USSR. At one time, we had our noses in everything around here. Those days are long gone, but old habits die hard."

"Kenny said you might be able to help me find Francine."

He shrugged. "Maybe. First we locate Travis Knox. He will lead us to your sister."

"Where do you suggest we start?" As I spoke, I noticed two dark-skinned men standing under a street light. They were dressed similar to Yuri and eyed us from further along the seaside walkway. Cuban police, no doubt. My private *escorts*. "They've placed restrictions on my travel." I shifted my gaze back to the Russian. "I can't go beyond the city limits."

"That is about what I would have expected. You are lucky they didn't throw you in jail for falsifying your visit. But don't worry. Back in the bad old days, I often had to be in two places at once. I haven't forgotten the tricks of the trade." He turned and motioned to me. "Let's take an evening stroll. This time of night, the Malecón is beautiful and has cooled from the heat of the day."

As Yuri and I sauntered past the two government agents, they turned away and seemed to take an intense interest in the lights of fishing boats bobbing in the waves a few hundred meters offshore.

When we were out of earshot, Yuri chuckled. "They start out by being obvious to make sure you know you're being watched. There are others observing us that are not so obvious."

I casually glanced around at the dozens of strolling Cubans and tourists but could not discern which ones, if any, were government agents.

"The city has a history going back to the early 1500s," Yuri said. "It has seen many a pirate ship sail into this harbor." He gave me a broad smile. "Some still come today. If we can find your sister, that's how we will get both of you home safe."

My heart beat faster. "Pirates?"

"Smugglers."

"I thought the Cuban government was harsh on smugglers."

"Just the ones who don't work for them. The narcotics trade is a cash bull for them."

"You mean a cash cow?"

"That, too."

"So you think there's hope for finding Fran?"

Again he shrugged. "No guarantees. But I have a lead."

I felt a rush of excitement with his encouraging words as we left the Malecón, crossed a park, and took a side street into the heart of Old Havana and the Plaza de Armas. I noticed quite a few cafés and restaurants serving dinner. Many of the tables along the sidewalks were occupied by tourists, it seemed by the bits of conversations I picked up.

Suddenly, Yuri gripped my arm and led me into a small café called *Tres Palmas*. Rather than asking for a table, he guided me through the crowd to the back and down a hallway. We passed doors to the men's and women's *baños*, boxes of canned goods, stacked chairs, and the entrance to the kitchen. Before I knew it, we were out a back entrance and standing in an alley. Parked a few yards away was a well-worn, gray Lada.

"This way." Yuri pointed to the small Russian sedan. A few moments later, we had merged into the traffic along Paseo de Marti. "The agents are sitting in the plaza waiting for us to finish dinner and come out of the café while we are already blocks away. That's how you can be in two places at once."

"Where are we going?"

"To talk to Travis Knox."

CHAPTER 32 – LAS VEGAS
Las Vegas, 2 months earlier

"Carl, keep your eyes open and your mind clear," Applewhite said to his son as they approached the glittering city lights of Las Vegas. "Don't let the glitz and glamour seduce you. God has led us here, to Sodom and Gomorrah, on a mission."

"Sodom and Gomorrah? Father, I don't think God perceives this city as Sodom and Gomorrah. There are a lot of good people here, not just sinners. Some live here, some just visit for fun—good people. God-fearing people. There are even revivals that take place in this city."

Applewhite shook his head and patted Carl's knee. "You'll see. This place crawls with vermin, prostitutes, gamblers, thieves, heretics, blasphemers."

Carl edged his leg away. He wasn't sure just what this *mission* would mean or what his father's plan was, but in his gut he was uneasy. His father was in a delusional spiral, believing himself to be Abraham and having fanciful interpretations of the messages that came from an unnamed, unknown voice on the phone. Calls that were becoming more frequent. He wished he could make his father understand how irrational and impulsive his recent thinking had become. Carl looked at the man beside him—the man who was becoming more and more of a stranger every day. Maybe something from scripture would help untangle at least a single snarl in his father's mind.

"Remember Matthew 21:32?" Carl said. "*I tell you the truth, the tax collectors and the prostitutes are entering the kingdom of God ahead of you. For John came to you to show you the way of righteousness,*

131

and you did not believe him, but the tax collectors and the prostitutes did."
He paused a moment, wondering if his father made sense of the Biblical quote.

"My son. I have never said that God is unforgiving, nor that He can find no place in his mansion for prostitutes, fornicators, and the like. On the contrary. Our God is merciful. But to receive His mercy, the sinners must repent first." Applewhite pitched a copy of the *Las Vegas Sun* at him. "Look at it, then tell me again of your doubts."

His father's voice was patronizing and his tone condescending—it grated on Carl. He scanned the newspaper headlines. *Mob Museum Exhibit Hijacked by Cost Concerns.* He quickly reviewed the article as his father watched.

"The Mob Museum. They actually have a museum dedicated to criminals. See that, boy? This city is not repentant."

Carl didn't respond, keeping his eyes on the newspaper headlines.

25 Arrested in Alleged Sex Scam
Gang Members Detained After Gun-Battle
Swedish Ex-Police Chief Convicted of Sex Crimes
Suspect Sought in Two Separate Sex Crimes

He paused on the page filled with escort services and private massages, knowing his father watched.

Then Applewhite jabbed a finger in Carl's shoulder. "Look out there. See those girls? Those whores? They flaunt their bodies in short, tight mini-skirts, their breasts bulging over their clinging, low, revealing tops. Their spiked heels that make their legs appear to stretch long and lean up to their groin, which is just barely hidden beneath the fabric of their skirts, swishing against their flesh in an erotic whisper they know we can hear. Their hips undulate to tease. Scarlet soldiers of Satan bent on destroying mankind. Stealing souls so God may not have them."

In a moment they had passed the streak of women working the street. Applewhite glared out the rear window of the limousine, but Carl looked forward.

Applewhite groaned, a sound of disturbed dismay. "They titillate men and prey on our very instinct to procreate. They strive to unleash those primal responses God instilled in us so that we would go forth and multiply. Even at a distance they project their poison. I feel the arousal they have stirred in me—that sexual urgency and physical response. The need. The lust. I am only a man in a man's body, but I am also a man of God, and He protects me from the temptation." Applewhite's head jerked around so he looked at Carl, first glancing at his son's lap as if checking for a sign of arousal and then at Carl's face.

Carl felt a flush of awkwardness. "I didn't pay them that much attention."

"You can't learn to resist temptation if you run from it. Face it head on. Spit in its face. Tell Satan to get behind thee!"

"It's not like I haven't been here before, father. I've seen the Strip a number of times—the casinos, the nightclubs. I'm not really sure why you've brought me here tonight."

"To see it with new eyes."

"I'm looking, but all I see is what's always here. There's nothing new."

"You must see so that you can prepare for the mission."

"What mission, father? What are you talking about?"

"Don't you realize by now that I have become the Blade of Abraham? And you will be the dragon slayer. Together, we are warriors of God. We come here at God's command to see if this sinful place should be spared, just as was done with Sodom and Gomorrah. If we can find twenty or even ten who are righteous…"

Carl felt a chill. "But we aren't meant to judge. That is the right of the Father. And if God is all-knowing, then why do we have to do this?"

"We are His messengers. We are His scouts—His eyes and ears. Can't you see that, boy?"

Abruptly, Applewhite pushed the intercom button. To the driver, he said, "Pull over."

When the car came to a stop curbside, Applewhite told Carl

to get out. "I want you to wander the city. Take it all in. See it through the eyes of the dragon slayer. Find me ten who are innocent and I will tell God that goodness dwells here." He pointed to one of the huge casino hotels on the east side of the strip. "Start there."

Carl opened the car door and stepped out. "Where are you going?"

"In search of sinners who can be saved."

Applewhite reached for the door and pulled it closed.

Carl stood perplexed and at a loss as he watched the black limousine pull away. His father had proclaimed himself the new Abraham. Had he lost his mind? Somehow he didn't think praying for him would help.

CHAPTER 33 – NIGHT RIDE
Eastern Cuba

We drove out of Havana and headed east along the coastal highway. Passing through small towns packed with hotels and seaside resorts, I could see the Caribbean Sea to the north sparkling in the starlight. Yuri said the hotels were filled with Eastern European and Canadian tourists. Some Greeks, too. After an hour or so, we moved away from the resort areas, and the landscape changed to shanties reeking of poverty. We kept up a steady pace, passing through the town of Santa Cruz and into a mountainous area, where we crossed the Bacunayagua Bridge over a dizzying, gapping gorge. I was thankful it was too dark to see the bottom.

"You're starting to make me nervous, Yuri." We had left the highway and swung south on a smaller country road that ran alongside a river. "By now, the police must know that we're not still in the restaurant."

"Don't worry. We're almost there." He seemed unconcerned.

The terrain had turned to overgrown roadsides and dark hilly forest. Our headlights caught a few head of malnourished cattle that wandered among the brush. Banana plants and palm trees dotted the landscape.

"How do you know this place?"

Yuri seemed to be concentrating on navigating the cracks and potholes along the poorly maintained road. To the left I could still see the river.

"I continue to cultivate my contacts in the government. I

did a little bit of snooping before you arrived. Not too much to arouse suspicion, mind you. But I believe I know where Travis Knox is hiding."

"While I was in Manila, he contacted us through high-speed internet. It doesn't look like there would be such a thing out here."

"Not needed. He would have wideband access through a satellite connection. Don't be fooled by the remoteness of this place. With enough money, you can buy whatever you need. It's no secret that Knox has enough money."

I glanced at my watch and realized I was royally screwed. We had been driving for hours. The police would know that I was last seen with Yuri and soon after that we disappeared. They had probably started searching for me. This could only end badly. I might never leave Cuba if they found me. But then, my whole purpose was to find Francine.

Yuri slowed and turned into a narrow side road that wound down an incline in the direction of the river. Soon, a sprawling concrete block structure appeared in the beams of our headlights. It was a rundown single-story building—weeds and brush stood waist-high in all directions. In the distance behind the building I saw a broad wharf jutting out from the riverbank. I thought I spotted the outline of a large boat on the river—perhaps a big shrimper or small freighter—but it was too dark to be certain.

"What is this place?" I asked.

"Used to be a seafood processing company. That was years ago. Now it's mostly used by drug dealers as a stopover point for their shipments."

"Colombian?"

He nodded.

"How do they get around the Cuban authorities?"

"Who do you think is running this leg of the operation?"

"I guess it was a stupid question."

We stopped and got out. "Doesn't look like anyone's been here in a while."

"The smugglers often shift their drop locations. That's so

the American DEA doesn't see a pattern starting from any one access point."

"You seem to know quite a lot about this."

He shrugged. "Knowledge is power."

The Russian handed me a flashlight before leading the way down a narrow path that snaked through the thick underbrush.

"Have you been here before?"

"Once. But back then, they weren't just shipping drugs out of here."

"What else?"

"Guns, munitions, humans. Anything that could be sold for a profit."

We paused in front of a large wooden entrance door. Yuri grabbed the knob and pushed. With a rusty shriek, it gave and we entered.

The room was spacious—maybe four times the size of a two-car garage. The floor was concrete with bare concrete block walls. A scattering of trash including beer cans and newspapers littered the floor.

"I'm confused. Why are we here? I can't believe anyone lives in this isolated place, certainly not Travis Knox. What's going on?"

"Why don't you look around first?" He said it matter-of-fact, as if he already knew what I would find.

"And what are *you* going to do?"

"Cover your back."

"Sorry, Yuri, but I'm not buying it." My pulse accelerated. Like a fool, out of desperation to find Fran, I had ignored my basic instincts and walked right into some kind of a setup—a trap. I shined my light at his face. "You're not Yuri Kirkov, are you?"

CHAPTER 34 – THE DUEL
Eastern Cuba

The Russian shrugged and gave me a *you got me* expression.

The reality sparked every nerve in my body, like fire shooting through my flesh. "It wasn't you Kenny called. You knew I was coming because you work for Knox. What the hell's going on here? What's happened to Yuri?"

"You want to find your sister? Then take a look around. Don't worry who I am or who I work for or where Yuri is. Just check out the place. You might find what you're looking for."

I wanted to ram the flashlight down his throat. I took a step toward him but suddenly realized that in his free hand he held a small automatic—it looked like a Beretta Tomcat. He didn't point it at me, just held it so that I knew it was there.

"What do you hope to accomplish with this ruse?" My mind worked overtime but I still didn't understand what all this meant. But I knew this was not going to end well.

Using his gun as a pointer, he motioned to a doorway across the room. "Take a look around over there."

Realizing this was more of an order than a suggestion, I turned and moved toward the doorway. I glanced back but he remained in the same spot motioning with the pistol for me to keep going.

I headed through the door, my flashlight beam searching the bare walls. The opening led down a hallway and ended in a darkened room about the size of a large bedroom. My light revealed another doorway on the opposite wall, but the actual door had been removed. The only objects in the room where I stood were two milk crates, one stacked on top of the other to form a makeshift table. On top lay a pistol—I recognized it as a Glock 17. I shined my light on the gun. The clip was missing, but one 9mm cartridge lay beside the weapon.

Then I saw a man appear in the doorway across the room, his form lit by a low-wattage overhead bulb.

Heat rushed up my neck, my hand shook causing the flashlight beam to jitter. Adrenaline shot through my veins, my heart pounded like a hammer drill, and I fought to find enough oxygen. I had no doubt who it was even in the dim light. I'd seen his face on the laptop in Manila as well as pictures in Aaron's office.

"Hello, Maxine," Travis Knox said, an automatic pistol in his right hand dangling relaxed at his side.

I wanted to lash out at him, to curse him, to spit, to rage, to pound his sorry face. I wanted to inflict pain, to make him suffer. But I stood fixed in place as my pulse kettle-drummed in my ears.

"Why did you have to kill my cat?"

"I didn't kill it. I had your cabin burned to the ground and your cat happened to be on its ninth life. Some things are destined."

"Aaron's blood is on your hands."

"That's the best you can do? God, I thought you'd be calling me everything in the book by now. Maybe I had you figured wrong. Maybe you're just a pussy. Maybe you don't have the guts to pull the trigger again."

"What are you talking about?"

"Your one big chance. I know you hate me. You've got the bullet wounds to remind you every day. You think I'm a low-life piece of shit, right? And I'm the bastard who burned down your cabin and fried your fucking cat. Well, I'm going to give you the chance you didn't give Aaron. A one-time deal to get even."

"By doing what?"

"By deciding to take the first shot. Sort of like an old-time duel. You make the call. I'll read your body language, and when you are ready to fire, I'll return fire. If you don't kill me, I'll take you out. A modern-day O.K. Corral. Fair enough?"

"Why are you doing this?"

"You think you're the only one who wants this over with? Think you're the only one who has demons? This is the way it will end eventually, so why put it off? Let's get it over with. One of us will live, and one of us will die. Whichever the outcome, we'll both have satisfaction and some peace. Don't you want that, Maxine?" He paused a moment and his face slackened and his eyes narrowed. "By God, I do."

"Why don't you just shoot me? What's stopping you?"

"Doesn't seem like a fair match. No game that way. Besides, I need to give you a sporting chance to see the big bang."

This guy was over the edge. The big bang? What the hell was that, the end of the world? "But if I get off the first shot and the bullet hits the mark, there won't be any *big bang*, whatever that is."

The smirk grew, and it made my stomach roil.

"Here's your chance. Pick up the gun, load it, and shoot. You got the guts? Or are you just all talk?"

I stared at the Glock sitting on the milk crates, trying to bring it into focus as the madness swirled inside my head. Why did he bring me all this way? Something was wrong. But I couldn't figure out what it was. Maybe he was so insane he was actually going to let me shoot him. Was he going to fire as soon as I picked up the gun so he could claim self-defense? Or were *his* demons as haunting as mine and he really did want it to end? None of it made sense. Maybe he would kill me anyway if I didn't comply. But I might never get another chance at him.

I rested the flashlight on the plastic milk crate. Picking up the pistol, I gripped the slide and pulled it into the locked position exposing the chamber. Then I took the 9mm cartridge, inserted it into the chamber, and released the slide. I was ready to kill Travis Knox.

I planted my feet firmly. "How about I take aim and order

you to drop your weapon and put your hands up?"

"Because I won't. And once you move your hand, it's a fair call. Who gets off the first and best shot—simple as that. So have at it. Shoot me, if you can. You know you want to more than anything. Just take a deep breath, move fast, aim for my heart, and squeeze the trigger."

I did.

CHAPTER 35 – ROOM SERVICE
Omaha, Nebraska, 1 week earlier

"So there you have them, ladies and gentlemen, the four types of nuclear terrorism threats we face today." Dr. Geoffrey Ford surveyed the three-hundred-member audience and then glanced back at his notes. "To recap, they are the theft and detonation of an intact nuclear weapon, the theft or purchase of material to create a crude nuclear weapon, the attack on or sabotage of nuclear installations, and the dispersal of highly radioactive material by conventional explosives or other means—what's commonly referred to as a dirty bomb."

After a pause, he continued, "In conclusion, I want to thank the board of the National Nuclear Terrorism Study for inviting me to speak at the conference today. And now if there are any questions?"

"Dr. Ford?" A brown-haired man in a solid black suit stood up in the second row. "You said there are more than thirty thousand nuclear weapons in the world's arsenals. How confident are you that they are all accounted for?"

"Not very, I'm afraid. We have to accept the fact that there are some lost weapons—what some call Broken Arrows. These include intercontinental ballistic missiles. It is the short-range tactical nuclear weapons that are most tempting to terrorists because of their size and portability.

"So our worst nightmare is a terrorist who steals a bunch of these small weapons?" the man pursued.

"Even one WMD in the hands of a terrorist is chilling enough." Ford saw a hand go up near the back. "Yes, and please speak up so we can all hear you."

This time it was a middle-aged man in a short-sleeved white shirt and dark pants. Ford wondered if that was a pocket protector in his shirt pocket—the universal symbol of a geek—but couldn't tell from this distance. "Dr. Ford, if a terrorist were able to steal, say, a small nuclear artillery shell, wouldn't he still need someone of your skills to arm it?"

"Sadly, there is a great deal of information on the internet and plenty of military or former military experts with the knowledge to arm the weapon. Let's just hope it never comes to that."

He pointed to a woman in the first row. "Yes?" As she stood, he saw she was much younger than the average attendee—perhaps in her mid-twenties; about the same age as his daughter. Her blond hair was cut short, and she needed little makeup to accent her sculptured facial features. She wore a plunging white cowl-neck blouse and navy blue skirt. He had noticed during his presentation that she took numerous notes and seemed to hang on his every word. She was quite attractive, he thought.

With a smile, she said, "You've stated that a nuclear terrorist attack would most definitely come as a surface blast, not an air blast, and would probably be in the one-kiloton range. Can you tell us what that would be like and the damage it would inflict?"

"Certainly," Ford said, speaking directly to her. "The amount of explosive power from a nuclear explosion, or the *yield*, is measured relative to TNT, and is usually in the thousands of tons or kilotons of TNT.

"A small nuclear device would be a one-kiloton device, meaning it would produce an explosive yield equivalent to one thousand tons of TNT. For comparison, the size of the Murrah Federal Building bombing in Oklahoma City was equivalent to only two tons of TNT.

"What about side effects?"

"Good question. In addition to generating a devastating explosion, nuclear weapons cause extreme thermal and radioactive effects. Roughly fifty percent of the energy released during a nuclear detonation is used up in the blast, which can destroy even the most fortified structures."

"And burns?" she asked.

"Yes, about thirty-five percent of the energy released is in the form of extreme heat that would cause large infernos and lethal burns."

"Radiation?"

"In a surface blast, fallout would be maximized, resulting in long-term contamination in the blast area and perhaps hundreds of miles downwind."

"How lethal are the effects of radiation?"

"Even small weapons such as the equivalent of one ton of TNT would produce a five-hundred-rem dose of gamma radiation within a forty-five-mile radius. That exposure would likely kill more than fifty percent of the affected population within sixty days. And the economic damage from the blast and lingering radiation to a large city would be devastating."

The young woman appeared to have more questions, but his host was slowly approaching from the side of the stage. "Well, it looks like my time is up. Thank you all so much for your kind attention. Thank you."

The host took the microphone. "One more round of applause for Dr. Geoffrey Ford for taking time from his critical duties at the Los Alamos National Laboratory to be with us today."

The room filled with applause. Ford noted that the blonde was clapping enthusiastically. He gave a final wave to the audience, with a special nod to his new fan.

———

Ford was tired. He had an early flight back to Albuquerque and wanted to get to bed soon. He had finished his obligatory call to his wife. Since he had ordered room service before calling her, when the knock at the door came, he assumed his dinner had arrived and opened the door.

"Hello, Dr. Ford."

It was the front-row blonde. Standing this close, he realized that she was stunning, and for the first time in years, his breath caught.

"I hope I'm not disturbing you." She smiled. "I can leave if this is a bad time."

He stepped aside. "No, no, this is a perfect time."

CHAPTER 36 – THE ILLUSION
Eastern Cuba

The blast from the Glock was thunderous in the block-walled room—it flashed like a strobe at a rock concert. At this close range, I couldn't miss. I was certain I'd gotten off the first shot, and he had not returned fire. I expected to see Knox grab his chest and drop to his knees from the 9mm ripping through his heart.

Instead, his image shattered into a thousand pieces and crashed to the floor in a pile of silver shards. I had shot at his reflection in a mirror mounted at an angle and taking up the whole door frame. A woman stood where the mirror had been. She wore a blindfold and gag, jeans, and a white T-shirt. Her hands were bound in front, and her legs tied together at the ankles above her bare feet.

Then I saw the red start blooming on her shirt.

I had just shot—

"Fran! Dear God, Franny! What have I done?" I rushed to her. With frantic fingers I untied the rope holding her against a post mounted in the floor. My legs went limp as I sank with her in my arms.

I tore off her blindfold and gag. She stared up with fear and confusion in her eyes. Her lips formed my name.

My sister's face turned pale, and she lost focus. I had taken direct aim to inflict the most damage to Travis Knox. Instead, I had shot my sister. She was dying. Her blood looked like red paint pouring from the wound. Her head sagged and her eyes closed. *NO!*

146

As I screamed her name, I felt a needle prick my neck.

With my next breath, my body collapsed. I seemed to be sinking right into the concrete. I could no longer feel Francine. I tried to pull her to me but there was no strength left. The room faded.

———

I awoke to a constant, monotonous thumping in my head. It came from all directions, but mainly from below. I lay on my side on a hard surface, breathing in the overwhelming smell of diesel and oily dampness. I tried to move but discovered my hands were bound behind my back. My legs were tied, as well.

The thumping was brutal, like a boxer throwing endless left and right jabs to my head. Waves of nausea coursed through me, and I realized I had already thrown up—the smell of vomit suddenly overcame the diesel odor. I tasted both, and a sickening wave hit again and what was left in my stomach rushed up and out.

I labored at breathing, trying not to choke on my own puke. The putrid odor caused me to retch. I felt my throat contract and spasm. And adding to it all was the movement, the swaying back and forth, intensifying miserable sickness. I realized I was somewhere below decks on a ship.

As I lay in the dark, unable to move, hardly able to breathe, I remembered.

Francine.

The sickening rocking, the pitching and rolling, was no match for the flood of anguish that washed over me and caused me to throw up again. This time, my guts seemed to rip apart.

I cried. A wet, balling, slobbering, uncontrolled weeping, wailing. For the first time in my life, I didn't want to live another minute.

The images continued to form. Like a video playing in reverse, I felt the sting of the needle preceded by the dead stare in Fran's eyes, emptying of life, draining of her spirit. Then I saw the red blossoming across her chest, so bright, so final.

There would be no way to stop it, to put it back. She gazed at me in shock, as if it could not be happening. I was there holding her, and yet I had shot her. And then the video worked backward to the actual blast. My aim was true, dead bang, a kill shot.

I'd been fooled by a simple carnival trick with mirrors. How could I have fallen for this? My stomach heaved.

Travis Knox had used illusion to trick me into murdering my sister. There was a new monster in the sideshow tent.

I heard a door open. A second later, someone dumped a bucket of cold seawater on my face. I coughed as I tried to keep from breathing it in.

"You don't look so good, Maxine."

It was Yuri, or whatever his name was.

"Fuck you!" I spit out more salt water.

"Be thankful. At least you're not in Cuba anymore."

CHAPTER 37 – THE MISSION
Las Vegas, 1 month earlier

Applewhite ordered his driver to cruise the length of the Strip. He watched out the window as the limousine toured the flashy, gaudy boulevard from the north end where the needle-shaped Stratosphere pointed skyward, all the way to the imposing black glass pyramid of the Alexandria Hotel and Casino at the south—its brilliant beam of light also shooting into darkness. Satan's bookends, he thought, to Sin City. The replica of the Great Sphinx of Giza in front of the Alexandria distracted him for a moment with its giant marquee that read: King Tut Experience. They'd built a monument to a failed civilization that worshiped false gods. Applewhite had no patience for those who bowed down to golden idols.

The Strip was packed with tourists, gamblers, partygoers and hookers—a mass of sinful disgusting humanity roaming Sin City under cover of darkness.

"Drive down some of the side streets," he told the driver. It didn't take long for Applewhite to see a small cluster of what were obviously *working girls*. "Pull over here." Almost instantly, the stretch limo rolled to the curb.

Applewhite stared through the dark glass at the flashes of youthful alabaster and ebony skin, the sway of curved hips, the fleshy tease of bosoms that made his mouth water. It was as if he anticipated the first bite into a succulent piece of fruit. He realized that his breathing had become heavier and that a tugging sensation crossed his lower belly.

The driver interrupted the pastor's thoughts. "Excuse me,

Father Abraham, but this is not a safe place to park. We need to move on."

It was only then that Applewhite became consciously aware that he was touching himself. *Oh, these harlots know well the ways of Satan.* Perhaps he could find one, just one, whom he could bring to salvation. Isn't that what God wanted Abraham to do in order to save Sodom and Gomorrah—find one righteous person? If he could do that, perhaps God would allow him to show mercy on this vile and depraved place.

He pushed the intercom button. "I'll call for you."

Applewhite stepped out into the night, and the fetid blend of tobacco, alcohol, body sweat, and cheap perfume engulfed him. Not only could he smell the odors, he could taste them, sour on the back of his tongue. And the very air had texture and weight, like a greasy sheath coating his skin and invading his lungs.

"Hi darlin'," a long-legged redhead said, bumping against him, then licking her lips. Her eyes roamed him from his forehead to his crotch, then back to fix on his face. "Wanna party?" She inserted her index finger in her mouth before slowly withdrawing it through pursed lips.

Applewhite shook his head, reached out and palmed her forehead. "Be gone, Satan!"

"What the fuck?" The redhead recoiled. "Fucking nut job!"

The pastor stepped forward, his hand still extended.

"Get away from me, you prick."

Applewhite took a step toward her.

"Hey! I said get the fuck away from me!" She was loud enough to attract attention.

A man with three thick gold chains dangling around his neck, one suspending a large cross, appeared. He came squarely in front of Applewhite, smacked his broad hands on the pastor's shoulders, and shoved. "You got a problem, man?"

Stunned, Applewhite began quoting scripture.

"You in the wrong place for that shit, dickhead. Turn your Bible-thumping ass around and get the fuck outta here before I make you wish you had." He stared into Applewhite's face, "Hey, ain't I seen you someplace before?"

Applewhite balked. "No problem, sir. A misunderstanding." He retreated, one hand held up in a surrender gesture. "No offense meant."

"Get your fucking ass outta here. Don't want to see you preachin' any of that holy crap around here. Get it, jerk-off?"

Applewhite nodded as he turned and hurried away, heading down the street. He glanced over his shoulder. The redhead was already busy enticing another would-be john.

The next time he looked up, he was staring at the Tumblin' Dice Hotel, one of the many off-the-Strip casinos. He remembered that this one had once been a Best Western but had fallen on hard times. Now it catered to the Vegas regulars wanting to avoid the tourists. Along with its casino, it had a three-hundred-room hotel.

He wandered across the parking lot past the "temporarily closed" sign on the entrance to the swimming pool area and entered the lobby. From there, he headed to the casino. Taking his time, he moved through the rows of slot machines with their insidiously constant robotic music and chink-chink-chink. The smoke was heavy, as was the smell of alcohol. Standing behind a man with long, dark hair wearing a biker's jacket from a club in New Mexico, Applewhite staked out a blackjack table. As he watched, a blonde, past her prime, bumped against him, and he moved away. But a moment later, a thirty-something black girl, slender but voluptuous, grazed his backside and slid her hands down his thigh. She didn't say anything, but without a doubt got his undivided attention.

She gestured for him to follow her, and he did. In the elevator, behind a group of four men and one woman, she slid her hand to his crotch, cupping him.

His instant arousal made him believe this was the one, the potential righteous convert. He could bring her to redemption, to salvation. God had given him this instinct, this primal reaction for a reason and he would see it through. The pulsing in his groin convinced him that this was the Almighty's intention, that he would fill this wayward woman with grace and bring her to everlasting life. And through her, God would show mercy on Sin City.

He needed to put his thoughts out of his mind and let God's work be done. His arousal was becoming out of control, and he feared if he continued his train of thought his release would be premature. Right here in the elevator without ever having the opportunity to—*Oh sweet God, your mission is so divine.*

Applewhite followed the prostitute to a room.

"Three hundred for an hour," she said, once inside. "Eight hundred for the night, or more if you want something...different."

She was already stripping, and Applewhite had to turn away for fear of ejaculating then and there at just the sight. No, first he had to bring her to redemption. *My mission. God's mission.*

"Whore," he said, stripping his clothes.

Naked, she trailed her fingers down from her breasts to her pubic bone. "Whore?" she repeated, then smiled. "Yeah, I'm your whore, baby." She moved closer. "That cock says I'm *your* whore. You like that, don't you?"

"On your knees," he said.

"Sure, baby."

"Pray with me, now. God will fill you with his grace."

She took him in her mouth, and he capped her head with his hands.

"In the name of the Father."

He gasped.

"And the Son."

Another gasp and then release as waves of pleasure swept through him.

"God is great, God is good."

CHAPTER 38 – OVERBOARD
Gulf of Mexico

The seas turned rough as a storm battered the ship. Lying in the pitch-black hole with the awful stench of my own vomit and the endless rocking of the ocean brought me renewed waves of nausea. I prayed to die.

Along with the seasickness was the heart-wrenching image of Francine dying in my arms. The last of my family was now gone. I was alone.

A couple of times, the Russian came back to check on me. If he or Travis didn't want me to die, they had a strange way of keeping me alive. I wished they'd just kill me and get it over with.

I had no way of knowing if Travis was even on the ship. I asked the Russian but his only answer was to throw another bucket of cold saltwater on me. Each time he left, the room turned back into a sea-going tomb.

During one of his visits, I caught a glimpse of what looked like machinery being transported in the hold. Long metal arms with large rocket-shaped objects attached. All were painted bright yellow. And the device had wheels, as if it were part of a trailer. But the saltwater blinded me, and the light from the open doorway was too faint for me to make out any clear details. Still, I was certain that I lay in what must be a shipping compartment below the deck of a small freighter. It might be the ship I'd spotted when we first arrived at the abandoned building. What was our destination? I drifted off to sleep, or maybe into unconsciousness, having nothing left in my stomach to throw up and no more tears to cry.

———

I came to and managed to sit up and lean against the steel hull of the ship. There was no way to know if it had been a few hours or a few days since I was drugged and brought aboard. I couldn't even tell if it was day or night. I was dehydrated and hungry, weak and dizzy.

The constant pounding of the waves shook and rattled the ship like thunderclaps. Judging from how it was tossed around, the vessel could not be very large—my guess from the memory of the boat anchored in the river would be two hundred feet at the most. I remembered the faint outline of a wheelhouse near the stern and a single derrick-crane tower near the bow.

So far, little of what had happened made sense. Travis Knox had drawn me out of retirement with the eBay offering of the Old Testament relic. He destroyed my home, then enticed me to Manila and baited me with the picture of Fran. Then he conned me into going to Cuba only to make me shoot and kill my sister. *Animal.* Was all this some sort of a grand plan—a lead-up to what he kept calling his *big bang?* Or was he just insane? Or both? No matter which, I'd been played…repeatedly. I hated myself for that. I'd struggled to regain a shred of self-confidence after Iraq, but that fledgling and fragile belief in myself was now crushed. I was right the first time, and the recent events were proof positive. Stupid and naive. An easy mark. A target. A fool.

With my mouth dry, my stomach aching from hunger, my body racked with bruises from being tossed around, and the cold metal floor feeling like ice, I slumped down and drifted back into the dark recesses of sleep. It was a better place to be than reality.

———

My dreams weren't fantasy nightmares. Instead, I wallowed in a depressing dream that was the recounting of a time I wished I could forget. I lay naked next to Kenny, and he was kissing my shoulder saying everything was okay and how much he loved me. I was crying. We'd had an argument—one we'd had quite a few times. Kenny was anxious to have children. Being ten years older, he was ready for kids, but I wasn't. I was climbing the rungs to a successful career so I wanted to postpone having children. I'd said some terrible things, accusing Kenny of being like all the other macho-driven guys in the world who believed they could trumpet their sexual potency by keeping the wife pregnant. He didn't understand that I believed having a family at the point would hold me back. Couldn't he love me completely even if we never had children? Wasn't I enough?

The sound of the bulkhead door clanking open awakened me. I saw the Russian framed in the dim light and realized the sea had calmed to a gentle rolling—the long storm had subsided.

"You're going to need this." He shoved a plastic bottle to my lips, letting me drink. The water tasted sweet.

Once I'd emptied the bottle, he tossed it aside and pulled me to my feet. Reaching down, he sliced the ropes binding my ankles. I wanted to fight back, but I was weak and barely able to stand. Then he shoved me through the doorway.

"Let's go." He pushed me up the steps to a steel grate platform that led to another set of stairs. At the top, he thrust me through an opening onto the outside deck. It was a moonless night, and the ocean appeared like crude oil rolling in swells against the ship. A second man stood next to the railing, his face chiseled and taut, and his build like a young Schwarzenegger. He slid a portion of the railing to the side in front of me so that there was nothing but the edge of the deck and the ocean below.

"Take a look." The Russian pointed out over the water. "See those lights?"

I squinted and could just make out tiny pinpoints twinkling on the horizon.

"Where is my sister? What did you do with her body?"

"Fish food. Don't worry, I said a prayer before we dumped

her over the side."

He laughed, and all I could do was imagine putting a gun to his temple and blowing his brains out. I'd have given anything at that minute to coldly and calmly snuff out his life without a flinch.

"So now you're going to bury me at sea, too?"

"Depends. We're only a few miles from shore. You know how to swim, right?"

"Yes, but I can't with my hands—"

"Janko, cut her loose."

I saw the flash of a knife blade. The big man gripped my arm like a vice and turned me sideways. The blade sliced through my wrist bindings in one quick pass. Holding me in his iron grip, he forced me to the edge of the deck. The waves rushing by the hull grew louder as they curled away from the steaming ship.

"I don't understand," I said to the Russian. "What do you expect me to do?"

"Sink or swim."

Then I was airborne. I swung my arms and legs trying to keep from cartwheeling. The fall lasted only a second or two before I was immersed in the cold darkness of the deep. I kicked and stroked until I realized the bubbles set aglow by the ocean phosphorus revealed which way was up. I followed them until my head broke the surface.

Gasping and coughing, I treaded water and watched the imposing bulk of the freighter slip by and disappear into the night, the foam from its prop wash hissed like a sea serpent. Soon, the thumping of its diesels and the points of its running lights faded, too.

I turned toward the shore lights, but it was impossible to keep a steady clear view of them in the six-foot swells. I bobbed around and seemed to swallow almost as much saltwater as air. Catching my breath, I started a slow but determined breaststroke in the direction of what I hoped was land. Exhausted, often I was forced to turn on my back and float, but the idea of being washed back out to sea quickly made me return to a combination of the American crawl, breaststroke, and an occasional feverish dogpaddle.

At first, my mind filled with images of hungry predators prowling the blackness below. I envisioned rows of jagged teeth opening wide to feed or the long stinging tentacles trailing the Portuguese man-of-war. I had never felt so small and defenseless. As the tide flowed in my favor, I tried to clear my mind of razor teeth and poisonous stingers, and concentrate on an image that I'd seen for only an instant when the Russian came for me.

It was a word painted on the side of the machinery in the ship's hold. Red lettering on a yellow background in a style that was almost cartoonish. The word was *Tapas*.

CHAPTER 39 – DESERT
Omaha, Nebraska, 1 week ago

"I don't think I caught your name earlier," Ford said, closing the door to his hotel suite. The blonde walked past him into the middle of the room, turned, and waited. Her trailing fragrance tugged on him like an invisible lasso. He didn't remember the dip of her blouse going that low at the conference. Now there was an even more generous portion of creamy cleavage and the hint of black lace.

Her arrival was much more convenient than his usual routine of scouring the internet for local escort services. And cheaper. After all, he'd paid up to a thousand dollars an hour in the larger cities—it was one of the main reasons he never turned down an invitation to lecture at an out-of-town meeting or conference. Ford would be the first to admit that at his age, having young, beautiful women attracted to him came with a fee. But this luscious beauty seemed free. So far, at least.

"Sarah," she said. "Sarah Walker."

"Nice to meet you, Sarah." He joined her. "What is it exactly that you do?"

"I'm a freelance writer, Dr. Ford."

"Geoffrey."

"Of course, Geoffrey, I came here hoping I could ask you a few follow-up questions in the privacy of your room." She languorously tossed her head, flipping her blond tresses over one shoulder. "You know, without distractions or interruptions."

"Pardon my manners." Ford couldn't believe this

stunningly sensual woman had just walked into his room. He watched as she ran her finger from the hollow of her throat down through the cleft of her cleavage. This was going to be a night to remember.

He motioned to the sectional couch taking up a corner of his suite. "I already ordered room service, but if you'd like to join me for dinner, I could call down and add whatever you want to the order. Perhaps wine or Champagne?"

"Champagne would be lovely."

"No problem. I'll just—"

There was a knock at the door.

"Seems their service is unusually fast. I'll have it brought in and then send down for a bottle of Krug. Unless you prefer Dom Pérignon."

Ford strolled to the door, still reeling from the rush of this alluring beauty flirting with him. He expected to find a hotel staffer holding a tray of food. Instead, he was greeted with the sight of two men.

"I think you have the wrong room," Ford said, and started to close the door just as he heard quick, muffled steps on the carpet behind him. Before he could turn, he felt a sting on his neck, like a mosquito bite, making him feel like an old fool.

The blonde had been too easy.

———

Ford opened his eyes. They hurt. Everything hurt, exceeding the worst hangover of his life. He lay on his back in a bare-walled room. As he painfully turned his gaze, the space reminded him of a prison cell. He lay on a single, cot-size bed, while nearby was a stainless steel toilet, matching sink, a non-glass metal mirror, and a wooden stool in front of a small writing surface that folded down from the wall. The overhead bulb was encased inside a wire-frame fixture. Near the ceiling, a narrow horizontal window emitted a slot of light—daylight.

He slowly sat up and edged his legs over the side of the bed. He hadn't felt this sore since high school football decades ago—every muscle seemed bruised and battered.

His memory came back in scattered fragments—the blonde, the two men, then blacking out.

He had awakened a few times and got the feeling of motion, as if he lay in the back of a vehicle. Maybe a truck or a van, but large, not a standard car. Someone gave him a drink of water. Blackness followed. The next time he awoke, the vehicle was traveling at high speed as if on an interstate highway. Once more, he remembered awakening when the truck had stopped. He heard the sound of distant traffic and the clunk of what he thought was a fuel nozzle being removed after refueling. Then they were moving again. This time for many hours.

His next memory was waking up in the small jail cell. He saw a bottle of water on the fold-down table and managed to stagger over and drink.

A key clanked in the metal door to his room. When it opened, one of the men he recognized from the hotel stood in the doorway, a small, hand-held Taser gun pointed at him. The man took a step forward.

"Go stand against the far wall, Dr. Ford, and put your hands behind your head. Don't move. Understood?"

Ford noticed the man had a distinctive Eastern European accent, perhaps Russian. "What's this all about? What's going on?"

The man raised the Taser. "Last warning."

Ford remembered seeing a network reporter on the news let the police Taser him as a demonstration. With that image of excruciating pain in his mind, he moved on shaky legs to the far wall. "I don't understand."

"Hands behind your head."

He did as he was told and waited. A moment later the woman who'd called herself Sarah Walker entered and placed a tray of food on the table.

"Why are you doing this?"

"All in good time, Geoffrey. You don't mind if I still call you Geoffrey, do you?"

"You don't know what you're getting yourself into. Kidnapping a federal employee is a serious crime."

"Enjoy your lunch, Geoffrey."

"What do you want?"

The answer was their exit and the sound of the door closing and locking.

Ford turned and found himself alone. He went to the table and studied the food tray—a white-bread salami and cheese sandwich on a paper plate, an apple, and a bottle of fruit juice.

This was insane. What could they possibly want? A ransom? Granted, after years of civil service to the Department of Energy, he made a handsome salary, but nothing exorbitant by any standards. His wife taught at the University of New Mexico. Their combined salaries kept his family in a comfortable lifestyle—nice home, vacation cottage in the mountains, two BMWs—and had put their kids through college. Their investments and savings came to a couple million. But most of the money was tied up in accounts that would require a heavy penalty for withdrawing early. And liquidating them to raise a ransom could take days or weeks. There was probably $10,000 in checking. Not worth this much trouble.

He didn't know how much time had passed since they took him from his hotel room, but it must have been quite a while, as he was famished and his mouth and throat craved water. His wife would have alerted the police when he didn't get off his flight from Omaha. The security people at the lab would be investigating by now, too. Someone of his esteem couldn't just disappear without a lot of people getting concerned. He bet, because of his high security position, the FBI would have already been called in. His kidnappers were crazy if they thought they would get a big payout from this.

So he wasn't rich. He wasn't famous. The only other asset he could offer was his knowledge of nuclear devices. Was that it? Maybe they wanted national security secrets. It seemed farfetched, but they might be exactly the kind of people he lectured about: terrorists. He went back to motive for most kidnappings—money. If that proved true, they were going to be disappointed. And he would be dead.

Ford wolfed down the dry salami sandwich and the green apple, then drank every drop of the juice. His hunger sated and his thirst quenched, he glanced at the long, narrow, rectangular window that stretched across the top of the wall. The light was fading. He'd like to get a look out that window before nightfall. At least get an idea of where he was being held.

He scooted the wooden stool over to the wall and painfully pulled himself up to stand on it. It was a couple of feet too short. He looked back at the fold-down table. It appeared thick and sturdy, being held up by chains. Would it hold his weight?

Stepping off the stool, he placed it next to the table and moved the food tray to the floor. Again, with a great deal of effort, he stepped onto the stool and then up onto the table.

He could see the sky—a deep blue with a few puffy clouds. But he needed a few more inches to be able to see the surrounding area.

Reaching down, he hauled up the stool and placed it on the table. Steadying himself with a hand on the wall, he climbed onto the stool.

What he saw was a tall chain-link fence topped with spirals of concertina wire. A great expanse of sand and sagebrush lay beyond. In the distance, mountains caught the last rays of the setting sun.

His hope faded, along with the light through the prison window.

CHAPTER 40 – RESCUE
Corpus Christi, Texas

"Hey lady, are you all right?"

Rain pelted the side of my face; my arms and legs stung as if hot peppers were being rubbed into raw wounds. I tried to open my eyes, but they felt swollen and glued shut. Then I heard another voice. This time it sounded like a child.

"Is she alive, Daddy?"

"Yes, sweetie."

Strong hands turned me on my back and brushed the sand and grit from my face and mouth. That's when I started a coughing fit and turned my head to the side, trying to spit out a gallon of seawater.

I opened my eyes to slits and realized it was daytime, but the sky was dark and overcast with a steady drizzle.

"Can you hear me?" It was a man—the daddy, I supposed. He leaned over me, his face hidden under the hood of his rain gear.

I gave a nod as I continued to cough and spit.

"Are you a mermaid?" the little girl asked. She was also hidden under an orange rain poncho. In one hand she gripped a fishing pole, in the other a large umbrella that she positioned to deflect the rain off me.

"Hush, sweetie. No, she's not a mermaid." Then he asked me, "What happened to you?"

I took a deep breath. "Where am I?"

"You're on Padre Island, south of Corpus Christi."

"Texas?"

"The Lone Star State," sweetie said with an air of pride.

"My arms feel like they're on fire."

"Jellyfish," Daddy said. "Well, not really a true jellyfish. From the welts, looks like Portuguese man-of-war. They got you pretty good. I've rinsed you down with buckets of salt water. Don't see any clinging tentacles left."

I tried to focus my thoughts. *Jellyfish? Is that what is stinging and burning?* "I need a doctor." My lips were dry and cracking, and I hurt all over. I knew I needed to be hydrated, along with serious medical attention. Then I had a passing thought as my memory flooded back. *Francine. Oh my god, I'm so sorry, Francine.* Maybe it would have been better if I'd just drowned or the sharks had gotten me. Maybe I didn't deserve to be rescued.

"Don't worry. I called nine-one-one as soon as we saw you washed up on the beach. Rescue is on the way."

I tried to sit, but only made it up on one elbow, my head dizzy and faint. "What are you two doing out here?"

"Fishing in the rain," sweetie said. "Daddy says that the fish love to eat when it's rainin' 'cause they don't think anyone will be out here."

I gave sweetie a smile but found I couldn't stay propped up, and dropped back onto the sand. That's when I heard the *whop-whop* sound emerging from the noise of the rain and surf. I turned my head to see a helicopter approaching out of the dark clouds, a big bright stripe slicing down its side like a Christmas ribbon.

———

"She's suffering from extreme dehydration and some pretty severe man-o'-war stings to her arms and legs." The voice was male and spoke with authority. "Good thing the guy who found her knew what he was doing. Dousing her with saltwater, not fresh, probably helped a lot. Most folks try old remedies like pouring vinegar on the lesions, but that can actually worsen the situation by making all the little remaining stinging nematocyst cells fire all at once. That can be bad. Real bad. She's lucky her Good Samaritan had a clue."

"How long before I can take her home?" It was Kenny.

I opened my eyes and found myself surrounded with tubes, monitors, and lots of white. The doctor stood at the foot of my bed with a clipboard in his hand and Kenny beside him.

"Ah, you're awake. I'm Doctor Ball." He came to the side of the bed. "You've had a rough go, Agent Decker. But I don't need to tell you that, do I?"

"Where am I?"

"Christus Spohn Hospital in Corpus Christi."

Kenny came to the other side of my bed and squeezed my hand. "I told you to never swim at night."

The doctor glanced at him, then seemed to realize Kenny was trying to comfort me with a feeble attempt at dry humor.

"Yeah, maybe I should start listening to you." I squeezed back. "How did you know I was here?"

"Before you passed out, you managed to tell the Coast Guard rescue guys your name and that you were with the OSI. Soon as we got the word, I flew down. You've been out of it for over twenty-four hours."

"Well, it looks like you're in good hands, Agent Decker," Dr. Ball said. "I'll leave you two alone."

"When can I go home?"

"Let's give it another day or so to build up your strength. And I want to keep an eye on those stings. Wouldn't want infection to set in. Sometimes there is a tendency for them to flare up. So, just relax and get some rest. You'll be able to leave soon enough."

I gave a nod of submission.

Once the doctor was out of the room, Kenny leaned over and gave me a kiss. Then he sat on the edge of the bed. I thought his eyes were a bit tearful, and that got to me. Big time. Kenny rubbed his hand over his face in an effort to hide his emotion, but I wasn't fooled.

"Max, you scared the shit out of me." A breath surged from him. Kenny recovered, drawing himself up straight. But I saw his Adam's apple move with a deep swallow. "Want to tell me what happened?"

I looked into his eyes and started crying. I was overwhelmed by everything—fatigue, pain, disappointment in myself, Kenny's obvious feelings for me, and my sister...my sister! "Francine is dead."

He stiffened. "Dead?" Kenny brushed the hair back from my face, and I saw the reflection of my pain in his expression. "Was it Knox? Did he do it?"

With tears flowing in rivers I shook my head.

"No, I did."

CHAPTER 41 – FLASH GORDON
Summit View, Nevada

Ford paced his cell. It had been well over a week, and in that time the routine was always the same—three times a day, the big man with the Taser would arrive, order Ford against the wall, and wait until Sarah had delivered the meal. They returned later to retrieve the remains.

No conversation or explanation of what this was all about. They supplied him with basic essentials, but nothing more. How he longed for a shower. A few days ago, they left a stick of solid deodorant. He must have smelled a little ripe for them to provide such a luxury.

There was no razor, either. As a result, Ford was growing a scraggly beard, and with his unkempt hair, his appearance was transforming from nuclear scientist to vagrant.

They had replaced his clothes with baggy orange prison garb. On the back and seat were stenciled the letters SVSP. What the hell did that stand for? he wondered.

They'd also given him socks and a pair of black rubber slides. The only sound in his cell was the soft flopping of the rubber against his heels as he paced.

Sarah and Taser Guy didn't seem at all concerned with the passage of time—no signs of frustration that a ransom had been demanded but not paid. So why had they kidnapped him?

Ford wondered what his wife was going through. A wave of guilt swept through him. His arrogance and his licentious infidelity, even though all those women had meant nothing, had now caught up with him. His wife must be on the verge of a nervous breakdown. By now the authorities would have set up camp in his home, waiting for the ransom call.

Ford had endlessly pondered how his captors got him out of the hotel. He may never know, but the bottom line was they did, and here he stood, helpless, isolated, and not too ashamed to admit, scared.

There was a rustling at his door. He glanced at the angle of the sun coming through the small window—not time for lunch, yet.

The door opened and Taser Guy filled the frame. "You know the drill."

Ford backed to the wall and put his hands behind his head.

The man moved in the direction of the table, and Ford assumed lunch was being served early. Taser placed a laptop on the table, opened it, and Ford heard a man' voice.

"Good morning, Dr. Ford."

A man's face filled the screen, probably using Skype or a webcam, Ford assumed. The stranger's profile was backlit, so there was little facial detail.

The man said, "First, I want to apologize for what you've gone through. I know you're uncomfortable and deeply concerned with your wellbeing and that of your wife and colleagues. Let me assure you that your spouse is fine—a bit rundown but holding up okay. Needless to say, your colleagues are also concerned with your disappearance. And the authorities are doing their best to find you. I can also guarantee you that they won't."

"Who are you? And where am I?"

"Telling you who I am would not be good for your health. Not knowing improves your chances of leaving here alive. To answer your second question, you're being held at the Summit View State Prison near Las Vegas."

"Prison? What about the other inmates?"

"You're it. You see, Dr. Ford, this facility was mothballed a number of years ago due to budget cutbacks."

"Then how are you able to be here?"

"We contract to perform basic maintenance on the

buildings for the state in case they want to bring it back to operational status sometime in the future. We're actually supposed to be here. Hiding in plain sight." He chuckled. "That's why no one will come looking for you here. Please understand our goal is not to hurt you or your family. But before we can let you out the front gate, we're going to need you to do an important job for us."

"What kind of job?"

"One for which you're well-qualified. You might even find it an exciting challenge, to say the least. You're definitely going to be intrigued." The face on the screen smiled. "My friend here will prepare you to be escorted to a work area. I'll be waiting for you there to explain what happens next."

"Then you'll let me go?"

"In due time. But I caution you that failure to follow orders or to complete the task I have assigned you will mean… Well, let's just say that the chances of your grave ever being found in the remote Nevada desert is slightly less than zero. Is that understood?"

Ford stared at the laptop.

"Would my friend's Taser help convince you?"

He shook his head. "No need. I understand."

"See you soon."

A moment later, a clink at his feet caused Ford to look down. Lying on the floor was a pair of handcuffs.

"Secure your wrists," Taser Guy said.

Ford did as he was told.

"This way." He let Ford go first.

Walking down the corridor, Ford saw that his cell was one of perhaps two dozen lining both sides. A line of lights ran down the middle of the ceiling, but only a random few were turned on.

The duo approached a metal door, with "Leaving Cell Block C. Entering Cell Block B" written above it in white letters. They walked through, and each new corridor they entered was lined with cells. They eventually arrived at a door labeled "Machine and Maintenance Shop." It stood partially open.

"Inside," Taser Guy said as he shoved on Ford's back.

Ford pushed on the door and entered into a dark space. He got the feeling it was large, but with no lights, he couldn't be certain. Behind him, the door closed with a loud thud, and he stood in total darkness.

His breath tightened and he felt his heart thrumming against his chest. What if they had lied? What if this was the end?

With a series of strident clanks, rows of overhead lamps blazed on, flooding the room with light. He stood in a space about the size of his old high school gym. He could tell by the caution lines and markings on the floor that it had probably once been filled with work benches, drill presses, and heavy equipment. But it was barren of all those now. A forklift sat near the middle of the room not far from a thick set of steel X beam supports, sort of a heavy-duty cradle. But what sat within the cradle caused his breath to catch.

The object was shaped like a cartoon rocket ship, almost like something out of an old Flash Gordon movie. He guessed it to be about ten feet long from its pointed nose to its set of tail fins. It was bright yellow and orange with green and blue stripes. Flames were painted down the sides, reminding him of the flames on antique dragsters at a car show.

On the side of the object, a portion of its metal skin was removed, exposing a large section of the inside mechanism.

Mesmerized by the uniqueness of the object, he was unable to take his eyes off it as he stepped forward. The closer he got, the more fascinated he became with the intricate complexity of its inner workings. Each step caused his heart to beat faster. This thing was such a mixture of textures and images: cartoon and machine, old and new, funny and…

Stopping a few feet away, Ford looked up at the big yellow *Tapas* rocket ship. Like a tsunami rushing over him, he suddenly realized what it was.

And he was overcome with paralyzing fear.

CHAPTER 42 – OUT OF AREA
Corpus Christi, Texas

I sat up in bed, staring out the window at Corpus Christi Bay. The hospital was right across the street from the water. I had finished telling Kenny everything that happened and choked back tears as the story ended.

"I'm so very sorry, Max," he said. "Being tricked into shooting Fran and then having her die in your arms is unbelievable." He shook his head. "What kind of sicko could do such a thing?"

"Nothing is beyond that bastard."

"Did I tell you I called Yuri to let him know you were coming to Cuba? But he called back the next day and said that when he went to find you, the hotel had no record of your arrival."

"I'm not surprised. The Cuban authorities must have been in on this. Knox has more influence than we realized."

I adjusted my arm with the IV to a more comfortable position. As much as I hated the damn thing stuck in me, I had to admit that I was feeling better—physically, at least. "So the big question is—what does all this mean? If his motivation is to punish me for shooting Aaron, it seems like he's gone to a lot more trouble than needed. I'd have to be an obsession of his, and somehow I don't think I'm that great of a magnitude to him. Nor was Aaron. Aaron loved his brother, but that was a one-way street."

"Do you really think so? Seems to me that you killing Aaron has put him over the edge."

"Travis is a sociopath—incapable of love or empathy or compassion. He's a master at using people to serve his own purposes. If I were the key to millions of dollars I would understand. But maybe it's no more than a perverted game to him. I'm like a Monopoly token he can push around the board. He simply likes it. Travis might get his rocks off by causing me pain or making me look like a fool. It could be a cheap thrill for him that makes him feel empowered. Even omnipotent or godly. I just have no clue."

Kenny pointed a finger at me in agreement. "You might be right. Otherwise why hasn't he just killed you if he wants to get even? He's certainly had the chance."

"The S.O.B. appears to know more about me than I do about him. And there's something else bugging me. This 'big bang' thing he keeps talking about. It's like he's baiting me for something, but I don't know what. Why? More cheap thrills for him." I glanced away from Kenny to the window and watched two sailboats gliding across the bay. The sight was calming but it didn't quite soothe me. "Whatever it is, putting the words 'big' and 'bang' together never sounds good."

"Did you ever get a look at the name of the ship?"

"Too dark. And I'd just been made to walk the plank." I sat up straighter and slapped my free hand down on the bed with a loud, emphatic, give-me-a-break *thwap*. "I was trying to stay afloat."

"Understood. How about the machinery in the cargo hold? Can you remember anything else about it?"

Now I was verging on not just being agitated, but exasperation was setting in. How many times was I going to have to answer the same questions—say the same damn thing repeatedly? And this wasn't even an official interrogation. "Like I said, it was big and yellow. Kind of reminded me of a carnival ride but all dismantled. Rockets or airplanes or spaceships, some shit like that, but I'm not positive. And also, like I said before, the word *Tapas* was painted on part of it. Maybe it said Topaz. Shit, Kenny, I was screwed up, dazed, frantic, dehydrated, sick, you name it."

Kenny didn't react to my lashing out. I guess I should be grateful for that, even though his lack of sympathetic response usually pissed me off. He reached into his satchel and brought out his laptop. He booted it up and sat it on my food tray so we both could see. A few moments later, he was online using the hospital Wi-Fi. He Googled the word *tapas*.

He scrolled through a few pages. "All I can find is somewhat general knowledge that *tapas* are Spanish appetizers. Not much help."

"Let me see it," I said, pointing at the computer.

Kenny shook his head to let me know he was insulted as he handed the computer to me.

"I just want to search, too. I might find something you didn't. Isn't that what they say about two heads being better?"

Kenny turned on a sports program on the television and sat back in the visitor's chair while I surfed the Web.

I found the same thing he did at first—*tapas* was a bunch of different Spanish appetizers. Then in some link to a Mexican restaurant I came across a reference to *tapas* coming from the Sanskrit word for *heat* or *fire*. Well, that was interesting and I continued down that rabbit hole until landing on a link that took me to a blog site about rumors and secrets of World War II. Didn't have any idea what *tapas* had to do with the war but I kept on scrolling through the blog for any reference. Four pages deep into previous posts, an entry caught my eye. Turning the laptop toward Kenny I said, "Flip off the TV and check this out." But I couldn't wait for him to read the whole thing, so I blurted it out. "It's a blog about World War Two. This guy, Old_Vet45, posted something pretty interesting."

"You know how many blogs are about the Nazis and World War Two. There are tons, Max. Half of the stories told are fictitious."

"I know, but just listen. By the end of World War Two, many of Germany's physicists had fled because they were Jewish. This article claims that of the few physicists left, a Dr. Kurt Strassmann had a top-secret bunker in the Austrian Alps in which was hidden Germany's answer to winning the war—

an atomic bomb ready to be dropped on London, but the war ended before they were able to accomplish the mission.

"Maybe it deserves investigation or it could just be—"

"Kenny, wait. Hear the end of this. Okay? Bear with me. At the news that the war was over, Strassmann supposedly destroyed the bunker, burying alive everything including his staff and soldiers. They found files and notes hidden in his attic decades after his death." A smile of discovery played across my face. "You'll never guess what old Strassmann called his pet project. A Sanskrit word that means *heat* or *fire. Tapas.*"

Kenny shoveled back his hair with his fingers, taking a moment to mull over what he'd just heard. "Think that's what you saw on the ship?"

I had to make sure I was being rational. I didn't trust myself. Turning the laptop back toward me I stared at the blog entry. I was pretty screwed up, but I clearly recall seeing the word *Tapas.* Hey, this is more than we had a few minutes ago."

"Okay, let's concentrate on the ship. We know it started in Cuba and you wound up getting tossed overboard off Padre Island. It doesn't make sense that they come to Texas, throw you in the water, and then head back to Cuba. So my guess is that they're headed south, maybe Mexico." He brought up Google Earth. "What are some of the ports that the freighter could be headed to?" He called up the region on the map. "There's Brownsville, Texas. Looks like after that it's Tampico, then Veracruz."

"That ship could have been headed anywhere, for all we know."

"Unless you can remember any more details, we've got little to go on."

I sank back into the pillows, feeling empty.

Kenny closed the computer. "What now?" he asked.

I shrugged. "No idea. I don't even have a place to go home to."

"That's not true." He took my hand. "As soon as you're feeling up to it, I want you to come and stay at my place in Virginia. I've got plenty of room."

"I don't know if that's such a good idea." The thoughts were already spinning in my head.

"No argument. It's settled. Otherwise I'll have the doctor force you to stay here with that." He pointed to my IV.

Kenny leaned over, and I thought he was going to aim for my lips, but at the last second he must have thought better and instead gave me a quick but soft peck on the forehead. "Sleep on it."

I opened the computer one more time and clicked back on the tab for the same blog site, scrolling down the list of comments. "Hey, Kenny, look at this from Austria. Didn't make world news but it's about the search for a couple of lost student hikers—"

Kenny's cell rang. He looked at the caller ID. "Out of area." He pushed *talk* and listened. "Who is this?" He looked at me with an expression of profound curiosity. "Yes, she's here." With uncertainty, he handed me the phone.

I held it to my ear. "Hello."

"Welcome home, Maxine. How was your swim?"

CHAPTER 43 – THE MACHINE SHOP
Summit View, Nevada

"What do you think?"

The voice came from the laptop Taser had brought along and placed on a table.

"Where did you get this thing?" Ford asked.

"We got it from the Nazis. Well, actually, we bought it from a man who found it. It was apparently the only atomic bomb built by the Germans. They were about to drop it on London, but they ran out of time—the war ended. So they shut their secret factory down and hid the weapon away. It was soon forgotten."

"And someone found it?"

"Yep, the guy who found it had enough connections to put it up for sale on the black market to the highest bidder, who turned out to be me. I'm sure his widow is still mourning his tragic death. Got run over by a piece of farm equipment. Sad."

"I'd heard stories of the Germans trying to build a bomb. I believe they called it the Uranium *Projekt*. A man by the name of Strassmann was the lead physicist, if I remember correctly. But it was more rumor than fact. And since nothing was ever found to prove it, no one knew for sure. But now this." He took a step closer and reached out to touch the weapon's metal skin, his initial fear shifting to intrigue.

"Any idea what its yield would be?"

Ford never took his eyes off the object. "If it was at all comparable to the bomb dropped on Hiroshima, I would guess thirteen to eighteen kilotons. But realistically, judging from Germany's limited enriched uranium capabilities at the time, it's probably around one kiloton, maybe less."

"So, can you make it go bang?"

Ford glared at the laptop screen, the uneasiness reappearing. "That's out of the question."

"Are you saying you can't?"

"I'm saying I won't."

"I already know it's doable. I just need someone like you to get it armed and ready."

"No. I refuse to have anything to do with it."

"Let's say for argument's sake that I can convince you to cooperate. Oh, and I need to be able to detonate it remotely using a cell phone."

Ford rubbed his shaggy head of hair. A back spasm made him lean his head to the side and stretch to relieve it. This was beyond belief. He was being held captive by a madman who possessed a nuclear weapon and intended to use it. His worst nightmare had come true—one man needing only one nuke. It couldn't get any worse.

"I won't do it. There's no way to convince me."

"Are you sure?"

Ford started to turn and walk away.

"Do you value your career?"

He stopped. "Of course. What kind of question is that?"

"How about your marriage? The respect of your children? You value those?"

"What are you getting at?" He prayed this lunatic wasn't going where he thought he was.

"How do you think your ultra-top-secret security position with the government and your thirty-year marriage would go if everyone found out about your dirty little secret habits on your out-of-town trips?"

Ford's stomach pitched. The air seemed to turn bitter cold. His brain ricocheted between having his family discover decades of cheating and the security risk he'd created for the Department of Energy and DHS by having exposed himself to blackmail. The defense secrets he kept stored in his head were priceless in the hands of the enemies of his country. If he didn't give them up, the scandal would mean a complete rupture within his family, the estrangement of his wife and children, the loss of his job. If he did reveal the secrets, he would most definitely be subject to federal prosecution and would go from this jail to a federal prison, with no stop in between.

"I'm sorry. I didn't hear your answer. Do you think your family and your employer—?"

"It would not go well," Ford said.

"Very good. Now you begin to see how I can convince you to make that thing in front of you go boom. You do that for me and no one will ever know about all the whores you fucked in the *privacy* of your hotel rooms."

How could this guy possibly know the hotels and the room numbers in advance? Ford thought. But then the events were always widely publicized. Still, did he really have videos? Was he bluffing?

"I don't believe you," Ford said. "There's no way you could know where I was staying and have enough time to install recording devices."

The man smiled. "Step closer, Dr. Ford."

He did, then saw a second window appear on the screen and a video started playing. The air left his lungs as he watched.

After about thirty seconds, the man said, "Let me know when you've seen enough."

"That will do." Ford wiped the sweat from his forehead.

"I have more if you like."

Ford shook his head, and the video window closed.

"I'll bet you're wondering which hookers worked for me. Frankly, it doesn't matter, does it? The outcome is the same. Can you imagine your daughters and your wife viewing the videos?"

He grew weak, his legs wobbled, and he felt on the verge of throwing up. Despite the room feeling arctic, he sweated like a man in a sauna. He quickly went over the faces of the last few women he'd paid to have sex. The madman was right—there was no way of knowing. And like he said, what did it matter in the end?

"So now that you understand your situation, let's talk about logistics."

"Like what?" His own words sounded to him like he was drunk.

"Speak up, please."

"What do you want me to do? And why me, anyway? There are others, particularly in the military…"

"I needed someone of your stature to prove that this is for real. You're the top authority, Dr. Ford. And as to what your job will be—I want you to examine the device, repair or replace anything that needs it, and create a mechanism that can detonate it by cell phone."

"What do you mean?"

"I dial a number. The cell phone you build into the trigger device rings. Boom! Should be simple for a man of your experience and ability. Right?"

Ford shrugged, wondering if his unsteady legs were going to continue to support him. Could he refurbish an atom bomb as old as this one and put it into working order? And make the detonation remotely controlled? And what about his own safety? For starters, how much had the containment devices degraded over the years?

"How did you get it here?" he asked the man in the computer. "You said it came from Austria?"

"Smuggled it in."

"Post nine-eleven? I don't see how that's possible."

"Dr. Ford, you're worrying about all the wrong things. Don't you realize you can smuggle anything into this country with enough cash? Just put it in the hands of the best smugglers in the world."

"Who are?"

"The Mexican drug cartel."

"Yes, but what about the radioactive signature that would have been detected at the border crossing? The authorities would definitely have picked up on that."

"Now, now, Dr. Ford, you still aren't paying attention to the right things. But if the information will end your distraction, I'll answer. It wouldn't have been picked up if the weapon was buried in the middle of a large shipment of medical equipment that also emits radiation. Equipment that's routinely allowed to cross. Plus, we wrapped it in a special blanket—a little secret I learned at the dentist's office. And it helped that I made a sympathetic ICE insider a very rich man along the way. I think he'll retire from the Immigration and Customs Enforcement now that he has such a big nest egg. The problem wasn't getting it into the country. The problem is for you to make it work."

"Well, I won't know until I start inspecting the mechanism. Almost seventy years in storage could have taken its toll on the inner workings or made it unstable or even unusable. But this is a very basic device. By today's standards, it's only slightly better than a dirty bomb. In fact, because of the technology at the time, it had to be a simple design—a gun-triggered fission device made up of a uranium target, a uranium bullet, what amounts to a gun barrel, and something to propel the bullet into the target, probably TNT. Strassmann and his technicians would have shaped the sub-critical mass of uranium into the bullet and placed it just in front of a quantity of propellant at the far end of the closed cylinder. The remainder of the uranium would go at the other end of the gun barrel. Detonation of the TNT would send the bullet down the barrel and slam it into the second uranium mass. The combined subcritical masses would go supercritical and set off a nuclear chain reaction. My guess is that the only thing that would need to be replaced might be the propellant. But even that could have survived the time in storage, depending on what was used. And I assume it's fueled with uranium-235, which has a half-life of seven hundred million years."

"So you don't see any difference between arming a first-generation nuclear bomb and this World War Two device?"

Ford shook his head.

"Good. Then we have a deal?"
"Do I have a choice?"
"No."

CHAPTER 44 – THE CLUE
Corpus Christi, Texas. Friday

"What do you want, you murdering bastard?" I held the phone away from my ear as I mouthed the words "Travis Knox." I put the phone on speaker and Kenny leaned closer.

"Just making sure you're okay," Knox said. "You know, it's not very smart going swimming at night in the Gulf of Mexico. There're all kinds of nasty critters out there. But I knew you could do it—you're a strong-willed woman in prime physical shape. And a hell of a shot, I might add. You nailed Francine with one bullet. Glad it wasn't me you were shooting at."

"Your time is coming."

"Should I consider that a threat?"

"Count on it."

"Excellent. I wouldn't want you to say it and not mean it. Revenge is a powerful motivation. And to be honest, Maxine, that's exactly what drives me, too."

"Haven't you done enough?"

"Oh, no. We're just getting started. Trust me—we've got a long way to go, yet. Before I'm done with you, you're going to wish you'd never heard my name."

"I'm way past that point."

"You just think you are. There are lots more surprises in store for OSI Special Agent Maxine Decker."

"You still haven't answered my question. What do you want?"

"All in good time. First you'll need to go on a little treasure hunt."

"Listen, asshole, I'm really not into games."

"No, but you are into the Blade of Abraham."

"What's that got to do with anything?"

"It's the key to everything, Maxine. I'm surprised you haven't figured that out by now."

"So I find the Blade, and I find you?"

"No. You find the answer to the riddle of the big bang. And by the way, I don't have the Blade anymore. I gave it away."

"To who?"

"Now you're on the right track. I would also recommend you read the Book of Genesis. Especially the part about Abraham. Did you know that he almost sacrificed his own son with that knife you're so fond of?"

"I'm well aware of the story," I said. "What are you—?" I suddenly sensed deadness on the line. "Hello? You still there?" He'd hung up.

"The man is certifiably insane," Kenny said as I handed back his cell.

"Testing all my buttons to see which ones to push. Problem is, so far he's zeroed in on just the right buttons. He has something much bigger in mind than tormenting me. Making me miserable is simply an added perk. This guy is a sociopath with no conscience."

"What he's already put you through is a hateful rampage. He's admitted that revenge drives him. But he's gone way too far out of his way just to cause you all this distress."

Kenny dropped into the chair beside my bed just as a nurse came into my room.

"How are we doing this morning, Agent Decker?"

"Good enough to check out of this hotel."

She gave me an understanding smile as she inspected my IV drips. "Looks like we're right on target."

"When can I be discharged?"

"I believe Dr. Ball said you could probably go home tomorrow."

I nodded a thank-you as she turned and left.

"Why is it that nurses and doctors always refer to patients as 'we'? How are *we* feeling? Looks like *we're* having a good day."

"They want you to know they feel your pain."

I was sure they meant well, but nobody could really feel my pain. I'd just killed my sister.

Kenny's cell rang again. He read the display. "It's a message from Knox. Says, 'These should help you find the treasure.'"

"These what?"

"He's sending over four photos." Kenny waited for the images to load, then he stood next to my bed so we both could look.

The first photo showed what appeared to be the inside of a grungy looking building. In the foreground was a cockfight—two roosters in battle on a dirt floor. Circling the fighting ring were tiered bleachers filled with men and women, even children, cheering for their favorite bird. Judging from the clothing and some signs readable in the background, it was taken somewhere in the Caribbean or Latin America, which made sense since the sport was legal in several of those countries. The picture was taken by someone sitting in the bleachers.

The next photo was basically the same, but the photographer had zoomed in on two men in the first row. The one on the left wore a hat pulled low and a pair of sunglasses. The one on the right wore a tropical flowered shirt and shorts. He was muscular to the point of appearing to be a bodybuilder. Although I could see his face, I didn't recognize him. What appeared to be a wooden box rested in his lap, his beefy hands on top of it. The box looked to be about fifteen or sixteen inches long and a few inches high.

Kenny pressed advance, and in the third picture the man in the hat now held the box in his lap. His face was still hidden behind the dark sunglasses and the shadow of the hat brim. The bodybuilder was gone.

The final picture must have been taken outside the cockfighting arena and showed a number of parked cars. The man with the hat and sunglasses was unlocking the driver's door to a late model Nissan. Cradled in his arm was the wooden box. I could clearly see the car's Puerto Rican license plate and number.

I glanced at Kenny. "There's our new owner of the Blade of Abraham."

CHAPTER 45 – INFESTATION
Las Vegas, Nevada. Saturday

Taser Guy pulled the Diamondback Pest Control van up to the back of Hershel Applewhite's grand Tudor-style mansion. "I'm here," he said into the Bluetooth mic attached to his ear as he scanned the service entry parking area.

"Any other vehicles?" The voice in his earpiece was Travis Knox.

"Two cars, no trucks. We're good."

In preparation, Knox and Taser had studied the mansion from every angle using programs like Google Earth. Ironically, there had been an AC repair truck in the satellite photo, so Taser knew exactly where to park. They had also gone to the county building department and made a copy of the architectural plans of Applewhite's house.

Knox had tracked down which pest control service Applewhite used, how often, and when the regular service call was scheduled. Today, the real technician had stopped for lunch at a diner in North Las Vegas, as he always did, before heading to his final customer of the weekend—the home of the famous televangelist. His lunch break proved fatal when a strikingly beautiful woman approached him asking for a ride. Minutes later, as they got into the van the woman reached over and plunged a needle into his neck. While she calmly got out and walked away, Taser was already climbing in through the back. As he stripped the man of the Diamondback uniform, he said into the mic, "Everything worked like a charm. Sarah had him drooling. He's out cold. You're a frigging genius."

"It's all about attention to detail," Knox had responded. "Genius isn't required. Just gotta be passionate and do your homework."

Now, as he sat in the van parked behind the mansion, Taser checked his watch. Two-twelve p.m. The Saturday service had started over at the Golden Throne Cathedral. He would have one hour to get the job done.

"Make sure your ID badge is easy to see," Knox said through the earpiece.

He fidgeted with it, admiring the duplication they had made using his photo. "Yep," he said, getting out. Opening the rear doors of the van, he glanced briefly at the body of the pest control technician—heavily sedated and bound hand and foot with tie wraps and duct tape. From among the cartons of supplies, he grabbed one of the larger sprayer canisters, then closed up the truck and locked it. With the dry desert wind on his face, he marched up to the mansion's service entry door and rang the bell.

A moment later a white-suited, middle-age gentleman greeted him.

"Diamondback Pest Control," Taser announced.

"Didn't we just have a treatment?"

"Five weeks ago, sir. Here's the work order." Taser handed the man the company form. "You never want to give a bug a decent break."

The butler glanced at the paper. "No, you're certainly right about that. Father Abraham detests insects." He swung the door wider and motioned for Taser to enter. "I don't recognize you from previous visits. Do you need me to walk you through the rooms?"

"Not necessary. We treat *every* room. Plus we maintain a floor plan back at the office of all our important customers. I familiarized myself with the layout before I came out. Need to be efficient."

The butler shrugged. "Suit yourself. But be finished before three o'clock, when Father Abraham returns from rehearsal for his service tomorrow."

"Not to worry. I'll be long gone by then."

Over the next twenty minutes, Taser journeyed from room to room in the sprawling house, moving quickly while he pretended to spray the baseboards and cubbies just in case anyone was watching. On the second floor, he found only one door locked. It had to be Applewhite's bedroom. Strangely, he noticed that in all the bedrooms and baths, there were few clothes and little evidence of personal belongings, except the son's. Taser knew which room was Carl's—it had a Bible inscribed to him from his father, an ornately framed Baptismal certificate, his college degree in theology, numerous graduate school textbooks, a laptop, and a scattering of personal items.

In the long hallway outside the bedrooms, Taser located the attic access for this part of the house. He knew from meticulously studying the architect's plans that there was no firewall between this section of the attic and Applewhite's bedroom.

Taser returned to the ground floor and tracked down the butler. "I hate to tell you, but there's evidence of a scorpion infestation. I'm going out to get some special stuff that should take care of it. But I'll have to go up into the attic crawlspace to apply the poison. You might hear a little noise and banging around since I'll need to bore a hole inside a few of the walls and apply a treatment of the chemical. Scorpions tend to love dark spaces. Be back in a minute."

Taser walked out to the van, stored the canister, and retrieved a backpack, which he suspended over his shoulders. Locking the van again, he returned to the mansion and headed upstairs. Wasting no time, he went directly to the attic access and pulled down the ladder. A few moments later, he was crawling along the ceiling joists, an LED utility lamp strapped to his head. Taser followed the electrical wiring conduit to where it turned down into Applewhite's bedroom. There he found the hollow space within the interior stud wall.

Sitting back on his haunches, he removed the backpack and withdrew a right-angle drill and a compact battery-powered vacuum. He fed the bit down in the open space a couple of inches and threaded the nozzle of the vacuum beside it. Then he pressed both triggers. The drill bit whirred and ground into the dry wall, popping through the masonry as the vacuum sucked up the small amount of dust and debris.

He withdrew both and set them aside, then took out a mini-projector, a tiny video camera, a wireless video transmitter, a roll of duct tape, and a piece of metal coat hanger with a one-inch, ninety-degree bend at the end. He set the projector beside the open space, attached its flexible lens, and bent it to match the wire. Next he tied a long string to the lens cap strap and held onto the other end. He fed the coat hanger down the hole as he kept the angled stub pressed against the dry wall. With a little manipulation and a few tries, he located the newly drilled hole. Gripping the string and wire in one hand, he slipped the projector lens inside the space, following the wire to the hole. He pushed the lens tube as flat against the masonry as he could, then gently tugged on the string until he felt the resistance give. The lens protector was now removed.

He carefully withdrew the wire and repeated the procedure with the flexible lens of the video camera. Done with that, he bent the top of the hanger back toward him, mashed it flat against the joist and used the duct tape to secure everything including the transmitter. The small hole he had bored was crowded now, and withdrawing the hanger at this point could dislodge or disturb the delicate equipment.

Last task was to hook up the projector, camera, and transmitter to the remotely activated power distribution switch. Finally, he attached a portable heavy-duty battery pack to the switch.

When he was finished, Taser removed a USB thumb drive from his pocket and inserted it into the side port on the mini-projector. Then he pulled out his cell and dialed Knox. Talking through the Bluetooth he said, "Power up."

A second later the devices turned on.

"Play." Taser saw the light on the thumb drive blink on and knew the projector was accessing the MPEG file. "We're good. Now try the camera and transmitter." Another LED, this one on top of the transmitter, glowed, telling him it was sending its signal to Knox parked on the highway a half-mile away.

Knox said, "It's pretty grainy, but I can see the room and the projection."

"It's a wrap, then," Taser said. "Shut it all down." He repacked the backpack and retraced his route out of the attic.

Moments later, he waved to the butler on the way out the service entrance. "That should do it. I've taken care of all the bugs."

CHAPTER 46 – VIVA LAS VEGAS
Corpus Christi, Texas. Friday

"Have you ever heard of a televangelist by the name of Hershel Applewhite?" Kenny walked into my room just as I finished shoving my meager possessions into a complimentary Christus Spohn Hospital tote bag. My doctor had left a few minutes earlier after having discharged me.

I considered Kenny's question as I surveyed the room for any missed items. Last evening, he had made a run to a nearby mall to get me some traveling clothes. "Those kinds of religious shows are not my thing, but I have caught bits and pieces of his Sunday telecast while channel surfing. He's the guy with the screwed-up hand, right? Quite full of himself, if you ask me, with all the billowing clouds—he even makes the choir members wear angel wings." I stopped and looked up at him. "Why?"

"Hershel Applewhite is the man in the photo getting into the Nissan. I had a meeting over at the FBI's resident agency. The special agent in charge was very helpful. The metadata embedded in those digital photographs Knox sent revealed they were taken nine months ago. Also the location coordinates were just outside Fajardo, on the eastern end of Puerto Rico. We traced the license tag number to a rental firm in San Juan. According to his rental application, Applewhite listed where he was staying on the island as the Ritz Carlton. The special agent called the San Juan regional office. Because we knew the date and name, they were able to confirm through hotel security video that Reverend Applewhite left the hotel on a day trip with no box but returned with it."

"So he's got the relic?"

"He did nine months ago—if in fact that's what was in the box."

"Where is this Applewhite guy?"

"He runs something called the Applewhite Ministry of Deliverance from the Golden Throne Cathedral in the desert outside Las Vegas. His headquarters are also there, along with a religious seminary. Viewership of his television ministry tops out at a hundred million worldwide. And they say he's got enough cash to buy the MGM Grand."

A candy striper appeared at my door pushing a wheelchair. "I'm here to take you down, Agent Decker."

"No need," I said. "I can walk fine."

"Sorry, it's hospital rules."

I glanced at Kenny but he just shrugged and took hold of my tote bag. As the girl wheeled me out of the room toward the elevator, Kenny said, "Looks like we're headed to Sin City."

I chuckled, then mumbled my best Elvis, "Viva Las Vegas, darling."

———

Las Vegas, Nevada. Saturday

Despite his subtle hints during the flight from Texas at the prospect of us sharing a room, I was dead set against trying to deal with my ex, sex, and close quarters along with everything else that had happened. His shoulders did their usual drop when I stood at the front desk of the Rio and requested two rooms. While the clerk checked us in, I turned to Kenny. "Get over it."

After meeting for breakfast the next morning, we hopped into our rental and headed north on I-15. It was Sunday and the traffic was light. Once we left the Strip and resorts behind, the "other" Las Vegas looked almost normal, with its sprawling suburbs stretching west to the edge of Red Rock Canyon and the mountains beyond.

I had never been a big fan of the desert. Whenever my job brought me west, I would carry a bag containing lip balm, eye drops, nasal spray, hand lotion, skin moisturizer, and anything else I could think of to wage battle against the paper-dry air. So I went fishing in my bag for my ChapStick as we headed away from the city into the desert to experience the Sunday morning services of the Reverend Hershel Applewhite.

We cruised past dozens of tour buses along the interstate headed in the same direction. "You don't think they're on their way to Applewhite's Golden Throne Cathedral, do you?" I asked as we passed the exit to Nellis AFB.

"Should know soon enough." Kenny kept the rental at a smooth eighty. "The church is not that far now—same exit as the Las Vegas Motor Speedway."

I glanced to the right at a series of buildings a mile or so off the highway. From the overpass I could see the facility was surrounded by high triple-tiered chain-link fencing and guard towers. But I could only see a few cars in the otherwise empty parking lots and just barely make out the name: Summit View State Prison. "Crime rate must be really low. Looks like nothing's going on there."

"Most likely another victim of the economy."

Kenny's cell rang. "Gates." He held it to his ear for a full minute, only saying *yes* and *okay* a few times. He ended the call with, "Thanks," then turned to me. "That was DC3. They got a call from Sergeant Dela-Cruz in Manila. He sent an investigator back out to take a statement from Paco Alvarez."

"The neighbor with the WiFi?"

"Right. The detective pressed the guy for a better description of the woman who paid him to set up the router. He finally admitted that it wasn't a woman after all, but a man. The man told the neighbor that a female American agent would be showing up with the PNP assault team and he was supposed to claim a woman looking exactly like the agent was the one who paid him."

With a deep sigh of relief, I said, "So Fran had nothing to do with it."

"No. It was all a part of the setup to get you to go to Cuba."

"Could the neighbor identify the guy?"

"The detective showed Alvarez a picture of Travis Knox, but he said it wasn't him. He did say the guy had a nasty scar on the side of his head and walked with a limp."

"At least I know now that Fran was an innocent pawn. That bastard is capable of anything."

"Did you ever doubt it?"

I shook my head. "So he's got an accomplice who's scarred and lame."

"That narrows it down to a few million men."

Ten minutes later, the Golden Throne Cathedral appeared like a mirage off to the left. Its chrome and glass exterior gleamed in the morning sun as multiple gothic spires pointed like needles into the Nevada sky. Along with a line of tour busses, we exited off the interstate and followed the four-lane parkway toward the church. Beyond it were other buildings that I assumed formed the headquarters and seminary of Applewhite's ministry. As we made the final turn into the parking area, attendants stationed at set intervals waved us into the *cars only* lot while the big busses were directed to the Bus & RV section. There were already hundreds of cars and dozens of busses lining up in the lots.

"This is quite an event."

Kenny nodded. "According to the brochure at the Rio, it gets repeated every Sunday." Kenny pulled our rental into the next available slot, directed there by a man in an orange vest who would have made a ground crewman at a major airport proud. "I've arranged for us to meet with Applewhite in his office after the service."

"Maybe we'll get religion."

"Probably too late for either one of us," Kenny said with a chuckle.

We got out and followed the gathering flock as everyone made their way toward the cathedral—all dressed in their Sunday best. I looked up at the imposing structure and had to admit it was impressive. Using the reflective metal and glass, the whole building seemed to shimmer. Even the expanse of the surrounding desert didn't diminish its grandeur. It was obvious Applewhite had spent a lot of money to create a grandiose impression. Over the majestic entrance doors, chiseled into the stark white marble was the inscription: God is Great, God is Good.

Inside we were directed to a bank of elevators.

"Balcony three still has plenty of seats," the attendant told us as he stood tall in his white tuxedo. "You'll be able to hear and see everything."

"How many balconies are there?" I asked.

"Five," he said proudly.

The glass-front elevators were in constant motion as they lifted groups of the congregation into the upper reaches of the six-thousand-seat megachurch. When we arrived at our seats, I got my first look from a dizzy height at the most impressive modern church I'd ever seen. Even my barely-in-control fear of high places didn't keep me from enjoying the view.

The lines of pews on the ground floor were shaped in a half-circle as they wound around a sanctuary that jutted out into the congregation—each seat filled. Even from this far up, I could tell that every age group was represented.

"Now that's an organ," Kenny whispered.

I followed his line of vision and my jaw dropped at the sight of the enormous-sized pipes taking up the entire back wall of the sanctuary. They reminded me of ICBMs ready to launch an all-out war against the devil. But the stunning size of the organ didn't come close to its enormous sound when the first notes filled the church. I thought of the scene in *Close Encounters of the Third Kind*, when the mothership let loose its full tones and the surrounding mountains must have moved a few inches.

Then the choir began "A Mighty Fortress Is Our God", accompanied by a sizable string and brass section along with King Kong, the pipe organ. If this was not what music sounded like in Heaven, God had the wrong music director. As

I watched, a ballooning mass of clouds rolled out across the sanctuary, and the lights dimmed. An ethereal golden beam channeled down and the clouds parted, revealing the desert deity, Reverend Hershel Applewhite.

CHAPTER 47 – NO MAN'S LAND
Las Vegas, Nevada. One week earlier

Bud, the Alexandria Hotel senior transfer guard watched the bank of video monitors as the Frontier Armored Services truck pulled up to the retractable electro-mechanical bollards in the underground tunnel below the hotel. All the casinos used armored services like Frontier to move excess cash offsite to banks.

"Morning," Bud said through a speaker box. Focusing on the monitor, he scrutinized the faces of the two men in the cab of the diesel truck and realized he didn't recognize the passenger. He'd seen the driver before—hard to forget that ugly scar running along the side of his forehead into his scalp. During an earlier transfer, when asked how he got it, the driver had said it was an Iraq war wound.

The driver held his ID badge to the barcode reader on the speaker box bringing up his picture on a screen for Bud. Then the passenger handed over his badge to be read.

"He's a trainee," the driver said, nodding his head toward the passenger.

A second transfer guard, sitting at a control panel, verified the IDs. "Clear."

Bud tapped a button on his console which retracted the bollards. A moment later, wall-mounted signal lights in the tunnel turned from red to green. The truck pulled forward into what was known as No Man's Land. Behind, the bollards returned to their extended position. The driver performed a ninety-degree maneuver before throwing the truck into reverse—the backup beep tones echoing in the bay. The heavy rubber bumpers lining the concrete lip of the dock stopped his progress.

"Alert status," Bud announced. His voice blared through speakers in the ceiling.

A metal door on the back wall of the bay rolled up. Out stepped two armed Alexandria security guards.

"Turn off your vehicle," one of them ordered.

As the truck died, the large garage fell quiet except for the distant whine of roof-mounted exhaust fans. "You're cleared to exit your vehicle."

The driver opened his door and climbed down. He walked with a limp as he climbed the steps to the top of the loading dock. Bringing a two-way radio to his lips, he gave a command to the trainee in the cab. The back doors of the truck swung open.

A throaty sound filled the dock area as a forklift moved to the back of the truck and gingerly delivered a pallet of four metal boxes, each about the size of a footlocker. Across their tops was stenciled *Alexandria Hotel and Casino.*

Bud walked out of the control room and onto the dock. "What's new?" he asked the truck driver.

"Taking the wife up to Lake Mead this weekend."

"Been up there before?"

"Couple a times. We love it."

"Yeah, me, too."

"You know, I gotta bring her by here to see the Tut Experience before it leaves."

"Better hurry, only a couple more days and the exhibit heads back east."

Once the forklift backed away from the truck and disappeared into the hotel, Bud held out an electronic device and the driver placed his ID badge over it, causing a beep as it read his barcode.

"Okay, my friend, the transfer is complete," Bud said. "Let me know what day you want to come, and I'll score you a couple of comp tickets."

"Hey, that would be great." The driver radioed to the trainee and the motorized doors to the truck closed. Then he made his way down the steps, carefully favoring his bad leg. He climbed into the cab and cranked the engine.

The bollards retracted, and the signal lights turned green. He pulled the truck out of No Man's Land and drove through the tunnel, up a ramp, and onto East Reno Avenue.

A few minutes later, once he'd steered north onto Las Vegas Boulevard, he turned to his trainee passenger. "See any problems?"

Travis Knox smiled. "Nope."

CHAPTER 48 – THE WHITE ROOM
Las Vegas, Nevada. Sunday

Applewhite stood when Carl ushered the two guests into his office and introduced them.

"These are agents Maxine Decker and Kenny Gates, from the United States Air Force Office of Special Investigations." He turned to the visitors. "May I present the Reverend Dr. Hershel Applewhite, pastor of the Golden Throne Cathedral and founder of the Ministry of Deliverance."

A tremor rattled through Applewhite as he wondered if their being here had anything to do with the harlot in Las Vegas? And if so, why the Air Force? He shot his son a look of disapproval for failing to call him by his newly declared name. He clenched his jaw, then briefly closed his eyes and gathered himself to a more relaxed state of mind. "Father Abraham," he corrected. He noted a startled look on the visitors' faces and thought that curious. Their eyebrows were arched and mouths slack. He didn't like that. "Sometimes my son is forgetful. Carl can be on the slow side." He focused on his son once again.

"I apologize, Father." Carl glanced at agents Decker and Gates, then lowered his head, but rolled up his eyes to fix his gaze on his father.

"He is a good son. Not like so many of the lost and damned children of this age who have no respect for their parents."

Applewhite came around his desk—four chrome pillars supporting a two-inch-thick slab of Plexiglas, six feet long. "It is a pleasure to meet you both." Still dressed in his white satin robe, he extended his hand. "Always humbling to meet the brave members of our armed services." He gestured toward two white suede and chrome chairs. As he went back around to take his seat, he motioned Carl to a chair on the right side of his desk.

When everyone appeared comfortable, Applewhite splayed his arms, palms down, on his desk. "Let us take a moment of silence to give thanks and praise to the Almighty for bringing us together on this glorious Sunday morning."

Without waiting for the visitors to acknowledge his request, he bowed his head, knowing the magnificence of his office overwhelmed them, like everyone else who first entered. This was how his flock expected him to live. The room was a sixty-foot-square space decorated almost totally in white marble and chrome. Even the sculptures and modern religious artwork all had a predominately white theme. But the most impressive element was the wall behind Applewhite—sixty feet of floor-to-ceiling glass showcasing a panoramic view of the great American desert. Nothing obstructed or distracted from the breathtaking scene stretching to the horizon.

"God is great, God is good," Applewhite said a moment later as he looked up to see the two agents staring intently at the desert landscape beyond. "Wonderful, isn't it? I chose this setting to build my church to remind us that God is the master of all creation."

"Impressive," Agent Decker said. "How do you ever manage to leave this office with such a view?"

"Sometimes it's hard." Pearls of sweat dribbled down his back as he wondered again if this was about the woman at the Tumblin' Dice Hotel. He had been a little too rough trying to bring her to redemption. Maybe she filed a police report.

"Must be an awe-inspiring sight during one of those rare desert storms."

"It can bring you to your knees, Agent Gates, to witness the mighty hand of God." He turned to Carl, who nodded. Applewhite paused to give his guests enough time to absorb the impact of the vista before them. He'd had enough of the small talk. "When my son came to me bearing your request for a private audience, I must admit, I was perplexed. I can't imagine what interest the Air Force would have with this simple servant of God."

"Are you familiar with the Office of Special Investigations?" Agent Decker asked.

"I'm afraid not." Applewhite tried to relax, hoping that perhaps this would only wind up being a request for a donation or even a personal appearance at some military base. Once a year, he hosted Armed Forces day at the Cathedral and filled the balconies with airmen from nearby Nellis.

"The OSI," Gates said, "is to the Air Force like the FBI is to the nation. Our job is to investigate crimes committed by Air Force personnel. All the branches of the military have their own version. You're probably familiar with the TV drama *NCIS*? It stands for Naval Criminal Investigative Service and is the Navy's version of our OSI."

"I will admit that I've heard of the show, Agent Gates, but as you can imagine, being the spiritual shepherd of such a large flock, I have little time to indulge in pulp television."

"Of course, Reverend. You have a big job to do, and we can appreciate the burdens you face."

"We all have our crosses, Agent Decker, but I embrace mine in the glory of God." He glanced at Carl, who acknowledged agreement. "Now, I must tell you that I have a rather busy schedule today, so if we could come to the purpose of your visit?"

Crossing her legs, Decker asked, "Are you familiar with the ancient religious relic known as the Blade of Abraham?"

Applewhite felt as if his heart had slammed up against his ribs. The question had come out of the blue, and he was unprepared for an answer. He only hesitated for a couple of seconds, but as he tried to figure out how to respond, it seemed like the pause lasted for endless moments. He needed time to reassess. "My goodness, pardon my manners." He turned to his son. "Why don't we have some refreshments brought in?" Back to the agents, he added, "Sometimes I get so lost in thought that I completely forget my social skills. I hope you'll forgive me? Would you like soda, coffee, tea?"

"Nothing for me, thanks," Decker said. Gates also declined.

"Well, I think we should at least have some sparkling water," Applewhite said to Carl. "Have some Fiuggi brought for everyone in case our guests change their minds."

"Right away, Father Abraham."

Applewhite cringed now at the title as his son rose and headed for a door to the private kitchen. But this distraction had given him time to organize his thoughts. He turned to Decker. "Now, you were asking?"

The woman said, "The Blade of Abraham? It's the knife many believe the prophet held as he was about to sacrifice the life—"

"Yes, yes, yes. Genesis twenty-two, verses one through nineteen. I know the story." He struggled to control his stress.

"Of course. I didn't mean to insinuate otherwise. The relic was stolen from the Cairo Museum over twenty-five years ago but recently surfaced for sale on the internet."

"Really?" Applewhite whipped up a shocked expression and tone as Carl returned with the water for everyone.

Kenny nodded a thank-you, accepting the drink. "We believe it was in the possession of a former Air Force officer who is wanted for desertion and attempted murder. He is also known to deal in stolen antiquities on the black market."

"That will be all, Carl," Applewhite said, dismissing his son. "That certainly is a disturbing story, Agent Gates. What is this world coming to? Nothing is sacred anymore. I wish I could help, but I'm afraid I don't know anything about the whereabouts of the relic." He was going to make this good. Being dramatic was second nature to him. He threw himself back in his chair as if he had taken an Evander Holyfield blow to his chest. He distorted his face to appear he was both stunned and mortified. Then as if having a distressing epiphany, he said, "Oh, no. Wait. You don't suspect I—?"

"Do you know a man named Travis Knox?" Agent Decker

leaned forward in her chair.

Applewhite was surprised. *Is that a name I should remember from the past?* "No," he answered, unsure if he was telling the truth. But he would commit the name to memory.

"So you have not recently purchased the relic known as the Blade of Abraham?" she asked.

"No," he answered honestly, since it was *given* to him. He tried not to sound nervous as adrenaline screamed through his body. Heat radiated across his chest. Now the other of Satan's agents leaned forward. "On a recent trip to Puerto Rico, did you receive a box from a man while attending a cockfight near the town of Fajardo? Was the stolen relic in that box?"

Applewhite felt blood pumping through the arteries in his neck. His temples pulsed, and the first hint of nausea crept into his gut. He forced out a nervous laugh. Thinking quickly he said, "Oh, now I see what you're getting at. And I can understand your confusion. Yes, I did receive a box during my trip to the island. But it contained nothing as exotic as your stolen ancient relic."

The reverend took a sip of his Fiuggi and tipped it too far as if by accident, buying him some time to create an elaboration to his story. "Oh, my. How clumsy of me." He dabbed his collar with the cloth napkin that had been brought with the water.

He continued. "It was just a carving by a local artist depicting Michael the Archangel defeating Satan. A beautiful rendering made from the wood of the local kapok tree."

"So you flew from Las Vegas to San Juan, rented a car, drove out into the country to a cockfight to receive a wood carving? Then you drove back, checked out of the Ritz Carlton, and flew back to Nevada?"

The evil woman agent kept on with her insinuations. Most certainly she was being instructed by the devil himself. Applewhite rolled his tight shoulders and snapped his head to the side to release a cramp in his neck. He wanted to shut her up. Gag her. Tether her to a pipe in a basement until he could release the demon in her. He swallowed hard. "Yes, I know it looks strange, so let me explain." He laced his hands on his desk in front of him. "You must understand that my responsibilities are great, and that can take a toll on a man. Now and again I need some respite, some time to meditate, to be alone with God for extended periods. I can't always do that here with the ministry. So I went to Puerto Rico for some spiritual R and R.

"I suppose you are curious why I, a man of God, would go to a cockfight. Seems a paradox, I'm sure. I attended the sporting event to experience the culture. We have become an intolerant species. The lesson to be learned is that we open our hearts to all, as the Almighty does. The artist at the cockfight was barely making a living with his carvings."

He shook his head to add some theatrics. "So sad. The island is beautiful, a true paradise, but speckled with shanty after shanty. Anyway, this man, this artist, had quite a few items with him that night, offering them for sale. Beautiful religious carvings whittled by his own callused hands. I purchased one. He asked ten dollars. I gave him twenty. Probably only worth five at the most. The Good Book tells us you get back more than you give."

He tried a confident smile. "And then, unfortunately I had to cut short my trip as I was called back unexpectedly. It was all perfectly innocent, I assure you."

Applewhite glanced at his watch feeling quite proud of himself. "Regrettably, I'm afraid that's all the time I have. My board of directors awaits me." He stood and strolled around the desk in a deliberate measured stride. "I can't thank you enough for your dedication and duty to our country." He shook their hands and noticed his were icy against their warm palms. "I sincerely hope you find your missing relic and catch the despicable individual who stole it. I ask God's blessing on you both." He motioned to the entrance to his office. "One of my assistants in reception will show you back to the public area. Thank you for celebrating this wonderful day with us." From the corner of his eye, he suddenly realized that Carl stood near the doorway and had probably heard everything.

As the agents turned to leave, Decker appeared to notice Carl, too. "Reverend Applewhite, just out of curiosity, why did you take on the name Father Abraham?"

Applewhite smiled as pleasantly as he could. "I didn't take it on, Agent Decker. It was the will of God."

CHAPTER 49 – CARL
Las Vegas, Nevada. Sunday afternoon

"I think Knox is just yanking us around," Kenny said as we sat in a booth in the Rio's lobby bar. "This is a wasted trip."

I watched Kenny sip his draft while I used my straw to play with the ice in my raspberry tea. His right leg bounced. I wanted to reach out and touch it like I used to. That's how I reminded him to slow down, but it was his body's way of releasing energy. And he had a metabolism I so envied. Didn't matter what the guy ate, he was as slim as he was when I first met him. And so many times that touch I gave him on his thigh to stop jiggling led to other more intimate things. Guess I never could stop at his thigh, nor did he want me to. Memories trickled through me. We had been so good together at least most of the time. Too bad we screwed it up. With that thought I put my brain back in gear.

"We came back from the Golden Throne Cathedral with nothing more than an impressive view of the desert. Applewhite fed us nothing but lies. We know he has the Blade and he knows that we know it. It would be useless to interrogate him again. The dear reverend will deny possession until he dies." I took a sip of tea. "I've been thinking—why would Knox be doing any of this? If he has some weird grand plan, why feed us clues? This is all wrong, Kenny. There's something really askew."

"Maybe it's all a game to him."

I rubbed my forehead with my fingertips as if it would clear my mind. "We've been through this before. It's got to be more than that. He's gone to too much trouble. Are we just plain stupid for following the scraps he tosses us? I feel like a dog playing fetch with some sadistic master. If Knox was simply out to screw with me, he's done that. Not only ripped the rug from under me, but took away my life and my only remaining family." I massaged the back of my neck. "So what *is* he up to?"

Kenny sat quietly, knowing better than to try to give me some lame rationale that would just piss me off. Our relationship had never been anywhere near perfect, but Kenny had learned to read my moods fairly well. There were times he knew it was best to withdraw and wait.

"Knox is still playing us," I said. "Over and over and over, and we keep right on going down the same path. He's dangling carrots knowing he can snatch them out of our grasp whenever we get close. Are we idiots?"

"What other choice do we have? He's got to figure you realize all this, but he keeps at it because he knows we can't just sit on our hands. If he throws enough shit around it'll wear you down, and after a while you won't know what to chase—how to sort the meaningful from the crapola."

"Maybe."

"Sociopaths are hard to read. They're unpredictable. They don't think like we do."

"So we don't have any choice but to act on every clue he hurls at us in hopes we'll come up with something, catch some mistake he's made. And he will. He's so brazen and full of himself he's going to trip up."

"Maybe that's *our* plan, Max. Go along with him so his self-confidence gets out of control and he thinks he's invincible. That's when they all mess up. In the meantime we dig deeper into everything he's told us or hinted at. Knox thinks he's so friggin' smart."

"Play his game?" I said.

"Exactly."

"Maybe his carrots have clues embedded. That's what we need to figure out. I don't know why, but Applewhite sure seemed edgy when we dropped the Blade question. And that story of going to Puerto Rico for some relaxation and a wood carving was a load of crap."

"Agreed," Kenny said. "I'll wager he made that up on the spot. I just don't understand why Knox would send us those photos? Why bring us to Las Vegas unless this is where the Blade is? And why would he want us to find it? That's what I mean. He's up to something and he's using us. And the reverend is lying, which is not a good characteristic of a man of God."

"He sure enjoys his pomp and circumstance. He had to build that huge church just to fit his ego under one roof." I looked up to see Carl Applewhite standing beside our booth. Round, boyish face, clean-shaven, and dressed in his button-down Hagar, khaki Dockers, and brown penny loafers, he definitely looked the part of a crisp divinity student. I wondered how much of the conversation he'd heard.

"Hey, Carl," Kenny said. "Good to see you again."

"Yes," I said. "Want to join us?"

He seemed to hesitate, but when Kenny moved over, Carl slid in beside him.

"How did you find us?" I asked.

"One of our traffic attendants told me you had a Rio Hotel parking pass on your dash. I hope you don't mind that I came here."

"Of course not." I waved to our waitress. "Would you like something to drink?"

"I'll have what you're having." He motioned to my tea. I was thankful I had resisted a Johnnie Walker this early on a Sunday afternoon. Waiting until the waitress took our order and left, I said, "So, we're really glad to have met your father today, and you. It must be quite interesting work, especially in such magnificent surroundings."

"I'm really worried about him," Carl said.

Kenny cocked an eyebrow, and I tilted my head as if to say *What do you mean?*

Carl cracked the knuckles of his left hand with one crushing squeeze from his right, obviously anxious. "I think he's going insane."

"Why would you say something like that?" Kenny asked.

"Because it's true. My father has always been…eccentric. I would guess most men in his position would have to be cut from a different cloth than the rest of us. But lately, in the last ten or so months, he's really changed, like he's drifting further and further from reality. Ever since the calls started."

I shot Kenny a look. "What calls?"

"My father believes they're from an angel or even directly from God. And he was spending hours and hours on the internet searching for something, but he wouldn't tell me what, only that he was doing the work of the Heavenly Father. Then that suddenly stopped. The work of God on the internet? It's all so odd. He's not himself, and I'm afraid for him."

Suddenly I realized the young man might be placing himself in danger by being here with us. "Listen, Carl, maybe we would be better off discussing this in a more private place. Would you be willing to come up to one of our rooms before we continue?"

I think the thought of danger occurred to him, as well. He glanced around with a trace of concern on his face. "You're right."

As we left the lounge and headed for the elevators, I said, "You're studying to be in the ministry, right?"

"Already received my degree in theology and started my first year of graduate work."

"At your father's seminary?"

"Yes. We offer masters and doctorates in all areas of Evangelical Studies."

"So you don't even have to go away to college," Kenny said, but Carl didn't smile at the attempted humor.

We stepped onto Kenny's floor and headed for his room. I took a quick appraisal as we entered and gave Kenny an approving smile that he hadn't left it in his usual state of male mess. All the rooms at the Rio were suites, so we took our places on the large sectional outside the bedroom.

"Carl, why don't you tell us what's really on your mind?" I said.

His expression filled with pain. "This is really hard for me. I love and respect my father very much. But I'm also concerned for his emotional and spiritual stability—and frankly, his sanity. This person who keeps calling is manipulating Father Abraham."

I held up my hand. "Mind if I ask why you refer to him in that way? His name isn't really Abraham, is it?"

"No, he took up the name—actually he declared it to the world—soon after he obtained the relic."

"So he *is* in possession of the Blade?" Kenny asked.

Carl looked down at his fingers that were digging into his thighs and gave a half nod. "He made the trip to Puerto Rico specifically to bring it home."

"Do you know how much he paid?" The first wave of excitement ran through me as I sensed the trail suddenly heating up.

"That's the crazy thing. My father has paid exorbitant prices for relics and pieces of ancient art nowhere near the value or notoriety of the Blade. But in this instance, he paid nothing. Not a dime."

"What?" That made no sense.

"The man on the phone—the *voice,* as Father Abraham calls him—gave him the relic as a gift."

I leaned back into the couch, deep in thought. It was beyond belief that Knox would give the Blade of Abraham away for free. Not after selling much lesser objects on the black market for hundreds of thousands if not millions of dollars.

I said, "Tell us about what this man on the phone has told your father. Why are you so concerned?"

"He's convinced my father that God has anointed him as the new prophet Abraham, the avenger of the Almighty. Father believes that it's his responsibility to carry out God's justice on what he considers the modern-day version of Sodom and Gomorrah—Las Vegas, Sin City."

"He's preaching fire and brimstone from the pulpit?" Kenny asked. "Condemning what goes on in Vegas?"

"Yes, although that's not necessarily a new theme for him. But privately, to me, he's insinuating that the city must be destroyed, just like the cities of sin in the Old Testament."

"Carl, what do you mean by *destroyed*? Are you talking metaphorically?" I asked.

"I don't know for sure. I'm hoping it's just a figure of speech."

"Okay," I said, "for argument's sake, let's say we're talking about a religious movement to clean up the city. That's understandable—many preachers become obsessed with cracking down on the wicked, using social movements, community protests, even attempts to change laws. This could be nothing more than expressing moral outrage at the current state of affairs in Vegas and his attempt to make it a better place. That's possible, isn't it?"

"I don't think so."

"Why?" I asked.

"The last time the *voice* talked to my father, he promised to deliver a solution to the abominations of Sin City. A total solution."

CHAPTER 50 – THE TUT EXPERIENCE
Las Vegas, Nevada. Sunday afternoon

Bud's shift had ended. After changing into his street clothes, he walked through the main casino of the hotel, soaking up the chink-chink-chink sounds and major scale melodies flowing from the slots—sounds he loved because they provided him with his livelihood. It was the music of money, and he never tired of its song. He'd been at the hotel for five years, working his way up to senior transfer guard of the *Ramses Tomb*, as they like to call it—the heavily secured, underground loading dock where pallets of cash moved in and out of the hotel. With the Alexandria's Egyptian theme so prevalent, everything, including the behind-the-scenes areas, bore the names of distant pharaohs and ancient monuments.

He wandered over toward the exhibition wing, the place that for the last two months had featured The King Tut Experience: select artifacts on loan from The Egyptian Museum. The centerpiece was King Tutankhamun's solid gold death mask, which had been allowed out of Egypt for the first time in decades. The lines to get in were longer than normal, since it was the last day to view the attraction. He watched the visitors' queue snake back and forth through a theme-park-style rope labyrinth. Bud had been through the Tut Experience a number of times, including once after hours with a couple of security guard buddies. He found that because there was so much gold in the exhibit, he quickly tired of it and focused instead on the less famous pieces that became his favorites. Items that were specially crafted for Tut when he was a child, such as a delicate ebony chair and a small alabaster chest. He would be sorry to see the exhibit go.

Two men caught his eye as they made their way to the end of the line—one walked with a limp. Bud recognized the Frontier Armored Services driver and the new trainee. "Hey, how's it going?" he said as he approached the two.

"Looks like we made it just in time," the driver said.

"I thought you were going to bring your better half."

"She came down with the flu. I don't think I properly introduced you. This is my new partner, Travis."

Bud shook the man's hand. "Pleased to meet you. And you're right, you did just slide in under the wire. You may even be the last ones through. They're gonna close the line any second now. Tomorrow, it all starts coming down."

"By the way, thanks for these," the driver said as he held up two tickets. "I owe you a beer."

"You're on. Well, you guys enjoy the exhibit. You're not going to believe what's in there. But remember, no touching the merchandise." He waved as he turned to wander back through the casino and out to the employee's parking lot. Must have been a hell of a fight, he thought, still picturing the nasty scar on the side of the armored car driver's head.

———

It took thirty minutes for Travis Knox and the driver to make it into the King Tut Experience. After sitting through a short movie on Howard Carter's 1922 discovery of the tomb in the Valley of the Kings, they followed the last of the visitors into the main exhibition. The displays, along with the surrounding props, were dramatically lit, giving the illusion that the two men had entered the hidden passages of the boy-king's tomb.

Travis and the driver stopped before an alabaster chalice in the shape of a single white lotus bloom. Next came a child-size ceremonial chair adorned with detailed hieroglyphics, with the Egyptian god of eternity depicted in gold on the arms. One after another, they passed air-tight, climate-controlled laminated glass display cases containing chests, carvings, furniture, necklaces, daggers, rings—an abundance of gold and other precious materials.

The two men stood before the death mask of King Tut, its surface shimmering in the light. Like all the previous artifacts, an accompanying movie was projected onto the side of the case, showing photos of the inside of Tut's tomb and the original location where Carter found each item.

Both men remained silent, staring at the mask. Since they were the last in line, there was no hurry to move along.

The driver rubbed his chin. "It says that's a priceless artifact."

Travis shook his head. "I don't know about that. I've got an exact figure in mind."

CHAPTER 51 – ANOTHER CLUE
Las Vegas, Nevada. Sunday evening

"So our deduction that Reverend Hershel Applewhite is a liar has been confirmed," I said after Carl left. I stood at the window staring at the imposing pyramid-shaped Alexandria Hotel in the distance. I'd read somewhere that the forty-two-billion candlepower spotlight at the top of the hotel could be seen from space. The same guy who designed it—I couldn't remember his name—built similar pyramid hotels with beacons in South Africa and China. Claimed he wanted his lights to be seen from every corner of the world.

"Carl is really scared of the old man." Kenny joined me to take in the view. "But why would Knox give the relic to Applewhite anyway?"

That had been the question dominating my thoughts since Carl told us. "The most obvious answer is that he needed to make us come here looking for it."

"Okay, so now that we're here, what do we do?"

"I guess we wait." I started to head for the door. "I'm going to my room for a nap. Jet lag and those days in the hospital are catching up with me."

Kenny put both his strong hands on my shoulders and began to massage my stiff muscles, working out the tension I wasn't even aware of until his magical fingers started releasing it. I remembered his hands, how he could find the very sinew that tensed inside me. We certainly had some memorable moments in the past—or at least I did. Without warning I slid back in time.

I hadn't meant to, but an audible moan of approval escaped my lips.

"Feel good?"

"Mmm," was all I could manage, yielding to his expert touch.

"Come on, Max. Let go a little. You need to relax."

He walked over to the bed. Stretch out right here. "No monkey business, just a good rubdown."

I hesitated, and then he was guiding me to the bed.

"No monkey business," I repeated.

"Promise."

I lay on the bed face down, and Kenny straddled my thighs, then started doing his miracle work on my back and neck.

"It's a little rough on your skin like this. I have some lotion."

My warning alarms went off but were muffled by the pleasure of the massage. "You want me to take off my blouse?"

"Only if you're comfortable with that." He chuckled and dug his hands into my stiff muscles. "Not like I've never seen your naked back before. It's up to you."

With that, the heels of his hands found tender spots that loosened with his touch. I imagined how much better it would feel if his hands glided over my flesh rather than being bound in fabric.

I hadn't even answered when I felt my blouse being plucked over my head. I knew I should protest, but I didn't.

Kenny spread lotion on his hands and then slid his palms with pressure along the edges of my spine from my lower back up to my neck. I was luxuriating in the moment when I started drifting off. I thought I was dreaming when I felt a warm kiss on my shoulder and then my neck.

Half between sleep and awake, I didn't want to fall into either. This was the perfect state of being.

I turned on my back to find Kenny's shirt was also off. He gazed into my eyes. "No monkey business," he whispered, and turned away on his back. I scooted over to him and lay atop him, my head nestled in the small concave space above his sternum. God had to have created it just for me because I fit so perfectly.

Flesh to warm flesh we lay there. Nothing safer, more content than this. I think I would have given in to *monkey business* at that point, but Kenny didn't press. Maybe I was even disappointed. But nevertheless, this felt like home.

A few hours later I awoke. Kenny was sleeping with his right hand on my head as if he had been stroking my hair, his other draped over my back.

I was tempted to stay right there, but changed my mind. Gingerly, I crept out of the bed and Kenny's embrace. Beside him I stared down. Where had we gone wrong? Why had I been so headstrong? *Well, dear Miss Decker, you had your career and look what it got you.* That grand biological clock had been ticking away all the time I was climbing the golden career ladder. What a waste. What a goddamn waste. But that was water under the bridge, as the cliché goes.

I gathered my blouse and put it on. As I buttoned it, Kenny awoke.

"Where you going?"

"To my room."

"Why don't you just stay here?" He pulled back the covers.

"You know."

"Max…"

"I've gotta go." I planted a peck of a kiss on his forehead. "Thanks for the massage."

"You sure?"

I struggled with my thoughts, then headed for the door.

"Yeah, I'm sure." I wasn't really sure, but I couldn't let myself think about it now. Not now.

A few minutes later, I was in my room starting to strip off my clothes while eyeing the king-size bed. Bottom line—I was exhausted but pleasantly relaxed, thanks to my ex.

Just as I reached to pull down the covers, my cell phone rang. I looked at the caller ID. Out of Area. I'd had to buy a new phone after my trip from Cuba but I kept my old number.

Much as I didn't want to ever hear from Knox again, I knew I had to keep my number until this was all resolved. Cautiously, I pushed the talk button.

"How's the queen bitch of the universe?"

"What do you want?"

"You always ask me that. And I keep telling you the same thing. I want you to hate me so bad that nothing will stand in your way of trying to kill me."

"And I keep telling *you* I'm already there and more." As I held the cell to my ear, I moved around the bed to the phone on the night stand. Easing the receiver off the hook, I pushed the number to Kenny's room. When I heard him pick up, I said into the cell, "Knox, why don't you just come out and tell me what this is all about? No more games. You've already caused me more pain than you can imagine. Enough."

I heard the click of Kenny hanging up and knew he was already running out of his door.

"So what did you think of our mutual friend, Father Abraham?" Knox said.

"I think he's a deeply troubled man who's being manipulated by a psychopath. I feel sorry for him, and I think it's disgusting what you're doing to the man. Do you know that he thinks he's talking to God when you call him? How sick is that?"

"Excellent. I'm even better than I thought."

I heard a soft knock on my door and quietly opened it.

"Maxine, is Kenny Boy there? Why don't you put us on speaker so he won't feel left out?"

I clicked the speaker button.

"Knox, give yourself up." Kenny said. "It's only a matter of time until we find you."

"By the time you find me, it'll be too late. Plus, why would you want to miss all the fun?"

"Your stupid games are getting old," I said.

"Now you're starting to catch on, Maxine. It's a game—a very deadly game. And the object is to find the solution to the game before the big bang. I give you guys so many hints and you just keep scratching your heads like you don't get it. Do I have to spell it out for you?"

"Go ahead," I said. "Have at it."

"Here it is as plain as I can make it. The big bang is going to bring the wrath of God down on Sin City—at least that's how Father Abraham will justify it."

"You're still talking riddles," Kenny said.

"What kind of game would it be if I told you *everything*? Look, just find the Blade in time and you win the game."

"I thought we already did," I said. "Applewhite has it."

"You guys ever read *The Da Vinci Code*? Remember how everyone thought they were looking for a particular object? Well, this is like that book. Good luck, gamesters."

The cell call ended.

"The bastard's hung up."

"Let me see your phone." Kenny pulled up the Calls Received list. The caller ID showed Out of Area, but rotated to the actual number. "Country code forty-four. He was calling from the U.K." Kenny pushed Talk to automatically redial the number. After close to sixty seconds, he shook his head and hung up. "No answer." Next, he took out his own cell, scrolled through his list and made a call. He waited for an answer, then said, "It's Gates. I need you to run a reverse lookup on a number in the U.K." He read the number off my cell. After a moment, he said, "Okay, thanks."

"What's the word?"

"Burn phone. Knox probably already tossed it. And it's not a given he's in England. Even those disposable phones can come with features like three-way calling. All it would take is for someone in the U.K. to call Knox, put him on hold, then call you and bring him back online. He could be in the next room, for all we know."

I nodded.

"But we both know it would be next to impossible for him to enter the country with all those arrest warrants."

"Kenny, I entered the country from Cuba by simply swimming ashore. He's a lot cleverer than that. If he really wants to come into the United States, he will. The guy has made millions on the black market. Money talks."

Kenny rubbed his stubble. "Let's say he's here, maybe even in Las Vegas. What was all that bullshit about *The Da Vinci Code*?"

"Did you read it?"

"No, I prefer a good western anytime—Louis L'Amour, Zane Grey, Tony Hillerman."

"You should have been a cowboy." I sat on the bed. "I read Brown's book. It was about the search for the Holy Grail. Only it turned out that the Grail wasn't what they thought."

"So the Blade is really something else? If so, what?"

"I think we already know."

CHAPTER 52 – VESPERS
Las Vegas, Nevada. Sunday evening

Applewhite knelt beside his cot, the grains of rice biting into the thin, tender flesh of his knees. He thought of this nightly ritual as his evening vespers. First he began with the Lord's Prayer and then the chanting of the Trisagion or a hymn or psalm that stirred him. Like his nondenominational ministry, he also incorporated bits and pieces from a mixture of the world's religions. Applewhite assembled prayers that called out to him with special meaning. They were prayers that roused his soul and often reduced him to tears. But he believed that was the way prayer was supposed to affect him if he were truly a man of deep faith. It was a process of cleansing the soul. He found no indignity in his weeping.

After the commencement prayer and the Trisagion chant of *Holy God, Holy Mighty, Holy Immortal, have mercy on us*, he asked for God's blessing and followed that up with a confession of all his impure thoughts. Next was a plea for forgiveness for all his past shameful or less than humble deeds. At this point he usually wept. When he could get his voice back again, he recited the Twenty-third Psalm. Exhausted from the intensity of his vespers, he would flop onto his cot for the night's sleep.

Applewhite had just ended this evening's vespers, and his tears were only beginning to clear when his cell phone rang. He rose to answer, brushing the grains of rice away that clung to his skin.

"Yes."

"Abraham." The voice was muffled and echoing as if

coming from far away. "Lift up thine eyes."

Applewhite looked around the room, blinking away the final tears.

Again the curious whisper on the phone said, "Abraham."

"Who is this?"

"Lift up thine eyes."

The preacher heard the connection go dead.

What did the caller mean by *Lift up thine eyes*? Was he supposed to see something? Applewhite scanned the bedroom, quickly becoming aware of a dim swirling light forming in the center of the room. In disbelief he vigorously rubbed his eyes.

He looked again, and the wavering form persisted. It appeared much like a desert mirage or heat radiating off blacktop in the summer. As he watched with incredulity, a vague three-dimensional figure of a man took shape inside the eddy of light. But it was too hazy to discern clear features and details.

Applewhite trembled, his eyes fastened on the bizarre apparition before him. Then miraculously, an exotic combination of symbols and glyphs materialized. They were crisp, unlike the figure engulfed behind them inside the light. He thought the symbols might be Sumerian cuneiform. Something archaic, for certain. The glyphs soon dissolved, followed by the appearance of script. The words were in English and seemed to circle around the image of the man. The letters looked as if they were aflame. He thought of the burning bush from the Book of Exodus. Shockingly, the oscillating light became emblazoned with his name.

Abraham.

Was he in the very presence of the Almighty?

"Yes," he cried out. "I am here." He felt his body teeter on shaky legs as he fought to focus on the swirling image.

The text dissolved away, then more appeared, scrolling about the image, flames leaping from each burning letter like red, yellow, and orange tongues.

Speak not. Lift up thine eyes. I have found favor in you.

The words dissolved and were replaced by more.

You possess the Blade of Abraham because I have great faith in you. And so I bestowed his name upon you. Abraham. The father of great and mighty nations.

Dissolve.

Command your flock, and your household to keep the way of the Lord. You will do justice and judgment.

Dissolve.

I have heard your cry from Sodom and Gomorrah, and it is great, and their sin is grievous.

Dissolve.

*I would spare the city of sin if you found fifty who were not wicked, or forty or twenty.*Dissolve.

Still more text spit fire before Applewhite.

I will speak this once. If even ten were found righteous within the city, then I would spare it. I would not slay the righteous with the wicked. But you found not ten who were righteous. You found not one.

Dissolve.

Applewhite realized the nails of his one hand had dug into the other, gouging the flesh open. "Are you God?"

No response.

Go forth, Abraham. You know the city of which I speak. The Sodom and Gomorrah. And you will witness the destruction of the wicked.

Applewhite's mouth was as dry as the desert surrounding his home. He was ashamed because God had commanded him not to speak and he had. And he was frightened by the task God had just bestowed upon him.

He flinched at the knock on his door before it opened.

Carl stepped inside, his jaw agape and he dropped to his knees as he saw the apparition. "My God!"

Applewhite raised his hand to silence his son.

Dissolve.

Witness the destruction of Sodom and Gomorrah.

Dissolve.

On the third day at sunrise.

Dissolve.

Follow the brilliant star that shines unto Heaven until it is extinguished atop the mountain of Moriah.

CHAPTER 53 – REVELATION
Las Vegas, Nevada. Sunday evening

On his knees, spellbound by the flaming text and the nebulous form of a being in the otherworldly light, Carl felt his spirit surge. As the last word dissolved and the light and spirit within it faded, rapture filled him. Overcome, he bowed his head, and the need to pray compelled him. The flood of words came to Carl in a deluge and spilled forth in a whisper. "The spirit of the Lord God is upon me because He hath anointed me to preach good tidings unto the meek. Merciful Lord, I beseech thee to cast thy bright beams of light upon this ministry, that by being illuminated we may walk in the light of thy truth."

Carl could hear his father's weeping and murmurings and knew this must have been how Father Abraham felt each time he had heard the *voice*. Had he also seen *it* before but not informed his son, believing Carl had not consigned himself to absolute, undoubting faith with the same sincerity and passion as his father?

Again the compulsion to pray prevailed. Nothing else mattered. Not earthquake nor fire could have thwarted him. He had been wrong about his father. He'd been deceived by those who would blind him to the truth—his faith had been tested and he had failed. "Almighty God, who sees that we have no power of ourselves, keep us both outwardly in our bodies, and inwardly in our souls that we may be defended from all adversities which may happen to the body, and from all evil thought which may assault and hurt the soul."

"Carl?"

It was his father's voice.

"Yes."

Applewhite flipped the bedside light on. "Did you see, my son? It has all come together. He has taken me slowly down His path, feeding my soul small portions of His manna. If He had just come to me and disclosed everything at once... Oh, that would be too much for any man, no matter how strong his belief and dedication to the Lord. Too shocking. So He began with the Blade. The first step in leading me up to this moment. He wouldn't identify Himself on the phone, even when I asked. Perhaps I would have quickly, but falsely, concluded the caller was a crackpot. I don't know. You can't second-guess the Almighty. Little by little, He has brought me along—given me my name, knowing He would give me the same task as Abraham. And now this, this most glorious vision of Him."

Applewhite paced, driving his maimed fingers through his hair. "Yes. Yes." He threw back his head and gazed at the ceiling in revelation. "I see it all now. Everything!"

The minister spun about to face his son. "You do understand, don't you, Carl?"

Still dumbfounded, Carl could only nod.

"And why did you come to my door, son? Why at that moment?"

"I was bringing you your schedule for tomorrow. And there was also a visit from the police about the pest man. He's missing or something, and the authorities are retracing his steps."

"And you felt it necessary to relay that to me at the very instant you did?"

Carl shrugged, not certain what the point of the question was. "I guess so."

"Why is that? Didn't you answer their questions?"

"Yes, but...well, yes."

"Think, my son. Think."

Carl swept his hand over his face. What did his father want him to know? Why didn't he just come out and tell him? His palms were clammy, and he rubbed them on his pant legs.

Applewhite stepped closer and put his arm around the younger man's shoulders. "It was no coincidence of timing, Carl. You were called to my door by our Heavenly Father. His will be done. Praise the Lord. Glory to God in the highest."

"You mean I was supposed to witness the…"

"Yes, yes, yes! And do you know why you can find no word to depict what you saw? Because there are no words to describe the countenance of our Maker. We could only see a vague form, something surreal." Applewhite's expression changed to one of incredible contentment. "Dreamlike." His eyes drifted up as if he heard choirs of angels singing in his ears. "It is impossible to look upon His face. Exodus 33:20, *You cannot see my face, for no one may see me and live.* Our eyes are not created to see the spiritual things on this Earth, nor can our bodies possibly endure beholding the awesomeness of our God."

"But Father, there are many times in the Old Testament when God revealed himself. To Adam in Genesis, Jacob at Bethel, Abraham, Israel and also Gideon, in Judges."

"You make me proud of your Bible studies. You are correct. And also Solomon in Kings, Isaiah, and Ezekiel. But those were only manifestations of God. He could only be seen in the best way we can envision him. But once we enter the Kingdom of Heaven, our limitations will depart. Then we will see His full glory."

Carl looked away. "Destroy Sodom and Gomorrah. Does He really mean Las Vegas?"

"It is a wicked place, writhing with loathsome acts against God's word. His creations have brought Him such deep sorrow. And He would have spared the city if there had been but ten righteous among them. But there was not even one. Our Lord trusts in us, Carl." Applewhite clasped both hands on his chest. "My heart swells, and I feel His spirit moving within me. Do you not?"

"I do."

"Then we will do as he asked. On the third day."

CHAPTER 54 – RED ROCK
Las Vegas, Nevada. Monday morning

"I can't believe how beautiful this place is," the mother said as she stared out the window at the rock formations and sandstone peaks among the Calico Hills.

"Breathtaking," the father said. He snapped another digital picture of the view along the thirteen-mile loop through Red Rock Canyon west of Las Vegas. "Every picture's a postcard."

They sat in the comfort of the air-conditioned Desert Tours mini-bus as it cruised along at a steady twenty miles per hour with the eight other tourists and the driver. Large windows gave everyone a panoramic view of the colors making up the one-hundred-eighty-million-year-old formations.

"It's hard to believe this was once at the bottom of an ocean," the mother said as she read from the guide book.

"You mean this *desert* was once under water?" their teenage daughter asked. She sat across the aisle and glanced up from her iPhone as she reacted. The girl had been texting since they left their hotel.

"Oh, so your ears do work," the mother said.

Without losing a beat, the girl rolled her eyes, shrugged and went back to the phone.

The father shook his head. "It's a lost cause. I can only hope someday she'll learn to appreciate her surroundings." He pulled his last picture up on the camera's LCD. "I'm gonna post this one on Facebook as soon as we get back to the room."

"You're such a geek," his wife said with a smile.

"Take a look at these amazing colors." He pressed the zoom to show her more detail.

"Sweetie, I'm right here looking at the real thing. I don't—"

"That's strange. It looks like…"

"Looks like what, dear?"

"Oh, my God." He shot from his seat. "Hey, driver, stop! STOP!"

———

"I'm at a total loss," I said to Kenny. Then I scrutinized my scrambled eggs and corned beef hash as we sat at the table in my hotel room. Room service had just delivered our breakfast. "I can't figure out what Knox is up to. It's so screwed up. And why would he want us to snoop around some delusional misguided televangelist who likes collecting ancient relics and thinks he's an Old Testament prophet?"

Kenny sat across from me folding globs of cream cheese on his toasted bagel. The muted flat-screen TV nearby showed a network game show.

"I wish I had an answer for you, Max. This has gone way beyond my computer forensics skills. I think you're right, Knox is getting his jollies out of screwing with our heads and manipulating the two of us any way he wants. And doing it in the cruelest of ways."

I pushed a piece of paper across the table. "I made a list of all the clues—big bang, *Tapas*, the Blade, Applewhite— everything Knox has thrown at us. On the surface they might look meaningless but there must be a connection. There has to be info cloaked inside."

My gaze drifted to the TV. I took a sip of my coffee and started reading a breaking news story scrolling across the bottom of the screen. "Hey, check it out. They found that nuclear scientist."

"The one that's been missing?"

I nodded.

Kenny read aloud. "The body of Dr. Geoffrey Ford, Los Alamos Director of Nuclear Weapons Research, was found by tourists in Red Rock Canyon." He looked at me. "Turned up dead right outside of Vegas. Well, now that's interesting. We get pulled here by Knox, then this. Coincidental?"

As my eyes followed the words, my thoughts shifted from Travis Knox to Dr. Ford.

"No coincidence," I said and pushed my breakfast away. I motioned to the additional details scrolling across the screen. "There's proof."

———

We were on the way into the Lake Mead Boulevard office of the Special Agent in charge of the FBI's Las Vegas regional headquarters. When I heard the agent's name I felt like someone had knocked the wind out of me.

Kevin Fender.

I'd been accused of involvement with the artifact theft and fiasco in Iraq—that I'd shot my partner in order for the operation to be successful. Kevin Fender was the principal investigator from the Office of the Inspector General who led the Department of Justice's efforts to prosecute me. He'd done his best to pin something on me, and was less than pleased when I left OSI after no formal charges were brought against me.

After we had been ushered through the building, Kenny rapped on Fender's open door.

The agent stood. "Come in. Good to see you, Agent Gates." He nodded to me. "Hello, Maxine." Then, while shuffling papers on his desk, he said, "Have a seat."

"Congratulations on your promotion," Kenny said. "This has got to be better than the Washington meat grinder."

Fender glanced at me. "Well, I'm still out here trying to catch bad guys." He gave a half-hearted smile, then said, "How's retirement going, Maxine?"

"Quiet, until recently."

"And I take it that's why you're here."

"Agent Fender," I said, "if we could set our history aside for just a moment, Kenny and I have information we think might help in your investigation of the kidnapping and murder of Dr. Geoffrey Ford."

He spread his hands as if showing the length of a fish he'd caught and said, "Just like in the past, Maxine, I'm always entertained by your interesting theories."

I wasn't there for a fight. So without waiting for any more sideways comments from Fender, I related everything that had happened, starting from the eBay auction and ending with our meeting with Carl Applewhite. By the time I finished, he seemed to be showing signs of genuine interest. "I am sorry about your sister. It's sad when innocents are involved."

It took everything in me to say, "I appreciate that," knowing it wasn't really a sincere sentiment but rather a harsh stab. I felt my face blaze with anger. Fender's intention was to remind me that I had *killed* Fran. Kenny rested his hand on my leg, approving that I had let the remark go. He made me feel a little better.

"Kenny and I believe that Ford's body was purposefully placed right by the roadside so it would be easily discovered."

"Could be."

I asked Fender specifically more about what was written in the dirt by the body.

"The word was definitely *Tapas*." Fender made a few notes on a desk pad. "And you say it's an ancient word meaning fire?"

"Correct." I answered.

"Do you remember anything else about the equipment in the ship's hold?"

"I wish I did, but I was in pretty bad shape. All I know is what I've already described."

"Well, it's a start. I'll have the folks at TSA and the Border Patrol start investigating shipments coming to the Las Vegas area that originated from the east coast Mexican ports within the dates you mentioned."

"What's your evaluation of Applewhite?" I asked.

"That's a tough one." He gave a quirky smirk. "On one hand, he draws a lot of visitors to the area, and he donates quite a bit of time and money to the community."

I got the impression that Fender was searching for the right words.

"On the other hand, he's…peculiar."

"That's a nice way to put it," I said.

Fender shrugged. "Got to be PC these days." He looked at Kenny. "You heading back to DC3?"

"To be honest," I said, reminding him I was *with* Kenny, "the *Tapas* connection is way too much of a coincidence. We're going to stick around at least for a few days and do some more digging." I handed Fender my card. "My cell is on there."

Kenny gave the agent his card, too. "Call if you think we can help."

Fender stood and shook Kenny's hand. I got a shallow nod.

For clarification, Kenny asked, "The news said Ford was shot?"

"Execution style, in the back of the head."

"That's interesting," I said. "If he was killed execution style, there's very little chance he could have survived long enough to write anything in the sand."

Fender nodded. "That was our conclusion, too."

"Which means the killer most likely left the *Tapas* clue," I said. "Was there ever a demand for a ransom?"

"No." Fender hesitated for a moment. "But there's something we haven't released." He looked at me as if debating whether to trust me or not. Then he said, "Ford's clothing had higher than normal traces of radiation."

CHAPTER 55 – ANONYMOUS CALL
Las Vegas, Nevada. Tuesday morning

I studied the reflection in the mirror. Zigzag lines crisscrossed the face staring back at me and formed hard-edged patterns. Slowly, blood seeped from them, and I felt an overwhelming sadness wash over me. Then the jagged streaks separated and floated apart like scarlet autumn leaves caught in a slow-motion wind. They hung suspended, as if riding a thermal current, for what seemed like hours before crashing to the ground.

I went to cover my ears only to find that in one hand I held a pistol, its barrel still smoking. I had just fired it into the mirror—

The shattering of broken glass transformed into ringing. Shaking and bathed in sweat, I emerged from the nightmare, my eyes tearing with the memory of Fran's death. The ringing was not glass breaking, it was the sound of my cell phone.

I had closed the thick drapes in my hotel room before going to bed, but I could now see the glow around the edges—the sun had risen over the desert. "Yes?" Gravel filled my voice.

"Maxine, this is Special Agent Fender."

I strained to focus on the digital clock. 7:52 AM. How could I have slept so late? And why was he calling *me*?

"What can I do for you?"

"I tried Agent Gates, but there was no answer. We received an anonymous call, a man claiming he had information about the doctor's death. The caller directed us to the location where the source of radiation came from on Dr. Ford's clothing. He also referred to something called the 'big bang'—an event that he threatens will kill millions."

Suddenly I was wide awake. Jumping from the bed, I stood and went to the window, yanking the drapes open so the light would help me clear my brain.

"He actually said *big bang*?"

"Yes, and I remember you mentioned that phrase in my office."

"Did you identify the caller? Was it Travis Knox?"

"No way to confirm it. But the caller did say one more thing concerning the big bang."

"What?"

"That from here on out, he would only communicate with you."

———

The approach to the Summit View State Prison took on a totally different appearance from Sunday when Kenny and I passed it on our way to Applewhite's Golden Throne Cathedral. For starters, I-15 was now shut down for ten miles in both directions. After passing through checkpoints set up by the State Police and the U.S. Army, we were in the only civilian car on the highway as Kenny and I followed our Humvee escort. Second, the once virtually empty parking lot in front of the prison buildings was now filled with military, law enforcement, and first-responder vehicles, including tractor trailer trucks from the Army and the Department of Energy and a couple of unmarked black uplink satellite trucks. I counted five helicopters on the ground near the facility and two overhead, all military.

Fender's conversation with me was crisp and to the point. I knew he hated to have to call me, and it must have pained him even more to relate that I was the only one with whom the terrorist would communicate. At this point, I was willing to do anything to find Knox and bring him to justice. I'd find a way to deal with Fender.

We followed the Humvee onto the exit ramp and down the long road to the prison gates. Every hundred yards or so we passed a parked, combat-ready Humvee. He glanced over at me. "You look tired."

"I am. After staring at your laptop screen all afternoon trying to find anything more on the Nazi bomb and *Tapas*, my sleep was filled with nightmares. I must have relived killing Fran a hundred times."

Kenny reached over and placed his hand on mine. He started to say something but seemed to change his mind.

At the prison gate checkpoint, we showed our IDs and were directed to park near a collection of city and state police cars.

"There's Fender," I said as Kenny pulled up beside a Nevada Highway Patrol Dodge Charger. The agent gave us a wave. Beside him stood a tall, dark-haired man in brown trousers, orange polo shirt, and blue windbreaker with a government seal on the breast. He wore wire-rimmed glasses and a serious expression. As we got out of the rental, Fender and the other man approached.

Shouting over the noise of the circling helicopters, Fender introduced us. "Agents Gates and Decker, this is Dr. William Martin, Deputy Secretary of the Department of Energy."

So now I'm an agent again? Funny how things change when my "interesting theories" start to have legs.

Martin shook our hands. "Thanks for coming so quickly."

"You got here fast, too," Kenny said. "Isn't your office in the Forrestal building in Washington?"

"Just so happens I was at a briefing over at the Nevada National Security Test Site. It's only sixty-five miles from here—a quick chopper ride. I came as soon as I got word of the discovery."

"What exactly have you discovered?" I asked, my voice nearly drowned out by the helos overhead.

"Two things, actually. Let's go inside," Fender said.

Martin looked at us. "Don't worry, it's safe. We've done a complete sweep of the entire facility. There are elevated radioactive traces concentrated in only one area, but even there it's within the safe range."

Kenny gave me, an *I hope he's right* glance as we passed through the main entrance to the prison. "Agent Fender, you mentioned at your office that Dr. Ford's clothing had radioactive traces. Do you now know how that can happen?"

Fender glanced at Martin, who responded, "We think so. Basically there are a number of ways to pick up traces of radiation—everything from exposure to medical devices to space travel to accidents at reactors to the manufacture and disposal of nuclear weapons. Even cross-country flights expose passengers to higher levels than standing on the ground."

"I take it Dr. Ford was not recently on the International Space Station?" I said.

"No," Fender said. "We think he had somehow come in proximity to a significant amount of enriched uranium."

"Specifically, uranium-235," Martin said.

The entrance area of the prison was stark and utilitarian— exactly what I expected. Beyond the reception area and security checkpoints were a series of heavy metal doors and unadorned white hallways with an abundance of security warnings and surveillance cameras.

As we walked, Martin continued. "U-235 can oxidize, leaving a white, powdery material that can cling to skin and clothing. This is what we found on Dr. Ford's body. Our mobile lab, which you probably saw in the parking lot, was able to analyze the substance and identify it as coming from U-235."

"Would Dr. Ford have had to come in direct contact with uranium-235?" I asked. "And would that have caused his death?"

"He would have had to touch it, which is no big deal if he's wearing protection. Some of the oxidation residue must have been transferred to his clothing. But it was the nine-millimeter slug to the back of the head that killed him," Fender said.

"Lead poisoning," Kenny mumbled.

"So you were going to tell us about your discovery."

"We're almost there," he said. "You'll see soon enough."

"Is this an active facility?" I asked.

"No," Fender said. "It was shut down two years ago due to cutbacks in State funding."

"Who has access to it?" Kenny said.

"A private contractor is responsible for maintenance," Fender said. "They usually inspect on a monthly basis. Their company records show that no one has been here for twenty-eight days."

"So the cars I saw in the parking lot two days ago were—"

Fender finished my sentence. "The vehicles driven by whoever is responsible for this." He pointed to a door labeled Machine Shop as we rounded a corner in the corridor. A number of people in hazmat suits were just coming out.

"You're sure it's safe, Doctor?" Kenny said.

Martin turned and nodded. "How about I go in first?"

Kenny stepped back. "Be my guest. I don't want to wind up glowing in the dark."

"If you do, Agent Gates," Martin said, "it'll probably be because you sprayed yourself with DayGlo paint."

We entered a large room big enough to house about half an Olympic-size swimming pool. Rows of overhead floods bathed the empty space.

"This was an inmate's training area before the State closed down the facility and removed all the work stations." Fender motioned. "That's the discovery."

My eyes were drawn to a large set of steel X-beam supports in the center of the room, obviously built to cradle a sizable, heavy object.

"What's that?" Kenny looked at Martin.

"We believe that a military-style weapon, perhaps a bomb, recently rested atop those supports," the assistant director said. "And we think it was the source that exposed Dr. Ford to radiation."

"So we're talking about a nuclear weapon?" I asked.

Martin gave a nod.

"I thought most modern nuclear weapons were rather small

and compact—you know, warheads and such," I said. "This thing looks like it was meant to support something much larger than contemporary weapons."

"And that's what's got us stumped," Fender said.

"Are there any military weapons known to go missing recently from old or current stockpiles?" Kenny asked.

Fender shook his head.

"How about any recoveries?" Kenny asked. "Like the H-bomb lost off Tybee Island."

"I'm sure the folks of Georgia would be happy if it was found," Fender answered. "But no, no recoveries that I'm aware of."

"Recoveries? Plural? How many have we lost?" I asked.

Fender smacked his lips. "The U.S. has lost eleven nukes in *accidents* since 1945."

"That's not very comforting." I wondered how many nuclear weapons, not just from the U.S., were out there floating around. And Fender emphasized the word accidents, probably not wanting to disclose the total number. How many were just lost and unaccounted for?

My worst fear appeared substantiated. The revelation jolted through my brain. Some of the puzzle was coming together. Worse than a nightmare. Knox *did* have a nuclear weapon! *Big bang* was a colossal understatement.

"I think I know what we're dealing with." Everyone looked at me.

"The blog you found while in the hospital in Texas," Kenny said.

"I came across a post written by a war veteran who mentioned the *Tapas* reference. He said it was the code name of a secret project by the Nazis headed up by a German physicist." I worked to remember the details. "Strassmann. Dr. Kurt Strassmann. This old vet on the blog said that Strassmann and his group were building an atomic bomb during World War Two, in a secret bunker hidden away in the Austrian Alps. Rumors spread after the war, but the whole thing eventually died away."

I watched Martin nod an acknowledgement. "I'm familiar with his work. He disappeared after the war. They found his secret files hidden in his house years later."

"How did this blogger manage to find out?" Fender asked.

"Purely by accident," I said. "Apparently two Canadian student hikers went missing in the Alps not long ago. One of their parents was in the Canadian government and pushed the Austrians to conduct an extensive military search. That's how the authorities eventually discovered the bunker, by retracing the last few days of the hikers. They found evidence of recent activity in an area and dug through the rubble to reveal an old bunker where the young hikers' bodies were found, both shot to death, inside the buried Nazi fortress. And they also discovered the skeletons of dozens of Germans soldiers and lab personnel, along with tons of files and data that documented the development of the weapon by Strassmann. The story of the missing hikers was regional news so it never made headlines over here. Neither did the discovery of the bunker. Old Nazi bunkers are found occasionally, and since there was no actual atomic bomb, the news stayed local."

"Who murdered the students?" Fender asked.

"They suspected a local guy—hold on a minute. Let me make sure I get this right. I saved the info on my phone." I took a minute to retrieve and read the information. "Okay, here we go. Josef Haupt and his wife ran a hostel along the hiking trail in the Alps that catered to hikers needing a place to eat and spend the night. After the authorities discovered the bodies, they went looking for Haupt to question him. They found his body on his family's farm near the city of Leoben. Some kind of an accident with a tractor. A few days later, his wife's body turned up at the bottom of a mountain ravine. Official word was also an accident. But here's the kicker. Josef Haupt was a retired prosecutor who had a pretty long list of court actions dealing with the black market. It's not a stretch to believe he could have put together a potential buyers list for the weapon."

"So what happened to the bomb?"

"They've got no idea, Agent Fender. Haupt supposedly blew up the entrance to the bunker, burying everything. But when the missing students were found, there was no bomb." I shook my head, knowing I had suddenly made another connection between Knox and the threat to Las Vegas. "I think Josef Haupt or whoever murdered the two kids took the weapon and sold it to Travis Knox."

Glancing at the other three, I realized they were coming to the same conclusion. We were dealing with a nuclear threat. "You mentioned a second discovery?"

"That." Fender pointed to an open laptop sitting on a nearby table. "The anonymous caller said not to touch it until you arrived. The dogs already sniffed for explosives and we checked for radiation."

As I took a step toward the laptop, its dark, blank screen suddenly blinked to life and a face appeared. A thin, metallic voice cut through the big room. "Well, look who's here. Maxine Do-Gooder and her sidekick, Kenny Boy."

CHAPTER 56 – DEMANDS
Las Vegas, Nevada. Tuesday morning

"All right, Maxine, here's how this is going to work." Knox's voice came from the tiny speaker in the laptop. "First, tell everyone including Kenny Boy to leave. I only want to talk to you."

I walked past the steel X-beam support cradle until I stood within a few feet of the computer screen that displayed his disgusting face. "I'm not in charge. I have no authority to order any of these people to do anything." I spoke loud enough so that Kenny, Fender, and Deputy Secretary Martin heard me. I adjusted the angle of the laptop so Knox could only see me.

"You're right. You're not in charge. I am. Don't worry, you'll understand everything soon enough, including the fact that I'm running things now. So unless your friends want to see the Strip rendered uninhabitable for a hundred years, tell them to leave."

I edged to the side, out of the laptop camera's range and moved to where the three stood. "Are you guys tracing his connection?" I whispered.

"Let's go, Maxine," Knox called. "You're on the clock."

"It's a generic USB network card," Fender said. "You can buy them at any electronics store. As untraceable as a burn phone."

"And I'll wager he's bouncing the connection through a dozen anonymous international routers," Kenny added.

"Then we have no choice but to comply." I nodded in the

241

direction of the doorway leading to the shop exit. As they turned and headed toward it, I went back to the laptop and aimed it so Knox could witness their departure.

"That's better, Maxine. Now we can be alone and intimate. Let me see your pretty face."

I planted myself in front of the laptop camera lens. "I'm sick of your endless sophomoric games. Just get to—"

"There's an armed nuclear device hidden somewhere in Las Vegas. I'm prepared to detonate it if my demands aren't met. The result would not go well in promoting the tourist and gambling business, I can assure you. Sin City would become Dead Zone City. Let's see, we could have the Chernobyl Casino and Country Club or maybe the Three Mile Island Hotel and Resort. Or how about a Fukushima Fun Park?"

"Okay, I get it. What do you want?"

"There are one hundred and twenty-two casinos in Las Vegas. In order for me to provide them with a comprehensive insurance policy against the detonation of a one-kiloton atom bomb, they must pay me a premium of one million dollars each. That's nothing more than petty cash for each casino but a hundred and twenty-two million will go a long way toward my island retirement fund."

"You'll never get away with it."

"Trust me, Maxine. Getting away with it is the easy part."

———

"Before he killed the connection, Knox said we have until sunrise to come up with the cash." I stood in the hallway outside the prison machine shop with Kenny, Fender, and Martin, along with a dozen other federal, state, and local authorities. "The funds are to be transferred to a numbered Swiss bank account. I'm to come back here as soon as the money is confirmed and he'll give me the account number then. But first, I have to show my face and pan the location with the camera in his laptop."

"And he'll only talk to you?" Kenny asked.

I nodded. "We need to have the money ready for transfer

tomorrow at sunrise, otherwise he detonates the bomb."

"That's the dumbest plan I ever heard," Fender said. "He knows that even if it's an anonymous numbered account, the bank still knows the owner's name. Swiss bank secrecy never protects criminals, and it's promptly lifted if somebody is proven guilty beyond reasonable doubt of a criminal offence. I think trying to blow up Las Vegas qualifies."

"Don't underestimate him," I said.

"He could be bluffing."

"You willing to bet lives on that?" I asked.

"Max knows this guy," Kenny said. "You should listen to her."

"Yes, I recall," Fender said. Another hint that he still didn't trust me. He contemplated our remarks for a moment, then turned to the group of fellow FBI agents. "Contact the casinos and start the process of getting the funds collected into a single account. Tell them at this point there's to be no publicity whatsoever. In the meantime, let's pull up the emergency response plan and start looking for that bomb. Notify the Secretary of Homeland Security that I'm authorizing phase one of Operation Stagecoach. Start bringing in evacuation busses to the staging areas. Alert the National Guard to anticipate the governor's call-up. And send the warning to the casinos to prepare for a complete shutdown. If we have to evacuate the hotels, we want everything in place in twelve hours."

Fender turned to me. "Keep your phone on, Agent Decker. Wouldn't want you to be unavailable if this guy calls again."

A few moments later, as the two of us headed out of the prison to our car, Kenny said, "Can you believe they intend to evacuate the whole city? Talk about asking for widespread chaos and panic."

"Not if we can find the bomb first."

———

The military had reopened the interstate since the risk of radiation from the State Prison was no longer considered a threat. We drove back to the I-15 junction and headed northeast toward Applewhite's Golden Throne Cathedral and Ministry headquarters. Our plan was to drop in without an appointment so he would have no time to prepare.

"You think Knox is crazy enough to blow up Las Vegas?" Kenny asked.

"He's not crazy. He's a sociopath and a very smart one. He knows right from wrong. He makes choices knowing the difference. I think he's cunning enough to do just about anything. Look at his record so far."

I stared out the passenger's window. Not far from here was the Nevada National Security Test Site that Martin had referred to, where hundreds of nuclear tests were conducted back in the fifties and sixties. I wondered if the flash and mushroom clouds of those above-ground detonations could have been seen from where we were right now. So many years later, here was the chance of yet another nuclear explosion in Nevada—but in a crowded city instead of the desert. And definitely unplanned. An explosion that could kill hundreds of thousands of innocent people. Knox had somehow managed to bring the worst threat imaginable to a place dedicated to fun and entertainment.

Kenny accelerated to pass an eighteen-wheeler.

"Down in the cargo hold," I said. "What I saw must have been the weapon. It was a big yellow object, and it did have the word *Tapas* on the side. I must have been lying right beside an atomic bomb. It was shaped like a rocket. Damn, I wish I could remember more. I was so out of it."

"Don't kick yourself. I can't remember what I had for lunch yesterday, and I wasn't drugged." He settled back into the outside lane. "It's going to be interesting to see this Operation Stagecoach unfold. I can't imagine clearing out the hotels and evacuating all the people in this city."

I started thinking out loud. "Knox has made buckets of money on the black market. A hundred and twenty million is a huge amount by anyone's standards. But when I went through his records at DC3, I discovered he was suspected of making close to a hundred million selling a dozen stolen Renaissance masters a few years back. So why isn't he asking for more? He could have just as easily demanded five million or ten from each casino. And they would have gladly paid. And there's something else."

"What?"

"The thing Fender said keeps bouncing around in my head. Something I'm starting to agree with."

Kenny turned to me. "Tell me."

"Knox's demands. It's the dumbest plan I ever heard."

CHAPTER 57 – THE VISION
Las Vegas, Nevada. Tuesday

"This place is impressive," I said as we rounded the wide circular drive of Applewhite's mansion. A fountain in the middle displayed four angels spewing water from trumpets into the middle of the pool.

"Pretty much everything he does is bigger than life," Kenny said as he parked the car.

We got out and made our way up the two-tier stone steps to the double stained-glass front doors depicting God creating Adam, reminiscent of the Sistine Chapel. Two large marble archangels guarded the entrance, their swords and shields at the ready. Inlaid in the stone at our feet was *God Is Great, God Is Good.*

We pushed the chime button and a moment later the door swung open, revealing a stately gentleman dressed in a white suit. "Yes?" he said with a hint of annoyance.

"I'm OSI special agent Maxine Decker." I held out my ID wallet containing my badge and photo. "This is special agent Kenny Gates. We'd like to speak with Reverend Applewhite."

"Do you have an appointment?"

"No," I said, putting my ID away. "We met with the reverend a few days ago at his office, and he invited us to contact him with any additional questions. We only have a few and won't take up more than a couple of minutes."

The man seemed to consider what I'd told him. "Father Abraham has requested that he not be disturbed while he is in holy meditation."

"Would it be possible to wait until he is available?" Kenny asked.

The man looked at his watch. "Well, I don't know—"

Carl appeared in the doorway. "It's all right. I'll take care of this. I know agents Decker and Gates, and I'll be happy to meet with them."

"Of course." The butler ushered us into the foyer, a soaring three-story white marble vestibule that commanded visitors to look to the heavens. Above our heads, a skylight framed a patch of pure blue Nevada sky.

"Follow me," Carl said, and led us into a formal living room with a fireplace large enough to stand in.

"You have quite a home, Carl," I said, trying to take in all the leather sofas, Persian carpets, and original paintings and statues. It was like walking through a museum—I couldn't imagine anyone actually plopping down on one of the couches and watching TV. But then, there was no TV that I could see. I felt I should be whispering out of respect for the grandeur of the room.

"Thank you." Carl motioned to a grouping of couches and chairs off to one corner.

Kenny and I sat together while Carl faced us from a chair across a stone coffee table. Resting on top of the table, I recognized a statuette of Pazuzu, an Assyrian wind demon. I wanted to examine it to see if it was authentic but didn't dare. "That's a beautiful piece."

"Father Abraham has a sizable collection. That's just one of many."

If it were mine, I thought, I would give it a bit more protection, considering it's probably close to three thousand years old.

Carl leaned back in the chair. "So what did you want to talk to Father Abraham about?"

I sensed that Carl seemed different from the last time we met. At the hotel he was skittish and somewhat fearful for his dad. Now he seemed relaxed, almost peaceful.

"Has your father received any more calls from the

mysterious *voice* you told us about?"

"He is in union with...our Heavenly Father. I am no longer concerned with the method in which God speaks to Father Abraham, only that he does so. We are blessed."

I glanced at Kenny, who said, "Well, that's good news, Carl. We were as concerned as you that someone was trying to influence or manipulate your father."

"We're really happy that you're not worried anymore," I said. "You're saying that he hasn't received any more calls?"

"He has received a great deal more than just phone calls."

I waited for an explanation. When it didn't come, I said, "So he has been contacted again?"

"Agent Decker, not only has Father Abraham spoken to our Heavenly Father, but God has come down from the heavens to this very place and appeared before him."

"Really? When did this happen?" Kenny asked.

"Sunday night."

"And your father said that God appeared to him...in this house? Could he be mistaken?"

"No, Agent Gates. There is no mistake. Almighty God appeared to Father Abraham in an apparition Sunday night upstairs in my father's bedroom."

"I'm sorry, Carl," I said, "but I have to ask. How do you know?"

"That it's true? That he's not crazy? Because I saw the vision, too."

CHAPTER 58 – THE THIRD DAY
Las Vegas, Nevada. Tuesday

There was silence as my mind raced in so many directions. Carl had just admitted to seeing an apparition of something he thought was God in his father's bedroom. Had he been hallucinating? But it was both of them—Carl and his father. Maybe some kind of group hallucination. Perhaps on drugs? Or maybe Carl was lying to cover up his father's bizarre behavior? Chances were he was just as nutty as Applewhite— the old adage about the apple not falling far from the tree. The irony of apple and the name, Applewhite, was not lost on me, and I nearly chuckled aloud. I was afraid to glance at Kenny for fear that we might both overreact and be tossed out for disrespect. I had to proceed carefully.

"Carl, I have to tell you that what you've revealed to us is hard to believe. But knowing your deep devotion to God, your church, your faith, and your father, I want to try to understand just what you experienced."

"The Almighty works in mysterious ways, Agent Decker." Carl's face filled with an expression of serenity. "For some, God speaks through others and guides their souls along the path of life. But for a select few, God communicates directly to them, laying out His plans—His mission. Father Abraham is one of the chosen few God has visited here on Earth. It was only by fate that I stumbled upon this most miraculous event and was able to share the experience with my father."

"You say you saw the vision?" Kenny spoke in a quiet voice, doing a remarkable job of feigning reverence. "Can you tell us about it?"

"I needed to deliver Father Abraham's appointment schedule for the next day, and my intention was to slip into his bedroom and leave it on his nightstand. And there was the matter of the police inquiry."

As I started to ask him to clarify, he said, "They're investigating a missing person—an exterminator who sprayed our house. We were the last customer on his Saturday route. After he left here, he disappeared. I think he'll turn up eventually. Las Vegas is not your normal town. People do crazy things."

"Okay." I said. "So you went to tell your father about the police investigation and deliver his schedule?"

Carl hesitated. "I knocked softly on the door. When he didn't answer, I assumed he was deep in prayer, so I cautiously turned the knob and pushed the door open. That's when I saw it."

Carl's eyes teared. His voice caught.

"I know this is highly emotional for you," I said. "Just take your time."

He wiped the tears from his cheeks and sighed deeply. "I saw Father Abraham beside his bed. His eyes were fixed on something in the middle of the room. As I shifted my gaze, I saw it. And fell to my knees. A man—no, more like a ghost or a spirit. The figure was taller than a normal man, maybe eight feet, and clothed in a long flowing robe. His body was surrounded by a glowing swirl of clouds, and he seemed to drift in and out of focus. The image shimmered as if it was made of a mixture of light and fog. And around the figure appeared words that glowed like they were on fire."

"What did the words say?" I felt myself getting caught up in the story as I tried to envision what he described. And what could have caused it.

"Father Abraham told me later that I had come upon the vision just as it was ending. The words I saw were the last of the message from God."

"You could read them?" Kenny said.

"They said, *Witness the destruction of Sodom and Gomorrah on the third day at sunrise.*"

"That was it?" I asked.

"No, there was something else. I didn't understand, but my father appeared to know the meaning. It said, *Follow the brilliant star that shines unto Heaven until it is extinguished atop the mountain of Moriah.*"

———

"I think you need to get out here," I said to Agent Fender. I'd called him on my cell the moment we walked out of Applewhite's mansion and got into our car. I repeated all of what Carl had told us. "Have you any idea what 'mountain of Moriah' and the stuff about the star extinguishing means? There's something familiar in the back of my mind, but I can't put a finger on it."

"Not a clue," Fender answered. "So, Maxine, what do you expect me to do? He thinks he sees God—talks to the big man upstairs. Applewhite and his kid are just another couple of fanatic religious kooks. There's no crime in that."

"Listen, somebody is dicking around with Applewhite's head. Knox is going to blow up Las Vegas at sunrise and the preacher is being set up for some part in that plan. Carl already told us his father more or less expressed to him that Vegas is Sodom and Gomorrah and now says the *vision* spelled out *Witness the destruction of Sodom and Gomorrah on the third day at sunrise.* I'm telling you we've got a ticking clock counting down to massive devastation."

I waited a moment for Fender to say something. *Nada.* I wondered if his slow response indicated he still has a problem with me over the Iraq ordeal. I thought that had finally all been resolved. If not, he needed to dump any lingering personal issues if we were going to stop Knox.

"That's all you could get out of the kid? Nothing more substantial?"

"Nope, that's it." I held my hand over the phone and turned to Kenny. "What does this guy want, an invitation carved in stone and delivered by Moses?"

Kenny shrugged as he started the car and flipped the air conditioner's fan to high.

"Listen," I said to Fender. "Pretend it's someone else giving you this information, okay. I know you must be thinking I'm trying to pull something over on you, but I give you my word I'm telling the truth. You're a very bright guy, so don't let the past interfere with your judgment. I'm convinced that Travis Knox is manipulating Applewhite, and I want you to be, too. Who knows, maybe Knox has been recruited by al-Qaeda or some other terrorist group. God knows he's spent enough time in the Middle East. And he doesn't do anything on a small scale. Getting a measly million from each of those casinos is a spit in the ocean to Knox."

"I'm assuming sunrise of the third say is tomorrow since that's the deadline for the money to be delivered," Fender said. "That gives us little time."

Is he finally starting to believe me?

"You can bet he's got an escape plan to disappear as soon as the cash is in the account." I said. "That's why he's not revealing the account info until the last second. If I were him, I'd have the money retransferred out of the Swiss account into numerous other accounts all over the world within minutes." Then I added, "By the way, are you aware that the locals are conducting a missing person's investigation at Applewhite's place?"

"Who's missing?" Fender asked.

"A pest exterminator. He treated Applewhite's place on Saturday then disappeared, company truck and all.

"Hang on a minute."

I heard what sounded like Fender chewing out someone and a muffled voice responding. When he came back, he said, "Guess I'm a little behind on that matter. Nobody brought it to my attention. Anyway, that mystery is solved. They found the van and the driver about an hour ago at the bottom of a lake near Henderson, east of here."

"Was it an accident?" I asked.

"The ME's out there now. Should know something soon."

"I can't believe it's just another coincidence that this guy went missing then wound up dead right after leaving Applewhite's."

"You're right. It's a small world, but not that small. Sorry. Hang on again."

I turned to Kenny. "They found the bug man and his truck at the bottom of a lake."

"Maxine?"

"I'm still here."

"ME is calling it a homicide. The body was found in the back of the van, stripped down to his briefs. His arms and legs were bound. The rear doors were locked from the outside and the guy's uniform is nowhere to be found. He was murdered—cause of death was drowning."

"You need to come out here and question Applewhite."

"I can't come myself—I'm buried in dealing with the search for the nuclear device and finalizing Operation Stagecoach. You two sit tight."

"There's no time to sit tight," I said. "Knox's plan is not only blackmail, it's a national security issue—a terrorist threat. So let's you and me get on the same page."

There was silence on the other end of the line. I was a dog with a very chewy bone and wasn't going to give it up. "Knox is preying on Applewhite. What if it's the reverend that Knox is prepping to flatten Sin City? And why Applewhite? Remember I told you of Knox's reference to *The Da Vinci Code*? Another clue. I'm supposed be searching for the artifact, the Blade of Abraham, but all of this is just a metaphor. Applewhite is Abraham. Could it be that the Blade of Abraham is an atomic bomb built by the Nazis at the end of the Second World War and not the artifact at all? Agent Fender, you question Applewhite and you'll get answers that will enable you to thwart a disaster."

I stopped. There was nothing else I could say to convince the man.

CHAPTER 59 – THE ATTIC
Las Vegas, Nevada. Tuesday

I hung onto the cell phone, praying Fender would see my points. I met Kenny's gaze and shook my head.

Finally, Fender said, "Okay, I'll admit that there's an overwhelming amount of evidence pointing toward Hershel Applewhite. It's circumstantial, but maybe enough to get a federal search warrant. Let me pull some strings and I'll have an agent out there to meet with you within thirty minutes. We'll get a photo of the dead guy from the pest control company and show it to Applewhite or his staff to make a positive ID. I'm shorthanded, so I'll need your help."

Now he's asking for my help. "Thank you, Agent Fender. We'll be right here waiting."

A half hour later, almost to the minute, a black SUV pulled up beside our rental in front of Applewhite's mansion. Kenny and I got out and waited for the driver to join us.

"Special Agent Gibson," he said as he approached us.

"OSI Special Agent Gates." They shook hands. "This is Special Agent Maxine Decker."

Gibson was young, perhaps late twenties, and a little shorter than most agents. He had a round baby face, but there was nothing baby about his build. I had no doubt from the looks of his arms and the way he filled out his blue FBI polo shirt that he had more than a casual attendance record at the gym.

"Were you able to get the search warrant?" I asked.

He held it up. "I also got a photo of the victim faxed over

from Diamondback Pest Control. They confirmed that the body in the van is that of their missing technician. Now we need Applewhite to ID him as the guy who came out here Saturday."

"Then let's do it," I said.

"This is quite a place," Gibson commented as we walked up the steps to the stained-glass front doors.

"You haven't seen anything yet," I said.

Agent Gibson rang the bell. A moment later, our buddy, the butler, swung open the door. He eyed Kenny and me with obvious annoyance.

"I'm Special Agent Gibson with the FBI. We're here to speak with Hershel Applewhite and his son."

"I'm afraid Father Abraham is not available."

Gibson glanced at me, a question in his eyes.

"That's what Applewhite calls himself these days," I said.

"Who are you?" Gibson asked the butler.

"I'm Douglas, Father Abraham's personal assistant."

"Okay, Douglas. This is a federal search warrant. Please go get Mr. Applewhite and his son, Carl, and tell them to make themselves available to us immediately."

Douglas glared at the piece of paper as if it were a poisonous snake. "Well, if you must…come in."

As Gibson did the mandatory gawking at the skylight view overhead, Douglas marched off and disappeared up a flight of stairs. "The religion business must be good," the agent said as we wandered into the expansive living room.

Almost five minutes passed before Douglas returned. He appeared agitated and perplexed as he approached. "I'm sorry, Agent Gibson, but I can't seem to locate either Father Abraham or his son."

"If they're not here, can you try calling them?" Gibson asked.

"Actually, I did, but neither is answering his cell."

"Anyone leave while you were waiting for me, Agent Decker?"

I shook my head. "Carl was here less than an hour ago

when we interviewed him. He said his father was meditating. We saw no one leave since then. But we were parked in the front, and it's a big estate. They must have gone out the service entrance in the back."

"Excuse me." Gibson pulled out his cell phone and walked away as he dialed. A moment later, he returned. "The state police have issued a BOLO for Hershel and Carl Applewhite.

Douglas paled and looked apprehensive after hearing that the state police were looking for his boss.

Gibson held out a picture I assumed was of the dead pest control technician. "Douglas, do you know who this man is?"

The butler stared at the picture, but I got the feeling his thoughts were elsewhere.

"Yes, I recognize him."

"Were you here Saturday when the Diamondback Pest Control technician came and treated this house?"

"The bug man? Yes, I let him in and he left about forty minutes later."

"Is this the man?" Gibson held the picture closer this time.

"No. He has serviced us in the past but it's been a while. He wasn't the one who came here last Saturday."

"You're absolutely sure?" I asked.

He nodded. "The man on Saturday was much more robust, like a weightlifter, if you know what I mean." He pulled the photo closer. "He had an accent, if that matters. Romanian, Russian, something like that." The butler tapped the picture. "This one was much slimmer and always looked anemic."

"He looks worse, now," Gibson said. "He's dead." The agent waited a beat to let the news sink in.

Douglas blanched.

"What did the technician do while he was here on Saturday?" I asked.

"Uh…the usual things they always do, I assume. He sprayed around all the baseboards and windowsills. Every room was treated. Organic pest control, of course."

"And you witnessed him perform all those tasks?" Gibson placed the photo back in his pocket.

"Well, no. I saw him part of the time while he was down here on the ground floor. I felt no need to follow him about. He was on his own most of the time, especially upstairs."

"Why don't we start with a search of those upstairs rooms?" I said. "The ones where he was unsupervised. Can you show us?"

Douglas hesitated, as if conflicted about showing us through the place without his employer's consent. After a moment, he reluctantly led the way.

Falling in behind him, we climbed a long sweeping staircase and entered a hallway lined with half a dozen doors.

"This is Father Abraham's private study and library." Douglas pointed to a door on the right.

"I'll take it," Kenny said.

"And this one is Father Abraham's bedroom."

Gibson motioned toward it. "Agent Decker, you want to start there?"

"Sure."

"Excuse me, but Father Abraham doesn't usually allow anyone in his personal quarters," Douglas said. "Not even the cleaning staff is permitted except in his presence. He's *very* private."

I didn't comment, but I sure had some thoughts about the Right Reverend fitting the bill of a nut job. I tried the knob but a dead bolt held the door secure. "Do you have a key?"

"I do, but I'm certain Father Abraham wouldn't approve."

"You have no choice." Gibson held the warrant out as a reminder.

Douglas fished a ring of keys from his pocket. He sorted through them before inserting one into the lock.

"Which one is Carl's?" Gibson asked.

"There." Douglas indicated a door across the hall.

Gibson nodded at me. "I'll take the son's."

I heard the dead bolt retreat. "Thank you." I opened the door and walked into a dark room, leaving Douglas in the doorway. Evidently he was a bit spooked at entering Applewhite's forbidden sanctuary.

Spotting the light switch, I flipped it on and was shocked by what I saw. For a second, I wondered if the room had recently been stripped bare. I would have bet that cloistered monks had more creature comforts than Hershel Applewhite's bedroom. It was a huge contrast to the lavish ground floor.

"He lives quite simply," Douglas said, still in the doorway. "Father Abraham believes in moderation. All but his private quarters are to satisfy the public's expectations."

Simply and *moderation* were gross understatements. The floor was of rough pine, with no rugs or carpet. The bed, which looked like a military cot, had only what appeared to be a sackcloth covering. No pillow or blanket. The table on which the lamp rested was a wooden vegetable crate standing on end. A windup alarm clock ticked away beside the lamp.

Although the room was large, about the size of my entire mountain cabin—my former cabin—it was almost totally void of objects. A metal folding chair sat beside a series of windows, all of which were boarded over with planks to block out the daylight. An unpainted chest of drawers sat against a far wall with a hand mirror and hairbrush being the only objects on top. A second light, this one a pole lamp, was positioned near the folding chair. A Bible rested on the floor nearby.

The room was strikingly tidy. Not a visible wrinkle in the folded cloth on the cot. Even the *Good Book* left on raw wood floorboards somehow seemed purposefully placed.

I noticed what appeared to be a scattering of white particles on the floor beside the bed. Walking over, I bent for a closer look. Grains of rice. Not sure what that was all about. A further look under the cot found no dust bunnies, but I did locate the source of the rice. A Mason canning jar filled with the grain. Odd.

I turned toward the center of the room. So this was where the *vision* took place, Applewhite's *burning bush* moment when Almighty God came down from heaven and appeared to an unworthy sinner. On this spot, God commanded the new prophet Abraham to witness the destruction of Sin City.

Bullshit.

This was the site where a mega-egotist got stroked by an expert con artist. I just needed to figure out how.

I moved to the chest and slid open each drawer. Of the six, three were filled with more neatly folded sackcloth, along with thin towels and washcloths. The next drawer contained meticulously folded socks and to my surprise, silk underwear, apparently a rare indulgence. The remaining two drawers contained black-and-white composition notebooks, cheap ballpoint pens, pencils, a couple of pairs of reading glasses, a flashlight, one pair of gloves, a small battery-operated radio, a box of cufflinks, tie clasps, and a plain silver woman's wedding band, none of which appeared to have much value. It reminded me of what to expect on a card table at a yard sale, except that it looked like someone with OCD had arranged them. All the pens lay side-by-side, caps at the top. The recently sharpened pencils were lined up with erasers level, the *Ticonderoga* branding face-up. The stacked notebooks' edges matched perfectly, and even the fingers of the gloves were aligned with preciseness.

There was a large walk-in closet, but aside from a few dress shirts, pants, jackets, and typical clergy robes, the rungs held only empty hangers. Some cardboard boxes rested on the shelves above. I took each down and opened them to find mostly copies of Bibles and study books of various religions.

A quick inspection of the bathroom revealed an almost empty medicine cabinet—a bottle of store-brand aspirin and a box of Band-Aid bandages sat on the glass shelves. A toothbrush and a generic tube of paste rested by the sink.

Leaving the bathroom, I went to an area by the wall under the windows. There I knelt, bent and sniffed where the baseboard and floor joined. Despite the claim that the bug poison used by most professional exterminators was odorless, there was always a slight residual smell left behind—at least for a few days. The wood only had a weak hint of Pine Sol or some similar disinfectant, not the after-scent of recently sprayed poison.

I moved to the opposite side of the bed, where I spotted a

tiny trace of white powder accumulated on the narrow ledge of the baseboard, as if it had drifted down from above. It was hardly noticeable, but like the rice, it was something that didn't sync with the otherwise spotlessness of the room. I touched it and squeezed the gritty substance between my fingers.

Drywall.

Standing, I took the flashlight from the chest and let the beam follow a direct line of sight from the powder residue up the wall almost all the way to the ceiling where I detected a small black hole easily lost in the darkness of the bedroom.

It couldn't have been more than a half inch wide, and was located about a hand's width below the ceiling.

I retrieved the metal folding chair, and after stacking a couple of the thick study books on the chair, I carefully climbed atop. Wobbling, I braced myself against the wall with one hand. Slowly rising on my toes, I held the flashlight up to the hole. "Well, I'll be damned." I saw two tiny round lenses reflecting the light.

Suddenly Applewhite's heavenly vision was starting to lose its supernatural luster.

I hopped down and asked Douglas if the exterminator had gone up in the attic.

"Why yes," he said as he watched me from the open door. "Apparently he found traces of a scorpion infestation and needed to go up there to apply a special treatment."

Gibson had finished checking out Carl's bedroom and stuck his head in. "What did you find, Agent Decker?"

"I think the bug man was *planting* a bug rather than killing one." I joined the two men in the hallway. "Douglas, where's the attic access?"

"I believe it's just down here." He led us back the way we had come.

I spotted the access door on the ceiling outside Applewhite's private study where Kenny was still inside nosing around. "Bring me a sturdy chair," I called to him.

Once he did, I stood on it and pulled the access door open and the fold-out ladder down. Hot air rushed out.

"What you got?" Kenny asked.

"Not sure yet. Be right back."

Climbing the ladder to the top, I shined the flashlight in all directions but saw only rafters and an ocean of pink insulation. Turning toward the direction of Applewhite's bedroom, I entered the attic and bent low as I cautiously worked my way from rafter to rafter while holding the flashlight in one hand and steadying myself on the joists with the other.

Dust covered everything. Everything except the path I followed. I clearly saw where someone had recently walked across the rafters—the dust was disturbed or swept away.

Then, out of the darkness, a small bundle of shapes emerged—two or three boxes, each about the size of a brick and all bound together with duct tape. I aimed the flashlight beam down, revealing wires interconnecting the electronic boxes. Two flexible tube extensions ran down into the space between the walls and studs.

A moment later, I stuck my head over the rim of the attic access entrance and stared down at Kenny, Gibson, and Douglas with the biggest shit-eating grin I could produce.

"I know that look," Kenny said. "Find any scorpions?"

"No, but I did find God."

CHAPTER 60 – THE BOX
Las Vegas, Nevada. Tuesday

Kenny and I stood in Hershel Applewhite's bedroom along with Agents Fender and Gibson, Dr. Martin from the Department of Energy, and the newly-arrived Secretary of Homeland Security with a couple of her assistants. Less than an hour after I notified Fender of the devices I'd found in the attic, an army of FBI agents, state police, local investigators, and public safety officers swarmed over Applewhite's mansion like ants on road kill. Now as we watched in collective anticipation, an FBI technician triggered the hologram image to appear from the mini-projector in the attic.

After the image faded, the Secretary asked, "Any idea who planted the projector and camera?"

"We found one partial," Gibson said.

"You got the results already?" I asked.

"Cut through some red tape. Not hard to do with this type of threat."

"Did it belong to Knox?"

"No, Agent Decker." Gibson held his iPad, and opened his email. "According to Interpol, it belongs to Janko Azarov, a former helicopter pilot in the Ukrainian army. Served in Kosovo and Lebanon before being arrested in southern Russia for weapons smuggling. He was convicted and sentenced to ten years in military prison but escaped before the end of the first year. Hasn't been heard from until now."

"Agent Fender," the Secretary said, "I want you to place all available resources into finding Azarov, along with Mr.

Applewhite and his son."

"Already being done, ma'am," Fender said.

Something clicked in my brain. Janko? Where had I heard that name before? "Do we have a photo of Azarov?"

Gibson scrolled, then turned the iPad so both the Secretary and I could see. "Applewhite's assistant already identified him as the fake exterminator from the pest control company."

"Son-of-a-bitch!" I blurted out.

"Something to add?" the Secretary said as everyone glared at me.

"I know this guy." I looked at Kenny. "This is Yuri's buddy from the ship—the jerk who threw me overboard."

"Would you care to explain?" The Secretary crossed her arms as she gave me her undivided attention.

"Sorry, Madam Secretary. I'm just shocked to see this man's face again." I gave her and everyone else in the room the abbreviated version of my relationship with Travis and Aaron Knox, the shooting in Iraq, the eBay scam, the history of the Blade, Manila, my cabin, Cuba, Texas, the murder of my sister at my own hands, Knox's demands, and how all of it brought us together in Hershel Applewhite's bedroom watching a hologram.

"I'm so very sorry about your sister, Agent Decker," the Secretary said. "You have my deepest sympathy. It seems obvious, now that we have heard your whole story, that you may hold the answer to solving this threat. And finding the hologram projector just might have saved Las Vegas and thousands of lives."

"Thank you, Madam Secretary," I said, "but we still have to find the bomb. There's no doubt in my mind that Travis Knox is behind everything."

"Well, you've convinced me." She turned to Fender. "Include finding Knox a top priority." She smiled at me. "Nice work." Then the Secretary and her group left the bedroom, along with everyone but Gibson.

"We're heading over to search Applewhite's cathedral and offices. You two want to join me?"

"Kenny, why don't you go with Agent Gibson? I want to stay here and see if I can come up with anything else."

"I'll stay, too," my ex said. He waved to Gibson. "Call if you find anything."

"Let's go to work," I said. "There's bound to be some places I missed on my first search."

"How about we check the rest of this floor again?"

I followed Kenny to the bedroom door and was about to flip off the lamp switch when I glanced back at the vegetable crate. The open side of it faced the wall.

"Hang on." I pulled the crate out and looked inside.

And there it was.

I was so stunned I couldn't move. It was almost a magical moment. I remembered the box from so long ago when, as a young girl, I stared into the display case in the Cairo Museum.

Kenny pulled a pair of latex gloves from his back pocket.

I felt a surge of exhilaration as I watched him slip them on. In just a moment I would be looking at the Blade of Abraham.

Stooping, Kenny gently lifted the box from its hiding place and rested it on the bed.

The wood was old and worn, but nowhere near as old as the relic itself. My guess was that someone had made the box long after the death of the prophet and placed it inside his tomb to protect the Blade.

A simple latch secured the top. "Open it, Max," Kenny said, touching his gloved hand to my cheek. "You should be the one."

I quickly donned a pair of gloves, and as Kenny watched beside me, I slowly opened the lid. Dark blue cloth filled the inside, and an indention showed where the relic had rested for thousands of years.

But the Blade of Abraham was gone.

CHAPTER 61 – THE LIST
Las Vegas, Nevada. Tuesday

"Why did he take the Blade?" Kenny commented as I closed the box.

I placed the container under my arm. "Good question. What could he be planning to do with it?" I didn't like the thought that was coming into my head. "Applewhite is a stickler for the scriptures. Maybe he feels that becoming the new Abraham also includes recreating the part of the story where he sacrifices his son Isaac—which in this case, is Carl."

"But didn't God stop Abraham just before he killed Isaac?"

"Yes, he sent an angel to keep the prophet from cutting Isaac's throat. Wound up sacrificing a ram instead. Let's hope Applewhite remembers that part of the story, too."

We walked out of the bedroom and into the hallway. Kenny asked, "What if Applewhite is so convinced things will go the same this time around as they did thousands of years ago, so he's counting on an angel showing up again to stop him?"

But there won't be any angel this time.

We paused at the entrance to the private study. "And I'm afraid that means Carl is going to be a victim of his father's sick mind."

Kenny pointed at the study. "Let's check in here one last time."

"Good idea. It's certainly appears to be where he keeps most of his valuable personal stuff." I went to Applewhite's desk while Kenny headed for the rows of bookcases and file cabinets. Placing the relic's box aside, I took in all the objects covering the desktop. There was a silver cross on a stand, a copy of the King James version of the Bible, an appointment calendar, a onyx box containing a collection of Montblanc pens, and a yellow legal pad with what appeared to be notes for a future sermon or event.

I sat in the thickly padded executive's chair and slid open the middle drawer. There were paper clips, rubber bands, rulers, a magnifying glass, business cards, and a host of other items common to a businessman's desk.

Next, I checked the slide-out drawers on each side. Both contained file folders labeled with church functions and sermon topics. I noticed a space behind the file rack in the right-hand drawer and pulled it all the way open to reveal a small, black notebook resting in the dark of the drawer's bottom.

Picking it up, I saw embossed on the front in gold the word *Notes*. I opened to the first page to find it blank. Same with the second. Why did Applewhite tuck away and hide a book with blank pages? Maybe he had plans to keep a journal but never got around to it.

I fanned through the pages just to make sure they weren't all blank. Halfway through, I spotted script.

There were two pages of handwriting. The first bore the title, *The boys who rejected salvation* printed in shaky block letters. Below the heading were two columns. The one on the left was a list of names; the other column contained corresponding dates. Beside the top name the date was over twenty years ago. I panned down the page and noticed that the dates progressively got more recent. The last entry was dated eight years ago. The color of ink and type of pen—ball point, fountain—varied, telling me the entries were probably true to the dates and entered separately. None of the names were familiar. Whatever the reason was for keeping these lists ended eight years back.

The second page also bore a heading. This one read, *The boys who embraced God*. And again, there were two columns— two dozen names on the left along with dates to the right. The dates were approximately in the same range as the preceding page and spanned two decades. My eyes scanned the list, then I closed the book to return it back into the drawer.

That's when my hand froze. I slowly reopened the book and reread the *embraced God* list. My gaze fell on one name halfway down the column. I read it three times to be sure before looking up.

Kenny was across the room on his knees searching through the bottom row of books on a floor-to-ceiling bookshelf. Instinctively he sensed my gaze and turned around. "Find something?" he said.

I nodded. "The connection between Knox and Applewhite."

CHAPTER 62 – THE DESTINATION
Las Vegas, Nevada. Tuesday

Applewhite's veined, sweaty hands gripped the steering wheel of his Lexus LS. He hadn't brought anything other than the relic and his cell phone. That was all the Lord told him to take along—well, that and his son, Carl. He corrected himself. *I mean Isaac.* He was Abraham, and his son was now Isaac.

He'd been given further instructions just this morning, but he hadn't related nor explained the newest phone message to his son. The call had come while Carl—Isaac—had been downstairs speaking with those heathen agents of Satan who had come to discuss, converse, question, or whatever euphemism they chose to call their harassing interrogation.

"You know what you must do, Abraham," the *voice* had said. "You must walk in the shoes of the one who came before."

The commandment issued was more than clear. The Old Testament story of Abraham and his son, Isaac, was his destiny, and he would remain loyal to scripture.

The bulk of his questions had been answered, though he still had a few. But he trusted all would be revealed as the Lord saw fit. There would be one more call when he reached his destination. Everything would soon be unveiled to the chosen one, the new Father Abraham.

Applewhite glanced over at his son, who was leaning against the door, gazing out the tinted window. Could Isaac possibly comprehend the magnitude of his father's or his own transformation? Even as his son possessed a profound depth of conviction, it was unlikely he could conceive of the consummate honor.

God had not made this easy, testing him over and over, even making him solve mysterious riddles. After spending day and night searching on the internet, falling down one rabbit hole after another, he'd come to understand the meaning of *Moriah* and the brilliant star. He didn't have to travel the planet to find the mountain—it was here, nearly in his backyard. And the star… He, Abraham, had unraveled the curious message, and it all made sense—one puzzle piece locking into the next. The Almighty had tested his worthiness again and he had triumphed.

Applewhite pulled the Lexus to a stop. "Isaac, we have arrived at our final destination."

CHAPTER 63 – DIRECT LINK
Las Vegas, Nevada. Tuesday night

"We ran the names on the first list, Agent Decker." Fender's voice came through the speaker on my cell phone as Kenny and I pulled into the valet parking entrance to the Rio Hotel. "All were reported missing years ago—most considered runaways. Because they're all now over the age of eighteen, those cases are closed."

"And the second list?" I asked. "The one with Aaron Knox's name?"

"Those were wards of the state in the foster care of Hershel Applewhite. Most all are accounted for except several who are missing or location unknown. A few are deceased due to military action, disease, or accidents."

"So now we have a direct link between Aaron Knox and Applewhite." I switched off the speaker and put the phone to my ear as we got out of our rental and entered the hotel.

"How do you read it?" Fender asked.

"I think something happened to Aaron as a youngster while in the foster care of Applewhite, and now Travis Knox is setting up the televangelist for revenge." Once inside the lobby, Kenny and I headed for a secluded table in a far corner. Fender didn't say anything for about twenty seconds. "You still there?" I asked.

"Yes, sorry. Just thinking. So we've got a guy who's trying to destroy your life out of revenge for shooting his brother. The same guy who appears to be manipulating Applewhite into taking part in detonating a nuclear device just to get back at him for doing something really bad to that same brother. And to top it off, you just might have uncovered a serial killer of young boys in the person of the Reverend Hershel Applewhite."

"Looks like we're finally on the same page, Agent Fender."

"What keeps nagging at me, though, is Knox's lame plan of transferring the ransom money from the casinos into a number account."

"It's obvious that he didn't come up with this whole scheme on the spur of the moment. This was well thought out for many months, perhaps years." I watched Kenny lean in to hear now that we were back on speaker. "The way I see it, the weakest part of his otherwise brilliant plan is the ransom money."

"Exactly," Fender said. "Why come up with something so complex, then top it off with a move that will never work."

"He knows it won't work," Kenny said. "Knox is too smart to base his plan on the weakest link."

"What now, Agent Fender?"

"We've got every cop in Las Vegas looking for Hershel and Carl Applewhite. There are multiple teams of federal experts combing the city for traces from the nuclear device. And we're within hours of pulling the trigger on Operation Stagecoach. I suggest you and Agent Gates get a good night's sleep. You'll need to be at the command center before dawn."

"Call me if there's any news."

"Sleep well." He ended the call.

———

As Kenny and I sat in my suite, he said, "There are so many things about this that just don't make sense."

"At least we're starting to get a clearer picture on motivation."

"True. If Applewhite abused Aaron as a child, I suppose that's enough to drive his big brother to seek revenge. But blowing someone up with an atomic bomb along with thousands of others is a bit of an overstatement, don't you think?"

"Like I've said from the beginning, there's more to this. I don't believe Travis had the ability to love Aaron enough to generate this whole scheme. He's a socio-path with no conscience. And I'm sick of dealing with this psycho. We've got to find that bomb and nail the bastard. The military has some high-tech sensors that can locate the weapon before the deadline. Knox must suspect that, too."

"He's smart enough to have smuggled it into the country, so he must have found a way to hide the radiation signature," Kenny said.

I tapped Applewhite's notebook I'd placed on the coffee table. "We're missing something. The money isn't enough, and the motivation is half-assed to be talking about an atomic bomb. He's gone to a great deal of trouble to position us like chess pieces." I took a slug of my beer. "It makes no sense."

———

I looked at my watch—3:55 a.m. Kenny and I stood staring out the window, watching what seemed like endless lines of tour-style buses moving east along Flamingo Road toward the Strip. Operation Stagecoach was well underway.

A dozen or so buses were already pulled into the Rio. The alarms continued shrieking throughout the hotel. A recorded announcement kept instructing the guests to calmly proceed to the lobby and exit the building. No further explanation. I assumed the same thing was happening in the other hotels, casinos, bars and restaurants across Las Vegas.

I dropped into a chair and opened Applewhite's notebook. Turning to the page with the second list, I touched Aaron's name. *What did this man do to you, my friend? What could have been so bad that it brought us all to this point? What revenge could be worth taking so many lives?*

Kenny went to the writing desk, opened his laptop and started typing. A moment later, he said, "I Googled blast zone stats. If the weapon *is* the Nazi bomb, which Martin estimated to be about one kiloton, the detonation will produce a two-hundred-mile-per-hour blast rushing out from ground zero. According to this blast effect calculation, it would pretty much destroy everything in all directions within a four-mile radius. At eight miles, it would severely damage free-standing structures. And at thirteen miles, blow out windows and take off roofs."

"But we're also talking about heat and fire, not to mention radiation."

"Right," he said. "Probably most of Las Vegas would be destroyed or on fire. The deaths from radiation come later."

I glanced at the streets below and the endless glitz of the Strip. I could see the lines of busses at other hotels, some pulling in and others leaving loaded with people. I wondered if we were fools and should have been on one of them. The flashing of red and blue emergency lights seemed to blend into the glitter of the hotel marquees and attractions. It was a bizarre combination of excitement and danger. The constant evacuation warnings from the hallway speakers only added to the craziness.

Kenny closed his laptop. "I wonder if Applewhite realizes that destroying Sodom and Gomorrah may also destroy everything he has. Depending on the exact location, the detonation could flatten Applewhite's church, headquarters, seminary, and home. I'm more confused than ever. Knox gave Applewhite the Blade, and now he wants to kill the reverend?"

"At least destroy Applewhite's world. But the reverend and Carl aren't there. The place has been searched and is under constant surveillance." I stared at the skyline, an ocean of lights. "They're down there somewhere in the city."

Suddenly, the brilliant beacon atop the Alexandria Hotel extinguished. I looked at my watch: four a.m. I had read that the hotel started turning the forty-two-billion candle-power spotlight off at four a.m. rather than sunrise to conserve power. And then it hit me.

CHAPTER 64 – MOUNTAIN OF MORIAH
Las Vegas, Nevada. Wednesday morning.
Sunrise minus 2 hours.

"Moriah! It's Moriah!"

Kenny glared at me like I had suddenly gone berserk. "What the hell are you talking about?"

"I couldn't remember until just now—the name of the guy who designed the Alexandria pyramid and the others around the world. His last name was Moriah."

"No shit!"

I grabbed my ex by the shoulders. "*Follow the brilliant star that shines unto Heaven until it is extinguished atop the mountain of Moriah.*"

"Great catch, Maxine."

"The beacon on top of the Alexandria—the mountain of Moriah—was just extinguished. That's where we'll find Applewhite."

Seconds later, I was charging out of my room with Kenny right on my heels. There were stragglers wandering the hall, many looking confused as the evacuation announcement perpetually blared from the ceiling speakers alternating with a warbling siren. I would have bet that some of the most muddled guests were the ones just coming back after heavy partying. I didn't envy the hotel staff trying to herd the worst of the lot downstairs and out to the waiting buses.

At the bank of elevators, I pushed the down button repeatedly.

"Maybe if you do that a little harder, it'll make it open

faster." Kenny said.

I pressed it one more defiant time. "Thanks for the tip."

"We're going to have a tough time getting to the Alexandria. The cops must be shutting down the streets by now."

"We can just grab our rental from the valet and start flashing our badges."

The elevator doors opened, but we faced an overloaded car and a wall of unfriendly faces daring us to try to board. A second later, another set of doors opened with a similar sardine-can grouping.

"We're only twelve floors up," I said. "Let's take the stairs."

Kenny glanced around before pointing. "There."

I rushed down the stairs, trying not to trip and break my neck. Along the way, we passed a handful of guests and a few staff members, all attempting to get someplace else. Bursting into the lobby, we ran head-on into a mass of people milling about, all highly vocal at the inconvenience of being ordered to leave the building, especially those who were being pulled out of the casino.

Working our way through the chaos, we made it out the front entrance to the huge drive-up portico. Kenny handed his claim ticket to one of the valets.

"Sorry, we're not allowed to retrieve any cars during the emergency evacuation. Police orders." The young man held up both hands up as if Kenny were pointing a gun at him rather than a parking stub.

"We are the police." I shoved my OSI identification and badge in his face, then pulled it away before he had enough time to see we weren't Las Vegas's finest. We had no time to explain what the OSI was.

"Doesn't matter," the valet said. "I'm not allowed to bring up any cars."

Kenny stepped forward. "Then give us our keys and we'll find the car ourselves."

Someone yelled over at the guy and he started to turn away.

"This is an emergency." Kenny blocked the valet from

leaving and counted out a hundred bucks. "Get me the keys."

The valet looked at Kenny, then at the source of whoever yelled at him, then back at Kenny. Snatching the parking stub and the money, he said, "Okay, but you didn't get them from me."

He trotted over to the parking booth window and shoved the stub at the cashier. "They're cops," he said and thumbed at us over his shoulder.

A moment later, the woman produced a set of keys. "Thanks." Kenny grabbed them and we both sprinted toward the entrance to the parking garage.

Kenny suddenly stopped and looked at the paper tag on the keys and then the location markers on the cement columns. "Next level." He pointed to a ramp. Running in the direction he indicated, he called out, "Fifty-five B."

At the top of the ramp, I spotted our car. A minute later, Kenny backed us out and shot down the ramp with the tires squealing and echoing in the big, hard-walled garage.

"Forget Flamingo Road," I said as we left the hotel. I brought up the GPS on my cell phone for directions. "Stay on Dean Martin. It parallels the interstate and will get us south the fastest."

Despite the evacuation, the traffic was light at this time of the morning. I saw the blue lights of emergency vehicles scattered across the landscape. Kenny flew past the slower traffic and soon the black bulk of the Alexandria appeared in the distance ahead on the left, its sloping sides lit against the night sky. Vegas was deceiving. Because the hotels were so big, they always looked closer than they were. Even though we could see the Alexandria, it was almost two miles away according to the GPS. Now it was just a matter of getting off Dean Martin Drive, then going under the interstate and onto Tropicana. Kenny ran the red light as he whipped us left on Tropicana and gunned it east.

Even though there was an effort to keep cars off the street so the busses could move along, still the traffic slowed and thickened as we headed back in the direction of the Strip. The cars crawled past the Excalibur on the right and the huge New York, New York roller coaster on the left. We hit the intersection of Las Vegas Boulevard and swung south. A few minutes later, we picked up speed and made it through the intersection at Reno Avenue.

"There it is," I shouted.

The pyramid loomed out of the night, its massive shape guarded by an equally huge replica of the Egyptian Sphinx. The entrance road was jammed as evacuation buses lined up. There was no way we were going to get the car close to the hotel.

"Just pull up on the curb," I said.

A tall obelisk, almost at the edge of the street, pointed skyward, and that's where Kenny stopped our rental. A wide walkway ran through a tunnel at the base of the obelisk. I grabbed my Maglite from the glove compartment and shoved it in my pocket.

"What's that for?" Kenny asked.

"The lights might be out up at the skybeam. And it makes a great faux gun barrel, if you recall."

We jumped out, hopped a low hedge, and raced along the walkway toward the hotel in the distance.

The closer we got to the hotel entrance, the bigger the crowds grew. Like at the Rio but only in reverse, we found ourselves battling the logjam of guests coming out of the building. A line of staff and security formed a barrier funneling the evacuees toward the buses.

Getting the attention of one of the security officers, I said, "I'm a federal agent and need access to the hotel." I held up my badge and ID.

"Sorry. No one is allowed back in the building. Police orders."

"I understand that. But this is an emergency. I have to get inside."

"Step back and follow the lines to the buses," he said, his face stern.

"You don't understand—"

"I won't tell you again."

Kenny grabbed my shoulder. "Max." As I turned, he motioned us over to the side of the crowd and said, "I've got an idea."

"What?" I was annoyed with the security guy and intended to go back and try again.

"Work your way around the crowd and get as close to the entrance as you can."

"What are you going to do?"

"Just trust me. I'll create a distraction so you can get in. Be ready to move inside fast."

Before I could argue, he shoved me away and walked into the crowd.

I did what Kenny wanted and made my way to the last of the doors that spread across the entrance to the Alexandria. I stood waiting, not sure what to expect. Then I heard someone screaming at the top of his lungs.

"Stop! Thief! He stole my wallet. Help! Police!"

CHAPTER 65 – FIGHT OR FLIGHT
Las Vegas, Nevada. Wednesday morning.
Sunrise minus 1:40

Hotel security was drawn in Kenny's direction as he bellowed about his stolen wallet and the thief who was getting away. He was a convincing actor, I had to give him that.

I slipped through the doors into the lobby, knowing I had to get to Applewhite fast, certain that in some way he was the key to everything. Even as I did, I prayed I wasn't falling into another one of Knox's traps.

Moving through the lobby, I swiftly came to the realization that even if this was a good idea, I didn't have a clue how to get up to the skybeam. "Hey," I called out to someone wearing a hotel uniform. At first I thought it was a man, but as I came closer, I saw it was a wire-thin woman with dark, short-cropped hair. "I need your help," I said, producing my badge. "Which elevator do I take up to the skybeam?"

"You no go there." The woman spoke with a heavy Hispanic accent and was dressed as though she might be part of the housekeeping staff.

I showed my badge again. "Just tell me where to get the elevator."

When she attempted to move away, I grabbed her wrist.

The woman glanced to the hotel entrance. She obviously wanted to get out and on an evacuation bus with everyone else. Then her eyes landed back on mine.

"No elevator," she said.

She had to be kidding. "Then how does anybody get up

top?"

"Stair."

"There has to be a faster way. A service elevator for maintenance?"

"No. No elevator."

"Okay, where are the stairs?"

She grimaced and chewed her bottom lip. "Please. Evacuation."

"That's why I need to get to the skybeam—the light at the top of the hotel. It's an emergency and many people could be injured." I tried to clarify without causing her to panic or make us a center of attention. "I don't have much time."

She tugged at her arm, pulling away. Poor woman was frazzled and by now we were acquiring some looks of interest from bystanders.

Checking her ID badge I caught her name. *Ileana.* "Ileana," I said, lowering my voice, "lives are at risk. You have to help me."

She hesitated, once more eyeing all the people moving past us toward the exit. Then she returned her attention to me. "I will get in big trouble. Lose my job."

"No, I promise. Just show me how to get up to the skybeam and you can go to the buses."

Taking one more look at my badge, she motioned, "This way."

Following her, we skirted the crowd, some who were simply scared and fleeing cooperatively, others arguing with officials about having to leave their luggage behind.

Beyond the lobby, she led me through an *Authorized Personnel Only* door into a long hallway leading to a maze of more hallways and corridors. Ileana stopped in front of a service elevator and punched the *up* button.

"I thought you said there were no elevators to the skybeam."

"Must take this to floor thirty-one, then climb stair."

"How many floors are there?"

She seemed to think for a second. "First thirty for guests.

Service elevators go to thirty-one."

I'd been ready to send the woman on her way, but realized I needed her. If the top floor wasn't accessible to guests, I would require a special ID code to get off on thirty-one.

"I can't get to the thirty-first floor, Ileana. Can you?"

She blanched and dropped her head. "My boyfriend, he work maintenance. He give me code card to see him lunch break."

"Then let's do it."

The door slid open, I took her elbow, and we stepped into the service elevator. I checked the floor buttons. They ended at 31.

"Swipe your card. Hurry, please."

Ileana resisted at first, but finally produced a card from her pocket and swiped it in the card reader, punched 31, then retreated to the side, as far away from me as she could get, burrowing into the quilted pad that lined the elevator wall.

When we landed on the thirty-first floor, I jumped out, but Ileana only cautiously slipped forward, peeking her head through the portal. "*Allí*," she said, pointing.

I stared down the dimly lit hallway. The noise of the elevator doors gliding closed made me turn back. Ileana was gone. Couldn't blame her.

I jogged down the hall, checking the labels on each door. The first said *Electric*. I turned the knob gently, then pushed. Flipping the light switch, I saw that the room was fairly large and filled with dozens of metering boxes. Moving along, I found the next few rooms were either locked or contained access to mechanical or heating and AC controls, or were storage. None led to any stairs.

Shit! Where the hell is the passage up to the top of the Alexandria? Maybe Ileana just screwed with me to get away.

Time was definitely running out. Sunrise was just over an hour away. Heading for the next door, a nearly paralyzing thought ripped through my mind, knotting the fiber of my gut. *What if I'm wrong?*

Then at the halfway down the hall to what was probably the

middle of the pyramid, I found it. I could have kissed the name plate screwed to the door. *Skybeam.*

Swinging it open, I felt a blast of fight-or-flight chemicals shoot through my bloodstream. My heart stuttered at what I saw.

CHAPTER 66 – MAGLITE
Las Vegas, Nevada. Wednesday morning.
Sunrise minus 1:15

I cringed at the sight of the narrow, frail metal ladder rising into the darkness. I thought of it as the skeleton of scaffolding. I guess Ileana hadn't really meant traditional stairs. Lost in the translation. I took out my Maglite and shone its bright beam on the ladder. The rungs couldn't be more than three-quarters of an inch in diameter—a wraparound metal cage would surround me, but gave little comfort.

I aimed my light into the blackness. The ladder seemed to go on forever until it disappeared in the darkness above. I was never a big fan of heights. Staring at the task caused my heart to palpitate. I hadn't yet begun the ascent, and already I was sweating. I wondered if I was reacting from my fear of heights or the fear of what lay ahead.

I turned off the flashlight and tucked it back in the pocket of my jeans. If someone was up there, I didn't want a flicker of light to give away my approach.

I drained my lungs and then hauled in as deep a chest full of air as I could. Blowing it out, I forced myself to remain calm.

Shakily, I reached for a rung above my head, wrapped both hands around it, and stepped onto the ladder. *Don't look down, Max, not even when you are in the dark.* Despite my best mental assurances, just thinking of the climb ushered a fleeting wave of dizziness. Darts of adrenaline fired down my arms. Keeping my eyes open and looking up, I distracted myself by counting the rungs as I climbed. Even though I could see little of anything in the darkness, I was acutely aware of the increasing height and the lack of concrete walls—only the round, metal cage protected me. My hands turned slick with perspiration and my knees felt untrustworthy. Time was running out, and if I faltered and fell, all would be lost. I fought between emotionally wanting to rush the climb and intellectually knowing I had to factor sureness into my actions.

Hurry up, but keep your head, Max.

I moved faster, but still kept each step steady and firm, making certain my feet and hands were solid.

A few moments later, I approached a small landing with a handrail. "Fifteen, sixteen, seventeen, eighteen, nineteen." I believed the rungs to be about a foot apart. That meant this first set of steps had taken me up about twenty feet. Not there yet. The landing was just wide enough to stand on, then more rungs. *How much farther?*

Holding the cold rail, I peered down. My response was not nearly as bad as I expected. A few distant security lights showed some detail. With not much to see, the height wasn't as daunting.

Okay, Max, hit it. Ramp it up.

Another set of forty rungs, a landing, but wider. Panting, I stood on the top platform in front of a door with a sign that read: *Skybeam. Authorized Personnel Only.*

As far as I was concerned, I *was* authorized. That's when I noticed that the door was slightly ajar. Not much, hardly noticeable, just that it wasn't secure. Gently, I pressed on it. For the first time since Iraq, I wished I had my SIG Sauer. What had I thought I was going to do when I got up here if things got dicey?

As the door granted me a glimpse, I cocked my head and looked through the slit. Dim, nondescript objects and surfaces. I had to open it more.

Grateful there was no groaning or squeaking of the hinges, I pushed until I had about six inches clear. It wasn't much of a wide-angle view, but I could see silhouettes of many large metal boxes, each about the size of ice chests. Then I realized from the article I'd read, they were the fixtures holding the enormous xenon lights that together formed the brilliant skybeam.

I still didn't see or hear anyone, so I opened the door wider as doubt flooded my head.

With enough clearance to pass through, I stepped onto the skybeam platform enclosure atop the Alexandria Hotel. Above I could see the steel-beam framework that formed the tip of the pyramid. Through large openings on each of the four sides, nearby hotels and casinos shed enough light for me to be able to see.

Shrouding the bottom third of the pinnacle of the pyramid's otherwise open skybeam rooftop was a covering of quilted foil, thick like a blanket. I was thankful it prevented me from seeing over the edge and down the sloping glass walls.

I took a few guarded steps forward. Then I heard a voice, but the wind whistling through the open rafters muffled the words. It had to be Applewhite. And yet, at his age, could he have made the same climb I just did? We were both on a mission. The answer had to be yes.

Pausing, I evaluated my options and realized I really only had one. All I could do was keep from startling him and try to talk him down. No threats, no weapons. He had the Blade and I had nothing except a Maglite. He might even have a gun, for all I knew. But most of all, he might know the location of the bomb.

I moved to one of the xenon light housings and crouched down. I could hear more clearly, now.

"We live and die by God's holy word. Do you understand, Isaac?"

It was definitely Applewhite. No reply to his question that I could hear.

"God has called me into His mighty army, and I am obligated to prove my loyalty. My devotion. Just as Abraham did in the Old Testament."

"But, Father—"

285

"Quiet, my son. Accept your destiny. You and I have been honored by God himself."

I peered over the metal lamp housings. Applewhite was dressed in a white robe, his hair blowing helter-skelter in the wind, the Blade poised in his outstretched hand, city lights winking off its edge.

I shifted my focus and saw that Carl's hands were tied behind him. A chill of terror washed over me. What Kenny and I had feared appeared to be about to happen. Applewhite was attempting to relive the scriptures as if he were the Prophet Abraham. He was prepared to sacrifice his son!

"Behold, Isaac," Applewhite said, moving to the perimeter. He held the Blade above his head then slashed through the foil blanket. The gash heaved, and a flap of the foil hurled out and flailed in the wind. "Behold Sodom and Gomorrah! Do you see, Isaac? Come close and witness the city of sin sprawled at our feet."

Obeying his father's command, Carl crept closer to the edge.

"Look there, my son. Gaze upon the reviled city that must be destroyed. And I have been given the gift to be an actor in God's grand theater. I will see the wrath Our Lord evokes. He is so pained by man's ill doings. By the fornication, the vileness, the disgrace."

Carl's hands squirmed. "Father Abraham, you must hear me. I believe the voice you have heard—"

"Still thy tongue, boy! Come to the very edge and look upon the final moments of the damned."

Carl stepped to the precipice of the rooftop, staring down at the city below. Just behind him, Applewhite raised the Blade. His intent was clear.

I chose the only weapon I had, my Maglite.

CHAPTER 67 – THE ANGEL
Las Vegas, Nevada. Wednesday morning.
Sunrise minus 1:05

"Dear God," Applewhite cried out as he turned around. He dropped to his knees from the glare of the light shining in his eyes. "Oh most merciful, God, You have sent forth Your angel, just as it is written. God have mercy upon me."

The revelation that God had again come to him caused the evangelist to break into sobs.

He looked up, shading his eyes with his hand as the angel spoke to him.

"Abraham. Abraham."

The light seemed blinding—God's holy light. Pure heavenly, angelic light. Through his choking throat, Applewhite answered, as did Abraham in scripture. "Here I am."

"Do nothing to your son. Lay not a hand on him."

The angel's voice was soft and compassionate. He'd trusted that God would intervene, send an angel to stop him from sacrificing Isaac. He'd been tested, just as the previous Abraham had been.

"Release your son. Set him free."

Applewhite used the Blade to sever the rope that bound Carl, then glanced about the rooftop. Where was the ram? The ram he must sacrifice instead of his son?

The angel spoke again. "Abraham, hear me. The voice that has been speaking to you on the phone is neither God nor one of His angels or messengers. It is the voice of an evil man."

Applewhite got to his feet. Carl had backed away from the edge of the rooftop and clung to one of the warm lamp casings. As the light was not shining in his eyes, he faced the angel and stared, mouth agape.

"No," Applewhite said. "That's not true. You speak lies."

The angel drew closer, the light burning. "I speak the truth."

"God will smite you for such blasphemy. Be gone, Satan!"

Approaching footsteps made them all turn as a new form appeared from the darkness.

"Who the hell are you?" Applewhite said.

CHAPTER 68 – BEST SERVED COLD
Las Vegas, Nevada. Wednesday morning.
Sunrise minus one hour

I turned and shined my flashlight toward the sound. "Travis?" When he stepped forward, I noticed the man had a pronounced limp. I studied his face a little closer. It was disfigured by a scar. Dumbfounded and shocked, my heart threw an extra beat. What was coalescing in my mind couldn't be possible.

"Aaron?"

"The one and only," he said with a chuckle, gun in hand. "I have to say, I'm as surprised to see you here as you are to see me."

My thoughts were scrambled, coming in starts and stops. "You're alive? I don't understand. Why have you let me think...? All this time I've had to live with..."

"Oh, poor, poor Maxine. Hey, you thought you killed me, so I let you believe it." He grinned. "I was your partner for years. Hell, we worked so closely that at one time we could finish each other's sentences. I know what makes you tick and how you think. I didn't have to do anything, really. Your conscience was going to eat you up. Who was I to interfere? What sweet revenge—now served cold, of course. You needed to suffer. Now maybe you've had a taste of what my life has been like."

His expression turned sour. "Look at me." Aaron ran the end of the gun's barrel down the jagged scar on his face. "See what you did? Maimed and disfigured. I walk around like a gimp. I look like a freak. I scare little children when I pass by, and people look away. You had to pay, Maxine. It's only fair." He turned toward Applewhite. "Both of you have to pay. Remember me, preacher?" He stepped closer to Applewhite. "Well, maybe not. I was only a boy then. One of *your* boys. One of so many."

Applewhite squinted and looked hard at Aaron. "No. You must be mistaken."

"I don't think so. But it doesn't matter. If you don't remember me as a boy, then maybe as God. Telephone God. Hologram-vision God. Recognize the voice?" He threw his head back and laughed. "Got you, didn't I, preacher?"

Aaron nodded toward Carl. "Sorry about you. You're the only one who didn't do anything to deserve what's about to happen. You can thank your old man."

He pivoted toward me. "You disappoint me, Maxine. I figured you'd put together all the crumbs I threw your way. You were supposed to be out at the prison right now. Nice and close to the Speedway."

"Speedway?"

"Yeah, there's big doings going on out there this weekend. Family Appreciation Day or some shit like that. They're bringing in a carnival for the kiddies."

This was all too much for me to comprehend. Aaron alive. A bomb disguised as part of an amusement ride at the Las Vegas Motor Speedway.

"Oh, come on, Max. I was counting on you to follow instructions. All you had to do was show up at the prison command center at sunrise and experience the big bang up close and personal."

"So there *is* a bomb?"

"Duh. You were lying right next to it in the hold of the freighter. *Tapas.* Remember? And now it's a mere stone's throw from the prison, not to mention this righteous asshole's fancy church and mansion and university. You were supposed to be blown to bits along with all his worldly possessions. Your stupidity has kind of foiled my plan. So rather than you getting vaporized, I'll just finish the job right here."

I felt a twinge in my throat. Aaron, my partner, I had trusted my life in his hands. "What happened to you, Aaron? You were such a good man."

"Ask the reverend, here. He knows. I was just a kid. He stole my childhood and my innocence. I learned early on how to feel and think one way and act another. Live a lie. It's called survival so you don't self-destruct."

"But somewhere in there is still the man I knew. My partner."

"You never really knew me, Max. Good acting on my part."

"I don't believe that. You don't have to do this. Do what you told me to do in Iraq. Turn and walk away."

"Too late. Can't stop the bomb from going off." He checked his watch. "Travis is waiting. The beauty of this whole thing is I get what I want, and he gets what he wants."

"If this was your plan, what's in it for Travis?" I asked.

"No harm in telling you at this point. Right now, down in the basement of this building, my brother is pulling off the heist of the century. King Tut's death mask. That was his part of the plan. Pretty cool, don't you think?"

"And all the rest?"

"You mean who thought up burning down your cabin that killed your fucking cat? Who came up with the idea of tricking you into blowing away your sister?" He turned to Applewhite. "And who conceived the hologram and the voice on the phone?" He spread his arms and took on a broad grin. "You're looking at him."

Aaron glanced back and forth between Applewhite and me. "Okay, time's up. You're first at bat, preacher. Max, I'll take care of you last."

Aaron waved the gun at Applewhite and strode even closer to stand within a foot of him. "Finish the deed, Abraham. Cut Isaac's throat. That's what you're here for."

Applewhite's eyes glazed.

"Get to it, preacher man. You need to pay your debt. First, you're going to sacrifice your son, and then you get to watch your whole world turn to ash—your home, your church, the whole she*bang,* Father Abraham. Get it? SheBANG! I've waited a long time for this. Served up cold. That's the best. You do it or I will. Either way, once you're done for, you're going straight to hell."

"My father is a decent man," Carl said. "You've taken advantage of his goodness. Leave him be."

"Not as easy as that, boy."

"I said, leave him alone." Carl stepped forward.

Aaron took a long stride, choking the space between them.

Suddenly, Applewhite dove at Aaron, a wild scream echoing off Mount Moriah.

As they toppled to the metal-grated floor, Applewhite thrust the Blade into Aaron's chest. Both men landed perilously close to the edge where the foil was torn, with nothing but open air below. Even over the shrill whistle of wind I heard the splintering of bone. Aaron managed to squeeze off a single shot. Then as if in slow motion, Applewhite quaked with a convulsion and tumbled to the ledge. He rolled to the brink, hung there for a moment, and then disappeared over the edge.

A gust of wind howled through the gaping opening, the insulation foil flapping like a wounded bird. My eyes were frozen on the gap where Hershel Applewhite had been a second before but was now gone.

Carl rushed to the ledge. "No, no, no!"

I heard Aaron sucking in a wet breath. He wasn't dead, only wounded. With surprising strength, he sat up and managed to aim the gun at me. That's when Carl turned and kicked, striking Aaron's wrist and sending the automatic clattering across the grate toward me.

With a roar of vengeance, Carl dropped and wrapped his hands around Aaron's neck.

Aaron grabbed the Blade lying on the floor. As he brought it up to plunge into Carl, I snatched up the gun and fired. The bullet hit Aaron Knox in the head. The Blade clanged as it dropped onto the grate.

Carl pulled back then stood slowly, his body shaking, his hands covered with Aaron's blood. He used his shirtsleeve to wipe away the mix of tears and blood splotching his face.

"I'm so sorry, Carl. I know you loved your father."

"What was that man talking about when he said he was one of my father's boys? Did something happen to him? Did my father do something?"

"Listen, I'll explain everything later. But right now we have an even bigger problem. Something terrible is about to happen. That man and his brother have planted a bomb at the Las Vegas Speedway. It's going to explode and do great damage unless I can stop it. Millions are about to die if we don't act. First, we need to get out of here. Once we climb down, you've got to get on one of those evacuation buses and get away from the city. There's very little time left."

Carl gave an unsure nod.

I slipped Aaron's gun under my jacket in my belt at the small of my back. We were leaving the skybeam grating when Aaron's cell phone chimed.

"Go," I told Carl and shoved him toward the ladder. "Get out of here."

I returned to Aaron's body and fished the phone from his pocket. The LED screen was lit with a text message. It was from Travis. *Got the prize. Get your ass down here right now.*

I pressed reply and typed: *Aaron can't make it. I just killed him. Again.*

CHAPTER 69 - DECOY
Las Vegas, Nevada. Wednesday morning.
Sunrise minus 40 minutes

"Fender!" I said his name into my cell phone so loudly I drew stares from those around me as I fast-walked through the Alexandria lobby. My legs still shook from the climb down from the beacon platform. I had heard Carl in the dark scrambling down the metal ladder but by the time I reached the ground floor, he was nowhere in sight.

"What, Agent Decker?" He had lost some of his calm demeanor, instead sounding edgy—which was more than understandable.

"I know where the bomb is." This time I kept my voice low and cupped my mouth with my palm. "It's at—"

"I know where it is, too. Our mobile and airborne sensors discovered a suspicious radiation signature less than ten minutes ago. I've got teams from the Army and the DOE on the way. Now if you'll excuse me—"

"They're going to the Speedway?"

"What the hell are you talking about? We've pinpointed the weapon on the roof of the new Utopiana Hotel. The building is under construction but one of the big cranes could easily have lifted the device onto the roof. The damn thing is twenty stories up, right in the center of the city, Agent Decker—the perfect detonation point. We've got less than an hour until sunrise to get this thing disarmed."

"It has to be a decoy. I've got solid proof that the device is at the Motor Speedway."

"We've already done a fly-over out there. No traces of radiation. Your intel is wrong."

"You don't understand. It was Aaron Knox—" I realized the connection was dead. "Shit!" I shoved the phone back in my pocket as I slipped through the crowd and stood under the Alexandria portico. Rising on tiptoes, I spotted Kenny off to the side of the lines as they snaked toward the buses. Making my way around the bulk of evacuees, I touched his arm and he turned, his face awash with relief.

"Max, you okay?"

I nodded and he took me in his arms.

"What about you?" I said.

"Worried sick. I've been mingling in the crowd keeping a low profile, trying not to be forced onto one of the buses."

I welcomed his embrace and wished it could have lasted longer, but I knew we didn't have the luxury of time. Before stepping back I said into his ear, "Applewhite's dead." My heart raced at the thought that I was the only one who knew the real location of the Nazi weapon.

"How?"

"I'll tell you the whole story on the way. First, we've got to get to the Las Vegas Motor Speedway." I lowered my voice. "That's where the bomb is."

Kenny pointed toward the tall obelisk on Reno Avenue. "The car's that way."

"Let's hope it's still there."

We worked our way along the edge of the crowd trying to avoid direct contact with security.

We darted between two buses, then broke into a run down the walkway leading to the street. Aaron's pistol, wedged under my belt, pressed hard against the base of my spine with each pounding step.

"I heard you yelling about your wallet being stolen."

"Once I was surrounded by enough security officers and I was sure you had time to get past the entrance," Kenny said as we huffed along. "I suddenly *found* my wallet in my other back pocket and apologized to everyone. They gave me a hard time but eventually let me go. Like I said, I was about to come out of my skin with worry. What happened up there? Applewhite's dead? What about Carl?"

"He's okay, but you don't know the half of it."

"Well, along with everything else, there was a big commotion and I heard that someone either jumped or was pushed out a hotel window."

"I'll tell you all about that, too."

I thought Kenny was going to stop cold, but I waved him on.

As we came out of the passageway through the base of the obelisk, I realized the car was gone. Probably towed. "Just great." My lungs burned from the run.

Kenny wiped the sweat from his forehead. "Try calling Fender. We've got about thirty minutes to find the bomb and get him and his crew to disarm it."

I could see the mountain ridges forming the eastern horizon. A soft glow behind them signaled the approaching dawn. I dialed Fender's number but went straight to voice mail. My gut tightened, knowing there might not be enough time.

To my left, the lights of the Strip and the surrounding city shone like a nighttime mirage—a fantasyland of color against a dark, foreboding sky. There was a strong possibility it would soon be anything but a fantasy as the shock wave from the blast rushed across the desert and brought Sin City to its knees. Tens of thousands dead. Millions more injured. There's no way they can get everybody out in time. And think of the billions in damage. Sodom and Gomorrah, Sin City destroyed. All because a thief wanted to steal a priceless Egyptian treasure—King Tut's Death Mask. And with little time left, we were about to go to ground zero and hope to stop it from happening. The good news, I told myself, is that if we're too late, we won't feel a thing.

I glanced back at the pale outline of the approaching day.

Kenny grabbed my arm. "Max, over there."

I looked where he pointed. Sitting alone in the vacant lot across from the hotel was a MedStar helicopter, its three-man crew standing idly by, probably staged to await any call of assistance during Operation Stagecoach.

I reached around to make sure Aaron's pistol was still secure in my belt.

"Come on, Max, our ride's waiting."

CHAPTER 70 - THE CARNIVAL
Las Vegas, Nevada. Wednesday morning.
Sunrise minus 30 minutes

"This is an emergency." Kenny held out his badge. "We need the use of your helicopter."

The EMT pilot, a tall, slim man with a bushy mustache, leaned in and shined his penlight on Kenny's ID. The two crewmen, both critical-care paramedics according to the breast patches on their blue jumpsuits, stood by waiting for the pilot's reaction. "Sorry, sir," he said, "but we're taking part in a county-wide operation and are under orders to remain here unless told otherwise."

"We know all about Operation Stagecoach," I said. "What we need your helicopter for directly affects the success of the evacuation."

"I wish I could help you," he said, looking at me, "but I'd need authorization from dispatch first."

"There's no time." My voice rose in volume and anxiety.

"Sorry, but that's the way it is."

I ripped Aaron's gun from my belt and pointed it at the pilot. "Wrong. This is the way it is."

"Jesus, Max!" Kenny took a step back as did the crew. "Where did you get that?"

"It's Aaron's."

"Aaron's?" Kenny's eyes grew wide. "Aaron Knox? He's alive?"

"Was. I killed him."

The pilot brought his hands up in surrender. "Lady, I don't

know who you are or what you want, but you need to put that down."

I extended my arm until the gun barrel was level with his eyes. "Start this thing and get us in the air." I shifted my aim at the two paramedics. "You guys take a walk—leave your com-helmets here."

"No problem," one of them said. They removed their helmets, handed them to Kenny and then started back-stepping. A few yards away, they turned and walked briskly toward the street.

"Inside." I motioned with the gun toward the pilot. "Let's go."

He opened the side door and climbed into his seat. I went around and hopped in the co-pilot's seat while Kenny jumped into the back and slid the side door closed.

I pulled on the com-helmet and adjusted the mic to be in front of my mouth. "Where do I plug in?"

The pilot pointed to a multi-jack, then did the same for Kenny. "Okay, lady with the gun, where are we going?"

"Las Vegas Motor Speedway, as fast as this thing can fly."

"I'll need to get ATC clearance." The pilot was already flipping the switches to start the jet turbines that drove the rotor on the EC-145 EMS air ambulance.

I held up the gun. "Here's your clearance."

He stared at me for a moment then nodded. "Good enough for me."

In less than a minute, we were at full power and the machine lifted off to about a hundred feet. The pilot rotated the helicopter to check for any approaching aircraft before he dipped the nose slightly and shot us into the dark sky. Once we had leveled out, he said, "What's this all about?"

"What's your name?" I asked him.

"Mosrite. Mo for short."

"Okay, Mo. You're going to help us save millions of lives and the city of Las Vegas."

He gave me a long, hard stare, then turned back to his instruments.

"Max," Kenny said through the com system, "what's this about Aaron being alive—or dead?"

I held my hand up for Kenny to hang on. "Mo, how far is it to the Speedway?"

"About fifteen miles, but we have to go around Nellis. Only adds a few extra minutes."

I turned in my seat toward Kenny. "When I got to the beacon platform, Applewhite was there with Carl. He had the Blade and was going to sacrifice his son, just like in the Scriptures. When I showed up, he said his prayers had been answered, and that I was the angel sent by God to stop him."

"And Aaron?"

"I'm getting to it." I proceeded to explain everything that had transpired on the rooftop. Kenny recognized the catch in my voice and apparently understood how deeply saddened I was over Aaron.

"I'm so sorry, Max."

"Yeah, me, too."

"So the body they thought was a jumper was Applewhite's?"

I nodded as I saw a scattering of work lights from the Speedway ahead and assumed there was already activity in preparation for the coming day's events.

"Where do you want me to land?"

"We're searching for something that looks like a circus or carnival—particularly with amusement rides."

"Family Appreciation Day," Mo said. "There's supposed to be that kind of stuff out here all weekend. They usually set up just outside the front gates north of the entrance."

Mo banked the helicopter and swooped in over the grandstands. Even in the darkness of the predawn, I spotted it—the carnival covered about half the open area outside the entrance gates. I saw a long midway lined with booth attractions and tents, and an amusement ride at each end. One was a decent-sized rollercoaster, the other a multi-armed ride with rocket-shaped cars at the ends of each arm—the whole thing resembled a giant spider.

"That one." I pointed. "Get as close as you can to the yellow one."

Throwing up a cloud of desert sand and dust, Mo set the helicopter down in a clear area next to Speedway Boulevard. I turned to him. "You got any portable lights?"

He pointed to two heavy-duty nine-volt lanterns attached to the inside wall of the cabin.

"Thank you," I said. "Now, I would advise you to fly as fast as you can directly away from this place. Don't stop until you get an all-clear from your dispatch that Operation Stagecoach is over."

"You're the boss." Mo gave a small wave. "Good luck."

As Kenny grabbed the lanterns, I yanked off my helmet and was immediately assaulted with the high-pitched scream of the twin jet turbines and the spinning rotors. Throwing open my door, I jumped out. Seconds later, Kenny and I ducked under the rotating blades and ran from the helicopter toward the carnival midway and the big yellow amusement ride. I didn't have to look back to know that Mo was already lifting off. I only hoped that if we couldn't get the bomb disarmed in time, he would be far enough away to survive.

There was a waist-high fence around the yellow, multi-armed ride. A rocket-shaped, two-passenger gondola was attached at the end of each arm.

We ran round the perimeter of the fence until we came to a large, thick metal archway marking the entrance to the ride. Standing a few feet away, I shined my light on the name spread across the top of the arch. Spelled out in light bulbs was: *Tapas Ride to the Stars*. Behind the sign, resting on top of the heavy steel support of the arch, was an elongated object about ten or twelve feet in length, concealed beneath what appeared to be a padded mover's blanket covering its entire surface. The blanket was secured in multiple places along the length of the object by tightly bound ropes.

"That's it!" I said. I had been right next to this thing on the ship. Somewhere along the way, maybe in Cuba, Knox had the archway built with the ride's name. Kind of an *in my face* thing for him. He must have sold it to the carnie owner cheap or paid him off to put it here. How ever he got it here didn't matter now. Quickly I looked around for a way to climb up.

"We need a ladder," Kenny said.

"No time." I handed my light to him and stood at the base of the steel archway. Twice in one night I had to climb. I could feel my skin breaking out into a sweat. My legs grew weak. This sucked.

Reaching out, I gripped the metal latticework running up the side of the arch and started climbing.

"Hey, what do you think you're doing?"

I turned to see a man trotting toward us. He was dressed like a security guard. Fortunately, I didn't see a weapon in his hand, only a radio. In the other he held an industrial flashlight. Ignoring him, I went back to the job of climbing to the device over the arch.

"I asked you a question." He stopped a few feet from Kenny.

My ex pulled out his ID. "We're federal agents. This is an emergency, a matter of national security. Stand back."

I was level with the sign and just below one end of the elongated object. Balancing myself as best I could and trying not to look down, I reached and pulled on the end of the rope hanging from the first knot. It was tight but within a few seconds it loosened and the rope gave way. I yanked it free and let it fall to the ground.

"I'm going to need more info than that," the guard said. "You're trespassing on private property."

I grabbed the end of the blanket. It was way thicker and heavier than I expected and reminded me of something I'd felt many times over the years when I had dental X-rays. The object was wrapped in a lead blanket. I knew immediately that's what had kept the government's sensors from detecting the radiation.

"We suspect that someone has planted a bomb in this amusement ride," Kenny told the guard.

I extended to reach the next knot and worked to untie it.

Soon, the rope fell away and I used all my strength to pull up a portion of the heavy blanket.

"Kenny, shine the light up here."

As his beam fell on the exposed metal, I clearly saw the bright yellow surface with the word *Tapas* written in a circus-like red font. More of Knox's artistic talent. I pulled my cell phone from my pocket and speed-dialed Fender.

"Bomb?" the guard asked.

Kenny began explaining to the guard what we were up against.

As I waited for Fender to answer, I forced myself to look down at the security guard. He seemed to have lost some of his courage as he stared up at the object.

"Yes, Agent Decker?" Fender's voice was strained—obvious frustration seeped through.

"Let me guess—the device on the roof of the Utopiana was a decoy."

He said nothing.

"How fast can you get your Army guys out to the Motor Speedway?"

"What have you got?"

"The bomb is part of a carnival amusement ride. It's concealed as a big yellow rocket, and the word *Tapas* is written on the side."

"But how did they—?"

"It was wrapped in a lead blanket. Like at the dentist's office, only bigger. That's why you didn't pick up the radiation."

"Son-of-a-bitch."

"According to my watch, you've got about thirteen minutes to get out here and disarm this thing." I hoped thirteen wasn't an unlucky number this time around.

I heard Fender start shouting orders to whoever was around him. Finally, he said, "We're on our way."

"That's a bomb?" the guard said, taking a hesitant step backwards.

"Afraid so," Kenny said.

"What kind?"

I looked down from my perch, wishing I were wrong. "Atomic."

CHAPTER 71 - DESERT SUNRISE
Las Vegas, Nevada. Wednesday morning.
Sunrise minus 10 minutes

I heard the helicopters coming. As they banked and circled, my gaze was drawn to a solid string of emergency lights appearing in the distance on the interstate. When the first Blackhawk touched down, Agent Fender jumped to the ground and ran toward me. He was followed by a half-dozen men, all wearing protective hazmat gear.

Fender came to a halt beside me. "Where?"

I pointed to the long yellow object mounted above the entrance to the *Tapas* ride. I had worked on the ropes while waiting, and the lead blanket now hung down, only covering about half the bomb.

Fender spun around, taking in everything. His gaze stopped on the security guard. "We need ladders or some other means to climb up there."

The man had just about recovered from the initial shock that he was within a few yards of an atomic bomb. But he now reverted back to a wide-eyed stare at the sudden appearance of the Blackhawks loaded with men rushing toward him dressed like invading aliens from UFOs.

Fender went to the guard and yelled in his face, "Ladders!"

The man seemed to suddenly notice the FBI agent. "How about a forklift? We've got one that can lift a platform up that high."

"Perfect." Armed soldiers poured from more Blackhawks and formed a perimeter around the amusement ride. Fender called to two of them. "Go with him. On the double."

"There's definitely a positive reading," one of the Army techs said, his voice muffled from behind his headgear. In his hand, he pointed a portable device toward the bomb. I saw a couple of its LEDs lighting up.

Kenny turned to face him. "Agent Decker was just up there next to that thing. Is she... ?"

"In danger from radiation?" The tech shook his head. "No risk being in proximity to nukes unless they detonate."

Relieved, I turned to Fender. "What was on the roof of the Utopiana?"

"A large industrial air conditioning frame filled with radioactive medical equipment parts. Probably from your Cuban ship or at least the stuff they used to conceal the bomb at the U.S.-Mexican border. Just enough to set off our detectors and cost us a couple of hours on a wild goose chase."

"Next time, maybe you'll listen to me."

Fender glared at me but his expression quickly softened. "Let's hope I get the chance."

One group of techs was already setting up banks of high-intensity floodlights. Soon, the bomb was lit up like high noon.

I heard a roar and turned to see a bulky forklift rumbling down the middle of the carnival midway. It was huge, like those in an auto junkyard, and its vertical rails were more than high enough to reach the weapon. Not a surprise to find it at a raceway. Someone had placed a wooden platform across the two steel forks. As soon as it arrived in front of the archway, a couple of the Army techs in hazmat gear stepped on the platform with their toolkits, and the driver engaged the motors, lifting the men to within a foot or so of the bomb. Within seconds they had cut the remaining ropes and let the heavy blanket fall in a heap below.

I watched the sky changing from cobalt to a dark orange like the shade of an overripe persimmon. It seemed to be growing brighter by the second. I glanced at my watch.

"Four minutes," Kenny said, reading my thoughts.

"That is, if Knox keeps his schedule." Fender never took

his eyes off the men on the platform.

I heard the whine of cordless drills. A few seconds later, the techs lifted a portion of the bomb's metal skin away and began probing the device's inner workings.

The area was now awash in a sea of emergency lights and brave first responders all prepared to do their jobs no matter what the outcome. My guess was that most didn't realize the enormity of the event. But it was impressive to see such dedicated men and women at the ready.

I heard the sound of another helicopter approaching. As I glanced at it, I realized it was an EMS air ambulance. It landed a few hundred yards away. Once the rotors slowed, Mo and the two paramedics hopped out and walked toward us.

When he stood in front of me, he said, "Had to go back and get my two guys. Just in case you need some help."

I nodded to them with a smile. "Thank you, Mo. I'm sorry I had to be so…demanding."

"Having a gun pointed at me is always good motivation."

"Two minutes," Fender called out. As a group, we fell still and silent, knowing if those techs didn't get this right, at least in the end, there would be no pain. One moment we would be here and the next there would be no *here*.

Then Fender's radio crackled.

"They're using a cell phone as a trigger," one of the techs said through the small speaker. "It's amazingly simple. Probably didn't count on us finding it in time."

My phone rang. I pulled it from my pocket and held it up. "A text from Knox." I read aloud, "Big bang time, bitch. This one's for Aaron."

I reached to take Kenny's hand. We looked at each other and I wanted so much to tell him how sorry I was that I had succeeded at my job but not our marriage. For an instant, his eyes let me know he understood. Then I saw reflected in those eyes the glow of the sunrise shooting across the desert.

CHAPTER 72 - SECOND CHANCES
Las Vegas, Nevada. Wednesday morning. Sunrise

"It's time," Fender said—his voice so soft, I barely heard the words.

The air stood still, causing the carnival pennants atop their poles to go limp. No one moved. It was a snapshot of the final second of our lives. I tried to visualize the atoms in my body instantly vaporizing in a cloud of plasma hotter than the sun. If there really was a next life, I wondered if my body would reassemble there. Or would I drift like a cloud in eternal ether. I pictured Francine and hoped to see her again a few seconds from now.

I held my breath.

"Got it!" the tech called from overhead.

I looked up at the man standing on the platform. He had swiveled around. With wires dangling, he held a cell phone over his head like an Olympic champion hoisting gold.

And in the next instant, breaking the paralyzing stillness of the desert air, I heard the cold, unfeeling, soulless ring of the cell phone in the tech's hand.

Travis Knox had dialed its number to trigger the detonation of the bomb. He would have killed us and millions more. Without hesitation.

No one dared move. We all must have realized that we had just come within a few heartbeats of eternity. Then, one by one, people looked around as if awakening from a deep, dark dream. The chilling sound of the phone was suddenly replaced with whoops and hollers. Calls and cries.

I felt someone hugging me and realized it was Agent Fender. He was quickly followed by the strong arms of my ex-husband.

"Max," Kenny whispered in my ear, "we just got a second chance. Not many can claim that."

I knew he meant that in two ways. I stepped back and placed my fingers on his lips to quiet him. "I know."

Then we started taking in the joyful commotion among the soldiers and first responders. It was a sight and sound I'll never forget.

Mo came and shook my hand. "Thanks, lady with the gun. You're my new hero."

I tried to say thank you, but the words caught in my throat. A nod would have to do—I'd never been anyone's hero before.

"The bastard was really going to do it," Fender said. "I want to personally track this guy down and see that he rots in prison for the rest of his miserable life."

"I never imagined Aaron was alive," I said, "and even if so, I wouldn't have thought he could hate me so much to do this."

"I don't understand." Fender rubbed his unshaven face. "Aaron who?"

"I'll be glad to tell you everything, Agent Fender, but first we have some unfinished business."

He gestured toward the *Tapas* device. "The bomb's defused. It's over."

"Not quite. There's the matter of the robbery."

CHAPTER 73 - INTERCEPT
Las Vegas, Nevada. Wednesday morning

"Aaron Knox was wearing a Frontier Armored Services uniform," I said as we rose into the sky aboard the Blackhawk for the short ride to Nellis AFB. Kenny sat to my left, Fender to my right. The remaining seats were taken up by members of the FBI Rapid Deployment Team—definitely some of the most serious-looking individuals I'd ever seen.

Fender had just finished the last of a quick series of cell phone calls including one to the Alexandria. He turned to me. "I must admit, this was a pretty slick plan."

We all wore headphones so Kenny could hear, too. "Tell us," he said.

"Frontier was hired to take the King Tut Experience pieces to a transport plane to fly to New York for the next stop on the tour," Fender said. "When the order came down to initiate Operation Stagecoach, the exhibit director called in Frontier to pick up the most valuable piece of the collection, the Tut Death Mask, and get it to the tour cargo plane as fast as possible. He wanted it out of the Las Vegas area in case the nuclear threat was for real. The armored truck driven by Knox showed up within minutes of his phone call, way ahead of the dispatched Frontier truck, and loaded the already-packed shipping crate containing the relic. Of course, the tour director had no idea he was handing it over to a thief."

"Where is it now?" I asked.

"Instead of transporting it to the tour aircraft, waiting at McCarran International, it was loaded onto a private jet at a rented hangar at the other end of the airport. It's already in flight headed south, probably for Mexico."

"Can you stop it before it crosses the border?" Kenny asked.

Fender nodded. "Two F-16s from the 65th Aggressor Squadron at Nellis just caught up with it over Needles, California. It didn't take much convincing from the fully armed fighters to convince the pilot to turn around."

I felt the helicopter start to slow and drop. Since we were only about two miles from the Air Force Base, we'd barely had time to get into the air before it was time to land. A few seconds later, we gently touched down in the middle of a sprawling tarmac. As the door slid open and we jumped out, I spotted a group of fighter jets in the distance parked in a series of straight lines. The area was already filling up with emergency vehicles and military police Humvees. The newly risen sun washed the runway, stretching out in front of us with a warm orange coating. My heart still raced with the adrenaline from the disarming of the bomb. It was a strange mixture of excitement, relief, and pure anger as I stood on the tarmac. I had survived the Nazi bomb threat, beaten the odds, and was now about to face the man I thought I hated most in the world—Travis Knox. But this had all been Aaron's doing. Travis never really gave a rat's ass about me. All he wanted was the Tut Death Mask.

Fender motioned to the south, and I watched a grouping of lights twinkle against the ever-bluing morning sky as three aircraft approached. It seemed to take forever before I could clearly make out the corporate jet, its landing gear extending as it slowly descended onto the runway. The two F-16s rode on each side, close to the jet's wingtips. Once its wheels touched down, the fighters continued on past us and swung into a slow arc to come back around, probably making sure the jet didn't decide to take off at the last moment.

"This way," Fender called as he led Kenny and me to a nearby Humvee.

Before I had a chance to close the door, we were racing

across the tarmac toward the rapidly slowing jet. Around us an army of vehicles all moved like a swarm of bees toward the aircraft. A new rush of excitement coursed through me as my heart beat faster. We were minutes away from ending this nightmare.

The corporate jet rolled to a halt, and the whine of its engines dropped in pitch as they were shut down. Dozens of military personnel surrounded the plane, all aiming their automatic assault rifles at the aircraft.

When the sound of the jet engines was finally lost in the desert wind, the side door opened and was lowered. From where we stood, I could see that seats had been removed and a large wooden crate sat in their place.

Someone had handed Fender a bullhorn. "Inside the aircraft. This is the FBI. Step out of the plane one at a time with your hands in the air. Do it now!"

I saw a man fill the entrance way, his hands on his head. He started down the steps. "That's the Russian," I said. "The one who claimed to be Yuri."

"Move away from the stairs and get on the ground, face down," Fender called to the man as he moved a few paces from the bottom of the steps. Then Fender said, "Next passenger, exit the aircraft with your hands up."

A woman moved to the top of the steps. Blond, slim, attractive. Knox's girlfriend? "No idea who that is," I said.

She took the steps gingerly in her stiletto heels and dropped down on the ground a few feet from the Russian.

"Okay, next passenger. Exit the aircraft. Hands where we can see them."

A man in the shape of a tree trunk filled the doorway and came down the steps. "That's Janko," I said. "He's the one who threw me off the ship."

"Janko Azarov," Fender called through the bullhorn. "Get down on the ground and don't move." There seemed to be no surprise on the Ukrainian pilot's face that his identity was known.

"Next passenger," Fender called out. "Exit the aircraft."

We waited a full sixty seconds. "Last chance," Fender called, "before we send in the dog."

Nothing.

The agent nodded to an Air Force police officer who had been standing by with a very eager German Shepherd. The officer unclipped the leash holding the K9. He shouted a command and the dog shot across the concrete and raced up the steps, its vicious barking filling the otherwise quiet tarmac.

The dog continued its angry yelp as it ran back and forth inside of the corporate jet before it appeared at the top of the steps, barking some secret language to his handler. The officer gave a quick whistle, and the dog bounded down the steps and ran to his side where he was rewarded with affectionate tousling of his fur and an encouraging, "Good job, boy."

Fender signaled and three armed soldiers moved cautiously up the steps, their assault rifles at the ready.

I held my breath as I saw them move past the round windows along the length of plane.

A minute later, one of the soldiers appeared at the doorway and stood on the top step. "That's it," he called, his weapon lowered. "There's no one else here."

CHAPTER 74 - THE CRATE
Las Vegas, Nevada. Wednesday morning

The corporate jet, a rented Gulfstream G450, was towed into a large hangar usually reserved for maintenance on Air Force F-15 fighters. I stood with Kenny and watched the various local and federal government agencies swarm over its interior. Fender and his fellow agents had taken the three passengers, Yuri, Janko, and the woman who identified herself as Sarah Walker, to separate holding cells for questioning. I was still trying to get a handle on all the facts and events in a logical and rational order. It was especially difficult when dealing with Travis Knox.

"Aaron, not Travis, was the main force in everything that happened to me," I said to Kenny. "He was screwed up from the get-go by Applewhite. I occasionally caught a glimpse of that imbalance in him when we worked together, but it was never enough for concern. Then, of course, the proverbial straw was my shooting and maiming him in Iraq. Aaron was absolutely obsessed with revenge for what I'd done. He's the one who burned down my cabin. And he's the one who thought up the idea of the mirror trick to get me to kill my sister."

I rubbed my face, realizing I was suddenly bone-tired. "And he wanted Applewhite to suffer for the abuse and torture the evangelist had put him through as a foster child. Perfect revenge—trick Applewhite into taking the life of his own son, then force him to watch as the televangelist's world is destroyed. Aaron was the voice on the phone calls to

Applewhite, by the way. Not Travis. But Travis had to stand in for Aaron when he was on the laptop with us and also in the photo in Cuba with Francine. I'd have recognized Aaron's voice and picture. Quite a collaboration."

"And as far as Travis was concerned, the whole bomb threat was just a diversion to steal the relic?" Kenny said. "For Travis, you were collateral damage."

I nodded. "The ransom money collected from the casinos would have been chump change compared to what I'll bet he was asking for the Tut Death Mask. There are more than enough mega-rich unscrupulous antiquities collectors out there willing to pay anything to possess one of the most famous relics in history." I glanced over at the wooden shipping crate sitting alone in the middle of the hangar floor. It had not been opened yet—Fender ordered it delayed until the Tut Experience tour director arrived with his authentication expert to identify the relic. A ribbon of crime scene tape surrounded the crate.

"But you couldn't show off something like that in your collection or tell anyone you had it."

"Wouldn't have to," I said. "Just the fact that you possessed it would be enough."

"Why do you think Travis wasn't on the plane?"

"That's the big mystery. I can't believe he would abandon the relic and leave it in the hands of those three."

"You guys doing okay?" Fender asked as he approached.

"Just another day at the office," I said with a smile. "Any luck with our friends?"

"Some. The guy who posed as Agent Gates's uncle in Cuba is actually Sergie Boiko. We matched his fingerprints to a former Moscow police lieutenant who's wanted for drug and arms smuggling. He's not saying much, but some of his old friends from Russia are on their way here to have a chat with him. Probably won't be pleasant. We already have a good bit of info on Janko Azarov, a former Ukrainian helicopter pilot. He was the one flying the Gulfstream."

"What about the woman?" I asked.

"Here's a bombshell. Sarah Walker was once Sarah Knox. For a brief time a few years ago, she was married to Travis Knox. They split, then got back together to pull off the Tut heist. She's wanted for counterfeiting and issuing false instruments—phony stock certificates. And are you ready for this?"

Fender didn't wait for Kenny or me to respond.

"Although she said very little, she did reveal the selling price of the Egyptian death mask."

"And?" I said.

"One billion."

"Dollars?" Kenny's jaw dropped.

Fender nodded. "No idea who the buyer was, but you can bet once the deal was done, King Tut's mask would never be seen again."

"No wonder everybody was willing to take big chances for a share of that prize." I glanced back at the crate. "Even something that's priceless still has a price."

"What about Carl Applewhite?" Kenny asked.

"He was questioned and released. Police identified his father's body as the person who fell from the top of the hotel. And they ID'd Aaron Knox from his military records.."

"And the Blade?" I asked.

"Missing."

"What?" For a moment I thought I'd misheard him. "But it was somewhere on the skybeam platform when I left."

"The entire skybeam area was searched. No knife found."

"Did anyone else go up there after Carl and I left?"

"We don't know," Fender said, "but we're checking surveillance video. Problem is, they have very few cameras in that area since only employees are allowed."

"How did Applewhite and Carl get up there in the first place?" I asked.

"He arranged it with one of the Alexandria staff—a devout follower of the Applewhite Ministry. The reverend convinced his disciple that he must go up to pray for God's forgiveness of Sodom and Gomorrah during the coming crisis." There was a sound of footsteps approaching. "This must be the people from the Tut Experience."

Two men approached, both dressed in dark suits and escorted by FBI agents. One carried a briefcase about the size of those used by airline pilots for their maps and manuals. "Agent Fender, I am Ahmed Hadidi, director of the Tut Experience. This is my associate, Hussein Karawan, professor of antiquities at Cairo University. We are here to open the container and identify the artifact."

"Nice to meet you, Mr. Hadidi." Fender shook the man's hand and then the professor's. "I'd like you to meet OSI agents Maxine Decker and Kenny Gates."

Hadidi took my hand in both of his. "Agent Decker, please accept my sincere thanks for all you've done, not only in saving our precious relic but our lives and the lives of millions in Las Vegas. I am forever in your debt."

"It was a team effort," I said with a quick nod to Kenny and Fender.

"You are too modest." Hadidi turned to Kenny. "And to you, Agent Gates, our heartfelt thanks and gratitude."

"That's why I get the big bucks," he said but I could tell he instantly regretted it. Fortunately, Hadidi seemed to get the joke.

"And now, let's see what we have." He led us over to the crate. Fender pulled the crime-scene tape aside to give Hadidi access.

Karawan opened his case and brought out a cordless drill with a bolt attachment. Within a short time he had unscrewed the ten bolts securing the top. The two Egyptians removed the heavy wooden lid to reveal a foam-fitted layer with rope handles embedded in the material.

"What you're about to see," Hadidi said, glancing at us, "is the gold death mask of the boy king, Tutankhamen. It's made of eleven kilograms—twenty-four and a half pounds—of solid gold inlaid with semiprecious stones and colored glass. The eyes are formed from obsidian and quartz. The back of the mask is chased with a series of spells and texts from the

Egyptian Book of the Dead. The mask was used to cover the face of the mummy of the pharaoh to ensure that his spirit would be able to recognize the body in the afterlife."

Karawan gripped the rope handles. With a gentle tug, he lifted the foam layer insert straight up. Beneath it was an object covered with a white linen cloth. Slowly he peeled the material aside and gave out a loud gasp.

Hadidi took a step back. "Dear God!"

CHAPTER 75 - DIRTY LAUNDRY
Las Vegas, Nevada. Wednesday morning

Hadidi looked as though he just stared into his own coffin. Karawan appeared unable to breathe.

I moved forward and peered into the crate. What I saw was a large black trash bag. "Doesn't seem fitting for King Tut's death mask to be in a trash bag."

Hadidi felt the plastic. "This can't be. I supervised the packing of the relic. It was perfectly fine when we sealed the crate. And this was not part of the materials."

"I packed it myself and sealed the lid," Karawan managed to mumble. "This is impossible."

I reached down and pressed my hands on the bag. It felt like it was filled with wadded-up cloth, like someone's dirty laundry. I turned to Fender and Kenny. "Guess who got here first?"

"Knox never intended for the relic to be on the plane," Fender said.

"So where is it?" Hadidi asked, his face turning the color of heavy cream.

Fender walked away as he brought a radio to his mouth and started spewing a rapid litany of orders. I caught some of the words—roadblocks, inspections, trucks and minivans, state police, airborne surveillance, all flights from McCarran.

"A billion bucks is a lot of bucks," Kenny said.

I nodded. "If he can smuggle an atomic bomb into the country, he can damn-sure smuggle an Egyptian relic out."

Hadidi and Karawan reverted to their native language as

they hurried away, noticeably upset. Fender had directed a CSI team to converge on the crate and search for any forensic evidence. As the activity around us intensified, Kenny and I seemed to become invisible.

"Not much more we can do here but get in the way." I pointed to a soda machine against a far wall. "Buy you a drink?"

"I'm buying," Kenny said. "It's the least I can do for the lady who saved Sodom and Gomorrah."

After we got our drinks, Kenny said, "You concerned that Travis will come after you?"

I shrugged. "Travis has what he came for. He's got to be more concerned with delivering the relic to his buyer than trying to hurt me."

"We'll find him," Fender said as he joined us at the vending machine. He slid a bill into the slot and grabbed the can from the dispenser. "We've cast a very wide net over southern Nevada and the surrounding states."

"When do you think he pulled off the switch?" I asked.

"Between the Alexandria and McCarran. I've just been informed they found the abandoned armored truck. There was evidence of packing materials in the back."

"Any surveillance video?"

"Not much. He picked his drop-off location wisely. There was a camera system on the private hangar, but it had been disabled. We have little to go on." He paused long enough to take a drink. "What are you two going to do now?"

"Back to my day job at DC3," Kenny said.

"What else do you need from us?" I asked.

"The locals will want a statement about what happened in the skybeam. They have to deal with two dead men, one of which you killed—in self-defense, but still there are the formalities. And I'll need a full report from you both."

"Sure." I finished my soda. "After that, I think I'll get on the first thing blazing out of Las Vegas."

"I don't blame you," Fender said. "Back to Colorado?"

I thought about it for a moment. "I love Colorado. I'd like

to rebuild my cabin on the spot where Knox burned it down—that is after I scrape up the money to pay for the construction."

Fender smiled. "I might have some good news for you in that respect."

"What do you mean?"

"Apparently there are a whole lot of folks in Las Vegas, including one hundred and twenty-two casinos, who want to show their appreciation for what you both did." He tossed his empty can into a recycle bin. "You just might be able to rebuild your cabin and then some."

I turned to Kenny and hoisted my soda can in a toast. "Viva Las Vegas."

CHAPTER 76 - GOSSAMER MIST
Big Bear Lake, Colorado. Eight months later

"They found the mask," Kenny said. He had just called as I was fixing my breakfast in my new kitchen. I'd been gazing out the window at the lake when my cell phone rang. The morning view was just as captivating as ever—thin veils of fog drifted off the glassy, deep indigo surface like gossamer mist. Once in a while, a circular ripple marked where a smallmouth bass sampled the morning air. Dark forest crowded the banks, and rocky ledges climbed slowly toward the distant mountains. I had yet to grow tired of this place. The only difference between now and before was my new cabin was about twice the size of the old one and equipped with the latest technology in electronics and appliances. And of course security.

The casino owners had been generous in their gratitude to Kenny and me. His first purchase was a red, midlife-crisis Italian sports car that everyone at DC3 made fun of, but secretly envied big-time. Both our bank accounts were fat with early retirement funding. Unlike Kenny, I already considered myself retired and was exactly where I wanted to be.

"Where did they find it?" I said into my phone as I took a sip of coffee.

"Fender called. Interpol, working with the IPS in India, located it in Mumbai. The result of an anonymous tip and a two-month undercover operation. They arrested the CEO of a petrochemical company."

"He could afford the billion dollar price tag?"

"His net worth is seventy billion."

"Was the Blade there?"

"No, but they did find an impressive private collection of art and antiquities, including a couple of Renoirs and a Monet, all missing for decades and worth a fortune. But the mask was obviously his crowning achievement."

I wondered how many of those treasures Knox had sold him.

"How are things in the backwoods? Everything done?"

"Just about. An electrician is coming out this morning to finish the motion detector floods. And I've got a little trim painting to do. But it's feeling more like home every day."

"It seems like forever since Las Vegas. How about I fly out and get the grand tour?"

"I'd like that. But I must warn you that you'll need to be patient with me. I'm still trying to cope with everything that happened. I'm doing pretty good, I think, considering."

I heard footfalls on the outside porch followed by someone knocking at my door. "Sounds like the electrician is here. Want to hang on?"

"I've gotta run to a meeting. Let's talk later." There was a hesitant pause. "I love you, Max."

I hesitated as well, but the words came out anyway. "I love you, too." And I meant it.

I ended the call, slipped the cell into my jeans pocket, and walked out of the kitchen through my new great room with its soon-to-be-used rustic fireplace. A curtain covered the diamond-shaped window in the middle of the front door. I pulled it aside and saw a man standing on the porch—his back to me as he seemed to be admiring the lake view. He wore heavy-duty khaki pants and a navy work shirt that had Summit Electric written across the back. I turned the knob and opened the door.

He spun around. "Ms. Decker. I'm Danny from Summit, here to finish your outside lights." He was young, maybe mid-twenties, with a dark close-cropped beard and long hair.

"Nice to meet you, Danny." I gestured to the fixtures on each end of the porch. Like tentacles, capped wires protruded from each. A pile of boxes was stacked under the porch swing containing the light fixtures, motion detectors, and bulbs. "They're all yours. Two more on the back of the house. Would you like a cup of coffee before you get started?"

"No, thanks. Appreciate it, though." He picked up his tool bag sitting beside his feet and grabbed his ladder that leaned against the railing.

I returned to the kitchen, turned the heat on beneath the skillet, and plopped in a pat of butter. As it started to melt, I heard a heavy thump from the direction of the front porch and figured Danny had dropped a tool. With the butter melted, I cracked open two eggs and eased them into the pan. The sizzle was a most comforting sound.

A couple of minutes later, two knocks came from the front door as I raked my sunny-side-ups onto a plate. Danny must have smelled my coffee and changed his mind. Setting the plate aside, I walked to the door and opened it.

I saw the barrel of the automatic a split second before the blast. It was just enough time for me to block the shot with the door as I stumbled backwards. A large chunk of wood exploded and blew a shower of splinters into the room. I hit hard on my back as I kicked the door closed. The latch caught. In the next instant, I rolled onto my hands and knees, jumped up, and sprang toward the kitchen.

I heard wood cracking when the door busted open. The second blast shattered the frame only a few inches from my head as I ran by. Wood slivers peppered my neck and cheek.

I flew across the kitchen to the door leading to the basement. As I yanked it open, the third bullet grazed the outside of my left leg and stung like an angry wasp.

I slammed the door and locked it behind me before maneuvering down the steps into the darkness of the basement. A fourth shot blew a hole in the wood, showering me with more small fragments. "Shit, next time steel doors," I cursed while trying to keep from spilling down the steps.

At the bottom, I felt my way along the wall past the washer and dryer to the workbench. There were tools on the bench and a collection of paints on a shelf above it. Working in the darkness from memory, I found what I sought and wrapped my hand around a heavy, ball-peen hammer. I crouched behind the workbench, my leg stinging like a son-of-a-bitch from the bullet wound.

The basement door opened, silhouetting a man backlit from the light of the kitchen windows. He held an automatic pistol in one hand and my breakfast plate in the other. It took only a second to confirm he wasn't Danny the electrician.

"Hey, bitch," Travis Knox called out, "your eggs are getting cold." He tossed the plate like a Frisbee. It careened into the wall and fell in pieces to the floor. "Hope you like 'em scrambled."

He reached for the light switch, but it didn't work. The basement was on the same circuit as the floods. I had killed the breaker earlier so the electrician could finish his install. "Okay, we can do this in the dark."

I remembered my cell phone. I knew the remote county I lived in had spotty service and no cellular 911 location services. So instead, I speed-dialed Kenny and hoped he would answer.

"Come on, Maxine," Knox bellowed. "Let me see your face like you saw Aaron's when you shot him. I want to see it just before I blow your brains out."

The next blast was deafening in the confined basement. The slug hit my brand-new Kenmore washing machine.

"You know it's only a matter of time. You don't have but one way out and that's past me. Give it up, Maxine. Don't you want to go see your sister?"

Knox moved halfway down the stairs. "Hey, bitch, I brought you a present. Come out and see it."

I had the advantage because of the backlight coming from the doorway. I saw he was aiming the gun directly at me, but he didn't seem to know it while glaring into the dark. As he swung the gun in another direction, I rose up and threw the hammer as hard as I could. It flew end over end and struck him on the side of his head. Lucky shot.

Knox staggered and groaned.

I had already dropped behind the bench when he fired again. This time the bullet hit a can of paint sitting just above me. It exploded and showered Benjamin Moore everywhere, including down on me.

Travis bent over, holding his head. I grabbed a large screwdriver and sprang across the basement floor. By the time he realized I was coming, I'd reached the steps and dove at him, jamming the tool deep into his thigh. He screamed in pain and fired the automatic pointblank at me.

The shot just missed my head, but the super-heated gases singed my hair. And I lost my hearing from the blast.

I smeared the wet paint from the top of my head to smother the flames, then threw myself on top of him, driving the screwdriver deeper into his leg.

He had to be in a great deal of pain but pushed back with amazing strength. Gripping his wrist, I tried to shove the gun away. His left hand tugged at the screwdriver.

I struggled to my knees and dropped onto his chest with all my might and weight, driving the air from his lungs. He gulped like a fish on a pier as he fought to aim the gun at me. Two more shots, but they sounded as if they came from under a pile of blankets—my hearing was all but gone.

Suddenly he thrust upward, wrangling me to an awkward sprawl on my side. As I stared into his eyes, he pointed the gun directly at my face. I wrestled my strength, freed one arm, and grabbed the barrel just as he pulled the trigger. I felt the click of the firing pen. The magazine was empty.

With his face filled with rage, he heaved me off the steps. I tumbled backwards, landing on the concrete, my head slamming into the floor. I reeled from the impact.

Knox stood over me, teeth bared, eyes wild like an attacking grizzly. I saw his mouth moving in rage but I heard nothing. He planted his boot firmly on my chest, tossed the gun aside, and started digging into his jacket.

And then I saw it. The light from the kitchen above reflected off its edge as he gripped the long, simple knife with its plain, leather-bound handle.

The Blade of Abraham.

He bent and held the ancient relic at my throat. His screaming voice faint in my deafened ears, sounding as if it came from miles away. "This is for Aaron!" Then Knox drew back his arm to slice the Blade across my neck.

I heard a muffled crack and felt something warm spray onto my face. *Blood? Mine? Was it over? Had he done it?* As I looked up, Knox's expression went from rage to shock to disbelief. A large hole had opened on the front of his neck and I realized it was his blood, not mine, that spurted onto my face and chest.

Travis Knox seemed to deflate. He slumped forward on top of me, the Blade slipping from his hand and falling next to my head.

With what little strength I had left, I chucked him off of me.

That's when I saw a man standing at the top of the stairs. He wore a dark green uniform and trooper hat. He stood in a shooter's stance with a gun held firmly in both hands. Smoke from the barrel drifted up like the gossamer mist on the early morning surface of Big Bear Lake.

CHAPTER 77 - THE PATH
Big Bear Lake, Colorado. Nine months later

I came over the last ridgeline and paused to admire my cabin nestled up under the thick oaks in the distance. From my vantage point I saw Kenny down at the end of the pier casting his new fly rod. Even with lessons from a local expert, he had yet to catch anything. But I admired his dedication.

As I continued along the path I pictured the still vivid image of the county medical examiner removing the body of Travis Knox. I thought then, and I still do, that the sight of that black body bag was like watching someone take out the garbage.

I sat in my porch swing that day while paramedics finished binding my leg. They wanted me to go to the emergency room, but I refused. Being in my home was the best medicine. It had taken a couple of hours for the ringing in my ears to go away and most of my hearing to return. Finally, everyone could stop yelling like I was a moron. I recall someone giving me a hat to hide my fashionable Benjamin Moore *storm cloud gray* hair color. I was so thankful the paint was latex and not oil-based.

Danny, the electrician, suffered a concussion from being knocked out by Knox but was back finishing my lights a week later. That time, he accepted my offer of hot coffee.

Apparently, as soon as Kenny heard the gunshots and realized what was happening, he had OSI call my local emergency dispatcher. Luckily, a Colorado State Trooper was on the county blacktop nearby and rushed to my aid. He was later declared a hero in the press and presented a commendation for valor. I had hugged him three or four times that morning—even more after the painkillers kicked in. I know his shoulders must have been sore from so many people slapping him on the back.

That afternoon and through the next couple of days as word got out, the phone never stopped ringing. Besides countless calls from Kenny, I also heard from Agents Fender and Gibson, Dr. Martin, Mosrite the EMT pilot, the mayor of Las Vegas, and the Secretary of Homeland Security herself, all wishing me well. I even got a call from a remorseful and apologetic Carl Applewhite, who expressed a desire to take over his father's ministry. One of the most exciting calls came last week from the Egyptian ambassador to the United States inviting me to take part in the formal presentation after the return of the Blade of Abraham and the King Tut Death Mask to the Cairo Museum.

One of my first questions to Agent Fender when he called was how Knox had gotten hold of the Blade. It was believed that Travis was so enraged when he saw the text message that I had killed Aaron, he parked the truck and made his way up to the skybeam. He must have grabbed it then.

In the days that followed the attack at my cabin, I did interviews with a number of TV networks and was later featured on the cover of *People* magazine. Kenny had it framed and hung it in my great room over the fireplace.

Thankfully, things calmed down as the death of international fugitive and terrorist Travis Knox faded from the headlines.

I came to the end of the path and stepped onto the foot of the pier. The forest around Big Bear Lake had started dissolving into dark and mysterious shadows—the sun long since dipped below the distant mountains.

"Any bites?"

Kenny turned and shrugged. "I'm not officially fishing. Just rehearsing. But if a trout decides to hook himself, I won't complain."

I stood beside him and looked into the evening sky. A

couple of stars were already out. "Instead of waiting for you to catch dinner, how about I open a bottle of Chianti and fix Italian?"

"Works for me." Kenny reeled in his line.

We turned and walked back toward the cabin. He slipped his arm around me and I laid my head on his shoulder. It still felt natural.

As we climbed the steps to the porch, he said, "Did I mention that we think we've got a lead on the location of Excalibur, the sword of King Arthur?"

"Not interested."

"But I haven't even told you the best part…"

ABOUT THE AUTHORS:

Lynn Sholes has worked as a writing trainer for Broward County Schools and Citrus County Schools in Florida. Before writing thrillers her interest in archaeology led her to write historical fiction under the name Lynn Armistead McKee. Lynn is a member of the International Thriller Writers, Mystery Writers of America, and The Authors Guild.

Joe Moore is a former marketing & communications executive and two-time EMMY® winner with 25 years' experience in the television postproduction industry. Joe is the president emeritus of the International Thriller Writers. He writes full time from his home on the banks of the Blackwater River in Northwest Florida.

AN EXCERPT FROM
THE SHIELD
LYNN SHOLES & JOE MOORE

PUBLISHED BY STONE CREEK BOOKS

"The presence of unidentified spacecraft flying in our atmosphere is now accepted as de facto by the military."
Relationship with Inhabitants of Celestial Bodies (June 1947)

~ Dr. J. Robert Oppenheimer
Director of Advanced Studies
Princeton, New Jersey
&
~ Professor Albert Einstein
Princeton, New Jersey

CHAPTER 1 - NIGHT VISITOR
Big Bear Lake, Colorado

I sat up, startled from sleep. My first muddled thought was earthquake. The walls and windows of my cabin shuddered, shaking a picture off the wall. But then I quickly recognized the thunderous roar of a turbojet helicopter. A beam of bright light shone through the window blinds. Instinct kicked in and I rolled to my side and snatched the SIG Sauer from the nightstand drawer.

The chopper's spotlight swept away and I used the opportunity to run to the living room with both hands locked on the 9mm's grip.

From the light seeping through curtains and blinds I could tell my entire front yard and surrounding area were lit up as if the sun had kicked the moon to the curb. The sound of the helicopter landing was unmistakable.

I stood flush against the wall, gun still gripped with both clammy hands.

A rap on the door made me flinch, and I took aim. I'd already been shot twice in my life and had no intention of this being number three.

"Maxine Decker?"

Another strident knock.

"Agent Decker?"

"Who's there? What do you want?"

"I need to speak with you regarding important government business."

I edged my way to stand beside the door and pulled on a

slat in the sidelight mini-blinds for a view of the porch. Backlit by the brilliance of the chopper's spotlight was a man of medium height and trim build. Other than that, he was nothing but a silhouette.

"Identify yourself," I yelled over the noise of the rotors.

"Peter Kepner. I'm with the government and I need to speak to you right away."

"You must be out of the loop, Kepner. I'm no longer a federal agent. I retired from OSI."

"I'm not OSI. I'm an emissary from Beowulf."

"Never heard of it. And if you're not OSI, then why do you want to talk to me?"

"In times of national security issues, Beowulf has executive authority to recruit CIA, FBI, NSA, even Air Force Office of Special Investigations agents. Retired or otherwise."

"Tell the pilot to kill the light and shut down the engine. And tell anyone else on board to stay put. Do it now."

The man relayed my demand through hand signals and his radio. The spotlight dimmed and the rotors trimmed down to a slow idle.

I switched on the front porch light and pulled back the blinds on the sidelight. "Turn around slowly."

Kepner did a 360.

"Show me some ID. And remember I have my weapon pointed at you."

"Got it. But for security reasons, I don't carry any special identification. I can show you my driver's license and a couple of credit cards."

"I'm not Walmart, so you're gonna have to come up with something better than that."

He pulled an envelope from his back pocket. "Agent Decker, I have something for you. I'm sliding it under the door."

I let the blinds snap back and saw the end of the envelope poke through. I picked it up and switched on the lamp on the foyer table. My curiosity was aroused by the embossed seal— the image of a fire-breathing dragon. *Beowulf.* I remembered the ancient epic poem I'd had to study in high school.

I checked to see that Kepner was still there. Then with a zip of my finger I slit the envelope.

I withdrew the stationery, shook it open, and held it close to the light. Seeing the letterhead, I whipped around and glared at the door.

CHAPTER 2 - THE LIGHT BRIGADE
Big Bear Lake, Colorado

My eyes swept the length of the paper. At the top of the stationery was the official White House letterhead. At the bottom was the supposed signature of Guy LeClaire, President of the United States.

Slowly I read the contents, then took a moment to digest it. I retrieved my cell phone from the charger on my nightstand and returned to the living room.

"You still out there, Kepner?" I called.

"Still here."

I did a quick Google search and came up with the phone number I needed to dial according to the instructions in the letter—the White House switchboard. When my call was answered, I continued to follow the directions I was given in the letter. "I'd like to speak with Tennyson."

"One moment, please," the operator said.

A few seconds later, a synthesized voicemail told me to leave a message. I glanced at the letter to make sure I would reply exactly right. "I have read *The Charge of the Light Brigade*."

Then I hung up and waited.

In a moment, my cell rang. "Maxine Decker," I answered.

"Ms. Decker, this is Guy LeClaire."

His words were steady and unmistakable with that distinctive, crisp Boston accent.

My voice had a small tremor in it, both because I was speaking with the President of the United States and because I knew that whatever the reason for Kepner's visit, it was of utmost importance. "Yes, Mr. President?"

"I apologize for this late-night visit and call. We have a critical matter that requires swift and efficient measures. You're needed to participate in a special assignment. Please invite Mr. Kepner inside so he can speak to you. He'll give you more details."

Before I could say anything else, he thanked me once more and ended the call. I stood there a minute trying to absorb what just happened. I unlocked the front door, thankful I wasn't the sheer nightie type, instead wearing long flannel pajama bottoms and a loose-fitting tee.

With a wave of my arm, I invited Peter Kepner inside. I decided to claim the overstuffed chair and leave the sofa to him. Even though I felt confident that the visitor was legitimate, I conspicuously rested the SIG on my lap, one hand atop it. With the kind of business I'd been in for so many years, if I'd learned one thing, it was never to let my guard down. Being betrayed by my partner a few years back had clinched that for me.

I gestured for my visitor to take a seat on the couch opposite me.

Kepner sat, eyed the gun, then looked squarely at me.

"Why the personal visit, Mr. Kepner? Why not a phone call? And why couldn't it have waited until morning? For drama's sake?"

Other than a condescending smile, Kepner didn't react to my jab. "What I'm about to disclose is top secret, and I can't emphasize that enough. As with all electronic communication, there is the outside possibility of unwanted surveillance. That explains my personal visit. And, we need to move on this ASAP. Waiting until the morning would delay our response."

Kepner leaned forward, his elbows on his thighs, fingers laced. "You were a hell of a civilian OSI agent. Top in the antiquities black market. That's why you're Beowulf's choice for this project."

"Like I said, I've never heard of Beowulf."

"And that's a good thing—the way it's supposed to be,

Agent Decker."

He wasn't going to let go of the *agent* title no matter how many times I said I was retired.

Kepner steepled his fingers then aimed them at me. "Here's the deal. There's been a serious breach of security at the Beowulf headquarters."

"Excuse me, but first would you elaborate a little more on what exactly Beowulf is? What's the function or mission?"

"I can't give you any more explanation until we are in a protected and secure environment. All I can do at this point is echo the request from the President that your assistance is needed to help with a potentially grave threat to our national security. The United States and its allies are at risk. I would like for you to get ready and leave with me as quickly as you can."

I'd promised myself I wouldn't return to my old occupation in any fashion. I'd consulted on one job after retiring and it had nearly gotten me killed. But this . . . this sounded like something critical that truly put the nation in peril. I felt my resolve softening.

"Where are we going?" I asked.

"I'm sorry, but I can't say."

"So you want me to take off with you to an undisclosed location to help with an undisclosed mission involving a government operation I've never heard of? Right now, in the middle of the night?" I plastered a *you've-got-to-be-kidding-me* expression on my face.

"That's about it."

I chuckled. "Who said the government doesn't have a sense of humor."

His expression quickly reverted to somber and so did mine. This was obviously a no-bullshit situation.

"Just one more thing. Don't pack a bag—no clothes or toiletries. But bring your ID, including your passport. Everything else will be provided for you."

I thought the request to take my passport was strange, especially since he carried so little. "Why my passport?"

"This may eventually require international travel."

I stood, holding the 9mm at my side.
He pointed to it. "And no guns."

CHAPTER 3 - BROKEN PIECES
Five days earlier. JFK International, New York City

The TSA officer watched the travelers passing through the international security checkpoint. A passenger had been asked to step aside after her shoulder bag was X-rayed. Apparently, something had attracted the attention of one of his inspectors. He observed the strikingly beautiful blonde in a fashionable business suit follow the inspector to a side table. There she placed her bag down and stood back while he unzipped it.

The officer wandered over to stand beside the woman and witness the bag search. The inspector was new on the job and the TSA officer wanted to make sure the search was being conducted by the book.

The bag, a leather satchel with a shoulder strap, contained an e-book reader, notepads and pens, some basic office supplies, and a loose-leaf binder full of what looked like design layouts for an advertising brochure.

While the inspector carefully checked the contents, the officer said, "May I see your passport, please?"

With a warm smile, the woman reached inside her purse and removed it—a Canadian passport in the name of Patricia Barney.

"What's your destination, Ms. Barney?" the officer asked.

"Amsterdam."

"Beautiful city."

"Yes, it is. Very European."

"Ma'am," the inspector said, "can you tell me what this is?" He held up a plastic baggie containing three small objects rolled in bubble wrap. He opened the bag and peeled back the bubble wrap. The objects looked identical—triangular in shape, slightly convex, and cream colored. Each was about five centimeters across.

"Those are pieces of a broken porcelain vase. I'm taking them to a specialist in the Netherlands while I visit friends, in hopes he can match the color so I can have a replica made. It belonged to my grandmother, and my goal is to have the new one made before she discovers it was broken." As the woman spoke, she calmly glanced from the officer to the inspector.

The officer took the package from his associate, examined the contents, and then rebundled it. After putting it back in the Ziploc, he held up the bag and jiggled it.

Patricia Barney flinched.

Then he gave it back to the inspector. "Sorry for the delay, Ms. Barney. Sometimes the sensors set off alerts randomly or if an object isn't recognized." He gave a slight nod to the other man and watched as the baggie was returned to the satchel.

"Good luck with finding that replacement," the inspector said as he handed the satchel to her.

"Have a nice day," the officer said. They both watched her rejoin the rest of the passengers and head for the KLM gate. When he returned to his station, he felt a slight tingle in his right hand. Shaking it seemed to make the tingle lessen. As he watched the line of travelers snake toward the metal detectors, he shook his hand again. Probably nothing, he thought, and turned his attention to the next passenger in line.

CHAPTER 4 - NIGHT FLIGHT
Big Bear Lake, Colorado

Did I have some kind of death wish? That was the question buzzing around in my head like a nuisance fly. Brushing my teeth before leaving with Kepner, I glanced in the mirror. What was I thinking to agree to this? I'd been enjoying my retirement. Life was good. The nightmares had dwindled, and I wasn't awakening in the middle of the night in a sweat, my heart exploding in my chest.

Even as I attempted to talk some sense into my brain, I found myself in the closet slipping into khaki pants followed by a pullover sweater and jacket. Next came my high-top hiking boots. As far as Kepner was concerned I'd be leaving my SIG behind, but not my Walther PPK as I slid it inside my right boot.

Fully dressed, I emerged into the living room. "All set." I shoved my license and other ID in my pants' pocket and slipped my cell into the inside pocket of my jacket.

Kepner opened the front door. "Let's go."

Stepping onto the porch, I felt the chilly Colorado night air. It was August and the mountains had the loveliest cool temps once the sun went down. I took a big fat lungful of air, knowing I was going to miss it.

Kepner signaled the helicopter's pilot and before we reached it, the turbos spun up and the rotors quickly approached full rotation.

I climbed in, followed by Kepner. He handed me a headset, put one on himself, and adjusted the mic.

The rotors roared and we were airborne.

"Where are we headed?" I asked.

"Grand Junction. Walker Field, to be exact. But that's all you need to know right now. Be patient, Agent Decker."

"Sure." I *was* being patient. What did he expect? I'd been dragged out of bed in the middle of the night because the President said I was needed. But that was basically all I'd been told. If they wanted me so badly, why couldn't they divulge more about *why* they needed me? From all the mystery surrounding tonight's event, I had drawn the single most obvious conclusion. Beowulf was black ops.

Something else was obvious. Kepner wasn't going to call me by my first name. During twenty years as an OSI agent, I never got completely comfortable with the military environment. After all, I was a civilian agent—a trained archaeologist—working on the fringe of the Air Force machine. My job was to locate and identify artifacts, relics, art objects, and antiquities suspected of being stolen or smuggled by military personnel. I did my job better than anyone else, and that's why my less-than-straight-and-narrow attitude was tolerated. Despite my frequent nonconformist approaches, they always kept sending me back into the field to track down the bad guys. And that's what I would still be doing on a regular basis had I not decided I was allergic to lead from one too many bullets. I'd finally had enough and retired to my remote Colorado cabin. But now, here I was. Again.

Thinking about the past, I started to get that old queasiness in my gut. And what made it worse was the dark feeling that the Beowulf operation was blacker than anything I'd come across before.

———

Just over an hour passed before we reached a private aviation area at the northwest corner of Grand Junction Airport at Walker Field. After jumping onto the tarmac, we walked a short distance to a small Lear business jet, its engines spinning at idle, the strobes and navigation lights washing the immediate area with color and flashes. As we approached, someone inside opened the side hatch and let it drop down, forming steps.

"Our ride," Kepner said.

I tried to pry more information about our destination but he wouldn't budge. "I'll fill you in once we're in the air," was all he offered.

Kepner's long paces and fast gait were difficult for me to keep up with. I double-stepped to almost each of his strides.

"Come on. Give me a break. I feel like a puppy at the heels of his master and I don't like it. Tell me what the mission is all about."

He turned and looked at me. "You are a persistent one."

"So brief me."

"I'm not sure you're going to like it."

CHAPTER 5 - FULL DISCLOSURE
Grand Junction, Colorado

I settled into one of the six leather seats in the small Learjet while Kepner sat across the narrow aisle from me. The pilot and copilot looked like recruiting posters for military fighter pilots—tall, with close-cropped hair, square jaws, and serious expressions. They acknowledged us as we boarded, and then briefly updated Kepner on the status of the plane, weather, and flying time, which would be just under an hour.

Within minutes, the jet screamed down the runway and pulled into a steep climb. One of my Air Force buddies had once told me that small business jets like this one were as close to a fighter as a private civilian could own. I believed it as we rapidly left the lights of Grand Junction behind and shot into the black Colorado night.

"I'm afraid there won't be an in-flight movie or cocktails served, Agent Decker," Kepner said as we quickly reached cruising altitude.

"Tight budget?" My question caused him to smile for the first time.

"I think you'll soon find that we spend our money where we can get the most bang for the buck."

"And where would that be?" As we banked left, I glanced out of the window and spotted the Big Dipper and Polaris swinging past. I knew we were on a southwest heading.

Kepner saw me establishing our direction. "The next leg of our journey ends in Flagstaff."

"Is that our destination?"

"No, only one more hop after that."

I peered back out the window at the sprinkling of lights from small farm communities interspersed with a black landscape. "I'm still waiting to hear what this is all about. And why me?"

Kepner seemed to consider my question.

"You can at least tell me something about Beowulf," I added. "Even if your prediction is right and I don't like it."

Kepner blinked and cocked his head to the side, then looked back at me. "All right," he finally said. "Let me start with this. The organization has been around in one form or another since the mid-1980s. It was one of the many offshoots of Star Wars."

"The Strategic Defense Initiative—Reagan's program?"

"Correct. One of many byproducts of SDI. Beowulf is probably the last one standing."

"Probably?"

He nodded. "The handful of other programs I knew about are all gone."

"So, you've been with Beowulf for, what, twenty-eight years?"

"No, I came onboard in 1993 when SDI was 'dissolved'." He formed quotes in the air with his fingers.

"You mean Star Wars went on even though the public thought it was shut down?"

"SDI didn't continue, but some of the darker programs did."

"Beowulf is a 'dark' program." I repeated his quote gesture. "I kind of figured that out on my own."

"We've covered as much as we need to for now."

"What do you do for Beowulf?"

Again, he seemed to ponder the question.

"Come on. Are you the boss or the night watchman? I at least deserve to know that much."

"Head of security."

"See, that wasn't so hard, was it? Would you like to know anything about me?"

"No need, Agent Decker. I know everything about you."

This ruffled my feathers a bit. "That doesn't seem fair."

"We don't recruit anyone without full disclosure of their history. You've been thoroughly vetted."

"Then you know all about my sordid past?"

In a dry, deadpan delivery, he said, "I know you grew up in Albuquerque alongside your twin sister, Francine. Your mother was a real estate agent and your father taught Economics at the University of New Mexico. You were president of your high school senior class and graduated with honors. You went on to study archaeology and got your masters in the same field. Your sister became an RN and later got involved with global disaster relief organizations.

"Nearing graduation, one of your professors suggested you become a civilian agent for the Air Force Office of Special Investigations. While in civil service, you met and married Kenneth Gates, a fellow OSI agent and computer forensics expert. The marriage ended in divorce. All told, you spent twenty years as an OSI agent before suffering serious gunshot wounds in Iraq—an event in which you shot and supposedly killed your partner, Special Agent Aaron Knox."

At this point I turned back to the window. My chest tightened at the thoughts of Francine and shooting Aaron.

"After recovering from your wounds, you retired to a mountain cabin until your ex-husband brought you back to OSI as a consultant to assist in tracking down an ancient relic called the Blade of Abraham. You wound up stopping a terrorist threat on the city of Las Vegas."

Kepner fell silent for a moment. As I turned back to him, he said, "Did I leave anything out?"

"You've covered enough." It was considerate of him not to mention how Francine died.

He nodded. "The main reason we need you is to use your talent for finding things that have gone missing, just as you did with the Blade of Abraham and so many other rare, stolen objects over the years. You are one of the best at what you do, and because of that, we are on a very important journey, one that could change the course of history."

CHAPTER 6 - THE ABYSS
Four days earlier. RAI Center, Amsterdam, The Netherlands

Patricia Barney walked across the sprawling entrance hall, had her ID badge barcode scanned at the security checkpoint, and proceeded along what seemed like endless carpeted aisles separating the hundreds of exhibits. Each interconnected building contained different areas of technology—television production, computers, internet, telecommunications, gaming, and others. The names ranged from the giants of technology like Sony, Harris, Panasonic, and Apple all the way down to small software developers and hardware manufacturers vying for attention. The booth Patricia sought was in Hall 4, companies dedicated to communication. She spotted the modest corner exhibit with its brightly colored sign that read Red Star Innovations.

Three Red Star employees, in matching polo shirts and slacks, were putting the final touches on the various product displays as she approached. The man she was to meet—in his late fifties with a dark, close-cropped beard, and dark eyes—saw her and stepped away from the others. He met her with a polite kiss on each cheek. As he did so, he whispered, "Were you followed?"

She shook her head.

"And you have them?"

"Yes."

"One moment." He grabbed a briefcase from behind a display counter and then waved to the two co-workers. "I shall return shortly."

A few moments later, they sat at a small table in the far corner of the food court silently sipping Douwe Egberts dark roast. His eyes roamed the area around them as if taking a mental picture of the hundreds of attendees moving in steady streams throughout the exhibition hall.

Finally, he placed his cup down. "Any complications?"

"The handoff at the motel went just as planned. My bag was inspected at JFK, but it raised no suspicion." Now it was Patricia's turn to scan the crowd of food court patrons.

"Is there any evidence of your meeting with him?"

"This was a small motel in a small Arizona town, so I doubt it."

"You are very good, Patricia." The man gave a sly grin.

"I believe that's why you hired me."

"So," he said, glancing around again, "it's time to finalize our business." He pointed at the satchel still hanging over her shoulder. "Shall we?"

She slipped it off and placed it next to his feet. At the same time, he reached into his briefcase, removed an envelope, and laid it on the table.

"In euros?"

He nodded.

"I don't suppose you'll tell me what the objects are in the parcel and why you have gone to such extreme measures to get them?" She watched him remove the baggie of triangular objects from the satchel and place it in his briefcase.

"You will be better off not knowing."

"Of course. How about this, then? The Beowulf staff has an exceptionally high level of security clearance. How did you get someone to smuggle the pieces out of the facility?"

"Everyone has skeletons in his closet, as the Americans like to say. Threatening to expose them is more than enough motivation."

"Those pesky skeletons." They both laughed as she retrieved the satchel. "I've been thinking about leaving the game."

"I can see why." He patted the envelope just before she

took it. "Is this the most you've made on a single job?"

She dropped the envelope in her bag and slid the strap back onto her shoulder. "If you call me for anything else and I don't return the call, don't be offended. I'm either on a beach somewhere in the South Pacific or . . ."

"Dead? You're much too beautiful and smart to be caught. Plus, you will get bored on that beach."

She winked. "Depends on who I have snuggled up beside me."

Patricia stood and started to leave but paused. "By the way, be careful how you handle the objects. They make your skin tingle."

"Good to know."

She made her way through the crowds on the long walk back to the entrance hall. Outside to the right was the taxi queue with a few people in line. Judging from their conversations, they were mostly booth-setup crews heading back to their hotels during show hours after working all night. A few businessmen and exhibitors also stood in line.

Patricia took the place at the end of the queue and waited her turn for a taxi. A few others came to stand behind her. The line moved along quickly and she soon found herself at the front. The taxi pulled up and she opened the door and slid into the back seat. She felt someone push in right behind her and slam the door shut.

Patricia turned to complain just as the taxi pulled from the curb. "What are you doing?" she asked the man in the suit next to her. "This is my—"

She knew in an instant she had just made the biggest mistake of her life. She was supposed to be a professional and yet she had let her guard down. So enchanted by the amount of money in her satchel and her new life on some tropical isle, she had neglected to scrutinize those waiting in the taxi queue. How convenient that the taxi had pulled into line ahead of the others. Full of her triumph, she didn't even notice the classic setup. Now she stared at the man pressing his hand against her neck. Patricia knew there was no point in fighting. A second after the sting of the needle, she felt herself surrender to the abyss.

CHAPTER 7 - THE EAST RIM
Flagstaff, Arizona

The jet touched down in the darkness of Flagstaff Pulliam Airport just after 4:00 AM and quickly steered to a collection of hangars south of the main passenger terminal.

Our *Top Gun* pilots taxied the Learjet off the single main runway onto the tarmac. As soon as we came to a halt, one copilot emerged from the cockpit, opened the hatch, and lowered it. Kepner motioned for me to get off. He followed.

He placed his hand at my elbow and hurried me to a helicopter parked around sixty meters away, its rotors spinning, its skin painted midnight black. As soon as we climbed in and buckled up, we lifted off. I saw that our Learjet was already racing down the runway. The whole transfer from jet touchdown to helicopter liftoff couldn't have taken more than three minutes.

Kepner slipped on a set of headphones and pointed to a pair hanging nearby. Once I had them on, I said into the mic, "I really wanted to hit the Flagstaff gift shop during our layover."

He gave me his now-famous blank stare

"How far this leg?" I asked.

"About seventy miles."

I estimated that we were heading northwest. Seventy miles would put us . . . "We're going to the Grand Canyon?"

"Very good. We're headed to a remote area on the East Rim."

"I've always wanted to see it by helicopter."

354

"Unfortunately, Agent Decker, you won't this trip."

———

Thirty minutes later, we landed. I couldn't see much except what the full moon illuminated. I noticed that before putting us down, the pilot slipped on what looked like a night vision device. This guy set the bird down with as much assurance as if he were pulling his car into his garage for the hundredth time.

Kepner slid open the side door and jumped out with me right behind. We ducked under the spinning rotors and walked briskly away from the helicopter across hard-packed sand and small stones. Once we were at a safe distance, the black machine rose, banked, and roared back in the direction we had come.

After the sand blasting from the rotor wash blew past, the night surrounded us like a cloak—moonlight swept across a brilliant, starry sky. A whisper of wind cleared the air of the dust from the aircraft's takeoff.

As my eyes became adjusted to the dark, I realized we were standing on a flat expanse of land. In the distance before us ran a dark zigzagging scar gouging the landscape. I assumed it was the Grand Canyon. Not far away in shadow sat a one-story structure the size of a neighborhood 7-Eleven.

"This way." Kepner started toward the building.

As we cut the distance in half, a number of high-intensity floods transformed our surroundings into daylight.

"One second," Kepner said, taking my arm.

We halted and stood silently in the bath of light for ten or fifteen seconds. Then the lamps blinked off, leaving us again wrapped in the blanket of night.

After a moment to let our eyes readjust, we continued on until we came to the front of the building. Even in the muted light I could make out a front porch built of rustic logs and rough-hewn lumber. Strange, I thought, there were no windows. As we stood on the porch, a light over our heads turned on. A plaque with the arrowhead-shaped emblem of the National Park Service was fastened to the wall next to the door. And below it, a sign read "Closed. No Admittance."

"Get many tourists up here?" I asked.

"It's restricted."

Kepner placed his face against the wall beside the door. I wondered what the hell he was doing, and then realized he had aligned his left eye with an iris scanner. An electronic buzz sounded and he pushed the door open. We entered a room about the size of a two-car garage. Fluorescent lights flooded the space.

The room was empty except for a small bare office desk and chair in the corner. I looked across the room. "Are those elevator doors?"

Because he didn't answer, I decided Kepner liked screwing with my head. Either that, or he was just an arrogant dick who didn't feel it necessary to answer my questions. It wouldn't be long before he really pissed me off and I'd bail on this whole deal, presidential request or not.

"Come on," Kepner said. As we walked toward the doors, I heard the click of the lock behind us. The front entrance was secured.

Kepner pushed the *down* button and the elevator doors parted. We stepped inside and he pressed the number 3 button on the control panel, the lowest of the levels. The lift motor spun to life and we dropped. I had no way of knowing how far we descended, but I guessed at least sixty meters, maybe more.

The elevator came to a smooth stop and the doors slid open. What lay before me caused me to take in a sharp breath.

Kepner stepped out, turned, and said, "Welcome to Beowulf."

CHAPTER 8 - CHAUCER
Beowulf Headquarters

Exiting the elevator, I noticed a security checkpoint manned by two ominous-looking men holding assault rifles. The Beowulf insignia patch adorned the breast pockets of their black jumpsuits. The floor, walls, and ceiling were a polished gray material illuminated with indirect lighting. A number of small black globes suspended from above told me we were under video surveillance.

Kepner led me past the two sentries and we entered a hallway like those in a modern corporate office, with a slight dissimilarity. The workstations and terminals that sat dark and empty weren't separated by the conventional portable partitions. Instead, they were divided by glass panels. This was very different from my old stomping grounds at DC3, the OSI headquarters at the Department of Defense Cyber Crime Center in Maryland. To carve this facility out of solid rock had to have been an amazing feat. Money had not been spared.

I assumed that whatever staff occupied these stations would be coming in later, since it was still an hour before dawn. I suppressed a yawn, thinking I should still be home, snug in my bed.

We stopped in front of a set of sculptured stainless-steel double doors that bore the now-familiar Beowulf shield. The nameplate read: Director.

"The director will take it from here. I have some other things to attend to. I'll check in with you later when I get back." Kepner tapped once then opened the door and gestured for me to enter. As I did so, I sensed that he stayed behind. I turned to check. Kepner was gone and the door softly clicked closed.

"Good morning, Agent Decker."

The greeting had come from a man sitting behind a glass and stainless-steel desk. I assumed the 50ish, silver-templed man was the director. He wore a jumpsuit similar to the security guards'. Other than the leather chairs, all the furniture and appointments in the office were also stainless and glass. I wondered what was up with the decor. *Fetish or functionality?*

"It hasn't been that good of a morning," I said. My adrenalin hadn't slowed much since Kepner arrived at my cabin. The shock of it all and lack of sleep were taking a toll.

He came from around his desk and shook my hand. Above the Beowulf patch was a nametag: Chaucer. As I tried to decide whether that was his first or last name, he picked up on my dilemma.

"Please, call me Chaucer."

I acknowledged.

"It's nice to meet you, Agent Decker. You have quite a reputation. All good, by the way."

He returned to his high-back chair, and with a wave of his hand invited me to sit in one of the chairs across the desk from him.

I thanked him for the compliment and sat.

"I have to say, Chaucer, your operation works fast. I feel like I zip lined here."

"Once we set upon a course of action, we waste no time in getting underway." He laid his hands palm down on his desk. "I'm sure you have lots of questions, but maybe I can answer most before you ask."

"Thank god," I said. "Your head of security stonewalled me."

"I apologize. He's very cautious not to give out too much info. Let me see if I can help you out. I'll start with my name. Chaucer isn't my given name. It's a code name."

An English poet. "Like Tennyson for the President?"

"Beowulf deals with extremely sensitive matters and is answerable only to Tennyson. We never reference the President or use his name. Because of the necessity to operate with ultimate covertness, we are different from other black operations. Congress is not even aware that we exist." He paused a moment, letting that settle in.

"Then how are you funded? Doesn't Congress have to appropriate funds even for black ops?"

"Yes. But not Beowulf. Before I continue, I need to impress upon you that what you are going to learn about Beowulf and our project must be regarded with the highest degree of discretion and confidentiality. Any suspicion of a lack thereof will result in the harshest of responses. You've been selected for your skills and for your character. Two other things were factored in. You don't break under even the most intense situations. And when it isn't easy, you do what you have to do."

I knew what he was referring to—the tragic death of my sister at my own hands, and when I'd been forced to shoot my partner.

"Do you clearly understand what I have just said?"

I gave an affirmative nod.

"Good, because if you can't agree with that, we won't go any further. Look me in the eyes."

Chaucer held my gaze and then continued. "Your help is needed in a critical matter, vital to this country's and others' security and safety. There may be times when you are on your own and things get dicey. I want you to be aware of that. So, if you're going to back out, do it now, not later. Once you're in, you're in."

"You mean I can't decide after you explain what the project is?"

"No."

Whatever the critical matter was, everyone had made it abundantly clear that it was a global-changing issue. If my country needed me that badly, how could I turn my back? My brain urged me to check out now, but my gut said *no way*. I had too many years of service with OSI embedded in me so my loyalty must have become part of my DNA.

"All right. I've come this far. It's a long walk home."

"That means you're agreeing?"

"Yes."

"Okay, Agent Decker. Glad to have you. First, I'll tell you we are a crew of only ten. The fewer who have knowledge of Beowulf, the more secure it remains. There will be no non-disclosure contract for you to sign. There'll be no paper trail that will connect us. This is a verbal agreement only. Please be reminded one last time that any violation will provoke serious measures."

Chaucer sat back in his chair, his eyes fixed on mine.

I got the picture. "Crystal clear."

"Then we'll proceed."

I heard my breath come out in a noticeable sigh. I'd been on some hazardous assignments in my time, but already I knew this was way beyond anything I'd ever been involved in.

"You asked about funding. I'll address that briefly, even though it is irrelevant."

I'd just been reprimanded. For now, I'd shut up and listen. This guy was no candy-ass, and this was no candy-ass operation.

"Every year the Department of Defense has single-line items in their budgets represented by a series of numbers and letters along with a code name—it might read Operation Dragonfly with a vague general description. These line items are simply covers for a black budget. It's a type of slush fund set up by the DoD. It keeps Congress's nose out of the DoD's business—in other words, no congressional oversight. Suppose 2.6 million is budgeted for Operation Dragonfly. But really only 1.2 million actually gets to that project. The rest is funneled to a blacker-than-black op like Beowulf. We are considered beyond black. We arrange to skim enough from each of those line items and, voilà, we have our funding."

"Sounds like government money laundering."

"If looking at it that way helps you understand Beowulf's

magnitude and the seriousness of what you'll be working on, then it'll benefit us both."

Chaucer rose and strolled over to a side credenza where a pitcher of ice water and glasses sat. "Would you like some?"

I declined.

He poured a glass and took a deep swallow before returning to lean against the side of his desk.

"Agent Decker, tell me what you know about the Roswell UFO Incident in 1947."

THE SHIELD is available in e-book. For more information on Lynn Sholes & Joe Moore, and their thrillers, visit www.sholesmoore.com and follow them on Facebook at www.facebook.com/sholesandmoore